A Safe Haven

Irene Northan was born on Tyneside, NE England and raised in Devon. Phyllida, published in 1976, was the first of 20 fiction titles and 1 non-fiction title written before her death in June 1993. Irene was a founding member of Brixham Writers' Circle, a member of the Romantic Novelists' Association, Librarian of Brixham Museum, and Reader for the South West Arts.

Also by Irene Northan

The Devon Sagas

To Dream Again
A Safe Haven
Daughter of the River

Irene
NORTHAN
A Safe Haven

CANELO

First published in the United Kingdom in 1991 by Headline Book Publishing

This edition published in the United Kingdom in 2021 by

Canelo
Unit 9, 5th Floor
Cargo Works, 1–2 Hatfields
London, SE1 9PG
United Kingdom

A CIP catalogue record for this book is available from the British Library.

Print ISBN 978 1 80032 494 7
Ebook ISBN 978 1 78863 322 2

This book is a work of fiction. Names, characters, businesses, organizations, places and events are either the product of the author's imagination or are used fictitiously. Any resemblance to actual persons, living or dead, events or locales is entirely coincidental.

Look for more great books at www.canelo.co

Printed and bound in Great Britain by Clays Ltd, Elcograf S.p.A.

1

Chapter One

1889

'Amy, I feel sick again!' Daisy's timorous blue eyes were filled with alarm as she made the announcement.

'Blimey, 'ow are yer going to manage that?' demanded Seth. 'There can't be nothing left inside you. You've already been sick once since we left Paddington, and wet your drawers twice.' His tone changed to a sing-song chant as he taunted, 'Daisy ain't got no drawers on! Daisy ain't got no drawers on!'

'I 'ave so!' cried Daisy, her nausea forgotten in her indignation. 'Amy lent me a pair of 'ers, didn't you, Amy? Make 'im stop!'

'Yes, you stop this instant, Seth Reynolds!' Amy rounded on him angrily. Then she put her arms comfortingly about the other girl. 'Just you look out at the view, that'll take your mind off things. Open the window a bit, Jed.'

Obligingly the fourth member of the quartet unhooked the leather strap and lowered the window, letting in the cold air. Amy was careful not to catch his eye. It had been Jed's idea to hang Daisy's bloomers out of the window to dry, not appreciating the strength of the draught caused by the speeding train. In a trice the wind had filled the stout calico drawers and wrenched them away, sending them whirling over the heads of a herd of bemused cows.

Daisy had been so distressed by the loss of her precious, if uncomfortable, underwear that Amy had sacrificed a pair of her own drawers to comfort her.

Amy swallowed the giggles provoked by memories of the incident, and gave her friend an encouraging hug.

'There now, Daise, don't that feel better?'

Hesitantly Daisy nodded, her eyes fixed on the wide expanse of water and mud-flats that were hurtling by. 'Is that the sea?' she asked.

'Shouldn't think so,' said Amy, looking too.

'No, it ain't big enough,' said Jed. 'We can see the houses and fields and things on the other side.'

'Ain't there 'ouses and fields on the other side of the sea?' demanded Daisy.

''Course there are, stupid!' Seth hooted with derisive laughter, but swiftly subsided under Amy's stern glare.

'Certainly there are,' she said firmly. 'They're just too far away for us to see.'

This was more than Daisy could comprehend, and a perplexed frown settled between her pale eyebrows.

'Amy,' she said at length, 'this place we're going to, what's it called again?'

'Brixham! It's called Brixham! 'Ow many more times!' declared Seth.

'This Brixham place…' Daisy continued, ignoring the exasperation in his voice. 'We are going to like living there, ain't we? I mean, it'll be good being there by the sea, won't it? Better than back in Lambeth?'

It was a question she had asked repeatedly on the long train journey.

'Gawd, not again!' Seth raised his eyes heavenwards.

'Shut up,' said Jed.

Amy shot him a grateful glance. He was the quiet one, was Jed. He recognized poor Daisy's need for constant reassurance. Come to that, they could all have done with a bit of reassurance.

'You are fortunate boys and girls,' the Master of Lambeth Union had informed them that morning. 'You are going out into the world to begin new lives. Be sure you make the most of this excellent opportunity. Be a credit to your country and to your great queen, Victoria.'

He had made it sound like a big adventure, and Amy had tried telling herself that that was what it was. The ploy had only been partially successful. A tight knot of apprehension in the pit of her stomach had accompanied her ever since they had set off from the workhouse that morning. She was going to work for a Mr J. Prout, boatbuilder. That was all she knew. A new life in a new place among new people! No wonder Daisy was in such a state!

''Course we're going to like it,' Amy said, her voice betraying none of her own doubts. 'It's a beautiful place, and the people are so k—' She got no further. The train shot into a tunnel, filling the compartment with pungent smoke and coal smuts. For a few minutes there was pandemonium as they coughed and spluttered while Jed hauled on the strap to close the window. By the time he had pulled it up they were out of the tunnel again, with cliffs of an incredible red at one side of them and at the other...

'The sea!' cried Amy. 'That's got to be the sea!'

Before she could take in the enormity of what she saw they were into another tunnel, and another, and another.

'I don't like it! Say there ain't going to be no more,' wailed Daisy.

'There, don't take on. They'll be gone in a minute, I dare say.' Amy took her hand and gave it a squeeze.

True enough, the tunnels came to an end. Now they all stared at the sea. There it was, stretching from the trackside away into infinity. No one spoke. They stood awestricken, their faces pressed against the grubby window.

'Blimey, it ain't half big,' said Jed, his voice low with wonder.

'I've been to the sea lots of times with my dad,' said Seth. ''E come for me in 'is carriage, and 'is coachman had a black top 'at, and they drove me...' His words faded into nothing. No one was listening. No one ever listened to Seth's tales. His dad, along with carriage, coachman and black top hat, existed only in his imagination.

'It's moving,' said Daisy stupefied. 'Why's it moving? Why does it keep splashing like that?'

'Just the wind, I expect.' Amy could not tear her gaze away from the sight. The sea looked so vast and cold and – and relentless. Suddenly her heart went out to Jed and Seth. They were going to have to make their living out on that great unknown expanse, as apprentices on board fishing trawlers. She pitied them, and could not help a twinge

3

of thankfulness that she was a girl. The prospect of her and Daisy's future lives in domestic service seemed blissful by comparison.

'I thought the sea was at this Brixham place.' Daisy still could not understand. 'What's it doing 'ere?'

'They laid it out special, so's we could 'ave a look at it, like,' said Seth. 'They'll scoop it up into barrels as soon as we've gone by, then send it on ahead by an extra quick train.'

'Oh,' said Daisy.

'Don't take no notice, he's pulling your leg,' said Amy. 'The sea's really ever so big. There's much more of it than this. It stretches all the way to Brixham and beyond.'

'Oh…' said Daisy, more uncertainly this time. She found Seth's version far easier to comprehend.

'Don't you go telling Daisy no more of your stories, Seth!' Amy admonished. 'You only do it to make fun of her.'

'What about you?' demanded Seth. 'Your stories ain't no more true than mine, telling 'er all that muck about 'ow marvellous this place is we're going to. 'Ow the bleeding 'ell do you know? You don't know nothing more about it than the rest of us.'

'Don't you swear at me, Seth Reynolds!' Amy was incensed.

'Shut up, the pair of you,' intervened Jed. 'You'll have the guard down on us, going on like that. Let's have a bit of hush. I could do with a kip.'

They subsided into silence and settled back on the seats. Amy contented herself with putting her tongue out at Seth from time to time, but after a while even this palled and her eyelids began to droop. She could not understand why she should be so tired. Maybe it was the excitement; she had to admit she had got precious little sleep the night before. Leaving the workhouse for good was a pretty big step. It had been her home for four years – though 'home' was scarcely an appropriate word. It was more accurate to say it was where she had lived ever since her mother had died. Remembering those long miserable years she felt certain that what lay ahead had to be better… It had to be…!

When she awoke it was almost dark, and the train was drawing to a halt at a small station. The minute it stopped the door of their compartment was flung open and a stout man in an impressive uniform demanded, 'Be you the lot from Lambeth Workhouse? Then out you get, and look lively!'

In bleary-eyed confusion they tumbled out on to the platform, clutching their few possessions.

'You stand there, under the light, where I can keep an eye on 'ee!' ordered the stout man. 'I'll come back soon's I've got this train off to Kingswear. Don't go straying off, do 'ee hear?'

'What's 'e say?' asked Daisy. 'I can't understand 'im.'

'I think he means us to wait here,' said Amy, drawing her into the yellow pool of light cast by the lamp. 'Stand still while I pull your hat straight, it's all cock-eyed; and do your coat up.' It occurred to her that in other circumstances Daisy would be very pretty, with her large blue eyes and hair as pale and as fine as dandelion fluff. If only she had more meat on her and those eyes weren't always so scared.

'Have we arrived? Is this Brixham?' Daisy demanded.

'Churston,' read Jed. 'It says Churston here on the board.'

'We've got off at the wrong stop!' cried Seth in panic. 'Quick, get back on the train! Come on!'

But he was too late. The last of the doors had been securely slammed shut, the stout station-master had blown his whistle, waved his green flag, and the train puffed sedately out of the station.

'What'll we do now?' wailed Daisy. 'What'll we do now?'

The departure of the train had caused the knot in Amy's stomach to tighten considerably. While the engine had stood in the station, emitting its regular puffs of smoke and steam, the place had seemed bright and alive. It had been a link with London and the life she had always known. Now, as the last carriage disappeared along the track, with its red tail-lamp swaying away in the distance, everything had grown dingy and ominously silent. No one else had got off and, apart from the rattle of a barrow somewhere beyond the ticket-office, there was no noise. No carts, no horses' hooves, no footsteps. Used to the city bustle, even from the confines of the Lambeth Union, Amy found the quiet unnerving. The enormity of the step she was taking suddenly became apparent to her and she was sorely tempted to give way and wail as loudly as Daisy. Then she pulled herself together. Where would blubbering and yelling get her? Nowhere!

Putting all her faith in authority she said confidently, 'The man said we was to stand here, under the lamp, and that's exactly what we'll do.'

'Quiet, innit?' remarked Seth uneasily. The lamplight shone down on his fair hair, emphasizing his sharp features and making him appear more frail and undersized than he was. 'Don't seem to be no town, no nothing. The back of beyond, if you ask me.'

'I reckon this is a junction,' said Jed. 'Yes, it must be. See the other set of lines? We're changing trains here, that's all.'

Amy heaved a sigh of relief. Jed knew about such things, he had moved about more than the rest of them. Just then the station master came bustling up.

'Right, which one of 'ee's got the tickets?' he demanded.

Jed dutifully handed them over.

'You'm the eldest, boy?' the station master asked.

Jed was not. At fifteen Daisy was a year older than the others, but she seemed much younger, while Jed's grave expression and observant brown eyes gave him a seriousness beyond his years.

'Right, then you'm to keep they three in order. Come on, I'll put the four of 'ee on the Whippet.'

They looked at each other in bewilderment, not sure they had heard correctly, until the station master snapped, 'Come on! I can't keep the train waiting all night.' He hustled them across to the other platform, chivvying them in front of him like an overgrown sheepdog.

What awaited them scarcely seemed like a proper train, not to folk who had travelled on a smart express from London, and whose eyes had drunk in the latest marvels of railway engineering the Victorian age could offer all the way from Paddington. It consisted of a small, elderly engine, one aged passenger carriage and a decidedly smelly freight wagon.

'On 'ee gets then!' The station master held the door open for them, slamming it securely shut as soon as they were on board.

'Please, mister,' said Amy, through the open window. 'How'll we know when we gets to Brixham?'

For the first time the man's self-importance cracked and his face stretched into a grin.

''Ee'll know, my lover,' he chuckled. 'No two ways about it, 'ee'll know sure enough.' Then he blew his whistle and they moved away.

It was dark for this last stage of their journey. There were no street lights, no illuminated trams clanking their way through the night, no lighted shop windows. Only the occasional glimmer from some house or cottage shone comfortingly in the blackness. Before they had been travelling for many minutes, rain began to patter against the windows.

'Amy, this place we're going to… It will be nice, won't it?' Daisy made another entreaty for reassurance.

''Course it will.' Amy slid her arm through her friend's. 'We'll be in proper houses with real families, just think of it! Not stuck in some bam of a workhouse with Matron on the prowl the whole time. And on our days off we'll get together and have such fun.'

'B–but what if they don't like me again?'

In her eagerness to give comfort Amy had forgotten that her friend had already been sent out into service once before. It had been a disaster. Within a week a near-hysterical Daisy had been returned to the workhouse by an irate employer who had plenty to say about the Guardians of the Union who foisted mental defectives upon the unsuspecting public. Before Amy could think of a soothing reply, Jed spoke up.

'Don't worry, Daisy, they're sure to keep you this time,' he said. 'No one'll pay your train fare all the way back to Lambeth, no matter how bad you are.'

Daisy gave him a grateful glance that changed to panic as the train began to slow down.

'Oh, my gawd, we're 'ere!' said Seth.

Three men awaited them on the ill-lit platform. The youngsters had barely stepped out of the train before the tallest man, dressed in severe black, came forward and inquired, 'Jediah Greenway? Seth Reynolds?' He spoke in the ringing tones of one accustomed to the pulpit.

'Yes, sir,' the boys replied in unison.

'You'm both bound apprentice to me. I be Matthew Burton. Come!'

7

Without further preamble he strode away, leaving the boys no option but to pick up their boxes and follow him. There was no time to say goodbye, no chance to wish them luck; but at the exit Jed did manage to turn and give the thumbs up sign. Then all three disappeared through the booking hall and were lost to sight.

'Well, and which of you nice little girls is Daisy Simms?' asked the smaller of the two men left on the platform.

Daisy stepped forward silently, too nervous to speak.

'Pleased to meet you, Daisy.' The man took her hand and held on to it. 'I'm Mr Floyd. You are going to work for me and my wife. My, won't Mrs Floyd be delighted when she sees what a pretty thing you are! We're going to be so happy. A proper family, that's what we'll be.'

All the time he had been speaking Mr Floyd had been gently shaking Daisy's hand. Now he released it with seeming reluctance.

'Which is your box, Daisy, my dear?' He went on. 'This one? Right, now say goodbye to your little friend. We must be on our way. Mrs Floyd will be impatient to meet you.'

Daisy turned in panic. 'Amy!' she cried, clutching at her.

'There, there, there.' Mr Floyd patted her shoulder. 'Don't fret. Brixham's not a big place; you won't be far from your little friend. Come along, my dear, let's be going.'

'Yes, you go along with Mr Floyd,' said Amy, gently releasing Daisy's grip on her arm. 'I'll see you again soon, when we have our day off. Everything's going to be all right – no, more than all right! Everything's going to be wonderful!'

She hoped she was right. With an uneasy heart she watched as a weeping Daisy was led away.

'That must make you Amy Kennedy, I reckon! I be John Prout.' The remaining man held out his hand and shook hers. He was in his thirties at a guess, moustached and serious-looking. His hand was hard, much calloused with work. It held hers in a firm grip then let it go.

'Pleased to meet you, sir.' Amy bobbed a quick curtsey.

'Right, my maid, let's be going. It bain't be far.' He swung her box onto his shoulder with ease.

'Please, mister, I can carry that,' she protested.

He regarded her slight figure, clad in a navy serge two-piece several sizes too large, and smiled. 'What, a slip of a maid like you? No, I'll carry un. It's light enough. You bain't got much in yer.'

'I ain't got much at all,' she replied.

Mr Prout laughed. 'Well, that's honest enough, any road,' he said. Then he looked at her curiously. 'What's happened to your hair?' he asked, 'You'm been ill?'

Self-consciously Amy put her hand up to her cropped light-brown hair.

'They cut it off like that at the Union,' she said. 'They do it to all the girls. In case of nits.'

'Ah,' said Mr Prout. 'Well, I dare say you can grow it while you'm with us.'

The opportunity of having proper long hair like everyone else was one benefit of being in service that had never occurred to her. Her heart rose as she trotted after John Prout into the rain, splashing through the puddles.

There seemed to be a large open space just beyond the station. They skirted it to reach a road which was cut into the hillside. The view to her right caught her attention. At first she thought there was nothing there, just emptiness. When her eyes became accustomed to the gloom she realized that what she had thought was a vast void was the dark sea stretching out to a barely discernible horizon. She wished they could stop so that she could get proper look, but did not like to ask in case she annoyed Mr Prout.

Her first impressions of her new employer were favourable. He was slow of speech, and she found his accent difficult, but instinct told her that he was a decent sort. Already she was thankful she was to work for him instead of Mr Floyd. There had been something about that man she had not liked. He had been too friendly, too determined to be agreeable, especially for an employer. And the way he had addressed them as 'little girl' and 'little friend' had set her teeth on edge.

She plucked up her courage and asked, 'Please, mister, where will Daisy be living?'

'You'll find her easy enough. Mr Floyd has a draper's business in Fore Street. That's right in the middle of town. They live above the shop.' He glanced down at her. 'You'm more bothered about that maid than about yourself, seemingly.'

'It's just that she scares so easy. I don't know how she'll manage. I've always taken care of her, ever since I went into the workhouse.'

'And how long might that be?'

'Four years, I was ten.'

'Were you now? That's young to be left alone. But don't worry about that friend of yourn. Her'll be fine.' He spoke with assurance. With a little too much assurance for Amy's peace of mind. So Mr Prout did not like Mr Floyd either!

'Yer us be! We'm yer!' John Prout stopped at a house in a terrace. It did not seem very large, and Amy was surprised that someone needing a servant should live in such a small place. A neat, plump woman with an abundance of blonde curls – Mrs Prout, presumably – had the door open for them even as they approached.

'You can come in the front way for now,' she said sharply. 'But remember, in future you're to use the bottom door.'

'Give the maid a chance,' said Mr Prout placidly. 'Her don't know top from bottom yet. And can us come in? This box be cutting into my shoulder.'

'You should have had the carrier bring it!' Mrs Prout stood aside as they entered a minute hall.

'What, that little step of the way? 'Sides, the maid'll need her things tonight, not sometime next week.'

Mrs Prout looked Amy up and down, and did not appear to like what she saw.

'We'd best show you your room,' she said, picking up the oil-lamp from the hall-stand.

Amy clutched at the handle of her box, while Mr Prout took the other end. He gave her a nod of encouragement, and they followed Mrs Prout up the twisting stairs.

'This is where you're to sleep.' With a wave of her hand Mrs Prout indicated the attic, then looked down at the box standing on the threadbare rug. 'I suppose you've got everything you need?' she said. 'Lambeth Union said I wouldn't have to provide anything.'

'Yes thanks, missus,' Amy replied. 'The Board of Guardians saw to that.'

In fact, it had been the Ladies' Relief and Working Party who had presented her with the required dresses, caps and aprons, and the underwear made of scratchy calico, all sewn by their genteel hands. She was about to suggest her new employer should look in the box and check but just in time she remembered that she did not have the required three pairs of drawers. She had donated a pair to Daisy on the train. Hopefully she crossed her fingers in case Mrs Prout decided to look. Fortunately Mrs Prout was engaged in lighting a candle.

'Do you read?' she demanded.

'Yes, missus,' replied Amy rather indignantly.

'Well, I won't have you reading in bed. That candle's got to last, do you understand?'

'Yes, missus.' Amy spoke in a more subdued tone. Frugality was something she understood very well indeed. Her heart was beginning to sink. Hopes that Mrs Prout might turn out to be as agreeable as her husband had already been dashed.

'Right, get yourself settled in, have a wash, then come downstairs for your supper.' Mrs Prout did not wait to see if Amy had any questions, she merely picked up the oil-lamp and left.

The attic looked smaller when illuminated by just the one flickering candle. Not that Amy minded. She was to have a room of her own, a privilege she had never expected. With something like awe she opened and closed the drawers in the rickety chest. She prodded the mattress on the narrow iron bed – it was a little lumpy, but there were plenty of blankets. She ran an appreciative hand over the wash-stand with its cracked tiles and its unmatched basin and jug, and her spirits rose. What if she did have to put up with a grumpy employer? She had a place of her own, somewhere private to put her few possessions, a luxury she had all but forgotten.

Almost reverently she unpacked her box, then washed in cold water poured from her own jug into her own basin. She regarded herself in the cracked mirror. Large hazel eyes set in a face pale with fatigue looked back at her. Her workhouse days were behind her, her new life had begun – for better or worse!

Only after she had combed her hair did she think to look out of the window. It was raining heavily now, lashing against the panes; she could make out very little save that she seemed to be high up, even higher than being in the attic warranted. That was one mystery that would have to wait until morning.

Taking up the candle she groped her way downstairs, not certain exactly where she was making for. Common sense told her that the floor below probably housed bedrooms, so she continued down another flight. With some relief she saw light filtering under a door and heard the murmur of voices. She raised her hand to knock but something made her hold back.

'I still say we're going to rue the day!' That was Mrs Prout. 'Why do we have to have someone from London? That girl could be any sort of riff-raff.'

'We agreed, didn't us, that 'twere only Christian to give some unfortunate youngster a home and a chance of something better?' replied Mr Prout. 'Goodness knows, the workhouse here be bad enough! What 'tis like up to London I shudder to think!'

'But why London? Aren't there unfortunate youngsters enough in Brixham? I know there was no one suitable in our workhouse, but there are plenty of others as would have done. Bessie Milton's girl for one.'

'You'd not tolerate Bessie Milton's girl for a day, and you know it!' There was humour in Mr Prout's voice. 'Her idn't got a brain in her head to bless herself with, poor soul. No, this li'l London maid seems bright enough. Give her a chance.'

Amy felt she had heard enough. Before Mrs Prout could argue further she rapped sharply on the door. Mrs Prout opened it.

'Ready then, are you?' she demanded.

'Yes, if you please, missus,' Amy replied.

'Come!' Mrs Prout bustled on ahead and, to Amy's surprise, led the way down a further flight of stairs. The house was far larger than it had seemed at first.

'This is the kitchen,' said Mrs Prout. 'The bottom door's through the scullery. That's the way you're to come in and out in future. Do you understand?'

'Yes, missus,' said Amy, trying to make out the features of the room by the light of the flickering candle-flame.

'Tomorrow morning I want you down here at half-past five, no later. You're to clean the range and light it – the blacklead and brushes are in that cupboard. Then put the kettle on to boil. Can you manage that?'

'Yes, missus,' Amy said confidently. Tending ranges was something at which she was much practised.

'Good.' Mrs Prout did not look so sure. 'I'll come down then and show you how we go on about breakfast. Now, I suppose you'll be wanting your supper. It's in the oven. You can make yourself some tea if you want, only don't throw the dregs out. Drain them and put them on that blue plate to dry. Wash up after yourself then go to bed.' Once more she did not wait to see if Amy had any queries or problems, but hurried from the kitchen, closing the door firmly behind her.

For a moment Amy did not move. It had been a long day, so many instructions and so many new experiences had left her feeling suddenly drained. At the thought of eating her stomach gave an uncomfortable heave; she looked in the oven all the same. Her supper proved to be a meat pie. It smelled temptingly savoury. She nibbled a little and found it tasted good. Her appetite returned with a vengeance and she consumed most of it before she felt full. For all that Mrs Prout was short tempered, she obviously fed her servants well. Nevertheless, Amy put the remains of the pie in her pocket – just in case.

By the time she had drunk her tea and cleared away she was so overcome by exhaustion she wondered if her legs would bear her up all those flights of stairs. Wearily she made it, then undressed and collapsed into bed, certain she would fall asleep at once. To her surprise she did not.

Amy had never slept alone before. Or, at least, not that she could recall. She may have had a room of her own when they had had the house off Hatfield Street. She had been little then, her recollections of those days were hazy, just a vague happy image of sitting on Ma's lap in front of the fire while Pa toasted muffins. That had been in the days when Pa had earned good money working for the Gas Company, before he had gone off. If she had slept alone then she could not remember it. After he had gone she had slept with Ma. For these last four years her nights had been punctuated by the moans, sobs, and snores of her sleeping companions. Thirty of them in one dormitory, beds tightly packed with barely standing room between them.

She found the attic eerily silent. Each creak of a floorboard, each easing of a rafter sounded abnormally loud, making her jump. The room was so dark, too, the corners filled with ominous impenetrable shadows. Too late she regretted blowing out the candle, for she had not brought up any matches. To add to her fears she began to worry in case she did not wake up in time the next morning. What sort of an impression would that make on her first day? And she was concerned for Daisy... and she missed her... and it was all so strange... Before she knew it she was sobbing bitter tears into her pillow. For four years she had dreamed of getting out of the workhouse. Now she longed to be back!

She must have cried herself into a doze – suddenly the room was filled with a light far brighter than her one miserable candle. The shadows were gone, the jug and basin were clearly visible on the wash-stand, she could even make out the faded roses on the scuffed wallpaper. Wide awake again, she got out of bed and went to the window.

The rain had stopped and the clouds had rolled back to expose a moon the like of which she had never seen in London. Vast and brilliant, it revealed what she had not realized – that from her bedroom window she could see the sea. A sea now transformed into a sheet of glistening silver by the cool rays. The outline of dark hills stretched away at either side, the piers and jetties of the harbour were clearly visible, even the vessels at anchor were silhouetted against the gleaming background. Here and there ships' riding-lights punctuated the scene with pinpoints of brilliance, like displaced stars. Never in her life had she seen anything so beautiful. She stood gazing out, awestricken, until cold and weariness forced her to return to bed. Drowsily she pulled the bedclothes about her and within minutes she was asleep.

She dreamed that Ma was alive. She and Ma were walking through the market, down New Cut. They had bought a penn'orth of roast chestnuts off the old man at the corner of Short Street. It was nearly dark, the barrows and stalls had their lamps lit, and everywhere was packed with cheery jostling crowds. Ma was wearing her nice hat with the cherries on it, and she was laughing, jiggling the chestnuts in her hand because they were too hot to hold. She did not cough once...

There were tears on Amy's cheeks when she awoke. She had not dreamed of Ma in a long time. It must have been thinking about the house off Hatfield Street that had done it. Blearily she squinted at the window, where a faint grey light announced the dawn.

The raucous cackle of seagulls made sure she did not go back to sleep. Wide awake now, she got out of bed and looked out of the window. Below her a russet-sailed trawler was edging its way into a harbour which was already bustling with activity. Much as she longed to, she dared not stay and watch its progress. Swiftly she washed and dressed, putting on the new print dress and cap. Just in time she remembered to wear her coarse hessian apron and take her tidy white cotton one with her. Then she made her way downstairs.

On the previous night she had guessed that the domestic quarters were below street level. Now she realized that the house was built into the side of a hill. That accounted for it being much bigger than she had at first thought. It came as a pleasant surprise to find the kitchen far less gloomy than she had anticipated. Its one window looked out on to a lower version of the view from her attic.

Less pleasant was the view of the kitchen range. Large, grey with ash, and strangely dead-looking, it dominated the room like a metallic monster. And it was her duty to breathe life back into it.

It was a long, hard morning. It took Amy no time at all to discover that her training at the workhouse had been thorough as far as it went, but was woefully inadequate for life in a normal household. She could light the range efficiently, but when coping with the parlour fireplace she overloaded the grate and hot coals tumbled out on to the hooked rug. She could scrub floors very well with soft soap and sand, but had no idea how to cope with carpets. When Mrs Prout told her to sprinkle tea-leaves on them she had used damp ones, earning herself a severe scolding as well as having to spend ages brushing them out. The kitchen pots offered her no problems when washing up, but the first fine bone-china cup she tried emitted an ominous cracking sound the minute she touched it.

'My patience is at an end! I can't take no more of you,' declared Mrs Prout, her genteel accent slipping in her annoyance. 'You can take Mr Prout his dinner. I'll be glad to have you out of the house for five minutes!'

Amy knew it was no use trying to explain to her employer that they did not have bone-china cups in the workhouse, or carpets, or such small fireplaces. And to be honest, she was eager to go out too. So much had happened that morning she felt she needed a breathing space to collect her thoughts. In addition, she would be out of doors by herself; she could hardly remember what that felt like. She grasped the handle of the basket Mrs Prout thrust at her, and listened to her instructions on how to find the boatyard: 'Go down, right round the harbour, then keep going,' sounded simple enough.

Thankfully she left the house – by the bottom door, naturally. She had hardly climbed the steps and set foot in the street before three boys barred her path. They were taller than her and a year or two older, at a guess. Mischief was written on all three faces. Her heart sank.

'Well, if it isn't the workhouse girl,' teased the tallest, a red-haired fellow.

'If it ain't then I must be someone else, mustn't I?' she retorted, hoping her voice would not betray how uncertain she felt.

'Oh my, ain't I!' The boys mocked her, imitating her London accent.

'What have you got in the basket, Workhouse?' demanded the redheaded one.

'Ain't none of your business, Ginger,' she replied.

'Then we'll make it our business, won't we lads?' he said. 'We aren't taking any lip from workhouse scum.'

The three of them moved forward threateningly.

Amy swallowed nervously, but she had survived for four years in a harsh world. 'Touch me or my basket and I'll kick your shins in,' she retorted.

The red-haired one ignored the warning and dashed forward, grabbing at the white napkin covering the basket. True to her word, Amy lashed out hard. She caught him under the knee with the toe of her boot. Giving a yell of pain that echoed along the street, he dropped to the ground, nursing his wounded leg. Immediately a sash-window from an upper floor was pushed up and Mrs Prout thrust out her head.

'Are you fooling about?' she demanded, glaring down at Amy and the red-haired boy – his two companions had disappeared. 'No, missus,' replied Amy innocently. 'This poor boy's just tripped over and hurt his leg bad.'

Mrs Prout did not look as if she believed the story. 'It's Daniel Newton, isn't it?' she asked, regarding the boy keenly.

'Yes, Mrs Prout,' replied the boy, getting painfully to his feet.

'Are you all right, Daniel?' She sounded different, more refined and quite concerned. 'Would you like to come in and rest?'

'No, thank you, Mrs Prout. I'm fine, honest I am.'

'If you are sure…? Please give my regards to your mother. And as for you, girl, Mr Prout wants that dinner today, you know.' So saying Mrs Prout withdrew her head and shut the window.

The boy pulled a face after her, then turned to Amy. 'Thanks,' he said. 'You're all right, Workhouse.'

By way of a reply Amy poked out her tongue as far as it would go, then hurried away downhill. He limped after her, but as she was no novice when it came to kicking, she soon left him far behind.

As she progressed down the slope a tense excitement began to take hold of her. With the excitement came anxiety. She was out walking, untrammelled, free! For four long years she had been restricted by the walls of the Union, but now she was permitted to go about the streets like any normal person. It was a heady freedom and for a moment she was tempted to run and run and run, just to celebrate such liberty. The weight of the basket on her arm was a reminder that her emancipation only went so far. However, she was determined to enjoy her outing. She suffered a temporary fit of indecision trying to decide which way to go, then common sense reasserted itself.

'Go right round the harbour,' Mrs Prout had instructed. All she had to do was to continue going downwards and she was bound to find the harbour sooner or later. Accustomed to the flat reclaimed marshland of Lambeth, she was fascinated by the hills which surrounded the port. What was at the top of each one, she wondered? The thought that one day soon she might be able to explore them and find out gave her a happy thrill of expectation.

She found the harbour easily enough. As she skirted it she grew quite bewildered by the clamour all about her and the new sights and sounds which assailed her. The shops and the tiny market had the novelty of long absence, but there were the boats too, anchored in the harbour, moored to the quays or dragged up on the beach. She was so busy drinking everything in that she tripped over mooring-ropes, ran into stacks of fish-baskets, and came close to getting entangled in fishing nets strung out to dry.

''Ee wants to watch where you'm going, my lover, else I'll brede 'ee into this yer net, and then where'll 'ee be?' remarked one old fisherman with whom she collided.

She did not understand what he was talking about, but she assumed he was making some joke about the net he was mending, so she just grinned and hurried on her way.

Mrs Prout's directions proved to be effective. Amy left the harbour behind and carried on along the road, confident that since the sea was never far away she would find Mr Prout's yard soon. What she had not anticipated was that there would be more than one boatyard along the same short stretch of coastline. At last she reached a beach which was tucked between cliffs and a breakwater. A few sheds stood well above the high water-line, while posts driven deep into the shingle supported the skeleton of a half-finished boat. There was the sweet smell of freshly cut timber about the place, and an air of well-ordered chaos. Most reassuring of all was the painted board which said: 'J. Prout. Boatbuilder.'

'How'm you managed this morning?' asked John Prout, as he accepted the food she had brought.

'Very well, thanks, mister,' she replied, not entirely truthfully.

He grinned. ''Tis all strange, I dare say. Not like you'm used to. Still,'m a pert maid. You'll soon get the hang of things.'

His sympathy brought tears to her eyes far more readily than all his wife's scolding. Swiftly she scrubbed away the tell-tale signs, but not before he had seen them.

'Tomorrow'll be easier, you'll see,' he said confidently.

Amy was not so sure, but she appreciated his kindness.

'Yer,' he said, taking a penny from his pocket. 'Get yourself some bulls-eyes on the way home.'

She was so astonished by such generosity that she feared she had not thanked him properly. She was back at the harbour once more before she remembered.

'Workhouse! Want a row across the harbour?'

A familiar voice made her jump. There was Daniel Newton sitting in a small rowing-boat by a slipway.

'Call me Workhouse again and I'll belt you,' she promised, adding as an afterthought, 'Ginger!'

He grinned. 'You win. Let's make a pact. If you don't call me Ginger I won't call you Workhouse. Now, do you want to be rowed across or not? I've been waiting for you specially. It'll save your legs a bit.'

She was tempted to be haughty and walk away; but the prospect of a trip in the rowing-boat was too attractive.

'How did you know I'd come this way?' she asked, carefully taking her place in the small craft.

'You were taking Mr Prout his dinner. You were bound to come back this way.' Daniel pushed the boat away from the slip with one oar, then settled to his rowing with easy, practised strokes.

Amy was impressed. 'You've done this before, ain't you?' she said.

'Of course I have, lots of times.' He smiled at her, then asked curiously, 'Why have you had your hair cut off?'

'Mind your own business,' she retorted.

By way of reply he shipped his oars and rocked the little boat from side to side, causing Amy to scream and clutch at the sides.

'See what happens when you're cheeky to me,' he said.

'I'll be cheeky to you if I like,' replied Amy. 'You ain't nothing special.'

He made to rock the boat again, but only half-heartedly. By the time Amy had opened her mouth to squeal he had resumed rowing. Another two or three long pulls on the oars and they were at the Quay. It had been a short journey and Amy regretted having spent so much of it arguing. Now it was over she felt she would have liked more time to appreciate it.

'Thanks for the ride,' she said, preparing to get out and negotiate the slippery-looking steps to the road.

'Wait a minute. I've got something for you. Close your eyes, open your mouth, and see what God sends you.'

'Gam,' said Amy. 'You must think I'm barmy.'

'Gam', he mimicked her. 'You must think I'm barmy. You will be barmy if you refuse this. It's a present. It won't bite, honest!'

Amy was not convinced, though he sounded very persuasive. Also, curiosity was getting the better of her.

'Just close your eyes and hold your hand out, then,' said Daniel.

'All right.' Screwing up both her courage and her face, in an effort to keep her eyes closed, Amy thrust out her hand. She was ready to withdraw it quickly in case he was playing tricks. He placed something on her palm, and cautiously she squinted through her long lashes to see what it was.

'Oh,' she said in surprise. 'Oh, ta very much.'

The 'present' was a twist of barley sugar. She was hesitant to take it, though. Sweets were a rare treat indeed and, much as she wanted it, she was reluctant to deprive him. 'Here, let's go halvies,' she said, preparing to break the stick in two.

'No need, I've got plenty,' he assured her. As if to prove it, he crammed an equally big piece into his mouth.

Unable to believe her luck she did the same. 'Got to go,' she said with her mouth full. 'Thanks for the sweet and the ride and everything.'

'You're welcome,' he said.

She was determined she would not look back at him; but she could not help taking a quick glance over her shoulder as she negotiated the hazards of the busy Quay. He was already halfway across the harbour, rowing with long, easy strokes.

He was a funny sort of bloke, she thought. One minute he was ganging up on her, the next he was being as nice as ninepence. It just showed what a good kick on the shin could do! He must be quite well off, she decided. Not just because of his generosity with the barley sugar. His clothes were neat and had no patches anywhere. Even his boots looked as if they had never been mended. And he could talk nicely too, almost posh. Amy could talk posh when she had a mind. Her ma had set great store by people speaking nicely it was something Ma had learned as a girl when she was parlourmaid to a grand family. Sadly Amy reflected how much her speech had deteriorated over these last years, with no one to remind her.

Trudging back up the hill to the Prouts' house she wondered if she would see Daniel again. Probably not... Suddenly she thought of Daisy, Jed, and Seth – how had they got on? She felt ashamed that she had spared them such little thought during the morning; there seemed to have been so much to occupy her, and so much to learn. Fervently she hoped that they had managed all right, particularly Daisy. If her own experience was anything to go by then she feared that poor Daisy might be having a hard time. Then her fingers closed over the penny Mr Prout had given her. Money in her pocket *and* a bit of barley sugar! Maybe this Brixham place was not so bad after all!

Amy's optimism was short-lived. It barely survived the afternoon. She managed the first part – cleaning the inside of the windows – fairly well. She was quite proud of the way she prudently removed all the plants and knick-knacks from the windowsills before commencing, and even prouder of the way she returned them all to their proper places without any accident afterwards. Then Mrs Prout announced it was time to begin cooking the evening meal.

'You can make a start on the potatoes, you'll find them in the shippen outside. Make sure you peel them thin, mind! No cutting off great chunks just to be quick. And don't start the cooking of them until I've seen them.'

'No, missus.' Buoyed up by her success with the windows, Amy felt that potatoes would present no problem.

Much later a tearful Amy waited in the kitchen, dreading the sound of the master coming home.

'Just wait until Mr Prout gets in!' Mrs Prout had been exclaiming repeatedly. 'I don't know what he's going to say about this, I really don't How could you be so stupid?'

And Amy could think of no reply save, 'It's different in the work-house, missus.'

The rattle of a key in the lock sent her employer hurrying upstairs.

'Just come and see what that girl's done now,' she heard Mrs Prout declare. 'Come on. It was your idea to have her. You come and see where your Christian charity has got us.'

'Can't I get my boots off first?' As ever Mr Prout was placid in his reply. 'And don't I get a kiss, coming in?'

'Oh you!' There was no coquettishness in his wife's reply, only exasperation.

With a sinking heart Amy heard their footsteps on the stairs.

'There!' announced Mrs Prout triumphantly. 'What do you think of that?'

Amy watched as Mr Prout's gaze took in the entire kitchen. There was a large pan of potatoes bubbling on the range. There were bowls of potatoes, white and peeled, covering the table. More peeled potatoes rested in buckets on the floor. Every dish, pot, and pail in the place seemed to be filled with peeled potatoes. They were everywhere!

'What the…!' exclaimed Mr Prout in bewilderment.

'A whole sack! She peeled a whole sack of potatoes for your dinner. Did you ever hear the like?' Mrs Prout's indignation was bubbling as vigorously as the potatoes in the pan.

Amy's eyes were fixed on Mr Prout. He seemed stumped for something to say. His lips were pressed together, and he scratched his moustache with a thumb-nail as if grappling with some great problem. Then the problem grew too much for him and he sank down on a kitchenand laughed until the tears ran down his face.

'Is that all you can do? Laugh like a mazed fool?' demanded his wife. 'She's got to go back. I don't care how much the train ticket costs, we're sending her back where she came from.'

'Please, no, missus,' cried Amy in a panic. She could remember all too vividly the way Daisy had been treated after she had been returned to the workhouse as 'unsuitable'. 'I didn't understand, missus, honest I didn't. I've got out of the way of doing things like ordinary people. I used to manage fine when my ma was alive. I looked after her proper, although I was only a nipper. I could learn to do it again, I swear. Just tell me exactly what you want and I'll do it. I'll do anything, only please don't send me back.'

John Prout mopped his eyes with a handkerchief.

'You'm not going back, maid, never fear,' he said. Then he looked at his irate wife. ''Twas only a few tatties, when all's said and done. They won't be wasted. I can think of some families where a bucket of tatties won't go amiss, specially as they're ready peeled.' For a moment his laughter threatened to break out again. 'Go on, Jess, see the funny side,' he pleaded.

'You're too soft for your own good, that's what's wrong with you,' replied his wife more gently. 'But as for you, miss, you can be the one as delivers the potatoes to all and sundry. You can start with Bessie Milton's lot down Penny's Row. And be sure to bring back the bucket!'

After her third trip out Amy's interest in the steep terrain of Brixham waned considerably. Her arms and legs were a mass of aches, and her boots and stockings were soaked from the water slopping out of the pails. She wondered how it was that all the needy families seemed to live at the bottom of the slope, while the Prouts' house was at the top. Wearily she was making her way up the narrow track of Overgang, thankful that this was her last trip, when a stone hit the bucket she was carrying. She swung round angrily, to find herself facing Daniel.

'Sorry! Can't stop!' he said. 'I've got elementary navigation with Captain Harris and he'll murder me if I'm late.'

Murder seemed an extreme punishment for missing elementary navigation, whatever that was.

'I'll come to your funeral!' she called after him.

He stopped and swung round. 'When's your day off?' he asked unexpectedly.

'Sunday, two till four,' she replied, surprised.

'Right, I'll meet you by King Billy at two!' He hurried on, apparently quite certain she would agree.

'Hang on,' she protested. 'Where's this King Billy?'

'You'll find it easily enough,' he called over his shoulder.

His casual manner almost made her refuse. Then she had second thoughts. She had never met anyone quite like him. He intrigued her, and she wanted to know him better.

'I'll have to bring my friend,' she said, belatedly remembering Daisy. He stopped again. 'Why?' he demanded.

'I ain't going nowhere with you alone,' she said indignantly. 'What sort of a girl do you think I am?'

He smiled at her, his quick brilliant smile. 'All right, bring your friend,' he said. 'See you on Sunday.'

Amy carried on towards the Prouts' house, her mind suddenly buzzing with recent events. She could never remember a day when so many things had happened to her. And now, the most extraordinary thing of all had occurred; not twenty-four hours in the place and already she had an admirer!

Chapter Two

The fishing smack, *Our Violet*, bucked as a squall caught her sails. Struggling to keep his balance, Jed lost hold of the bucket he was carrying and it rolled noisily across the deck. More by good luck than good management he snatched it up before it went overboard. Matthew Burton, who was at the helm, regarded him with scorn. Jed was thankful he was out of arm's reach, otherwise the incident would have earned him a blow, and his head was still ringing from the last one. Unsteadily he made his way down to the cabin.

'Ain't you got the boiler going yet?' Jed protested. 'The skipper'll flay you alive.'

The body curled up on the bunk moaned.

'Come on!' He shook Seth by the shoulder. 'You were told to tend the boiler. You'll feel better if you do something.'

'I ain't never going to feel better, ever again,' came the pitiful reply.

Jed tried to rouse him, but it was no use. Seth just fell back on the bunk.

'No wonder you feel bad, it's so hot in here!' Jed set about firing the capstan boiler himself, making the stuffy cabin even hotter. 'Skipper told me to brew some tea. You can take it to him. It'll give you a breath of fresh air.'

'Oh no!' groaned Seth miserably, and he curled into a tighter ball.

Jed gave a sigh. His stomach was heaving too, but he forced himself to concentrate on the job in hand. Once he had got the boiler started he turned his attention to the other source of heat, the cooking-stove. The kettle was boiling merrily, and he raised the lid to add a handful of tea leaves to the existing brew. He had earlier made the fatal mistake of emptying the kettle to start afresh. He was informed, by words and a clip across the ear, that the kettle was only emptied when there was no room for tea, for water, or for both. The black, bitter brew was a far cry from the tepid grey liquid he had consumed in the workhouse. At his first sip he had screwed up his face in disgust.

"Ee needs more sugar in it, boy,' Harry, the first hand, had informed him, taking a generous spoonful from the tin and stirring it into his mug for him. 'Keep 'ee going, that will. And put 'airs on your chest.'

Jed had learned the importance of tea during his few hours aboard the *Our Violet*. Matthew Burton might prohibit alcohol on his boat, but tea was evidently an essential commodity.

'Take the skipper his tea,' he urged Seth. 'He says he wants some before we take the trawl in.' Jed was merely repeating Matthew Burton's words; he had no idea what taking the trawl in would entail. It sounded good and seamanlike.

'All right.' Reluctantly Seth made a move, but immediately gave a stifled gasp and reached for a nearby bucket. Jed had no alternative but to brave the pitching deck and take the tea himself.

'What be the other un doing?' demanded Matthew Burton, accepting the mug without thanks.

'Tending the boiler, like you said, Skipper,' Jed replied promptly.

'He'd better be.' Skipper Burton's eyes bored into the boy, as if he saw through the falsehood. 'I've brought both of you with me this trip for a reason. I allus starts my 'prentices off myself, to make sure they don't get no slack habits. I begins the way I means to go on. Anyone as sails under me finishes up a first-rate seaman, else us parts company. When I'm sure you've made proper progress then one of you can sail with my boy, Isaac, on the *Jupiter*. Until then I'm keeping my eye on you, and don't you forget it.'

Jed nodded.

'Drop of tea going, boy?' asked Harry, as he made his way back.

'Yes, I've brought you some.'

'That be a proper job.' Harry clenched his pipe-stem between his teeth and took the drink. 'Bain't this the little un's job?'

Jed wondered why Seth was always thought of as the smaller and younger of the two of them, when in fact there was scant difference in size or age. Perhaps it had something to do with Seth's angelic blond looks.

Darker than Seth, Jed often seemed dour by comparison, but then Jed had a more serious turn of mind. He rarely smiled, and his brown eyes looked out at the world from under dark brows with a brooding expression.

'Seth's seeing to the boiler.' Jed kept to his fiction.

'Oh ah?' Harry's eyes twinkled in the dim light. 'Tell un to get a good 'ead of steam up; us'll need it soon. I'd not want to be in 'is shoes if 'e don't. Be sure to warn 'im like.'

'I will,' said Jed.

Harry took another pull at his pipe, then tapped its contents over the side in a cascade of red sparks.

'A last pipe and a mug o' tea afore us brings in the trawl! That's what I calls grand. You go and 'ave some yourself, boy. 'Ee won't get no time once us starts, I can promise 'ee that. Got some vittals?'

'Mrs Burton gave us some bread and cold bacon.' The thought of the food, particularly the bacon, caused Jed to gag and swallow hurriedly.

Harry laughed. 'Best thing out for seasickness. No, I be serious. Get a bit of food inside 'ee and a good mug of trawler tea. Revived many a dying man, 'as trawler tea. Make sure the little un 'as some too.'

Jed managed a wan smile and went below. He was not too hopeful of getting Seth to take anything. When he got into the cabin such a blast of heat hit him he reeled. How Seth could bear it he did not know. The thought of Mrs Burton's cold bacon grew even less attractive. As he expected Seth was not interested in such delicacies. Jed gritted his teeth, replenished the kettle, added more fuel to the boiler, then hurried on deck with his own meal. He tried manfully to swallow it, but it was not long before he had to make a dash for the side.

'Best get it over now, son!' Harry patted him on the back good-naturedly. 'Another ten minutes and 'ee won't 'ave no time for such pastimes.'

The first hand was right. Before long the skipper decided to bring in the trawl. It had been down a good six hours, scooping its way over the sea-bed, and in spite of his seasickness Jed was interested to see what they had caught. The winch was set going, then with infinite care the trawl was brought up.

''Ee did a good job there, boy,' said Harry encouragingly to a pale and unsteady Seth, who had managed to come up on deck. 'Tended the boiler real well. Important job that is, gets the trawl up in no time. I minds the days when us 'ad to wind it up by 'and. Three, four hours that could take, and it was back-breaking! Don't know you'm bom, you young uns. Got it real easy!'

If this was easy Jed wondered what hard work was like. From the moment the contents of the trawl were emptied on to the heaving deck it was non-stop toil, a seemingly unending session of sorting, gutting, and packing fish. The constant motion and the smell of fish offal did not improve matters.

Suddenly a fish caught him full in the face, almost knocking him off his precarious balance.

'Danged fool! Can't 'ee tell a mullet from a whiting?'

It was Cy Heath, the second hand, who spoke. He was an unpleasant individual, slack-mouthed and weak-chinned. What his expression lacked in intelligence it more than made up for in vindictiveness. Jed had already been on the receiving end of a barrage of smelly fish guts flipped at him by Cy. Less innocent was the flying rope-end, complete with metal cleat, which had narrowly missed his eye, and the 'dropped' gutting knife that had gouged a deep nick out of the side of his hand. There had been other 'accidents' too. Cy clearly saw Jed and Seth as suitable butts for his malicious jokes. Jed had other ideas. He knew the type all too well. The longer Cy was allowed to continue the worse he would get.

Waiting for a chance to stop Cy's games was the only thing that got Jed through the next few hours. His hands soon became so stiff and cold with handling the wet fish that they ached; his fingers slipped on the gutting knife and he cut himself more than once, wincing in pain as the salt water got into the wounds. Even the oilskins he wore as protection against the rain and the night cold contrived to hurt him as the cuffs of the stiff material chafed against his wrists until they were raw and bleeding.

Tired, sick, and with his hands paining him, Jed was thankful when the skipper ordered him and Seth to start clearing the deck of the brash, the accumulated rubbish from the catch. Surely that meant they were finished for the night and could return home?

'We'm going to shoot the trawl again. Stand by!' Matthew Burton's command struck dismay into Jed's heart. They had not finished. They were going through the whole exhausting, agonizing process once more. Beside him Seth gave a snivel. Jed had not cried since he was four, when his pa died. He prided himself on never betraying his distress. It took a superhuman effort not to join Seth and blubber away like a baby.

'Harry, you'm on watch. You two, go below and get some rest.'

Jed and Seth were only too happy to obey Matthew Burton's orders once the trawl was over the side again. Now that the boiler had died down the cabin had reached a reasonable temperature. Jed was so bone weary he felt he could have slept through anything. He slipped off his oilskins, wincing again as the rigid fabric scraped against his raw flesh.

'Hands bad, boy?' It was Matthew Burton, who had come down to the cabin behind them. He reached into a locker and drew out a green glass bottle. 'Yer, mb some of this in. The missus makes un. Got self-heal in it. Stops the sores turning to ulcers and such.'

Somewhat surprised at the skipper's concern, Jed did as he was bid. At first the lotion stung; then after a moment or two the pain eased considerably.

Seth held out his hands for treatment also. They were not nearly as chafed and painful as Jed's.

'Us don't need telling who does the work and who don't,' announced Matthew Burton in his best preacher's voice. '"Idleness is the root of all vices".' He glared at Seth, who shrank back in alarm.

Although Jed had had his fair share of blows and reprimands from the skipper Seth had already come in for the more severe punishment. He was his own worst enemy. Always so eager to be noticed, so desperate for attention, he would rush forward volunteering for anything and everything. Nine times out of ten he had had no idea of what he was taking on; he was constantly in trouble, either for making a mess or for leaving things undone. Seasickness had proved to be a blessing in disguise. It had rendered him incapable of getting himself into more scrapes.

Jed lay down to sleep. He did not occupy a bunk, like Seth. He curled up on the floor as he had seen the rest of the crew do. It was cooler there. He closed his eyes, but for a while his body ached too much with weariness for sleep to come.

He did not like the sea. That conclusion was uppermost in his mind as he lay there. Nothing in his already harsh upbringing had prepared him for this. The rigours and discomforts he had endured during the last hours were far beyond either his experience or his expectations. And today the weather had been reasonable, or so Harry had assured him. What would it be like in a gale or snow or frost? A deep depression settled on him as he contemplated that he must go fishing again tomorrow and the next day and the next for five long years at the very least. Five years was the span of his apprenticeship indentures. How he was to bear it he did not know.

Jed had tried not to be too hopeful about his apprenticeship. He had learned at an early age that optimism was foolish. Time and again, after the death of his parents, he had gone to relatives confident that he would be absorbed into a proper family and have a home. Instead, he had been resented as an extra mouth to feed, and pushed on to the next relation as fast as possible. This had been different, or so he had thought. After the two years he had spent at the Lambeth Workhouse, this had seemed like a miraculous release. A new life, a new job, a new way ahead! He should have known better. The Union Guardians had got rid of him, just as his relations had done. They had passed him on to Matthew Burton and to a future of unending misery. But they were not going to succeed, these folk who pushed him about like a counter on a penny board-game. Deep within him smouldered a burning resolution to shape his own destiny one day. He would do it alone, relying on no one.

Exhaustion brought him only a few hours sleep before things were astir again on board the *Our Violet*. He awoke to find Harry shaking him.

'Move yourself, boy, and get us a bit of breakfast. I've brought a pail of dabs down. They'm tasty fried.' Harry moved on to Seth and shook him too. 'Come on, little un, get this cabin cleaned up afore us eats. Us've the trawl to get up afore long.' Then he hurried back on deck.

Jed stared at the fish in dismay. He had not realized he was expected to cook. Making tea was one thing, but cooking…! Stiffly he rose to his feet. There were oilskins lying about, seaboots, discarded garments, and somewhere in among the mess were the tea-mugs.

'Seth,' he began. 'Find the mugs for us, there's a pal.'

There was no reply. Seth was fast asleep again, his face white and intense. It seemed a shame to rouse him after he had been so ill. Jed gave the cabin a quick tidy then turned his attention to the cooking. In the past his various relations had taken advantage of his sturdy arms and legs and made him chop wood or fetch water. Cooking was not something he had ever done before. Still, cooking was what was required of him now; so he had better make a start. Experimentally he put the frying-pan on the stove and added a lump of dripping, watching it slowly beginning to melt.

Boots stumped down the companionway and Cy Heath entered the cabin.

'Yer, what the 'ell's this?' he demanded, regarding Seth's sleeping form. 'Move yourself. This ain't no bloody cruise!' He swung back his foot ready to deliver a kick at the boy's defenceless back.

'Leave him alone!' cried Jed.

'Oh yes?' Cy turned slowly towards him, a look of malicious satisfaction in his eyes. 'And who says so?'

'This says so!' Jed grasped the heavy frying-pan in both hands and raised it menacingly. The dripping had melted, though it was not really hot. But Cy did not know that. He backed away.

'He'd not dare!'

'Just try me!' Jed joggled the pan up and down, ignoring the splashes of melted dripping which shot across the cabin. Some reached Cy and spattered down the front of his canvas frock.

'Watch what you'm doing, you damned fool!' he yelled, backing away hurriedly. 'Get yon idle bastard on 'is feet, that's all I've got to say.'

'Cy Heath! I'll not have foul language on board my boat, as well you knows!' Matthew Burton's voice boomed out from the top of the companionway. 'If I have to warn you again about that dirty tongue of youm you'll be looking for another berth the minute us reaches harbour. Do you hear?'

It would have been difficult not to near Matthew Burton, his voice would have been audible through a force nine gale.

Cy could only reply, 'Aye, Skipper!' and slouch away.

Hurriedly Jed replaced the frying-pan, trying to look as though he were innocently cooking. Inwardly he was triumphant at having scored over Cy.

'Boy!' came the Skipper's voice from the companionway again. 'Clean up that grease afore you does anything else. Accidents happen easily enough at sea without you giving them a helping hand.'

'Yes, Skipper.'

'Oh, and boy, if you'm determined to do the work of two while that other un sleeps, don't you expect double the money.'

'No, Skipper.' Matthew Burton knew a lot more about what went on aboard the *Our Violet* than Jed had realized. It was something he would have to watch in future.

The cooking of the dabs turned out better than he expected. No one complained about the end result. But consuming any himself was the last thing he felt like. He would have settled for just the inevitable mug of tea if Harry had not nodded at him encouragingly.

'Got to keep your strength up, boy,' he said.

Jed started on the fish, then to his surprise found he could manage most of it.

From then on there were no more urgent dashes to the side while the trawl was raised for a second time. A pearl-like dawn spread across the sky, making it easier to work on the catch. The darkness and the newness of the situation had meant that the first bringing in of the trawl had been a nightmare for Jed. Now, with the morning growing lighter by the minute, he could see what he was doing and so made fewer mistakes. The sea was calmer, too, causing the *Our Violet* to toss and roll less energetically. But there was no improvement to the pain in his hands as he sorted the fish, nor did he find the work less tiring.

'Wind's dropping.' Skipper Burton looked up at the rust-red sails. 'Us had best make for home.'

Jed felt he had never seen anything more welcome than the sight of Brixham nestling in its green hills, the houses clinging to the steep slopes. It seemed to take an interminable time coming closer; he feared they would never arrive. Not that he spent the homeward voyage in idleness. Matthew Burton found him an unending list of tasks to do – trimming and filling the lamps, cleaning the deck, and much more. By the time they rounded Berry Head and sailed in past the breakwater he felt weak with exhaustion. Only his pride and determination not to show how he felt kept him going.

''Spects you'm pretty weary, boy,' observed Harry.

'A bit,' was as much as Jed would admit.

'Ever been to sea afore?'

'No.'

''Ee've stood up to it very well. Better'n the little un.' Harry looked thoughtful. 'I suppose it must be 'ard, coming to everything new. Now me, I went out with my dad many a time afore I was properly took on as a boy. It didn't make the work no less 'ard, but I knowd what I were letting myself in for. To you it be proper strange, I dare say.'

Jed nodded agreement at such an understatement.

'Well, 'ee've been took on by a good skipper— Ah but 'e be!' insisted Harry, seeing Jed's look of incredulity. ''E'm an 'ard man, there be no two ways about that, but 'e'm fair. 'E'm a fine seaman, too. When we'm going round land, Land's End that is, in a strong sou'westerly, there's no skipper I'd sooner 'ave than Matthew Burton. When 'e's finished with 'ee 'ee'll be a danged fine seaman as well.' Harry gave a chuckle. 'Strikes me you'm quick on the uptake. 'Ee'll be all right, boy, don't fret.'

Harry was a kindly soul, and he meant his words to be heartening, Jed realized that. What the first hand could not know was, just at that

33

minute, being a seaman, 'danged fine' or otherwise, was the last thing he wanted to be.

They eased their way carefully into the harbour, just beating another smack to the best berth.

'Got our nose in fust!' said Harry triumphantly. 'Not that it matters much these days. Everything can get sent off prompt like. 'Twas a different matter afore the railway came. Then 'twas fust landed, fust off, and fust with the best prices. My Granddad used to tell me of the goings-on to get the catch landed afore the rest. You think the skipper's an 'ard man? 'Ee should've knowed some of they trawlermen in them days!' He chuckled at the memory, then he looked back out to sea. 'See that lot? That's what I meant by our skipper being a good un.' He pointed out to the horizon where a scattering of boats was barely visible to the naked eye. 'Missed the wind, they 'ave! Most of them won't be 'ome afore nightfall, while us'll be snug by our firesides, thanks to the skipper.'

Jed soon found that being in harbour still did not mean an end to work. The catch had to be unloaded. Larger vessels, like the *Our Violet*, did so on to smaller boats, which carried the laden baskets over to the fish market on the quay. After that there was the inescapable cleaning down. Not until Matthew Burton was absolutely satisfied did he allow Jed and Seth to go ashore.

To his dismay Jed found the ground beneath him move up and down, just like the deck of the *Our Violet*. Harry roared with laughter to see him stagger.

'Took 'ee by surprise, did un?' he grinned. 'Don't worry, 'twon't last. Best grab 'old of the little un, afore 'e falls. Come on, son' he said encouragingly to Seth. ''Ee'll be a new boy in the morning.'

''Ope so,' Seth muttered. 'Most of the old one went over the side today.'

'That's the spirit,' chuckled Harry, as they made their way unsteadily along the Quay.

'Not bad,' said Harry appreciatively, regarding their catch already set out in rows. ''Bout twenty pounds that should fetch, I reckon.'

'Twenty pounds shared between the skipper, you, and Cy!' exclaimed Jed.

'It dun't work like that, boy. I wishes it did. No, the catch is divided into eight shares – the boat has to 'ave 'er share – not to mention the gear and so on. New nets and new suits of sails bain't given away free. Cy and me, us gets one share each. Matthew Burton gets a bit more 'cos 'e'm skipper, and a bit more again 'cos 'e owns the *Our Violet*. If Skipper wadn't providing 'ee with board and lodgings you two lads ud get a three-quarter share each. Divided that way it don't sound so much, do it?'

'No, not really.' Jed felt dejected. For a moment he thought he had found some compensation for all the hard work and discomfort.

Harry laughed. 'Don't look so down in the mouth. What'm 'ee getting? Two bob a week and your keep? Then think yourself lucky, my lad. On days when us can't go out 'cos the weather's bad or there's no wind, us don't get paid at all, while 'ee and the little un'll still get your florins. 'Ee'll 'ave best of the bargain then.'

To Jed's ears it still did not sound like a very good deal, but he said nothing. He and Seth bade goodbye to Harry, then made their way to Matthew Burton's house in the centre of the town. As they walked, too tired to talk much, his eyes took in the rows of houses climbing the hills above them. Where were Amy and Daisy, he wondered? How were they getting on? He had a sudden longing to see them again. Despite his determined self-reliance, at that moment he felt that the sight of a familiar face would be very welcome indeed.

—

Amy was anxious about Daisy. For four days they had been in Brixham, long enough for her to discover what a small place it was. Yet in those four days she had had no sight of her friend. It was not that she did not go out often enough. The potato incident and her regular journeys to take Mr Prout his midday meal at the yard apart, she had several times been sent on errands by Mrs Prout. It had been easy to find Fore Street and Mr Floyd's draper's shop. Eager as she was to see her friend she did not like to risk knocking at the Floyds' house door, it might get Daisy into trouble. Servants were not supposed to have callers. She had hung about outside for as long as she dared, peeping in through the glass door, but there had been no sign of Daisy.

How she wished she could have seen her, just to satisfy herself poor old Daisy was all right. Amy was concerned about the boys, too, but less so. They were together, they would be a comfort to one another – though Jed would burst before he would admit to needing comfort. No, it was gentle, timid Daisy she was bothered about.

It did not occur to Amy that she might need comfort herself. Such an idea never crossed her mind. Throughout her short life it had always been she who had cared for other people and given them support. First it had been her ma, especially in those last few months before she was taken away to the hospital, and afterwards it was Daisy and anyone else in the Union dormitory who had needed sympathy. Many a new girl at the Lambeth Workhouse had been grateful for Amy's kindness during the first anguished weeks. Amy felt rather bereft herself now because she was on her own and had no one upon whom to pour her abundant affection.

Things were going better for her at the Prout household. She was quick to learn, and if the china and glassware still had a mysterious way of evading her grasp during the washing-up, she was managing well in other respects.

The food was very good, which was a great compensation to anyone brought up on rations considered adequate by the Board of Guardians. Whatever Jessie Prout's faults she was an excellent cook and prided herself upon providing ample meals, both upstairs and down. For the first couple of days Amy had slipped any surplus into her apron pocket and secreted it away in her room in case of future leaner days. There had been a big row when Mrs Prout had discovered her hoard in the corner of a drawer.

'Why on earth did you do it?' Mrs Prout had demanded. 'Don't I give you enough to eat?'

'Yes, missus.' Amy had stared at the floor, unable to explain that she feared such plenty could not last.

'Rats and mice! That's what we'll have up here next! Don't you know that? Hiding food up here! It's a disgrace! Are you hungry, is that it?'

'No, missus.' Amy had to admit she was full. She raised her eyes and looked into Mrs Prout's face. To her surprise she saw that her employer was more upset than angry. The complaints about the rats and mice had been a sham. What was bothering Jessie Prout was the suggestion that someone under her roof might not have enough to eat.

'I'm sorry, missus. I won't ever do it again, I swear.'

'See you don't! Now clear it out and take it downstairs with the rubbish. And don't leave a single crumb!' Mrs Prout had given an indignant sniff and swept away downstairs.

Since then Amy had noted at each meal there was now extra on her plate. She soon found she needed the nourishment, for she had to work hard. Jessie Prout was house-proud, and a stickler when it came to the scrubbing, sweeping, and polishing. Being on several floors the house was not easy to run. Amy lost count of the times she had to go up and down stairs, not to mention the extra effort needed to keep those staircases clean.

There was one other thing which made her new life more agreeable – the thought of meeting Daniel on Sunday. To have something to look forward to was a novelty in itself, and helped her get through the long days of non-stop work. She was so eager to see him again. Already in her mind he was beginning to acquire the golden aura of a being from some other, higher world.

It was an overcast grey morning when she entered the kitchen, not relishing her regular tussle with the range. It looked more dead and clogged with cinders than usual; she made for the scullery to fetch the ash bucket. Even as her hand went out to the doorknob she froze. A noise came from the other side of the closed door. There was a squeak of hinges, then the click of the latch. Someone was creeping into the house through the scullery. Silently she reached out for a weapon, her hands closing about the broom-handle. Thus armed she crept behind the door and waited, her heart pounding, broom upraised. There came a thud, followed by another, as if boots were falling to the floor. This interloper was a cool one, he intended to sneak about the place in his stockinged feet. Soft footsteps padded across the floor, and before her nervous gaze the doorknob began to turn. The minute the door opened she acted, bringing the broom down on the intruder's head with all her strength. At the same time she yelled at the top of her voice to rouse the household.

'Oo! Ow! What be this for? Stop it, I tell you! Leave off!' The intruder sank to his knees beneath the unexpected onslaught, his arms protecting his head from the blows.

Amy did not give up her attack – or her yelling – until hurried footsteps stumbling down the stairs told her that Mr and Mrs Prout were on their way.

'What be goin' on?' demanded Mr Prout, still hauling his braces over his shoulders. 'What's happened? Have you gone mazed, girl?'

Amy's grasp of the broom slackened in her surprise. He was not alarmed to see a burglar in his kitchen, nor was he pleased she had routed an intruder. He was looking at her in angry astonishment.

'Come on, answer the master!' Mrs Prout was behind her husband, craning her neck to see what was going on. 'What do you think you're doing, hitting Mr Prout like that?'

'I ain't hitting Mr Prout!' protested Amy in bewilderment. 'He's there, in front of you!'

'Not that Mr Prout!' Jessie Prout sounded exasperated at such stupidity. 'Mr Todd Prout! The master's brother.'

'The master's brother!' Amy's perplexed gaze went from the man on the floor, to her employers, then back to the man again. 'Oh my gawd!' she said.

'If I've said it once these last few days I've said it a score of times!' declared Mrs Prout. 'That girl is not suitable, not suitable at all.' She turned to Amy. 'What possessed you to hit Mr Todd like that?'

'I thought he was a burglar,' said Amy.

'You thought I was a burglar? That's rich!' Todd Prout rose gingerly to his feet, still rubbing his head. He was dressed in the blue canvas smock and trousers of a fisherman. Although he was taller and younger than his brother, and his dark hair curled vigorously instead of lying straight, there was a strong family resemblance. 'No, I idn't no burglar, my lover, I lives yer.'

'I didn't know. I thought only Mr and Mrs Prout lived here,' Amy said, close to tears. 'I'm sorry, mister. I hopes I didn't hurt you, but you came in so quiet like.'

'Didn't want to wake everyone,' explained Todd. 'Been fishing off Mount's Bay. We got back just afore dawn. You'll be the li'l Lunnon maid, I suppose?'

'Yes, she is,' retorted Jessie before Amy could speak. 'Though why we had to go so far to reap so much trouble I do not know.'

'Oh, don't be hard on the maid,' said Todd. 'Her was only doing what her thought best.' He gave a wide grin, making his weather-beaten face seem even younger. ''Twasn't as if you did any harm,' he informed a still dismayed Amy. ''Twas only my head as took the punishment. You knows what they say, don't you? "Devon born, Devon bred, strong in the arm, weak in the head."'

He was so cheery, in spite of the beating he had received, that Amy could not help smiling.

'That's better!' said Todd with satisfaction. 'For a minute you was looking as if the end of the world had come.'

'I'm real sorry, honest I am, mister,' repeated Amy.

'That's all right. Don't suppose you means to make an habit of it. Yer, Jessie!' He turned to his sister-in-law. 'You don't have no call for a watch-dog now, like you was always wanting. This li'l Lunnon maid's more'n a match for any burglar. And I'm hoping as her can turn her hand to cooking a bit of breakfast for a starving man, which is more than any dog could ever do.'

Both Amy and Mrs Prout took the hint, glancing in horror at the unlit stove.

'Best get a move on. We're going to be behind-hand because of this fiasco,' snapped Mrs Prout.

Amy did not know what a fiasco was, but she understood the order well enough, and hurried into the scullery for the ash bucket. When she returned the kitchen was empty. She could hear the family going upstairs. As usual Mrs Prout was complaining about having a workhouse girl in the house.

'Don't you realize she might have killed your own brother,' she was declaring.

39

'What, that li'l slip of a thing? It'd take more'n her to bash Todd's head in, wouldn't it, boy?' said Mr Prout. 'No, let her bide. 'Twas our fault us didn't tell her he lives yer too.'

'Surely her common sense...' The rest of Mrs Prout's voice was lost on the stairs.

The last Amy heard was Mr Prout saying, emphatically for him, 'No, us'll give the maid a proper chance. Let her bide, I say!'

There was a closing of doors upstairs, then silence. Amy found to her surprise that she was clutching the handle of the ash bucket so tightly it had made a deep weal across her hand. Slowly she released it, rubbing her palms together to ease the soreness. Mrs Prout still wanted her to go, Mr Prout still wanted her to stay. The precariousness of her situation made her swallow. She dreaded the thought of being sent back to Lambeth. As she riddled the ashes of the range she wondered if Mr Todd might make any difference. Whose side would he be on, his brother's or his sister-in-law's? It was something only time would tell.

Sunday may have been a day of rest for some, for Amy it involved a lot of extra work. Jessie Prout bustled about demanding to have everything done in extra sharp time so that she could put the beef to roast before going to church.

'I like to have the meat cooking, and the potatoes and vegetables all ready to put on the minute we get back,' she said.

''Specially the tatties,' said Mr Prout. 'Make sure you peels enough of they, won't you? About a bucketful should do.'

Amy smiled uncertainly, then she saw that his eyes were twinkling and her smile widened.

'I could put the things to cook while you're out, missus,' she said.

'You aren't staying here alone!' Mrs Prout sounded aghast at the idea. 'You will attend church with us!'

This was the first Amy knew of it. As she was sent up to the attic to wash and put on her Sunday best she was not sure whether she was to accompany the Prouts to church for the good of her soul or because the missus did not trust her by herself in the house with the silver. She changed into her one decent outfit, the hand-me-down navy serge jacket and skirt in which she had travelled from London. When she returned downstairs Mrs Prout looked her up and down critically and said, 'I suppose you'll have to do.'

Amy followed behind the family with a sense of anticipation. Hopefully she would see Daisy and the boys. The thought gave her a comfortable warm feeling which stayed with her right until she reached the steep slope up to the church door. Then it occurred to her that she might see Daniel inside. At this thought her anticipation and her comfortable warm feeling merged into something close to happiness.

Daisy was already in church, seated in a pew with the Floyds – Mr Floyd, small, plump, and looking unpleasantly ingratiating; Mrs Floyd, plain and sad-looking. There was an indeterminate number of little Floyds squeezed in beside them.

Although Amy glanced across at Daisy from time to time, never once did she raise her head. Jed and Seth were not there, and nor was there any sign of Daniel: with his height and his red hair she would have spotted him immediately.

After the service had finished the congregation filed out of their pews with a great rustling of Sunday best and a pervading smell of moth-balls.

'Did you enjoy the service?' asked Todd as they waited to leave their pew.

'Very nice, thank you,' Amy replied politely. Then, emboldened, she added, 'I did hope to see Jed and Seth here.'

'Jed and Seth? They two new lads with Matthew Burton? Oh, you won't never see them yer. Matthew Burton's chapel.'

So that was the explanation! She wished she dared ask if Daniel Newton was chapel too. She did not, though. She would have to curb her curiosity concerning his whereabouts until the afternoon.

To Amy's chagrin the Floyds left well ahead of the Prouts.

Fortunately, when they reached the road outside, she saw the Floyds in conversation with a stout gentleman. Daisy was standing apart, huddled and whey-faced. As they passed, Mr Floyd doffed his hat and beamed his oily smile in their direction, evidently eager to speak.

Mr Prout nodded in greeting and shepherded his small party smartly along the road without stopping. His uncharacteristic brusqueness confirmed what Amy had suspected, that her employer did not like the little draper. It meant that her chance to speak to Daisy was escaping.

'Please, missus,' she said in desperation. 'Can I have a quick word with my friend?'

Mrs Prout's mouth was shaped ready to say no, but her husband was too quick for her.

'All right. You can follow on after,' he said.

'Five minutes!' said Mrs Prout. 'Not one second later. You've the church clock up there, you've no excuse.'

'Thank you. I won't be late.' Amy turned swiftly and hurried back to where Daisy still stood.

She had been ready to ply Daisy with a score of questions when they met up, yet now that they were face to face she could not think of a thing to say.

'Well, then, how're you getting along?' Amy asked at last.

'All right. 'Ow about you?'

'Fine thanks. It's been a bit difficult at first, of course. The dinners are grand, though. Do they feed you well?'

'Not bad.'

'Have a lot to do, do you?'

'A fair bit.'

Amy felt as if she was having to draw the information from her piece by piece. She noted that frequently her friend glanced nervously in the direction of the Floyds, even though they were well out of earshot.

'Look, we can't talk here,' Amy said. 'Have you got time off this afternoon?'

'Yes.'

'Then I'll meet you at King Billy at about two.'

'I don't know where that is,' said Daisy.

Since Daniel had chosen it as their rendezvous, Amy had made it her business to find out.

'It's the statue down by the harbour. A king or summat. The seagulls perch on his head.' It was obvious that this still made no sense to Daisy so she said kindly, 'Never mind, I'll come for you. I'll wait outside the shop.'

There was no time to say more: the hands of the church clock were creeping round swiftly.

'See you then!' Amy gave her friend a sudden hug and hurried off up the hill.

Sunday dinners in the Prout household were special. Jessie considered it only proper to uphold the Lord's Day with the best meal of the week; but such consideration took time. Down in the kitchen Amy was torn between enjoying the sort of food she had formerly only dreamed about and being late for her meeting with Daniel and Daisy. Eventually the last roast potato had been consumed, the final slice of treacle tart and cream been declined by everyone with reluctant groans, and Amy could complete the washing-up.

'Please, missus, is it all right if I go now?' she asked, after she had taken the tea-tray upstairs.

'Go? Where?'

'Please, missus, you said I could have time off on Sunday afternoons.'

'So I did, but I didn't mean this Sunday. For goodness' sake, girl, you haven't been with us a week and here you are wanting time off!'

Amy's heart plummeted to her boots. It had never occurred to her that Mrs Prout had meant her time off to start next week. Daisy would wonder what had happened to her. And Daniel, too. He would think she was the sort who did not keep her word.

'Go on, let the li'l maid have an hour off.' Todd, sprawled in his armchair, beamed with well-fed good humour. 'What's her to do else? Sit in the kitchen and twiddle her thumbs?'

''Tis a nice day. Let the maid get a bit of fresh air,' urged John Prout.

'She's already had some fresh air, going to church,' protested Jessie. 'Oh, very well. You can have an hour. And think yourself lucky, my girl.'

'Thank you, missus.' Amy bobbed a curtsey and fled before Mrs Prout could change her mind.

She wished she had something pretty to wear. Her serge two-piece was unbecoming, it shrouded her slight figure. Yet beneath the severe lines of her black felt hat her face shone with animation, her hazel eyes large with suppressed excitement. Looking in the cracked mirror she noted with satisfaction that her cropped hair was beginning to curl under the hat brim. It did not make her a beauty, but it would do.

She was afraid she would be late, and she had to wait for Daisy. It was some minutes before her friend emerged from the house-door beside the shop.

'How's it going?' Amy asked, taking Daisy's arm and steering her towards the harbour. 'Really going, I mean.'

'Oh, all right.'

'Do they treat you well? They don't knock you about or anything?'

'No, they don't knock me about.'

Amy went on asking the same sort of questions she had asked after church, and getting the same non-committal answers. She had hoped that now they were on their own Daisy might open up more. But her friend volunteered nothing, nor did she question Amy about her situation. Most unusual of all, she did not seek constant reassurance as she normally did. A tight-lipped Daisy was both uncharacteristic and disturbing. Soon they were at the harbour, and there was no further hope of private conversation.

Because they were late Amy was afraid that Daniel would not be there. She was greatly relieved to see him. He was lounging against the protective railings of the statue that dominated the Beach. He saw them as they approached, and straightened up. Amy felt a thrill of pride that he should be her friend, for in his Sunday best he looked very handsome. He was even taller than she had remembered, and his dark red hair had been well-brushed. His smart tweed Norfolk suit with a belted jacket was a far cry from the hand-me-downs and patched garments worn by the other boys she knew.

'Ah, you found King Billy,' he greeted them. 'I thought you'd got lost.'

'I was late getting off. This is Daisy. Daisy, meet Daniel.'

'Pleased to meet you.' Daniel's response was automatically polite.

He's been nicely brought up, thought Amy with satisfaction.

Daisy, however, was too overawed to reply.

'Who was he, this King Billy?' asked Amy, gazing up at the statue of the rather dyspeptic-looking man above them.

'William of Orange. He landed in Brixham from Holland centuries ago, and went on to be King of England.'

'Didn't he have to go to London to be made king?' Amy asked.

'Yes, he marched there.'

'What, from here? All the way? Blimey!'

'Where shall we go?' Daniel was bored with past monarchs and wanted to move.

'Dunno. Where is there to go? I'd like to be by the sea. What about you, Daise?' As Daisy nodded Amy added, 'I've only got an hour, mind.'

'Come on then, don't waste any of it.' Daniel was already beginning to move off, and Amy and Daisy had to hurry to keep up.

'Where are we going, then?' demanded Amy.

'Would you be any the wiser if I told you?'

'No, but I won't be no wiser if you don't, either!' she exclaimed.

He laughed. 'You've got a point there. All right, we're going along by Oxen Cove and past the quarry. There, does that satisfy you?'

'It'll do,' said Amy, then because she was afraid she had sounded too grudging she said, 'Here, have a sweet.' She had bought some pear drops with the penny Mr Prout had given her, and now she offered them around. She was gratified to see Daniel observing the 'ladies first' rule and letting Daisy have first pick. She also noticed that, although he thanked her he was very casual about the way he put the sweet in his mouth and sucked it as if it were of no importance. In contrast both she and Daisy sucked theirs slowly, savouring each drop of the flavour, making it last. Amy was a little disappointed. She had wanted the pear drops to be as big a treat to him as they were to Daisy and her.

How the other half live! she thought to herself. He can probably have as many sweets as he likes. 'What d'you do?' she asked, curious to learn the source of his evident affluence.

'Do?'

'Yes, what's your work?'

45

'Oh, I'm not working yet. At the moment I'm studying.'

'Studying? What's that?'

'Well… studying.' For once he seemed stuck for an answer. 'Learning things. Having lessons. Being taught.'

Lessons meant just one thing to Amy.

'You're still at school? A big bloke like you and you're a schoolboy?' She was appalled. 'How old are you, for heaven's sake?'

'Fifteen, and there's nothing unusual in studying at fifteen.' He sounded somewhat testy. 'I'll have you know my cousin's twenty and he's still studying. He's at university.'

'Gam!' breathed Amy in astonishment 'What's there to learn about for all that time?'

'Stacks of things. He's doing Classics – Latin and Greek and things like that…' his voice faded as he realized she did not know what he was talking about. 'Did you go to school?' he asked politely.

''Course! Everyone has to now. I liked school.' For a moment she sounded wistful as she remembered the one pleasant aspect of life at the Union. 'Got on well, too. Not that we learned nothing fancy. Just reading, writing and 'rithmetic. What about you. Do you like your lessons?'

'They're all right. What I really want to do is go to sea, like my father. I should be at sea now. My father's commodore of the South Devon Line, and I was going to be taken on as a cadet last year, only I broke my leg.'

'Oh!' gasped Amy, full of remorse.

'No, not the one you kicked,' he grinned. 'The other one. The owners say I can join at the end of this summer. In the meantime, father said it would be a good thing if I improved my knowledge. I do elementary navigation, and trigonometry, and mathematics – oh, and some geography.'

'Ooh!' Amy was both impressed and bewildered. 'What's them? I mean, you said the other day about navvy… navvy summat. What's that?'

'That's learning to find your way about the oceans. There are no landmarks out there – you have to use charts – they're sorts of maps of the sea.'

46

'If there's nothing out there, what can they put on these chart things?'

'You'd be surprised. They put in bits of coastline and the depth of the water. It's very interesting how they do it...'

He went on talking, and Amy listened in dumb admiration. He was so clever. He knew about things she had not known existed. Until this moment she had always felt she had done quite well at school; now she became conscious of how little she knew.

They had left the harbour, packed with trawlers, behind them, and were taking a track between cliffs and the sea, with Daisy as their silent shadow. Amy had wanted to walk by the sea, but now she had it lapping a few feet from her she almost ignored it. Her attention was all for Daniel. He led them along a pathway which rose, suddenly bringing them out on a grassy slope dotted with hawthorns. Amy now knew they were hawthorns – Daniel had told her. The profusion of wild flowers almost took her breath away.

'Will you look at that, Daise!' she cried. 'Ain't it pretty? All them flowers – the pink ones and the white ones like stars, oh, and the blue ones – they must be bluebells, I bet you.'

'Yes, they are,' said Daniel. 'The pink ones are campions, the white starry ones, they're called milkmaids, and the small yellow ones—'

'Them's primroses! I've seen them before. There's a woman sells them down the New Cut every year!' Amy was determined not to appear a complete ignoramus. All the same, she was very impressed. Was there nothing Daniel did not know?

'You want to be near the sea, don't you?' Daniel said kindly. 'Let's go down on to the rocks. Don't worry, it's quite safe. I'll help you both down.'

The expanse of green rolled away to a fringe of rocks at the water's edge. In fact, the drop was not steep, and numerous small tracks showed where others had made their way on to them. Not for the world would Amy admit that she could have got down quite easily by herself. She preferred to have her hand grasped by Daniel and to have her feet directed into the exact spots where they must tread.

They sat down on the rocks, the salt wind in their faces, and ate more of Amy's pear drops.

47

She looked at the sea, blue-green in the sunshine and white-capped by the stiff breeze. It was beautiful, yet she still found it rather frightening.

'Do you really want to go to sea?' she asked Daniel.

'Of course. Why not?'

'What sort of a boat will you go in?'

'A ship,' he corrected her gently. 'The South Devon Line have ships. Schooners, to be exact.'

'What's the difference? Between a boat and a ship, I mean.'

He grinned, his green eyes sparkling. 'They say you can put a boat on a ship but you can't put a ship on a boat Does that answer your question?'

'Near enough. Will you have to go far?'

'Right across the world at times. The South Devon Line trades in fruit. Oranges, bananas, pineapples. They go to Florida, over the Atlantic to get them. It takes them weeks to get there. See that ship out there? The one just off the harbour? That's one of their schooners.'

'It is big,' said Amy, though privately she thought it was not nearly big enough to sail out of sight of land. Bananas and pineapples were only items in a greengrocer's shop window to her, but she had eaten oranges. They had been the annual Christmas treat at Lambeth Workhouse. One orange per child. She had enjoyed them very much, but looking at the size of the schooner she would gladly have forgone oranges for ever rather than have Daniel risking his life to fetch them.

'There used to be lots of schooners in Brixham when my father was my age,' said Daniel dreamily. 'They must have been a brave sight. Now there's just the South Devon Line and a few independent ones left. They've been killed off by the steamer trade. Of course, I won't be going on one of the Florida runs for my first trip, more's the pity. I'll probably only get as far as the Med.'

'What's that?'

'It's a sea. The Mediterranean Sea.'

'Cor, what a mouthful! Are you pulling my leg?'

'No, honest. Just a minute.' He rummaged in his pocket and pulled out a crumpled piece of paper. It was a page from an exercise book.

'This went a bit wrong,' he said, smoothing it out on the rock in front of them. 'But it will do.'

On the paper was a series of wiggly lines drawn in coloured inks. 'I can't make head nor tail of those, can you, Daise?' said Amy, still trying to include her friend in the conversation, though she had long since given up any hope of getting a response.

'I'll explain,' said Daniel pointing. 'Now this bit is the coast, and there's Brixham. This is the Mediterranean... I'll be sailing round like that.' With his forefinger he traced the line of his proposed voyage. 'We'll load up with fruit on the south coast of Spain – here.'

'What's that funny bit like a boot?'

'That's Italy. And at the end here's the Holy Land.'

'Where all the Bible stories come from? Cor!' Amy was impressed. She pointed with her forefinger and traced, just as he had done. 'There's Brixham, then round this bit to Spain. That bit's Italy, and that's the Holy Land where Jesus lived, and they're beside the Mediter-something Sea.'

'My word, you pick things up quickly!' Daniel sounded proud of his pupil. 'You've just done some geography, did you know that?'

'Have I really?' Amy was not sure which pleased her most, Daniel's praise or having tackled a subject with such a fancy name. Then she knew – pleasing Daniel!

A less pleasant thought was that her hour off must be almost up.

'You aren't far from the Prouts' house. I'll show you a short cut,' Daniel said when she said she must go.

'What about Daisy? She'll never find her way back alone.'

'I'll take her. I can go home that way,' said Daniel.

At this suggestion, however, Daisy clung frantically to Amy's arm.

'I reckon I'd better go with her,' Amy said apologetically.

The three of them made a speedy return towards the town.

'Will you only have an hour off next week?' asked Daniel.

'I don't know. I hope I'll have two.'

'Then perhaps I'll see you by King Billy again? I can't promise, because my father's due home.'

'I'll be there if I can, and you'll be there if you can. That's fine.' Amy beamed happily at the prospect then, waving goodbye, hurried Daisy back along Fore Street.

'Amy,' said Daisy suddenly, as they reached Floyd's shop. 'That King Billy, did he really march to London?'

'Daniel said he did. It must be true.'

''Ow long did it take, do you think?'

'Oh, weeks and weeks I should reckon!' Amy stopped abruptly as the significance of Daisy's questions sunk in. 'Daise, you ain't thinking of running away back to Lambeth, are you? Oh, don't even think about it. It's ever such a long way. You'd get lost. Say you won't try to run away!'

'Why shouldn't I?' demanded a suddenly resentful Daisy. 'Why should I take any notice of you? You said it'd be lovely 'ere and it ain't. You said the people would be nice, and they ain't. You tell lies, Amy Kennedy! It was better at Lambeth!'

Amy was astounded at such an outburst. She felt hurt and angry by turns. Then she saw the bleak misery in her friend's eyes.

'It's just because it's all new,' she said gently. 'Once we get the hang of things everything will be fine. Don't run away – please! They'd just send you back here again. Don't try it!'

Daisy muttered, 'All right,' with such a look of desolation on her face that Amy's heart went out to her. She wished she did not have to dash away, but the church clock was telling her she had very little time to get back to the house.

'Things will get better,' she repeated. 'And we'll meet up again next Sunday if we can both get off, eh?' Impulsively she thrust the paper bag which still contained two pear drops into Daisy's hand, then hurried towards Furzeham.

The misery in Daisy's eyes haunted her all the way up the hill. It took some time for her natural optimism to take over, and with it the happiness of being with Daniel. He was like no one she had ever met; she had thought it before, and now she was even more sure of it. He talked of things that were new and different, and he was good at explaining. Fancy, because of him she could pick out the Holy Land on a map all by herself. She could do – what was it? – Geography! Her world had expanded, and with it her heart felt full. With luck she would see Daniel again next week. Poor Daisy, wanting to go back to Lambeth. As far as Amy was concerned she was growing more and more determined to stay in Brixham.

Chapter Three

Amy was scrubbing the front steps when a large black spider suddenly appeared inches from her nose. She gave a scream and struck out at it with the scrubbing brush; then she noticed the bit of elastic fixed to the spider's back. Behind her someone started laughing.

'Oh, Mr Todd, you nearly gave me a heart attack!' she protested.

'Good, idn't it? Proper lifelike.' Todd jiggled the spider up and down experimentally.

Amy gave a shudder. 'A bit too lifelike for me.'

At that moment the bedroom window shot up and Mrs Prout put out her head.

'What's all the screeching?' she demanded. She caught sight of her brother-in-law. 'Todd Prout, what are you doing there? That girl's got work to do.' To Amy she said, 'I want those steps really clean this time. No leaving out the corners. If they're not satisfactory then you'll do them again and again until they are.' She withdrew her head and pulled down the sash-window with a thud.

Todd and Amy stood side by side on the pavement looking suitably abashed, Todd with his hands behind his back to shield the spider from Jessie's gaze. Then suddenly they both burst out laughing.

'Wait until Jessie sees what a surprise I've got for her!' chortled Todd. And he jiggled the spider again. Then he grew serious. 'I'm real sorry I've got you into trouble.'

'Don't worry, I was in trouble already.' Amy gave a sigh and wrung out her cloth. 'This is the second time I've had to do these danged steps. They weren't good enough first time.'

'That's Jessie all over, proper house proud. Her bark's worse than her bite, though. I minds when her and John was first wed, her was a happy enough soul then. I reckons it's not having childer. Desperate for a babe, she is, and John too. Her was expecting two or three times, but they came to naught. Poor Jessie, her'd make a fine mother. Life bain't fair, be it?'

Todd often felt the rough side of his sister-in-law's tongue, and Amy was touched by his gentle sympathy. He made her consider Jessie Prout in a new light. In her eyes Mrs Prout seemed to have everything – a good husband, a comfortable home, pretty clothes, more than enough to eat – yet obviously it was not so. The lack of a child was evidently a great tragedy to the Prouts.

'I s'pose 'tis more than my life's worth to go up this way?' Todd pretended to tread on a newly-washed step.

In retaliation Amy threatened him with the scrubbing brush, then hurriedly dropped it in the bucket, alarmed at what she had done. You did not pretend to hit one of your employers with a scrubbing brush, not even in fun. She waited for the stem reprimand. None came.

'Come to think of un, I'd best not go in the front, not in my sea-boots,' said Todd, quite unperturbed. 'Jessie'd never let me hear the end of it!'

He went down the stairs to the bottom door, as he always did after coming home from work. Amy followed him, smiling as she went. It was hard not to smile at Todd's antics. He was never serious for a minute, always up to mischief, like an overgrown schoolboy.

Todd had removed his boots and was now washing his hands at the big stone sink in the scullery. Despite his larking about he looked tired.

'Fishing seems a hard life,' she remarked. 'Did you never fancy boatbuilding, like Mr Prout?'

'Who? Me? I never had the skill for it, nor the brains! The fool of the family, that's me! Father said so from the day I was born.' He sounded remarkably unconcerned about being condemned at such an early age. 'Decided to arrive right on trawler race day, see. My fust big mistake, and I never got nothing right after.' He gave a cheery grin. 'Not that I minds! I enjoys myself, and that's the main thing. John's offered me a job many a time, but I'm happy where I be. Rest of the family's got on well, of course. Our Edward's up to Grimsby – owns a couple of trawlers there, and Joseph, he'm in America. He'm got more work'n he can manage, according to his letters. And of course there be John. He started out as a shipwright.'

'He must have worked very hard to get his own yard.'

'He did! Mind, he married the boss's daughter. That helped.' Todd's ever-present grin widened. 'No, that idn't fair. Proper soft about each other they were – and still are. Best day's work Jessie ever did was marrying our John, both for herself and for the yard. Old Man Taylor, her father, were drinking away the profits a deal faster than the men could build the boats. If John hadn't stepped in the lot would've gone long since.'

'Oh…' Amy had always thought Jessie to be a somewhat fearsome figure, but now she assumed more human proportions.

Being more human did not lessen Mrs Prout's authority over Amy, however. She bustled into the scullery in her customary way.

'I might have known!' she declared. 'You are not paid to gossip, girl. You haven't even started on the bedrooms, have you? Before you begin, though, I want you to go down to fetch Mr Prout's boots from the cobbler's. They were promised for this morning.'

Although she had more than enough to occupy her, Amy enjoyed running errands. Going anywhere near the harbour continued to fascinate her; there was always so much of interest to attract her attention. Her usual regret was that she seldom had time to linger. On this occasion, however, she was in luck.

'Mr Prout's boots? They'm not ready yet, my lover.' The cobbler had looked at her regretfully over his spectacles, 'Can you come back for them in ten minutes?'

Happy to dawdle she found herself a fine vantage point at the top of Overgang Steps, and regarded the busy activity below her. Many trawlers were already moored or at anchor, their red sails hanging limply to dry from the masts like leaves in autumn. Others were just entering the port, manoeuvring for position with infinite skill.

'Amy! Amy!'

The sound of her name caught her attention, and there below her was Jed. At the sight of him she rushed down the steps and flung her arms about him in an impulsive embrace, oblivious to the fact that he had just come off the boat and was far from clean. Hoots and whistles made her drop her arms swiftly and take a step back. The catcalls were good-natured enough, but you could never tell with Jed. She had no wish to embarrass him in front of the other fishermen. Fortunately he did not seem put out by her greeting. His face lit up with pleasure at the sight of her.

Before she could speak he demanded urgently, 'How are you? How're they treating you?'

His evident concern surprised her. 'Fine thanks. A bit strange at first, but I'm getting the hang of things better. How about you?'

'Not bad.' He said it quickly, as if not wanting to be questioned further. Nevertheless, she looked pointedly at the bruise on his cheek.

'That's an old one,' he said. 'I'm getting the hang of things too; I don't get thumped so often.'

Amy was appalled. 'Is Mr Burton cruel to you?'

Jed considered carefully before he spoke. 'He's very strict. Reckons he's got to turn us from the path of wickedness and such like. He's doing his duty, according to how he sees it, and I must admit I've learned a lot from him already. Harry, he's the first hand, says Mr Burton's one of the best skippers in Brixham.'

'Well, that's something, at any rate.' Amy tried to sound optimistic. It was typical of Jed to have summed up his skipper so thoroughly in so short a time. 'How's Seth?'

Jed's face grew more serious. 'He gets a lot more hidings than I do. It's the stories he tells; the ones about his dad having pots of money and a carriage and goodness knows what. Skipper considers them to be lies.'

'No one takes no notice of them stories. He just tells them to make himself feel more comfortable,' protested Amy.

'I know. I did try to explain to the skipper...' Unconsciously Jed touched his bruised cheek. 'But to the skipper they're lies, and "A liar be an abomination unto the Lord", or so he says.'

Amy was silent for a moment. She wondered how often he had had to step in to protect Seth, and how often he had been punished for doing so… But it was no use asking Jed, he would never give anything away. 'And how's Daisy?' he asked.

'She don't like it here.'

'Poor old Daise. She'd not like anything new.'

'Perhaps that's it. She's certainly taken against the place pretty strong for her – or maybe it's the folks she works for. And, Jed, she's talking of running away, back to Lambeth.'

'Daisy is?' The enormity of timid Daisy contemplating such a thing made Jed's jaw drop. 'I hope you talked her out of it.'

'I tried…' Perhaps she should not have told Jed of Daisy's intention, but sharing her anxiety with him had been a relief.

'Where'd you live?' asked Jed suddenly.

'Up there.' Amy pointed to the hill behind them. 'You can see us from the water. We're in the end terrace. A white house with brown paintwork.'

'I'll look out for it,' Jed promised.

'I always look out for you and Seth,' Amy said, 'I don't know which boat is yours – I wave to every one I see. What's your boat called?'

'The *Our Violet*. Her number's DH 151.'

'What's that mean?'

'Dunno exactly. That we're the one-hundred-and-fifty-first boat to be registered at Dartmouth, I suppose. That's what the DH stands for – Dartmouth. It's the next port dong the coast.'

'Why Dartmouth? Why not Brixham?'

'Don't ask me!'

'Right! From now on I'll know what to look out for,' said Amy with satisfaction. 'I'd better go now and fetch Mr Prout's boots or I'll have to look out on my own account.'

'I'm glad I've seen you,' he said. 'I've been wondering how you were getting on.'

'I've been wondering about you, too,' said Amy. 'I hope things get better for you, and that you don't get any more shiners like that one.'

'They're getting fewer all the time,' he said. Then he smiled his rare smile.

Jed would be fine, decided Amy as she ran back up the hill, the boots under her arm. He was tough, a survivor, like her. She wished she could say the same about Seth and Daisy. Well, she now knew which boat to wave at. It made her feel closer to the boys.

–

In a long, hardworking week, Amy's two hours of freedom on Sunday afternoon would have loomed large under any circumstances. The added prospect of seeing Daniel made the occasion doubly precious. For days before she was in an agony of anxiety in case Mrs Prout should curtail her meagre time off again, or stop it all together. Much to her relief, after Sunday dinner was over and everything was tidied away, Jessie Prout said, 'Well, I suppose you're desperate to be off. Mind what you get up to! You're to behave yourself, or I'll soon hear about it.'

With this warning in her ears Amy dashed up the numerous flights of stairs to the attic, to don her serge two-piece and her black felt hat. That morning she had managed only the briefest of words with Daisy after church. She had been relieved to see her; it had been a niggling worry to her that her friend might have taken it into her head to run away after all. Now Daisy was already waiting for her outside the draper's shop, and at the sight of her she thought the poor girl looked too exhausted to walk far, never mind run away.

'Perhaps we'll meet Daniel at King Billy again,' Amy said. 'He might not be able to come, though. Where shall we go today?'

'Somewhere where we can rest our feet,' was the uninspiring reply. Daniel was waiting at the statue, just as he had done the previous week. He looked so well-dressed, his tweed Norfolk suit immaculate. Clearly there was no 'popping' of his Sunday best at the pawnbroker's every Monday, like most folks. The sight of him caused Amy's heart to lighten, yet at the same time she felt uneasy, remembering Mrs Prout's parting warning.

'You're prompt. Jolly good,' Daniel said when he saw them.

'You're here! That's jolly good too,' answered Amy. 'What happened? Didn't your dad come home?'

'No. He won't be home for a few days. He sent a telegraph message saying he was putting into Falmouth. That's in Cornwall, to the west of us,' he added with a grin. 'I know how keen you are on geography.'

For all he was only joking, his words made her feel proud and happy. She felt that to have even a joking interest in something like geography set her apart from her drab background... Was he disappointed because his father had not come home? she wondered. It occurred to her that she had remarkably few friends with fathers she could inquire about. She had one herself, of course. Somewhere! Ever since she could remember Pa had disappeared from time to time. He had always come back eventually – loving, apologetic, and broke. All except the last time, when Ma had been really poorly and started coughing blood. He had gone away then and never come back. And good riddance, thought Amy.

'Where can we go?' she asked. 'We've both got two hours this week.'

'I suppose you'll want to be by the water again? All right, we'll go to Fishcombe. It's only a bit further on than we went last time. It's a nice little cove, you'll like it.'

'It sounds lovely, don't it, Daisy?' she asked.

'Yes, lovely,' replied Daisy without enthusiasm.

As they retraced their steps of the previous week, Amy felt she had to speak out. The unease which had been with her since leaving the house would not be silenced, no matter what it cost her.

'Daniel,' she said. 'You won't get into trouble from your folks for being seen with us, will you?'

'Why should I be in trouble?'

'You know – for being in the company of a couple of workhouse girls.'

'Of course not! And, anyway, you aren't workhouse girls any more. You are both in respectable domestic service.'

His reply sounded too confident to Amy's sensitive ears. 'Once workhouse, always workhouse,' she said firmly. 'You can't get away from it. I'll bet your ma'd kick up something awful if she knew you were with us.'

'Not Mother, she's a good sort.' He spoke with the confident assurance of an adored son.

'Your pa, then, when he comes home. What'll he say if someone tells him who you've been with?'

'But Father isn't home, is he? We'll cross that bridge when we come to it.'

She had been right. He knew perfectly well that his family would not approve. 'I don't want to cause you no trouble,' she said gently. 'Even if it means we don't see each other.'

'Don't you want to see me any more?'

She was flattered at how dismayed he sounded. ''Course I do. Only, as I says, I don't want to make no trouble for you.'

'And what about you?' asked Daniel. 'Are you sure Mrs Prout would be pleased to learn you'd been meeting me?'

Amy knew Mrs Prout would be anything but pleased. She had been conscious of the fact since she had agreed to meet Daniel that first time.

'There'd be all hell let loose,' she said frankly.

'Yet you came!'

'Yes, I came!' She looked up at him, her hazel eyes suddenly alight with laughter. 'All right, we won't worry until we've got something to worry about, eh? Until the fur begins to fly, let's enjoy ourselves.'

'That's the spirit! I knew you were a good un!' declared Daniel approvingly.

In that instant their friendship acquired an added edge of excitement, the extra attraction of forbidden fruit. They exchanged conspiratorial smiles, drawn closer in the knowledge that, just by being together, they were earning the disapproval of their elders.

Side by side they strode on, with Daisy following behind. Once past the quarry the wild flowers were as beautiful as before, scattered across the vivid green of the spring grass. Amy was tempted to linger and pick some.

But Daniel did not halt. 'We're nearly there,' he said, as they rounded a small headland. 'It's a bit of a drop down, I'm afraid.'

He was not exaggerating. Below them a small shingle cove was tucked in a cleft of the wooded hillside. The path they were on ended in a steep scramble down the rocks.

There was no pretence about accepting Daniel's aid this time. Amy was grateful for his strong grip. Somehow they manoeuvred a fearful Daisy between them until they reached the beach. Amy accomplished the last few feet in an undignified slither down the rocks, showing an indecent amount of stocking and leg in the process, and losing some skin on the sharp rocks.

When her feet touched the shingle, however, she was delighted she had made the effort. With cliffs and hilly slopes rising steeply above it on three sides, the cove had an air of seclusion about it, despite the harbour being just round the headland. Amy felt it was a perfect place for them to be, secretive and cut off from the eyes of the world. The sea beyond them was a cool aquamarine; where it lapped against the shore it was crystal clear, intensifying the delicate colours of the pebbles and making them shine. In no time Amy had quite a collection, marvelling at their variety – palest pink, soft grey, speckled white. She picked up a green stone, as translucent as a jewel.

'What's this?' she demanded excitedly. 'Is it treasure?'

Daniel smiled indulgently. 'It's a piece of glass,' he said. 'Probably a bit of broken bottle.'

'Gam!' said Amy, not believing him.

'It's true,' he laughed. 'It's smooth through being rolled about in the waves for goodness knows how long.'

'The sea really did this?' she said. She ran an exploratory finger over the rounded surface, now devoid of any sharpness or jagged edges. Then she slipped it into her pocket. To her it was a treasure cast up by the tide, no matter what Daniel said.

Daniel was playing skimming stones, sending small flat pebbles skittering across the surface of the waves.

'Did you see that?' he cried in triumph. 'That was a twelver! Did you see?'

'Yes,' declared Amy with admiration. 'How d'you do it? Show me!'

Although Daniel's instruction was patient, she couldn't achieve more than a sixer.

Laughing, they crunched across the pebbles to the large rock where Daisy had settled herself as soon as they had arrived.

'Blimey, she fast asleep!' Amy said softly. 'Poor soul, she does look wore out.'

'We'll let her sleep then,' said Daniel, equally softly. 'Come on, let's find another rock.'

They moved far enough away so that their voices would not wake Daisy.

'I've got something for you,' said Daniel. 'Close your eyes, hold your hand out and see what God sends you.'

'You always say that!' This time Amy trustingly closed her eyes at once and held out her hand.

It was not the expected sweet that Daniel laid on her palm, it was something larger and flatter. Amy opened her eyes.

'A book!' she exclaimed.

'It's a geography book. You seemed interested – I thought you'd like to read it. It's all about the Mediterranean and the lands round about.'

'The places where you'll go?'

'Some of them, certainly. Look, there are pictures and maps – far better maps than the one I drew.' Daniel flicked through the pages.

'Ooh thanks! Are you sure you don't mind me borrowing it? I'll be ever so careful.'

'I'm not lending it, I'm giving it to you.'

Amy's breath was almost taken away by such magnanimity. 'I can't take it!' she protested.

'Why not?'

''Cos books cost ever such a lot, that's why not! Your Ma'd likely go mad if she knew you was giving good books away.'

'No, she wouldn't. She was going to throw it out, along with the other school books I don't use any more. Amy, it's not a very good book. It's battered and torn. I just thought you'd be interested because of the subject. If you don't want it—'

'Don't want it? Who said I don't want it?' Amy was appalled at such an idea. 'I don't want you to get into more trouble, that's all.'

'Will you stop worrying about me? I give you my solemn promise that no one will mind me giving you that old book. Mother had put it in a box ready to go down to the church bring-and-buy sale. It's all right! Such a tizzy about one battered book!'

To Amy it was not battered. Until Daniel had mentioned it she had not noticed the ink-stained cover, the missing spine or the loose pages. To her it was something to be treasured even more than the pretty piece of sea-worn glass. Very few books had come Amy's way. Her schooling in Lambeth had been enough to give her a hunger to know more, but her circumstances had never allowed her to assuage that hunger. In her narrow world a book was something to be greatly appreciated. What made this one more valued was that it had been used by Daniel and was a gift from him. With something like awe she put it carefully in her pocket out of harm's way, and held her hand over it protectively.

'Thank you,' she said quietly. 'Thanks ever so.'

One look at her beaming face was enough to show how delighted she was.

'If it pleases you that much I'll see what else I've got,' said Daniel nonchalantly, happy to bask in her gratitude.

They sat in silence for a while. It was sheltered in the cove, and the spring sunshine was warm. Amy leaned back against the rock, her eyes closed, letting the sound of the lapping of the tide gently soothe her.

'Hey, don't go to sleep,' protested Daniel.

'I wasn't!' declared Amy, not quite truthfully. To prove how wide awake she was she sat bolt upright.

'The Prouts are still treating you well?' he asked.

'Yes, thanks. She can be pretty bad-tempered when she's a mind. But I like Mr Prout. And as for Mr Todd, well, there's certainly never a dull moment when he's about.'

'Todd Prout? He's a fool,' Daniel said disparagingly.

'No, he ain't!' exclaimed Amy so loudly that Daisy stirred in her sleep. 'He's a real nice bloke, and he's ever so kind.'

'Well, if you like him there's no more to be said.' Daniel spoke in an uninterested manner.

Amy regarded him anxiously. 'What's the matter?' she asked. 'You sound as if you've got the miseries.'

'Nothing's the matter with me,' he replied almost sulkily. 'I'm just glad you're getting on like a house on fire with the Prouts.'

Amy was afraid she had said something to upset him, though she could not imagine what.

'I wouldn't go that far,' she said carefully. 'And although things ain't bad there's one thing I don't like.'

'What's that?'

'I s'pose it's silly, and it ain't only the Prouts as does it, but I don't like the way everyone keeps calling me "maid". I know that's what I am and everything. All the same, it narks me to hear it all the time. I may be just a servant, but there's no need to rub it in. I've got a name, why can't they use it...? Why're you laughing...? What've I said...?' For Daniel was grinning all over his face.

'I suppose you wouldn't know, you only being a Londoner,' he chuckled. 'But "maid" is what we call a girl round here. It doesn't mean "servant" at all. Why, my sister often gets called "maid" and she doesn't object.'

'Oh!' said Amy, feeling rather foolish. 'I didn't know.' Then she swiftly went on the attack. 'What d'you mean, saying I'm only a Londoner? London's a grand place. The biggest city in the world! It's where the Queen lives and it's a lot better than this stinking dump.'

'Why did you come here, then, if London's so wonderful?' he teased.

''Cos I didn't have no choice,' she said, becoming suddenly serious.

'I suppose you didn't.' He became serious too. 'I'm sorry, I shouldn't have made a joke of it. There's something else I'm sorry about too. That first day we met I called you "Workhouse". I shouldn't have done that. It was rotten of me. I'm very sorry and I hope you will forgive me.'

She did not know what to say. For four long years it had been drummed into her that the inhabitants of the Union were among the lowest of the low, that it was not a misfortune to be poor, it was almost a crime. Yet here she was, Amy Kennedy, barely two weeks out of

Lambeth Union, hearing someone like Daniel Newton offering her his apologies. She could not believe it.

'I would forgive you anything,' she said softly.

Daniel smiled. 'Even this?' he asked.

Leaning forward he kissed her gently on the mouth.

Amy tried to say, 'Even that,' but the words would not come.

Kisses were a rarity in her life. Yet if they had been a daily occurrence, she was convinced no one else would ever have kissed her like that. The softness of his lips touching hers came as a revelation to her. She was bewitched by him, and by the experience. She wanted to return his kiss, but she was too shy. He was a lordly being in her eyes; for him to bestow favours was acceptable; for her to do the same would be presumptuous. The only way she could show her delight was by smiling back at him in sheer happiness.

The sun had gone off the cove, warning them that the afternoon was almost at an end. Reluctantly they roused a sleepy Daisy and headed back. When they had successfully scrambled up the slope and brushed the resulting mud from their clothes Daniel said, 'I won't be able to see you next week, I'm afraid.'

He did not explain why the arrival of his father should make a difference, though Amy could guess.

'Never mind,' she said, still too buoyed up with delight to be disappointed. 'It'll be nice for you, having your pa home.'

'Yes, it will.' Daniel's answer was sincere, and she was glad. It was good that he should be fond of his pa. She waited for the words she hoped would follow.

'We'll meet up the week after, shall we? Same place, same time?'

'Yes, all right.' Her reply was calm and matter of fact, belying the happy tumult inside her.

Daniel had kissed her! The ghost of his lips touching hers remained with her long after they had parted, long after she had seen Daisy safely home, long after she had returned to the seclusion of her attic in the Prouts' house. She was convinced the memory would remain with her for ever.

Amy found herself fitting better and better into her new way of life. She had grown used to sleeping alone at night; it was rare now for any unexpected noise to have her wide awake with her heart pounding. One thing she felt she would never get used to was the view from her window. Every night, after she had blown out her candle, she would gaze upon the scene. The sea still frightened her in its vastness and its power, but its ever-changing beauty held her with a relentless fascination.

One evening Amy settled herself by the range, glad of its warmth, for April was proving unseasonably cold. This was usually a respite in her busy day, the brief time between washing up the supper things and making the bedtime cocoa. She toyed with the idea of reading the book Daniel had given her, then thought better of it. If Mrs Prout caught her there would certainly be all sorts of questions as to how she had come by it. Already she had read it from inky cover to inky cover several times. There was little about the Mediterranean that she did not know, from climatic conditions to trade routes, from countries and capital cities to principal commodities. The only thing she could not really grasp was the true distance between Brixham and this far-distant sea; Daniel would be going there one day, and she wanted to know how long she would have to wait for his return.

A sharp rapping on the outside door made her jump. The callers who came down the bottom steps were usually tradespeople and it was far too late for any of them. Curiously she went to open the door. There, to her amazement, stood Jed and Seth.

'Hullo, Amy,' they said in unison.

'What are you two doing here?' she demanded. Then she laughed. 'My, didn't I sound sour then? I didn't mean to. I'm just that surprised to see you.'

'We've come to say goodbye. We're going away,' said Jed.

'Going away? But you've only just got here. Where're you going?'

'We're off to Wales in the morning,' said Seth. 'We're going to make our fortunes, and I shall 'ave a carriage with gold 'andles just like my dad's, only bigger.'

Amy and Jed exchanged glances. Mr Burton's hidings had not altered Seth one bit.

'I don't understand, why're you going to Wales…?' began Amy. 'And I don't know why I'm keeping you on the doorstep, neither. Come in.' Mrs Prout would create, no doubt, but she was willing to risk that.

The boys entered and stood looking about the kitchen, their caps in their hands.

'This is nearly as good as our place,' declared Seth. 'We've got a comfy armchair each, and a great big sofa, and carpets on the floor and—'

'You're nice and cosy here,' broke in Jed, before Seth's fantasy got out of hand. 'I like this.'

Such unexpected enthusiasm from Jed made Amy take in the details of the kitchen more carefully, something she rarely had time to do during the day. He was right, the kitchen was cosy. The range was glowing, casting a rosy light on the cream-painted walls and on the gleaming blue and white china neatly stacked upon the dresser. Warm and welcoming was how it seemed.

'Come and sit down, then tell me what this is about.' Amy pulled twokitchen chairs on to the rag rug by the fender.

Before the boys could sit down, however, Mrs Prout burst in.

'I heard someone at the bottom door—' she began, then she saw Jed and Seth. 'And who might you two be?' she demanded.

'If you please, missus, they're Jed Greenway and Seth Reynolds. They came from Lambeth the same time as I did,' said Amy.

'Haven't they got tongues of their own?' The way Mrs Prout was folding her arms across her plump bosom did not look promising.

Jed faced up to her, looking her straight in the eye. 'We're off to Tenby tomorrow, missus. We'll be gone all summer. We've come to let Amy know where we've gone. Mr Burton said we could if it's all right by you.'

'You're a bit late in asking if it is all right by me, seeing that you're standing in my kitchen,' snorted Mrs Prout, then she relented. 'You can stay for half an hour. No longer!'

'Thank you,' said Amy. Then, emboldened by relief, she asked, 'Please can I make them some tea?'

'Very well.' Jessie Prout regarded the boys. 'I've heard Violet Burton isn't much of a hand at cooking. You can give them what's left of the seedy-cake.'

'Wonders will never cease!' breathed Amy, as the door closed behind her employer. 'Here, sit down while I get the cups.'

The tea brewed, she took out a wedge of seed-cake and cut it in two. Jed looked at his slice. 'Ain't you having any?' he asked.

'No, I haven't room,' Amy replied.

He gave her the sort of look he normally reserved for Seth and his stories, and she laughed.

'It's true, I tell you,' she insisted. 'I've only just had my supper. We had meat pudding and taters, with apple dumpling to follow. If I eats any more I'll burst.'

Reassured, Jed tackled his portion of cake. Both boys ate with singleminded enthusiasm. Not until they had finished, and literally every crumb had been demolished, was there any hope of conversation. 'Why're you going to this place?' Amy asked. 'What's it called?'

'Tenby,' said Jed. 'Fishing there's good in the summer, they say.'

'Ain't it good here, then?' Amy asked.

Jed shrugged. 'Dunno. We're going, that's all I can tell you.'

'But all summer...' Amy was appalled. She had seen precious little of them since coming to Brixham, but knowing they were close by had been comforting. 'Where is this Tenby, then?'

'To the west. In Wales,' Jed informed her.

She was not much the wiser. Daniel was sure to know where Wales was. She would ask him.

'If you've got to go then there ain't no help for it,' she said. 'You'll have the good weather, that's one thing. It'll be nice being at sea then, seeing new places and all,' she added, determined to be optimistic.

'We're going to have a grand time,' declared Seth. 'Skipper's going to let me take the 'elm all the way. I'm the best 'and 'e's ever 'ad, and 'e's going to make me skipper of my own boat when we gets back.'

'That's nice,' said Amy absently, her attention on Jed. She was trying to determine whether he was truly getting on all right, but it was impossible. As ever his face gave nothing away.

'Things still going fine for you?' she asked.

'Not bad. I've not had a hiding for three days.'

'Well, that's got to be good!' Amy declared cheerfully. 'Mr Burton must be getting to like you.'

'It isn't only Skipper Burton, neither,' grinned Seth. 'Lucy's got 'er eye on 'im. Oh my, if 'er ain't!'

'Shut up, you!' retorted Jed, flushing.

'Who's Lucy?' Amy asked.

'Lucy Burton, the skipper's daughter,' said Seth. 'She's sweet on Jed, want's to marry 'im I shouldn't wonder.'

'How's Daisy these days?' Jed asked, changing the subject so deliberately that Amy wondered about this Lucy Burton. It was unusual to see him ruffled.

'Still not happy. I reckon she's being worked real hard. Last Sunday she seemed wore out. We went to this little cove and she fell asleep.' Amy did not like to mention anything about Daniel being with them.

'Shame!' Jed shook his head in sympathy. 'Pity there's nothing much we can do.'

''Til keep an eye on her,' Amy said.

The mood in the kitchen became serious as they contemplated their inability to help.

'Did I tell you about the trouble I had over the taters?' she asked, suddenly determined to cheer up the proceedings. The boys were going away for months, and she did not want their leave-taking to be gloomy. Soon she had them laughing with her description of all the buckets and bowls of peeled potatoes about the place. Then she went on to tell of Todd Prout's pranks.

'Honest, you never stop laughing when he's about...' Her voice tailed away at the unmistakable tread of Mrs Prout coming down stairs.

'Half an hour, I said!' Jessie Prout declared sternly, 'And that was five-and-forty minutes ago.'

The three of them scrambled to their feet.

'Sorry, missus, we got talking and didn't notice the time,' said Amy hurriedly.

'Yes, sorry, missus. We'll go now,' said Jed. 'Thank you for the tea and the cake.'

Seth would have charged out if Jed had not hauled him back with a muttered, 'Where's your manners?'

'Thank you for the tea and the cake, missus,' repeated Seth obediently. Then at the memory of the unexpected treat he beamed angelically. 'That was the best cake I ever 'ad in my whole life.'

For once he was not exaggerating, Amy thought. It was probably the only cake he had ever had. Jessie Prout did not know that, though. She smiled at him, an unexpectedly tender smile which softened her features to an extraordinary degree, making her look younger, prettier, more gentle.

'You're welcome, boy,' she said. 'You can both come and see Amy again when you get back, if you wish. Mind, I'm to be told the minute you come. I don't want anyone and everyone coming in through my scullery.' Her final comments were more like the Mrs Prout Amy knew, though the words lacked their customary sting.

On his way out Jed looked back. Amy had lit the lamp and its soft yellow light made the kitchen appear even more inviting. He was glad she had somewhere nice to live, where she was being treated well and the food was good. She was looking bonny. She had filled out and grown quite rosy. Her hair was growing too, and curls the colour of honey edged her white cap. He thought how nice and fresh she looked in her print dress and crisp apron: fresh, and wholesome, and very pretty. It was a picture he carried away with him. It stayed with him on the long, treacherous voyage round Land's End. It was still with him when they reached Tenby.

–

There was no denying that Tenby was a pretty place. Tucked within medieval walls it was a pleasing mixture of the stylish and the quaint. A ruined castle on its hill dominated the port, while tall, elegant houses fringed the small harbour. Jed liked the town, but to his mind the fishing off Tenby was no different from the fishing off Brixham. It was as arduous, as fatiguing, and as downright uncomfortable. There was not even the benefit of sleeping ashore to look forward to. A few men from the fleet of Brixham trawlers had brought their families with them, and had temporary homes in the town. Most, like Jed and Seth, lived aboard their boats. No one would ever consider residing in the Burton household to be easy living, but it was luxury compared to the cramped, stuffy, smelly conditions aboard the *Our Violet*.

To Jed's way of looking at things fishing had nothing much to recommend it. In Wales or in England it made no difference: it was a chancy way of making a living, with fickle catches and equally unpredictable market prices. What sort of a future lay ahead of him if he stayed with the trawling? A darned hard life, with precious little to show for it. He wanted something better. The trouble was that he did not know what. However, he had the next five years in which to think and plan there was no getting out of his apprenticeship.

One difference between life in Brixham and in Tenby was the pattern of Sundays. The few Sabbaths that Jed had spent at the Burton house had been dominated by chapel three times a day, and interminable readings from the Scriptures. Here, to Jed's surprise, the main service was an unexpectedly open-air affair. A harmonium of all things was brought ashore from one of the Brixham boats, and set up on the beach at the head of the harbour. The fishermen gathered round, ready to conduct their own service. Apparently this was no novelty, for many local people had gathered to join in the worship and to sing the hymns.

At last the final notes of 'Abide with me' drifted away across the water and an old Welsh woman who was standing by Jed dabbed a tear from her eye.

'Such a beautiful hymn,' she sighed. 'You Brixham men sing it every year, and I love to hear it.'

'It's special to us, for it was written in Brixham by the vicar of our All Saints' Church,' said Harry.

'Oh, there's lovely!' said the old woman with evident approval. 'You must be proud, belonging to a place where such a fine hymn comes from.'

'That we are, my lover,' said Harry. 'We be, bain't us, lads?' His beaming smile took in the half-dozen or so Brixham men who were standing nearby, and it included Jed and Seth.

Jed did not feel that he belonged anywhere, certainly not to Brixham. He wondered what it must be like to have some special attachment to a certain place. It was something he had never experienced: he had been pushed about from pillar to post too much for that. The two years he had spent at the Lambeth Workhouse had constituted the greatest security he had ever known, and there was no way he would ever have a special attachment for that place.

'We know the summer's come when we see your red sails off the coast.' The old woman gave a toothless smile.

'The only times we miss chapel is when you Brixham men come with your harmonium. Isn't that right, cariad?' said her husband by her side.

'That's right, and we hope you come for many summers more,' agreed the old woman.

The service over, the people began to disperse. Jed and Seth fell into step beside Harry, walking over the sand.

'You've been here lots of times?' asked Jed.

'Yes,' Harry replied. 'Us've been to the North Sea for a few summers too, mind. Grand fishing there if you knows where to go.'

'Don't you ever get tired of fishing?'

'What else'd I do?' Harry looked surprised at the question.

'There must be something easier.'

'Oh, yes, and there's lots a darned sight 'arder. With 'ard work and a bit of luck you can do well at the fishing. Some do very well...'

'If they've had a grand start!'

'No, not so.' Harry jabbed his pipe-stem in the direction of a man walking ahead of him. 'See 'im – George Beale? 'E were a work'ouse boy, too. 'E were 'prenticed like you. And now look at 'im. Owner and skipper of 'is own boat.'

Jed was incredulous. 'He never is!' he declared.

'I ain't joking. 'E'm owner and skipper of the *Faith*. You must 'ave seen 'er.' Harry swung round and regarded the trawlers at anchor off the harbour mouth. 'That be 'er, to leeward of the *Jupiter*. A good sound craft.'

Even at that distance the *Faith* did indeed look to be a good sound craft, as she rocked gently on the incoming tide.

'And the man who owns her came from a workhouse?' Jed still could not believe it.

'That 'e did. And from a Lunnon work'ouse like you, now I comes to think of it. 'E didn't 'ave no grand start yet 'e prospered.'

Jed did not reply, he was too busy thinking. It had never occurred to him that it was possible to attain so much from fishing. To be a skipper and an owner! That would be something! If George Beale had managed it, why couldn't he?

Once the idea took hold it gnawed away at his brain like a maggot. During the next week or two he watched the *Faith* and her skipper whenever he could. George Beale was a good seaman, he could see that for himself whenever he observed the *Faith* under sail or shooting her trawl. It was also evident that Skipper Beale was held in esteem by the other fishermen. If his name was ever mentioned it was with respect. He was clearly a man to emulate… And Jed wondered what was the secret of his climb to success. He had to find out.

It was on a fine May morning, when the trawlers were back in port and the catches all dispatched, that Jed chanced upon Skipper Beale. He was leaning over the harbour wall, smoking his pipe. It took the boy some time to summon up his courage, but eventually he realized that it was now or never. He gave a polite cough.

'Mr Beale, sir.'

The man turned. 'Yes, boy?'

He was a short man, thick-set and grey-haired, with vivid blue eyes set in a weather-beaten face.

Jed was not sure how to continue. 'If you please…' he began. Then he blurted out in a rush, 'Is it true that you were a workhouse boy?'

George Beale scrutinized Jed for a minute, as if trying to place him, then he said, 'You'm with Matthew Burton, bain't you?' There was nothing in his accent to tell he came from London.

'Yes, sir. I was apprenticed from Lambeth Workhouse.'

'So that's it.' The man's bright blue eyes twinkled. 'Yes, I was a workhouse boy, too, from Acton. Now I'm a trawler owner. And you want to know how it's done, eh?'

'Yes, please.'

'I tell you, I bless the day when I was apprenticed to a trawlerman, instead of some other trade.' Skipper Beale drew on his pipe. 'I didn't at the time, mind. I hated every minute. But I'd had nothing and been nothing all my life. I wanted to be something before I died. I worked hard, I saved, I got my skipper's certificate… And I made sure I was one of the best darned fishermen in the fleet! Then two of us bought a boat between us, a small one, just twenty-five tons, a mumble bee. Blessed if I knows why they'm called mumble bees. Daft name for a boat, I reckon. I suppose it's because they'm like the craft they have on the Welsh coast, up Mumbles way. Any road, when I could I bought my partner's share. Then I sold the mumble bee and bought a bigger dandy boat, the *Faith*. I've another smack being built now over to Prout's yard – she'll be the *Hope*… I ain't finished there. I means to have one more, and she'll be the *Charity*. I had charity at the start of my life and I'll have *Charity* at the end, but there'll be a wealth of difference between them. Ah, I sees you appreciates the joke. Yes, you knows what I mean, it's writ all over your face.'

'I want to get on too,' said Jed simply.

'Then fishing's your best bet. There ain't many occupations where you can drag yourself up from nothing to something *and* not have folks look down their noses at you. If you'm a good seaman you'm respected in fishing, no matter where you'm come from. You'm getting a good start. There isn't much about seamanship that Matthew Burton don't know. He'll help you save your money, too, 'cos with his eye on you, you won't get much of a taste for strong drink. You seem bright enough. And being from a workhouse you'll be used to hard living. Yes, you'm a fair number of things in your favour. The only other thing you need, apart from a bit of luck, is determination. Think you'm got it, boy?'

'Yes, sir.' There was no doubt in Jed's voice.

'Good, that's what I like to hear. One bit of advice I'll give you: don't get tangled with a wife and family too early. They can drag a man down quicker than anything I know.'

'I don't intend getting married,' Jed said.

'So you say now, boy.' A slow grin spread over George Beale's tanned features. 'So you say now... Well, I wishes you luck.'

'Thank you, sir. Thank you...'

Jed was scarcely aware that Skipper Beale had relit his pipe, nor that his own footsteps were leading him away, back to the *Our Violet*. His head was too filled with thoughts and plans. So far he had thoroughly disliked fishing. That had been in the days when he had seen it as an arduous, dead-end job. Everything had changed now. He could not wait to get back on board, to learn all that Matthew Burton had to teach him. He knew now where his future lay. It lay with the sea and fishing. He would be skipper of his own craft one day.

Chapter Four

All morning the mist, white and opaque as lamb's wool, had blanked out the bay. Gradually it had been dispelled by the hot sun, and at its retreat Amy's eyes had hungrily scanned the sea.

In the two years since she had come to live at Brixham she had come to dislike these sea fogs more and more. The old London pea-soupers she had known as a child had never had the uncanny element which pervaded the sea mists. Maybe it was the desolate wailing of invisible fog-horns out there on the equally invisible sea; or maybe it was the realization of the perils boats could be in when they could neither see nor be seen: she knew of too many vessels lost and good men drowned – run down by large steamers coming at them out of the mist. On this particular day, however, her chief grievance against the thick fog had been that it had impaired her view of the English Channel.

Thankfully, the sun was now blazing down out of a clear sky. Like a cloud of red-winged butterflies the trawlers were leaving harbour and skimming over the waves, eager to round Berry Head and make up for lost time. Amy paused in her task of hanging out the washing to watch them.

These days she did not need to see a vessel's port number to identify it, nor squint to make out the name on the stem. Each boat was easily recognizable to her by the particular shade of its red sails, caused by every Brixham skipper having his own recipe for the liquid in which the sails were regularly soaked to preserve them. The *Our Violet*, with Jed on board, and the *Jupiter*, with Seth, had been among the first to leave. Amy could make out the brownish-red of the *Vigilant*'s sails just quitting the harbour. She waved, though she knew Todd could not see her.

Impatiently her eyes kept going to the horizon, where the line between sky and sea was still smudged with a band of pale mist. It was not red sails she was hoping to see, it was the white sails of a schooner. Daniel was due home. Anticipation and excitement at the prospect of seeing him again had such a hold on her she felt as if she would burst. At times like this, when at any moment she hoped to see the sun glinting on white canvas far out on the horizon, she could forget how empty the world was without him. It was a different matter when he sailed away again and she knew she would not see him for weeks. She had no wish to think of departures, though. Daniel was coming home! That was all she wanted.

'If you don't get that washing out soon it'll be time to bring it in again,' remarked Mrs Prout.

The sharp edge to her words was caused more by habit than any genuine criticism. It had been a long, long time since she had threatened to send Amy back to Lambeth or declared bitterly that they would rue the day they had taken on a workhouse girl. Relations between mistress and maid were far from amiable, but they had fallen into a comfortable routine shaped by custom.

'When you've finished you can go down to Higgin's to see what's happened to those plums,' she continued. '"I've some lovely plums coming over from Dittisham this morning, Mrs Prout. I'll send the boy up with a chip the minute they arrive, Mrs Prout."' She mimicked the greengrocer's voice. 'Where've they got to, that's what I'd like to know? Mr Prout's set his heart on plum tart for his supper, but at this rate he'll still be waiting come Sunday.'

Amy pressed home the last peg then raised the line high with the clothes-prop to catch the growing breeze. 'I'll go right away.' Her accent had lost much of its London harshness, and was now softened by a hint of Devonshire burr.

'And while you're in the town you can see if Floyd's have got that waxed ribbon in he told me would be here last week,' went on Jessie, following Amy into the kitchen. 'He's another one whose promises are like piecrusts. Don't buy any, mind. I just want to know if it's in. Four inches wide and black, nothing else.'

The heat struck Amy the moment she emerged from the bottom stairs into the street. Here she was shielded from the sea-breeze by the row of houses and the sun blazed down on her relentlessly, making her glad to move into some shade. Halfway down the hill she met the greengrocer's boy struggling up, a chip of plums over his arm and an ominous bulge in his cheek.

'You eating the profits?' she demanded.

'What if I am? They idn't counted,' replied the boy.

Amy grinned and helped herself to a plum.

'All right, I won't tell if you won't,' she said.

The boy spat out his plum-stone and eyed her appreciatively.

''Ow about meeting me later? Us could go over Furzeham Green for a bit of courting.'

'Sorry.' Amy looked suitably regretful. 'I don't get off till eight, and that would be past your bedtime.' He must have been all of twelve.

'Yah!' The boy thumbed his nose at her.

'Yah!' answered Amy, pulling a face in retaliation.

It was not a very dignified thing for a young woman of sixteen to do, but she had not been able to resist it. She was still chuckling as she went on her way, unaware that the saucy errand boy was still looking after her with evident admiration.

In these last years her accent was not the only thing to have changed. Thanks to Mrs Prout's cooking she had grown taller, and her figure had become attractively rounded. To her irritation the summer sun had tanned her cheeks a pale gold; she would have much preferred to be fashionably pale and interesting, though a tan was infinitely preferable to the pinched features and city pallor with which she had arrived at Brixham. Her most pleasing attribute, as far as Amy was concerned, was her hair. It had grown splendidly, and it gave her great satisfaction to be able to put it up in a golden-brown mass and anchor it properly with hairpins. It did not matter that it was usually hidden under her cap. The main thing was that her workhouse crop was only a horrid memory.

There was no need for her to call at the greengrocer's; the plums would be safely in the Prouts' kitchen by now if the boy had not eaten them all on the way. Amy could have turned back; the inquiry about the waxed ribbon was not urgent, she knew. Once on her way, however, she decided to continue. It was too beautiful a day to ignore a chance to be out of doors.

Mr Floyd was already serving a customer when she entered the shop, much to her relief. The intervening years had done nothing to make her like the man more. Mrs Floyd regarded her from across the counter, a polite, slightly vague smile on her face. She had the distrait air of someone who was thinking of other things. 'Can I help you?' she asked.

'Yes, please. Mrs Prout would like to know if the waxed ribbon you were expecting has come in.'

'Waxed ribbon?' Mrs Floyd looked bemused, as if she had never heard of such a thing.

'Yes. Four inches wide, in black.'

'In black?' Mrs Floyd sounded as if black too was an unknown quantity. Then she rallied for a moment. 'If you don't mind waiting I will ask my husband as soon as he has finished with his customer,' she said, then lapsed into her day-dream.

To Amy's discomfort the other customer left almost immediately, and Mr Floyd came over. There was no regarding her over the counter for him. He came up to her and stood very close. She could smell the pungent scent of the pomade he wore on his scanty hair.

'Why, it's our Daisy's little friend,' he beamed, taking her hand in a moist grasp. 'What can I do for such a pretty creature?'

'She's inquiring about waxed ribbon. Black. Four inches wide,' said Mrs Floyd.

She had been paying attention! 'It's for my employer, Mrs Prout,' Amy said.

'Ah, yes! You can tell Mrs Prout that it is in and that it is tenpence three-farthings a yard. Very reasonable price for such quality.'

To Amy's discomfort he had begun to caress the back of her hand with a pudgy thumb. She pulled her hand away in disgust.

'I'll tell her,' she said, making swiftly for the door.

Mr Floyd got there before her and took hold of the handle.

'Please do. And when you've got a moment you might like to choose something for yourself. We've got some pretty things, and for a delightful young person like you I am sure we could come to some arrangement...'

'I'll think about it,' said Amy, determined to do no such thing. 'Now if you'll excuse me, Mrs Prout wants me back quickly.'

'Yes, of course.' He opened the door a little way, blocking most of the opening with his plump figure.

Amy saw what he was about immediately. He was forcing her to squeeze past him, so that their bodies must touch. The very thought revolted her. Under cover of saying goodbye to Mrs Floyd she surreptitiously took hold of the edge of the door, then gave it a sudden tug. Amy was fit and strong, and surprise was on her side. The door was wrenched from Floyd's grasp, grazing his knuckles painfully in the process.

'My, what a sudden gust of wind,' said Amy innocently. 'It's a wonder it didn't take the door off its hinges.'

She did not wait to find out if Floyd was taken in by her ploy; she left as hurriedly as she could, unconsciously wiping the hand he had held on her apron.

Poor Daisy, having to live with that! she thought.

Barely had she left the draper's shop when she saw Daisy herself coming along Fore Street, a heavily laden basket extending her stick-like arms to their limits. At the sight of her friend Amy's heart dropped. As she had thrived since coming to Brixham, so the other girl had declined. Daisy's slight body seemed ready to snap; her face was habitually drained of colour and her blue eyes were ringed with dark shadows. Although there had been no more talk of Daisy running away anyone could see that she was desperately unhappy.

'Hullo,' said Amy. 'You weren't in church on Sunday. What happened?'

Daisy looked a little bewildered, as if she were having difficulty in collecting her thoughts.

'I was needed indoors,' she said.

'I didn't see you in the afternoon, either,' Amy persisted. 'Aren't the Floyds letting you have your time off? Because if not, it isn't good enough. You ought to complain...' Even as she spoke she knew how silly her words were. The idea of Daisy complaining was ludicrous. And, besides, who would pay attention to a servant girl's grievances? 'Look,' she said gently, 'While the nights are light Mrs Prout sometimes lets me have an hour off of an evening. Why don't you ask Mrs Floyd if you can have a bit of free time, since you missed your Sunday? We could meet up and go for a walk, or just sit somewhere and chat. It would be like it was at Lambeth. We used to talk a lot in those days.'

'No!' said Daisy, with unexpected emphasis. 'It'll never be like Lambeth, ever again!' Then her voice took on its usual hesitant tone. 'I can't get away. They'd never let me.'

Time was pressing. Amy knew she would be in trouble if she did not get back home soon, yet Daisy looked so forlorn she could not leave her without offering some comfort.

'You don't have to stay with the Floyds, you know,' she said. 'We aren't apprenticed like the boys. You can find another job.'

'No I can't!' cried Daisy in distress. 'Not with the character the Floyds would give me. No one'd have me. No one!'

Amy bit her lip, upset to see her attempts at consolation fail. 'I've got to go,' she said. 'I'll see you on Sunday. We'll talk more then.'

'On Sunday...' Daisy repeated vaguely.

Her manner was something else that bothered Amy. She had never had a strong intellect, but recently she had become so distant it was almost as though she were losing her grip on reality. Her behaviour reminded Amy of someone. She was almost back at the Prouts' house before she realized who it was. It was Mrs Floyd.

The kitchen was a scene of hectic activity when Amy entered. Jessie had been inspired by the delivery of the plums to preserve the fruit as well as make tarts.

'Where've you been all this time?' Mrs Prout complained, her face already flushed with the heat.

'I went to Floyd's like you said, missus,' replied Amy. 'The ribbon's in. It's tenpence three-farthings a yard.'

'My stars! Does the man think I'm made of money? Here, you start stoning these plums, while I get on with the supper.'

There was no time for distractions during the next hour or so. The kitchen filled with the rich scent of cooking fruit. It was not until Amy went to open the window – which had been closed against invading wasps – that she saw the sight she had been longing for all day. The *Balmoral*, Daniel's ship, was entering the harbour. She was both happy and disappointed: happy because Daniel was home, yet disappointed because normally she delighted in following the progress of the *Balmoral* from her first sighting on the horizon until the vessel reached port. Illogically she felt as if she had been robbed of a portion of Daniel's leave.

There would be no meeting with him that night. The plums would ensure she got no free time and, besides, Daniel's first evening home was always spent with his family. They had become much more circumspect in the last two years, had she and Daniel. In the early days the knowledge that their youthful romance would be frowned upon had added a touch of spice to the relationship. Their attitude had altered as the romance had developed into a deeper love. They were careful not to risk that love. It had become too precious to them both to be wrecked by other people's disapproval.

It was not until the following evening that Amy felt free to say, 'Is it all right if I step out for a breath of fresh air, missus? I've done the supper things and the kitchen's tidy.'

She waited, trying not to hold her breath. Had she sounded too eager? Did Mrs Prout suspect she was meeting someone?

'I suppose so,' said Jessie grudgingly. 'You're to be back before dark, though.'

The sky was already flushed by the setting sun and bats were on the wing as Amy hurried from the house. Her route led her away from the town and along the narrow footpath towards the woods above Fishcombe Cove. There, looking down on to the sea, yet sheltered from prying eyes by a thicket of elderbushes, was their special place, private and secluded. They had found it by chance when a heavy shower of rain had sent them scurrying for cover. Now it had become an important element in both their lives.

Amy did not know if he would be there. Such uncertainty had been a major thread woven throughout their love. At the very least, however, he may have left her a letter under the roots of one of the bushes. Eagerness hastened her footsteps so much that her boots slipped and slithered on the stony track.

'That's scarcely a silent approach,' said a familiar voice, as much-loved arms enfolded her, sweeping her off her feet.

Amy's startled yelp of alarm was stifled by Daniel's lips crashing hers. For a long time they clung together, bodies entwined, mouths hungrily seeking one another, desperate to make up for the empty months of separation.

When the first urgency of their greeting was over, Daniel spread his coat on the ground for them to sit on, and the richness of crashed greenery filled the air.

'I thought you weren't coming,' he breathed, resting his cheek against her hair.

Amy nestled closer to him, scarcely able to believe that she was with him at last.

'I'm sorry. Supper was late.'

'I knew you'd come if you could. Oh, I've missed you so much!' His words came in an explosive sigh.

'And I've missed you. You know I have. I hate it when you're away.'

'That's the penalty of loving a sailor.'

'I suppose it is.'

'There are advantages, too, of course.'

'There are? Such as...?'

'This!' He tilted her head back and kissed her with a warmth and an energy that left her gasping. 'There, no landlubber can kiss a girl like that.'

'Is that true? I'll have to kiss more landlubbers to find out.'

'Don't you dare!' Seizing her firmly he rained kisses down on her.

'All right! All right!' she cried, laughing and breathless. 'I'll take your word for it, honest!' Then, suddenly serious, she put her arms about his neck and asked, 'How long are you home for?'

'A week. One whole, glorious week. Isn't that splendid?'

'Yes, wonderful,' she replied, though in her heart it did not seem very long, not compared to the months he was away at sea.

'You sound glum. We'll see each other every day, won't we?'

'I'll try to get away, certainly. It isn't always easy.'

'You'll manage somehow.'

'That's what you always say.'

'Well, it's true. If you really want to be with me you'll slip out somehow. Where there's a will there's a way!' He spoke confidently. Daniel was always confident. Accustomed to getting what he wanted, he still could not quite comprehend Amy's lack of freedom, even after all this time.

'I'll do my best. What about you?'

'I shall be here again tomorrow and the day after and the day after… right until I go back to sea. Mother can talk about "social obligations" all she likes. I prefer to be with you.'

'Oh dear, has there been trouble already?'

Just how much Daniel's mother knew about their relationship Amy did not know; he would never tell her. She feared Mrs Newton suspected her son had formed a liaison with someone unsuitable. Little things Daniel had let slip, such as his mother's frequent lectures about his social duties, and her attempts to keep him by her side, made it evident.

'Certainly not!' His reply was too emphatic. 'She did remark about me going out tonight, when she had invited friends in for a musical evening. I pointed out that I was at her disposal for twenty-two hours out of every twenty-four that I was home, and surely it was not unreasonable to want a couple of hours to myself.'

'And what did she reply? Didn't she ask how you intended to spend that couple of hours?'

'Of course.' Daniel's eyes sparkled with mischief. 'I simply gave her a hug and told her not to worry, that boys will be boys.'

'But didn't she—'

Amy got no further. Her words were silenced by a kiss.

'You're worrying about me again,' Daniel said with mock severity. 'Stop it this instant, do you hear?'

'All right, bossy boots! You aren't issuing orders from the quarter-mast now, you know!'

'Orders from the quarter deck!' corrected Daniel, collapsing with laughter. 'Issuing them from the quartermast sounds as though I was up a stick, like a monkey.'

'Very appropriate!' retorted Amy.

'Now you're cross,' he teased. 'Your lower lip is sticking out. Does that mean you intend to sulk?'

Amy pretended to consider. 'I haven't time,' she said. 'I've to be back before dark.'

'It's almost that now.'

As if to emphasize how late it was growing the whirring call of a nightjar sounded from deep within the woods. Amy and Daniel sat side by side, holding hands, and listening. Neither of them moved. It was too perfect a moment to spoil, with the air heavy with the scent of late honeysuckle and the bird's languorous note rolling through the warm summer night.

Amy rose with reluctance. 'You'd better not be late,' she said sadly. 'It's always the same. There are always a hundred things I want to ask you, and there never seems time.'

'Some day there will be all the time in the world,' Daniel replied softly, taking her face between his hands. 'When we can really be together. The rest of the world can like it or lump it.'

He spoke with such conviction she almost believed him. She had her misgivings but this was too special a moment to voice them.

'I forgot to tell you something very important,' she said.

'Oh, and what's that?'

'The fact that I love you very much.'

'You're right, it is very important. How come you didn't tell me sooner?'

'Because I was saving the best until last,' she said, pulling his face down gently towards her to kiss him.

Slowly, unwillingly, they parted.

'I'll see you home,' said Daniel.

'Better not. Just in case.'

'Does it really matter if anyone sees us together?' he asked somewhat irritably.

'Yes, you know it does.' She stretched up and kissed him again. 'That will have to last me until tomorrow, I suppose. I'll be waiting for you here at the same time.'

'I may not get away.'

'You'll get away.' He spoke as though the matter was in no doubt. 'Now go, before Ma Prout goes on the warpath.'

One last sun-ray streaked the sky as Amy reached home, and by some miracle Mrs Prout made no objection.

'I was wondering when you were coming back,' was her only sour comment. 'You can start the cocoa while I'm locking up.'

It was strange that Jessie Prout, who was normally so sharp, had not suspected Amy's love affair. She had actually found out about the girl's friendship with Daniel long ago – before Daniel had even gone to sea. Her anger, when she heard that her new maidservant had been meeting a boy, had been terrible. She had scolded Amy endlessly, lectured her, cancelled her time off for a month and threatened yet again to send her back to Lambeth. The one thing she overlooked in the heat of her fury was to extract any promise from Amy that she would never do it again. Amy had withstood the scoldings and the threats, fretted over her lost free time – and felt herself at liberty to continue meeting Daniel. The only difference was that they were more cautious about being seen.

The attic still held the daytime's heat when Amy went to bed. It was not the warmth which kept her awake, it was thoughts of Daniel. At first she relived every moment she had just spent with him, then gradually her thoughts drifted towards the future...

Was there a future for her and Daniel? He was convinced there was. She was less certain. The gulf between a servant girl and the only son of a well-to-do seafaring family would have been wide enough under normal circumstances. She had the added stigma of her workhouse years. She loved him desperately. More than anything she wanted to marry him one day. Yet how could she? A wife who came from the workhouse would be an appalling burden to him, both socially and in his career. Encouraged by Daniel, she did everything she could to fill in the gaps in her education – borrowing books, or buying them secondhand out of her tiny wage – just so that she would not be a disgrace to him. But it was no use, and she knew it. No matter how much she loved him, nor how much she tried to improve herself to be worthy of him, her past could not be eradicated. Once workhouse, always workhouse! The words pounded in Amy's head as she tossed and turned. It was a long time before she fell asleep.

–

Jed came ashore at the Quay, and slung the bag containing his stocker-bait – his share of the unsaleable fish – over his shoulder. He looked back towards the New Pier. The *Balmoral* was in, he noticed, and his mouth tightened. That meant the tall red-haired fellow would be home. He had hoped to go up to see Amy for half an hour that evening, as he sometimes did, but there would be no point now.

He did not know Daniel Newton personally, just by sight. He had seen him down by the harbour in his uniform, all sharply-tailored navy-blue and brass buttons, looking superior. It was only by chance that he had found out about the love affair between Amy and Daniel Newton. He had been in Fishcombe Woods after rabbits, when he had seen them together. Never had he let on that he knew about it, but it had not been easy. There had been times when he had been sorely tempted to warn Amy that in courting Daniel Newton she was courting trouble. He did not, however – he remembered the radiant happiness on her face as she looked up at Newton, and he knew he would be wasting his breath.

It was hot in town, and grew hotter where the sheltering hills cut off the sea-breeze. Jed felt dispirited as he reached the Burton house. He entered by the back door, put his Stocker in the scullery, then went across the yard to the quarters he shared with Seth. It was nothing more than an outhouse, freezing in winter, damp when it rained, and baking on a summer's day such as this. Jed remembered Seth once describing their accommodation to Amy in glowing terms, telling her they had a carpet on the floor, comfortable armchairs and much more. That was

Seth's exaggeration at its most extreme. Reality was an unadorned stone floor, two iron bedsteads with straw mattresses, two battered tin trunks, a wash-bowl and jug on a rickety stand and a piece of unframed mirror. The Burtons euphemistically called it the cabin, but it was still an outhouse.

For the moment Jed had the place to himself. Seth was not in yet, nor would he be for a good hour. These days Seth sailed on the *Jupiter*, with Isaac, Matthew Burton's son, and Jed had seen the vessel approaching the harbour as he walked along the Quay. He was hot and tired, yet he felt a certain satisfaction at having another week's fishing behind him.

They had trawled beyond the region known as the Scruff, off Portland Bill. Although it was only at the other side of Lyme Bay, it was an area they did not frequent often; Skipper Burton preferred to fish to the westward of the bay. Jed had registered every detail of the unfamiliar fishing grounds; the depth of water, the currents and the prevailing winds. Most of all he had registered the bottom-soil of the seabed, for it was that which most affected the type of catch and the ease of trawling. This information he stored carefully in his mind, ready for the day when he would be skipper. That was how he regarded his working life these days, as so many steps towards being master of his own craft. It was what made the danger, the discomfort, and the back-breaking toil worthwhile.

Wearily he pulled off his boots and scale-encrusted fishing clothes. Stripped to the waist he went into the yard and pumped cold refreshing water over himself. He was so engrossed that it was some time before he realized he had an audience. Lucy Burton was leaning against the kitchen door watching him.

It always amazed him how Matthew and Violet Burton could have produced a daughter like Lucy. The parents were both alike – thin, severe and spare – while their daughter could only be described as voluptuous. As far back as Jed could remember Lucy's bosom had loomed large in his vision. A couple of years older than Seth and him, she had been well-developed when they had first come to live with the Burtons. In the intervening years she had had no qualms about using her generous curves provocatively when the boys were about, especially Jed. She could be most embarrassing too in the way she showed her preference. Jed had long since grown adept at avoiding sitting next to her at meals, for beneath the shelter of the table, her hands were liable to stray caressingly across his thighs.

Now, as she leaned against the door, her rounded breasts seemed to strain the plaid cotton of her dress to bursting point. Her eyes were taking in every detail of Jed's near-naked body as die water trickled over his glistening skin. Her gaze was appreciative. Jed had become wellmuscled in the last year.

'Have you seen everything?' he asked, reaching for his shirt.

'I dunno, do I? What else 'ave you to show me?' Her dark; eyes were bold and inviting.

'Nothing that'd interest you.'

'Be you'm sure?' Lucy moved towards him, and began undoing the buttons on his shirt as fast as he did them up.

Jed's pride would not let him retreat from her. He snapped, 'Get off!' and thrust her hands away.

'If you'm shy us could go into the cabin. Seth won't be back for ages yet; our Isaac's always way behind Pa.'

'I'm not shy and I certainly don't want to go anywhere with you.'

'Why not? Us could have some good fun. There's a thing or two I could show you. You'd like that, wouldn't you?' She was close enough for her magnificent bosom to be pressed up against him, and the scent of her warm body filled his nostrils.

'No!' he said shortly. Her proximity was beginning to have its effect on him, exactly as she had known it would. Grasping her by the shoulders he pushed her firmly away from him. 'Behave yourself,' he said. 'I'm not going to play your games. Go and find someone else.'

'I don't want no one else,' she replied frankly. ''Tis you I got my eye on. Come on, let's go in the cabin, just for a few minutes.'

'No!' His answer was more emphatic.

'Why idn't you nice to me?' she asked curiously. 'Could be worth your while – if you was really nice to me.'

'A thrashing from your father's not worth while.'

'Oh, 'e'd thrash you right enough if 'e caught us. But then 'e'd have the banns called. I wouldn't 'alf fancy being Mrs Greenway.'

'I don't fancy marrying you.' Jed's reply was blunt. 'Even if I was old enough.'

'You'm nearly seventeen, bain't you? When our Isaac got Mary Anne into trouble 'e 'ad to get wed, and 'e was only just eighteen. Still, I don't mind waiting a while.'

'I'm not marrying you!' retorted Jed, surprised at the revelation about Isaac, who always seemed as dour as his parents. Clearly, there was a hot-blooded streak in the Burtons he had never suspected.

'You'm a fool,' replied Lucy without rancour. 'You'm idn't thinking straight. Marry me and you'm be doing all right for yourself. Pa likes you. Why else 'as 'e kept you on the *Our Violet* and sent Seth to the *Jupiter*? It's 'cos 'e thinks you've got something about you. 'E idn't getting no younger, you know. 'E'll have to give up the sea one day, and then who'll get the *Our Violet*? 'E wants to keep the boats in the family. There's only Isaac and me left, and Isaac's already skipper of the *Jupiter*. Think about un!'

Jed did think. Such a short cut to his ambitions had never occurred to him before. Marry Lucy and he could be skipper of his own boat in a few years.

Lucy regarded his rapt expression, a smile of triumph on her face.

'Think all you like,' she said. 'One way or another I means to make you wed me some day. You idn't going to 'ave no choice.'

Before Jed could stop her she had moved close to him again and, rubbing her body sensuously against his, she kissed him full on the mouth and whispered, 'You idn't going to 'ave no choice at all, my lover!' Then, laughing, she flounced off into the house, swirling her petticoats.

Stripping off his shirt again he went back to pumping cold water over himself. Lucy had given him a lot to think about in more ways than one. He tried to guess how much longer Matthew Burton would continue going to sea. The skipper's health was getting progressively worse, he might continue for another four – five years? Five years! By then Jed would be about twenty-one. Too young to get his skipper's certificate? Too young for the responsibilities? He did not think so. Excitement stirred in him at the thought. He could have his own boat much much earlier than he had ever dared to hope – if he were willing to marry Lucy.

Seth's arrival put an end to his deliberations.

''Struth, it's like an oven in 'ere!" Seth shook the door of the cabin, trying to promote a draught. He had changed remarkably little, apart from growing in height. He remained slight and sharp-featured, and looked far younger than his age. Of the four from Lambeth he had kept the strongest London accent. Jed had maintained the neutral tones of a man who belongs nowhere.

'The pump water's cold enough.'

'Then it's the pump water for me.' Stripping off as Jed had done he hurried away. And for a while the squeak of the pump-handle echoed round the yard. When he returned his skin was pink and his fair hair lay damply flat against his head.

'Lend us a clean shirt?' he asked.

'What's happened to yours?'

'Dunno. I can't find it.'

Looking at Seth's half of the cabin Jed was not surprised. In the few minutes since Seth's return it had been reduced to utter chaos.

'Try looking for it,' Jed said.

Seth obliged by stirring up the items into greater disarray.

'It's not 'ere,' he said. 'Come on. Lend me yours. I can't go about 'alf dressed. Lucy'd start getting ideas.'

Jed grinned. 'Anything's better than that,' he said. 'All right, but I want it back in one piece.'

'There, I looks the proper little gentleman,' Seth said, tucking the shirt into his trousers. 'All I needs now is a bit of the ready. I suppose you couldn't see your way to lending me a bob, just until Skipper pays us?'

'I loaned you sixpence last week, what do you want more for? We'll get paid in the morning.'

'It's night-school and I'm broke.'

'When did you last turn up at night-school?' Jed looked at him disparagingly.

'I've got better things to do with my time. Come to that I've got better things to do with my life. I ain't never going to be no skipper so there ain't no point in me getting no papers. You won't find me going to sea for one more day than I 'as to. I'd stay ashore now if I could, but I can't.'

The sudden vehemence in his tone made Jed look at him keenly.

'It's not that bad,' he said.

'Yes it is,' Seth retorted. 'Look, let's stop talking about the bleeding sea. It's bad enough having to go out there without jawing about it when we're ashore. Are you going to lend me that bob or ain't you?'

'You seem to need it pretty urgently. Who wants money off you? Cy Heath?'

Seth nodded.

'You're a fool, you know that, don't you?' declared Jed. 'Playing pitch and toss with Cy Heath! You're asking for trouble. And the skipper'll flay you alive when he finds you've been playing hookey from night-school. Between the two of them there's not going to be much left of you.'

Again Seth nodded. 'If you could just lend me that shilling it'd stop one of them 'aving a go at me, wouldn't it?' he said.

Jed gave a snort. 'All right, here's the shilling,' he said. 'But I'll have it back off you the minute we get paid in the morning, if I have to choke it out of you.'

'Thanks, you're a pal.' Seth pocketed the coin gratefully and left the cabin.

Although the *Our Violet* remained in harbour on Saturday morning, it was far from being a day off for Jed. Skipper Burton was a stickler for having the boat ready to set sail immediately. To go fishing on a Sunday was unthinkable, but it was not unknown for some boats, the *Our Violet* among them, to be heading for the fishing grounds soon after midnight if the wind was right. Lately Jed had noticed that the skipper had given him more and more responsibility for getting the smack ready. At first he had thought it was simply a result of his progressing from boy to third hand. Now, after his conversation with Lucy, he began to wonder; could it be that Matthew Burton was grooming him to be his son-in-law?

As he entered the house after work he heard an all too familiar sound. The repeated thwack-yell-thwack-yell that told him Seth was getting another beating.

'E'm been telling lies again,' said Lucy, answering his unspoken question. 'Great whoppers.'

Jed sighed. 'They aren't lies, not really,' he said.

'Pa thinks they are. Pa thinks 'e'm doomed to eternal perdition if 'e don't change 'is ways.' Lucy's tone suddenly assumed a winsome quality as she continued, 'If Pa was to find Seth taking liberties with me, 'e'd thrash the boy to nothing and throw what was left out for the gulls. Now if it was you...' Her fingers were beginning to walk playfully up Jed's chest. He pushed them aside.

'I don't intend to take any liberties,' he said, and walked away.

The beating had stopped, and he knew better than to go to the cabin just yet. Seth would want to be alone with his tears and humiliation for a bit. He felt Seth's shame. It was not right to be thrashed like a dog when you were sixteen rising seventeen. He went in search of Matthew Burton. He found him about to enter the parlour.

'Skipper, can I have a word?' he asked.

'What about?' The skipper's brows were still drawn together in anger.

'About Seth. He's been in trouble again, I gather.'

'He has been lying in the face of the Lord. How he could pollute God's pure air with such untruths... He dared to tell me, as boldly as you please, that his father was the Lord Mayor of London!'

Jed almost pointed out that, for all anybody knew, he might well be, then he thought better of it. The skipper was working himself up into a rare rage.

'He doesn't mean to lie. He doesn't think of it as lying,' he said.

'Oh no? And how does he think of it?'

'As stories in his head, to make himself feel better. He knows they aren't true, but he can't help himself.'

'In that case it behoves me to help him instead.'

'You won't do it by beating him.'

There was an ominous silence.

'Oh, won't I?' said Matthew Burton in a low voice. 'And who says so?'

Jed knew he was on delicate ground. No one challenged Skipper Burton's authority lightly.

'I mean no disrespect, Skipper,' he said. 'But you don't know what it's like to come from nothing and to be nothing. That's what we were taught in the workhouse. All Seth's doing is making up stories to fill in the blanks in his life. He doesn't expect anyone to believe him. He's done it for so long he can't stop, not if you were to beat him for ever more.'

'You are workhouse and you don't lie.'

'We're different, that's all. And he's not lying in the ordinary way. Please don't keep punishing him. It won't work.'

'Indeed? And how dare you tell me what'll work and what won't! You'm an impudent young dog, and you deserve some of the medicine I dished out to that friend of youm.' Matthew Burton's hands had already gone to his belt buckle. Unexpectedly he let them fall. 'However, you stood up for your friend like a man. You came out into the open with what you wanted to say; I can respect a fellow who does that. But don't you go trying to tell me what to do again. I won't be so soft another time. Be off with you now, and let me have some peace.'

Greatly surprised, Jed did as he was told. He had expected a clip across the ear, or worse, for being so outspoken. Skipper Burton's mild reaction made him wonder even more if he was being considered as a suitable husband for Lucy.

It was a terrible temptation. There were snags, of course. If he wed Lucy he would not be skipper of his own boat, he would be skipper of Matthew Burton's. He knew his employer far too well to expect him to relinquish one iota of control, even if he became aged and bedridden. Lucy herself was another snag. He thought of sharing the rest of his life with her, of waking each morning to see her beside him, and his stomach turned over with distaste. Living with her and fathering her children would be a heavy price to pay. But the *Our Violet* was a grand craft, one of the best in the fleet. He would have to work hard for most of his life to own a boat like that. Yet she could be his eventually — Matthew Burton was not immortal. All he had to do was encourage Lucy... could he pay that price?

In the weeks that followed, no one seeing Jed's impassive exterior could have guessed at his indecision. Temptation gnawed at him like a hungry rat. In the balance hung his entire future.

Chapter Five

The autumn gales came late, but when they arrived they brought the high spring tides, sending sea-water rushing up over the Beach to flood the huddle of low-lying houses beyond. Hurrying out to take Mr Prout his dinner, Amy was forced to make quite a detour in order to keep her feet dry.

Wet boots were the least of her worries. Daniel was at sea, outward bound for the Mediterranean. She had followed his route regularly in her threepenny atlas and knew it by heart. She hoped fervently that he would have rounded Ushant before the storms had begun and would be sheltering at Brest or maybe Lorient. Any poor soul unfortunate enough to be out at sea in these conditions had her prayers, but her constant concern was for Daniel. Her greatest dread was that he would be shipwrecked. Deliberately she turned her mind from such a terrible thought. It was the fear carried by every woman whose man went to sea. She had no option but to live with it.

Arriving at Prout's Yard provided a welcome diversion. The more she saw of boatbuilding the more she admired the skills of the men John Prout employed. Today the pungent odour of paint overlaid the more usual smells of tar and freshly cut timber.

'She's almost finished, then,' Amy remarked to Charlie Bowden, the foreman shipwright.

'That's right. She'll get her masts soon, the riggers are all ready for her.' Proudly he looked at the hull, still propped on its strong stakes. 'If George Beale isn't pleased with her he danged well ought to be. That makes three smacks he's got, so maybe all the novelty's gone out of being an owner for him.'

'I dare say a look in his money chest brings it back sharpish,' grinned Amy. She regarded the letters being carefully painted on the vessel. 'DH 234. Why do Brixham boats have to have Dartmouth port marks? I've never been able to find out.'

''Cos us idn't got no port marks of our own,' Charlie informed her. 'And don't go asking me why that is, I bain't no wiser than you.'

'In that case I won't ask,' she said, with a smile. 'I'll take the master his dinner.'

'I was wondering when you'd remember about me,' remarked John Prout as she entered the small stone hut that served him as an office. 'I saw you jawing away to old Charlie out there, with never a thought for my empty belly.'

'Sorry, Mr Prout.' She knew the reproof was half-hearted. 'I was admiring the *Charity*.'

'Ah, a grand craft, though I says it as shouldn't.' John Prout stood in the doorway, looking appreciatively at the nearly-finished boat. 'There won't be much weather she can't handle, even days like today. Is that my dinner, maid?'

'Yes, Mr Prout.' Amy had unpacked the basket. 'You've a pasty today, and some fruit-cake that missus made this morning. I'll be getting back now, if it's all right with you.'

John Prout, who was already tackling the large pasty, nodded his head.

Amy had started to leave when she remembered something. 'I'm going to the post office for missus,' she said. 'Have you anything for the post?'

John Prout swallowed hastily. 'Not for the post I haven't,' he said. 'But you can deliver this letter for me, if you will. 'Tis to Captain Newton. He lives just along the road yer, towards Berry Head. Big house with a darned gurt lamp over the gate. You can't miss it.'

Amy was unlikely to miss it. She knew the house very well. Of course she did. It was Daniel's home. She was so startled at the prospect of actually going there that she almost missed Mr Prout's final instructions.

'There idn't no need to wait for an answer, unless Captain Newton's to home and it's more convenient for him.'

Amy scarcely heard him; she was already hurrying away from the yard. Countless times on her days off, when Daniel had been at sea, she had come this way. Daisy had complained often.

'Why're we coming along 'ere again for?' she would whine.

Amy never told her it was because she was desperate for some contact with Daniel. Just a glimpse of the house where he lived gave her solace. Now she was to call there, and her heart pounded at the prospect. One half of her was keen to see inside, the other half would have run away given the least encouragement.

The house seemed bigger than she had remembered, and alarmingly grand. Gates wide enough to admit a carriage and pair were topped by a wrought-iron arch bearing an ornate lamp, just as John Prout had described. She began to go up the sloping drive.

'Yer, where'm you going?' demanded a voice.

She jumped with alarm. The man who had addressed her leaned on his spade.

'Where'm you off to?' he demanded again.

'To see Captain Newton. I've a letter for him,' she replied.

'Oh, you'm front door company, be you?' he asked sarcastically.

Then he jerked a calloused thumb down the drive. 'The gate you want's in the wall.'

Scarlet with mortification Amy returned the way she had come. Sure enough, a few yards further along in the high retaining wall was a small gate bearing the notice 'Tradesmen Only'. She went in and found herself on a narrow path, well shielded from public gaze by a high privet hedge. The door it led to at the back of the house was undeniably the servants' entrance. She knocked. The servant girl who opened it was about her own age, and wore a smart black dress with a frilled apron and cap in spotless muslin. She looked Amy up and down, taking in her shabby coat and her boots that were scuffed and dirty from the beach at Prout's Yard.

'Yes?' she asked in a superior tone.

Amy wished she could sink through the floor. She had always felt she was unworthy of Daniel. Now it seemed she was unworthy even to enter his kitchen. Then her dismay withered as her anger mounted. Who was this girl? Just a maidservant, like herself.

'Is Captain Newton at home?' she asked, her head held high. 'I've a letter for him.'

'All right, I'll take it.' The maid took it and would have closed the door if Amy had not put her foot in the way.

'There might be an answer. I'll wait,' she said, and stepped inside.

The maid looked as though she had other views on the subject. Instead of voicing them she closed the door and said, 'Stay here.'

As soon as she had left Amy gazed about, taking in her surroundings. She was in a neatly painted passage with a runner of coconut matting on the floor. Through an open door she could see into the kitchen. It was a great deal larger than the Prouts', and a woman in a voluminous white apron was rolling pastry on a scrubbed table, while a young girl fed the gleaming range with coal. The Newtons had at least a cook, a parlourmaid, a scullerymaid and a gardener. Amy was both impressed and dismayed. The parlourmaid's return made her stand erect, her head proudly raised. No matter what she felt, she was not going to let this creature in useless frilly muslin think she was inferior.

'You're wanted upstairs,' said the parlourmaid with a disapproving sniff. 'Follow me.'

Amy did as she was told, feeling extremely apprehensive. She could think of no reason why she should be summoned, unless – and the thought made her go ice cold with dread – unless Daniel's parents had found out that she was in love with their son.

The parlourmaid led the way through a green baize door and into a large hall. For a moment Amy thought she had stepped into another world. She had never seen such a beautiful room: the walls were hung with pale blue damask, while long curtains of a deeper blue velvet were looped back in carefully draped swags and held with gold tassels; a crystal chandelier hung from the ceiling; a Persian rug in soft shades of rose graced the polished floor, a porcelain bowl of late chrysanthemums on a small walnut table added a perfect splash of colour. Amy was so enthralled she came to a halt.

'Come on! The Captain's waiting!' The parlourmaid gave her an impatient tug. Obediently Amy followed the girl up a flight of softly carpeted stairs. They stopped outside a door of polished oak. The maid knocked and entered.

'The young person you wished to see, Captain Newton,' she said, then bobbed a curtsey and left Amy alone with Daniel's father.

Captain Newton was Daniel thirty years on. He had the same long lean figure, the same rich red hair, the same green eyes. Those eyes were looking at Amy now with a kindly expression.

'Come along in, my dear,' he said 'You are Mr Prout's maidservant, I take it?'

'Yes, sir.' Amy's voice sounded strained.

'Ah. Then can you tell me if Mr Prout will be at his work at six this evening, or is he more likely to be at home? I have urgent matters I wish to discuss with him.'

For a moment Amy's heart seemed to stop. Was he going to talk about her and Daniel? Then common sense reasserted itself. Of course he wasn't, not when he was looking at her in such a kind way. Most likely he wanted to see Mr Prout on a matter of business.

'He doesn't usually leave the yard until half-past six or later, unless the light's particularly bad, sir,' she said. 'He didn't mention coming home specially early today.'

'Good, then I shall catch him at his work. I've no wish to intrude upon his time at home. If you will wait a moment I will write him a short note, which I'd be obliged if you'd take back to him.' He settled himself at a large desk and selected a sheet of paper, then he glanced at Amy and smiled. 'Do sit down, my dear. I won't keep you a moment.'

Amy perched herself on the edge of a chair, her eyes taking in the small room. That it was Captain Newton's study was evident from the model ships and mementoes from his travels which decorated the walls and shelves, and from the brass telescope on a tripod that stood in the window. She imagined Daniel coming in here when he was younger. How he must have enjoyed it; there were many strange and interesting things from many places. She wondered if he had a similar room of his own, or were the souvenirs from his voyages laid out on display somewhere else in the house?

She could scarcely credit that this was where Daniel lived, where he ate, where he slept. It was the side of his life she knew very little about, and she was not sure she was glad to have it brought home to her. It was all very grand.

The door opened and a small lady bustled in. Her movements were brisk, causing the silken skirts of her fashionable gown to swish vigorously. Daniel got his looks from his father, but his formidable energy came from his mother. Amy rose swiftly to her feet, conscious that Mrs Newton was regarding her with considerable annoyance.

'Really, William!' declared Daniel's mother. 'Why on earth is this girl in here?'

Captain Newton looked up. 'Hullo, my dear. This is John Prout's maid. She's just delivered a letter.'

'Couldn't she have delivered it below stairs?' Mrs Newton's censorious eyes swept over Amy from her head to her boots. 'Just look at the state of her! Goodness knows what dirt she's tramped in over the carpets! Really, this is too bad of you!'

'I can't see anything amiss with the lass,' said Captain Newton. 'Her boots are remarkably clean considering the conditions underfoot. She must have wiped them most conscientiously before she came upstairs.'

'I still do not see why she had to come up here at all!' Mrs Newton's voice was stiff with disapproval.

'Because I wanted to speak to her, my love,' replied her husband patiently. 'I require an urgent word with John Prout about repairs to the *Windsor*. I needed to know his whereabouts this evening. There you are.' He put his letter in an envelope and handed it to Amy. 'If you would be kind enough to give that to Mr Prout immediately I would be much obliged.' His smile, as he dismissed Amy, was full of sympathy.

'Thank you, sir. I'll take it straight away,' she said, bobbing a curtsey first to Mrs Newton and then to him before leaving.

The haughty parlourmaid was waiting for her outside the door. 'I knew she'd get on her high horse about you coming upstairs,' she said, jerking her head in the direction of her employers. 'Come on, I'll show you the way out. And try not to get too much muck from those boots of yours on the carpet. I'm the one as has to clean it up.'

'I'll walk out on my hands if you like,' retorted Amy. 'Would that be clean enough for you?'

The parlourmaid glared at Amy, who glared back, unrepentant, then in hostile silence both girls went down the stairs and back through the green baize door.

Amy hurried away from the Newtons' house. Her initial shock at entering Daniel's home and meeting his parents began to fade, leaving in its place a depression which grew deeper with every step. She had always known that Daniel came from a well-to-do family, but she had never dreamed that they were so prosperous. Their house, their furniture – everything – far outstripped the Prouts' comfortable home in luxury. That alone had widened the gulf between his world and hers. But worse still had been his mother's attitude.

Mrs Newton had disapproved because a maidservant had tramped through her house in dirty boots. Amy still smarted with humiliation from the comments about her appearance and the way she had been discussed as if she were not present. What Mrs Newton's reaction would have been if she had realized that that self-same servant was her son's beloved she dared not imagine. Captain Newton had been kind and sympathetic. He might look upon Daniel's association with a servant, if not with approval, then with tolerance. But his wife was a very different matter. Amy could tell instinctively that if she ever found out, approval, tolerance and sympathy would not be part of Mrs Newton's vocabulary.

Amy delivered the letter to the yard and trudged back up to Furzeham.

'What's wrong with you?' demanded Jessie Prout. 'You look washed out. Not sickening for something, are you?'

'No, missus. I'm just tired. I reckon I need my dinner.'

She could not admit that all her dreams for the future had just collapsed about her like so much rubble.

'I'm not surprised. Have you seen the time? Where on earth have you been until now?'

'Mister wanted me to take a letter to Captain Newton. I had to wait for an answer.'

'The Newtons, eh?' Jessie's interest was caught immediately. 'It's said their house is like a palace inside. I don't suppose you saw much of it.'

'I saw a bit,' said Amy. 'I had to go upstairs to see the captain.'

'Well, what was it like?' Jessie urged.

'Beautiful and very grand. They didn't have paper on the walls, they had silk – well, it looked like silk to me. And there were pictures in huge gold frames, and the lamp was drops of crystal. It was grand all right. I've never seen anything like it.' Every word of description was an agony to Amy, yet she could not hold back. Each luxurious item, each thing of beauty, pushed Daniel further and further out of her reach.

'My! Silk, you say?' Jessie was impressed. 'Mind, it's not surprising. Captain Newton doesn't just sail with the South Devon Line, you know. He's a shareholder.'

This last piece of information, previously unknown to Amy, almost proved the last straw. She swayed ominously.

'Here, girl, sit down and get some food in you this instant.' Jessie Prout pushed her into a chair and, taking a pasty from the oven, put it on the kitchen table in front of her. 'I want you to turn out the cupboards this afternoon. I can't have you fainting about the place.'

Obediently Amy ate the pasty, though she did not taste a single mouthful. It might have been dust for all she knew. The food gave her physical strength, but nothing could ease the anguish in her heart.

Her love affair with Daniel had been absolute foolishness. Her hopes of their future life together had been nothing more than silly dreams. Just supposing they flew in the face of all opposition and did get married, what then? For the first time, she had seen the world he came from. What would the people who lived in that world think of her as the young Mrs Newton? Already she could hear the whispers: 'Daniel Newton might as well give up the sea right now, he'll never get any more promotion… Why? You mean you haven't heard? Because of his wife, of course…' 'He married beneath him. A tragedy in a young man with such promise…' 'A workhouse girl, you know, from Lambeth or Hackney, or some awful place like that…' Amy clapped her hands over her ears in an attempt to cut out the silent voices. She could never harm Daniel. He loved the sea and he was ambitious, she had always known that. The idea of ruining his career and his life, of watching him being dragged down simply because of her was too terrible to contemplate. There was only one course of action she could take. As she scrubbed out the cupboards she considered what she would say to him when he came home. With tears streaming down her cheeks she rehearsed the words that would tell him their love affair was at an end.

–

In the days which followed the weather was in time with Amy's mood of desolation. Because of the gales the harbour was packed with smacks that had been unable to go to sea for weeks, and faces in Brixham began to wear the pinched look that told of hungry mouths to feed and no money coming in.

The rain was beating against the house one night when Jessie came into the kitchen and began to lock up.

'Mr Todd's not in yet,' Amy said.

'That's his lookout. He knows what time we like to settle for the night.' Jessie's mouth was set in a hard line. 'Some folks have to go to work in the mornings; they can't all be fishermen and laze about when they choose.'

'The boats can't go out, missus, not in this weather,' said Amy, incensed at such unfairness.

'Then he should show more sense and not throw his money away. This is the third night in a row he's been out drinking. Well, he can take his bed down to the Buller's Arms and sleep there! I'm locking the door.'

'But, missus, just listen to that rain. He'll get soaked to the skin. Where's he going to go if he can't get in?'

In vain Amy begged and pleaded. Jessie was adamant. She stood there, her arms folded, and said, 'You can stop making all this fuss. Get yourself off to bed. I'm staying here until you do. I know you. You'd unlock the door the minute my back was turned, given half a chance. Well, you aren't getting that chance. Go to bed!'

There was no help for it. Amy climbed the stairs. She had already heard Mr Prout go up to bed. She was certain he did not know his brother was locked out in such weather. Should she appeal to him? As she paused on the landing opposite the Prouts' bedroom, summoning up her courage, Jessie came up behind her.

'Get to bed!' she ordered. 'I won't tell you again!'

Reluctantly Amy carried on up to her attic. The rain sounded louder up there, beating against the window and streaming down the slates into overflowing gutters. It was impossible to sleep. She kept thinking of Todd huddled in some corner, wet and comfortless. Her ears were strained for the sound of him returning.

Deliberately she had left her door open, and she was certain she heard the front door rattle. It came again, then a little later she heard a crash, as if someone had fallen down the steps. That was enough for her. She would not leave him out there. He was a fool, was Todd; but he was kind and good-natured. He was not staying out all night, not if she had any say in the matter.

Pulling her coat over her nightgown she crept downstairs in the darkness. Once she had closed the kitchen door softly behind her, she lit the lamp and went through the scullery. With infinite care, so as to make no sound, she slipped back the bolts and opened the door. There, sitting on the bottom step, seemingly impervious to the water that was streaming down from the road above, was Todd. He was very wet and extremely drunk.

'Li'l Amy,' he beamed. 'Knew you'd come… Couldn't get in! Door was shtuck.'

'Come on in, do,' she whispered. 'Quickly! The rain's blowing in.'

With great difficulty Todd got to his feet. Upright, he wavered so ominously that Amy was forced to support his unsteady footsteps into the scullery.

'Boots!' he said loudly. 'I idn't allowed in with my boots on. Jessie'd… Jessie'd kill me!'

'Hush, will you,' snorted Amy, 'or she'll kill the pair of us. Right, hold still while I get your boots off.'

She propped him up against the wall and tackled the difficult job of undoing wet bootlaces. Unfortunately, as soon as his boots were removed Todd's last bastion of stability went too. Slowly and without a struggle he slid down the wall until he was sitting on the floor, his legs outstretched in front of him.

'Oh, what did you do that for?' demanded Amy irrationally. 'Now how am I going to get you upstairs?'

'Sleep here...' beamed Todd. 'Nice and comfy...' His head began to droop.

Amy was having none of it. 'Oh no, you aren't sleeping here!' she protested. 'Not in those wet clothes.' With an effort she peeled his soaked jacket off him. 'Why on earth didn't you knock on the front door? Mr Prout would have heard you and let you in.'

'Didn't... didn't want to dishturb no one... John worksh hard... needsh his shleep.'

That was typical of Todd, decided Amy. As drunk as an owl and yet still considerate of others. With an effort she attempted to drag him into the kitchen but Todd's stockinged feet could get no purchase on the scrubbed floor, and kept slipping away from him.

'Go to... to bed... I... be fine yer...' he slurred.

'Don't be daft, I can't leave you half in the scullery and half out,' puffed Amy. She sat down for a minute to consider the situation. 'I can't get you up to your bed, that's for sure,' she said eventually. 'You'll have to stay here. I'll stoke the range up a bit to keep you warm. Wait there.'

Then she grinned at her last remark. Todd was in no state to go anywhere.

There was still a dull glow of red in the range. Encouraging it into a decent blaze while at the same time making no noise proved incredibly difficult. Time and again she stopped, her heart in her mouth, as a coal clattered to the hearth or a fire-iron hit the side of the grate with a metallic clang. When she had succeeded in mending the fire she returned to Todd, who was prostrate on the floor, sleeping peacefully.

'Up you come,' she said, pushing at his back to prop him into a sitting position. Then, putting her arms round his chest, she gave a tug. Suddenly her feet shot from under her and she fell backwards on to the wet floor, knocking over a chair in the process. The inevitable sound of footsteps hurrying downstairs followed immediately.

Jessie Prout took in the scene at a single glance.

'Oh yes, miss, and what do you mean by deliberately disobeying my instructions?' she snapped.

At the same moment her husband demanded, 'What on earth be going on? Todd, what be you doing down there, boy?'

'Isn't it obvious? He's drunk,' retorted Jessie.

'I can see that. What I wants to know is why he'm down yer at this time of night, soaking wet. He can't have been drinking till this hour. I idn't going to get much sense from Todd, so you can tell me, maid. What be these instructions you been disobeying?'

Amy looked uncomfortably from master to mistress, then back again. The last thing she wanted was to stir up trouble between husband and wife.

'Mr Todd got himself locked out,' she said.

'How'd he manage that, then? You can account for everyone afore you locks up, surely? He could have caught his death out there—'

'He has to put up with far worse when he's fishing,' Jessie cut in acidly.

John Prout had been about to lift up his brother. He paused and looked at his wife.

'But he wadn't out fishing. Judging by the water on this floor he was out there on the bottom steps.'

'What else can he expect if he gets drunk every night?' retorted Jessie.

'He can expect a good talking to from me in the morning,' said John Prout sternly. 'I idn't eager to have drunkenness in my home, no more than anyone else. But he shouldn't expect to be locked out, especially not on the worst night of the year. He'm my brother and, drunk or sober, my door idn't never to be locked against him. I hopes everyone understands that.' Having delivered his rebuke he turned his attention to his brother. 'Come on, boy,' he said, hoisting him over his shoulder. ''Tis bed for you.'

Next morning Amy expected repercussions but apart from being more silent and grim-faced than usual, Jessie made no comment. She suspected that there had been stern words exchanged in the privacy of the Prouts' bedroom.

Although it was gone eleven there was still no sign of Todd. Smiling to herself she decided that he was wise to delay waking for as long as possible. She was glad she had disobeyed Jessie. She liked Todd Prout. He showed no sign of growing more sensible, and was still likely to come home with impossibly huge false teeth sticking out of his mouth, or with some other silly toy to make everyone laugh. She spent a lot of time on her own, and she appreciated it when he came into the kitchen to chat with her and tell her jokes.

Loneliness was the biggest drawback in working for the Prouts. It was the penalty for being a maid-of-all-work, with few opportunities to mix and make new friends. Sometimes she thought about looking for another situation, somewhere larger perhaps, with more staff. Then she would reconsider. It was a big step to take and there were many worse positions than hers.

Until recently the one bright hope on her horizon had been that some day she would marry Daniel. While he had been her future she had felt she could tolerate the loneliness, the hard work, and Jessie's sharp tongue. That bright future was now lost to her. A tear trickled down her face and fell on the table she was dusting. Hastily she rubbed it away with her cloth.

Usually she enjoyed polishing the parlour. She used to think it a very grand room, with its shining brass, its crisp net curtains and its pretty ornaments. Not any more. She had been to die Newtons' house and now knew the Prouts' home, though extremely comfortable, to be modest by comparison.

Amy had to admit she had learned a great deal since coming into service, more than just cooking. Jessie Prout was a good needlewoman and had a deft way of making a room welcoming and attractive. Amy had taken note, preparing for the day when she would make a home for herself and Daniel. It had all been time wasted. When Daniel came home from sea it would not be to her. In years to come he would return to the sort of fine home he was used to, and to the sort of wife who was born to such things.

More tears threatened to follow the first, but Amy fought to hold them back. As she did so her gaze lit upon the bookcase in the corner.

That bookcase was one of the great consolations of life at the Prouts. It had taken her a long time to pluck up the courage to borrow a book. She had not asked Jessie's permission: she knew too well what the answer would be. She had slipped one out, moving the others along the shelf so that the gap would not be noticed. At first she had read fearfully, certain of a terrible retribution if she were found out. Miraculously no one had noticed. Since then she had frequently borrowed novels, devouring them in the privacy of her attic, and returning them with great stealth.

Now a longing for the solace of reading came over her again. She selected a book and slipped it into her apron pocket. At that moment she heard the parlour door open behind her. Cold with alarm, she swung round, fearing to be confronted by Jessie. She found herself facing a decidedly fragile-looking Todd.

'You'm looking guilty for this time of day, maid,' he said. 'What you been up to?'

'Nothing, Mr Todd.'

'Nothing?' His eyes went to the open bookcase.

Reluctantly she withdrew the book and handed it to him. 'I was only borrowing it. I'd have looked after it,' she said. 'Please, you won't tell the missus, will you?'

'No, I won't tell Jessie. For one thing, I reckon I owes you a favour for last night. And for another thing, tidn't naught to do with her.'

'What do you mean?' Amy was puzzled. 'I was borrowing one of her books.'

'No, you wadn't. You was borrowing one of mine.'

'Yours?' She stared at him incredulously. 'These books are yours?'

He gave a laugh at her surprise, then winced with pain. 'Don't look like that, girl. I can read, you know. Long words, too.' He laughed again, and did not find it any less painful. 'Yer, I'm going to have to sit down 'fore I falls down.' He slumped into the nearest armchair.

'They're all your books?' She was having great difficulty taking it in. 'You've read every one?'

'Yes. Most more than once.' He looked at the book she had handed to him. '*Ivanhoe*, eh? I'd have thought you knew un off by heart, the number of times you've read un.'

'You knew?' Amy was aghast. 'All the time you knew I was taking your books—'

'Borrowing my books,' he corrected her gently. ''Course I knowd. Do you think I couldn't tell when one was missing? 'Sides, *Ivanhoe*'s one of my favourites, too. More than once I've put my hand out for un, only to find un not there.'

'Oh,' said Amy in a small voice. 'I'm very sorry. I won't do it again, I promise.'

'Why not? If it gives you pleasure, you read un, my maid. Yer.' He went to hand the book back to her, but even that slight movement gave him pain. He closed his eyes and groaned.

Amy was full of sympathy. 'Is there anything I can get you, Mr Todd?' she asked. 'Would you like some breakfast?'

He groaned again, more loudly. 'That wadn't a friendly thing to suggest to a man in my state,' he said, his eyes still closed. 'A bit of bicarb's more what I need.'

'I'll get you some.' Amy made to leave the room.

'Yer, you take this and hide un somewhere.' He handed her the book. 'Us don't want you to get a flea in your ear from Jessie, do us? 'Sides, she'd likely have a go at me too, for encouraging you, and I don't think I could stand it the way I feels.'

'Thank you.' She slipped the book back into her pocket. 'I don't know what else to say.'

'The thanks should be from me. I be the one in debt. A night spent out on the steps in that rain wouldn't have done me no good, to my way of thinking. There's not many'd have braved Jessie's wrath to drag a daft drunk in out of the wet.'

'You aren't a daft drunk,' she protested.

'I wadn't exactly sober, was I?'

'No,' she admitted. Then she said in a rush, 'Why do you do it? Get drunk, I mean. It's the third time in a week it has happened. Missus was really vexed about it. Even Mister wasn't any too pleased.'

'Oh, I dunno.' Todd leaned back in the armchair. 'Same reason as I reads, I suppose, so's I don't have to think about how dismal life is. They both blots out the everyday world.'

Amy did not know what to say. She had never heard Todd express such sentiments before.

Cautiously he opened one eye and gave a tentative grin.

'That be die drink talking,' he said. 'Shows I should stick to reading. You don't have no hangover after that. Yer, be I going to get that bicarb or bain't I?'

'Yes, Mr Todd. Right away.'

She hurried off downstairs, still in a state of amazement. Everyone regarded him as a fool. Good-natured and likeable, yet a fool all the same. To discover a completely different side to his nature was bewildering.

During the next few days, in her scant free time, Amy lost herself in the medieval world of *Ivanhoe*. She agreed implicitly with Todd, it did blot out the everyday world. For her it almost blotted out a world without Daniel.

–

The next Sunday Daisy fainted in church and had to be carried out by the verger. Amy would have followed after, to care for her, if Jessie Prout had not restrained her with a firm hand on her arm.

'Poor maid, 'er idn't goin' to make old bones,' remarked a woman in the pew behind.

Amy feared she might be right. These days she was perpetually concerned for Daisy. Her friend was like a frail stem, ready to snap under the least pressure, and, distressingly, she had become even more silent. No longer did she constantly seek reassurance; she scarcely spoke at all.

That afternoon Amy was free. It was time she sometimes spent with Daisy, but frequently these days her friend made excuses that she could not get away or was too tired to go walking. After the morning's episode Amy did not expect to see Daisy. She walked up Fore Street, intending to knock boldly on the Floyds' door to ask how she was. Unexpectedly, as she stretched out her hand for the knocker, the door opened and Daisy herself came out.

'Are you better? Do you feel like coming out?' Amy asked anxiously.

'Yes!' Without waiting for a response Daisy set off towards the harbour, only to sway and almost fall after a few yards.

'You're in no fit state to be out! You're as white as a sheet,' exclaimed Amy, catching hold of her. 'Come on, I'll take you back.'

'No!' Daisy was unusually determined. 'I don't want to go back there. I wish I didn't have to go back there ever again.'

Amy was in a quandary. It was too cold for Daisy to sit about, yet there was nowhere for them to go.

'If I helped you could you manage it up to Furzeham?' she asked. 'Mrs Prout won't mind us sitting in the kitchen, if I ask her properly.'

The only answer she received was a nod of the head.

Their progress was so slow, with Daisy having to rest every few yards, that Amy began to despair of ever reaching home. She was very relieved when Todd overtook them. He gave Daisy a pitying look, and as good as carried her the last part of the way.

'Don't worry, I'll see 'tis all right with Jessie for you to have your friend yer,' he said, setting Daisy down on a chair. 'Pull yourself close to the fire, my maid. You'm shivering.'

He pushed Daisy, chair and all, nearer to the warmth, then left the kitchen. A few minutes later he was back, a glass in his hand.

'Yer, get that down you,' he said, handing it to Daisy.

Obediently she swallowed it in one gulp, making her cough and splutter alarmingly.

'What on earth did you give her?' demanded Amy, vigorously patting Daisy on the back.

'Brandy,' said Todd. 'Maybe I should have warned her to take un slow.'

'Maybe you should,' Amy agreed, wondering what result such a generous measure of spirits would have on her.

For a while there were no after-effects. After Todd had left them Daisy sat drowsily by the fire, her pale cheeks growing gradually more flushed with the warmth and the brandy. Amy, too, kept silent, her instinct telling her that her friend's immediate need was for peace and quiet and rest.

'I 'ates 'im! 'E's a dirty, disgusting animal!'

Amy was startled by the sudden announcement.

'Who is?' she asked.

'Dirty, disgusting animal. No! No animal'd be as bad as 'im!' Daisy did not seem to have heard her. She stared into the fire, her eyes unnaturally bright. 'I'll do for 'im! I swear to God I'll do for 'im one day, if 'e comes at me again with his filthy 'ands touching me, and 'is slobbering mouth. 'E's got a wife. What's 'e need to push 'is stinking body into me for? 'E does things to me I'll bet 'e don't do to 'er. Things you wouldn't believe. 'Ow 'e thinks of them I don't know. 'Is mind is as dirty and twisted as the rest of 'im. From that very first night we got 'ere, 'e was at it, pawing and touching and poking. I'll do for 'im! It's the only way I know of stopping 'im coming at me. I can't take no more!' Daisy suddenly crumpled up, and began to weep, her head buried in her hands, her thin shoulders shaking in desperate spasms.

Amy had listened to her with growing horror, too appalled to move or interrupt. Now she rushed forward and took Daisy in her arms, rocking her gently.

'That's terrible!' she exclaimed, tears streaming down her cheeks too. 'Absolutely terrible! You shouldn't have to put up with it! You don't have to put up with it! That awful, evil man!' She had no doubts about whom Daisy meant. It was Floyd, who else? 'You aren't going back there, do you hear? You'll stay here, I'll persuade Mrs Prout somehow...'

'I've got to go back,' Daisy raised a despairing tear-stained face. 'You don't understand. 'E'd come and make trouble, for you and for me.'

'Just let him try!' Amy was ready to take on a dozen Floyds rather than let her suffer such appalling treatment, but Daisy shook her head.

'I've got to go back,' she repeated, 'I can't stay with you. I can't stay with no one decent. I'm too wicked to be with ordinary folk.'

'Wicked? How can you be wicked?' demanded Amy in bewilderment.

'It's what 'e says. It's 'cos I'm wicked as makes 'im do those things to me.'

'It isn't you who's wicked,' Amy cried indignantly. 'It's that foul creature Floyd.'

Daisy shook her head again. 'I must be wicked, mustn't I? 'E wouldn't do it to no decent person. That was why I was in the work'ouse, 'cos I was too wicked to go nowhere else.'

'Listen to me, Daisy.' Amy gave her a little shake. 'You are not wicked. You are good and gentle, and you are the innocent one. Don't let that man persuade you otherwise. One thing's clear, you mustn't go back there. Not under any circumstances. Mr and Mrs Prout are decent Christian people. They'll help, I'm sure. I'll go and tell them what's been going on, they'll—'

'No!' Daisy's response was almost a scream. She clung so tightly that her fingers dug painfully into Amy's arms.

'Then go and see Dr Searle. You're looking really ill.'

'No, I ain't going to no doctor! They finds out things, do doctors.'

'But he's a kind man, he'd help you.'

'No, I ain't telling 'im nothing, and you mustn't tell no one, neither! There ain't no one as'd believe us, and I'd 'ave to go back and 'e'd be worse than ever.'

'Then tell his wife. Tell Mrs Floyd.' Amy was certain that something could be done. 'She wouldn't stand her husband doing such things under her own roof.'

'She ain't going to do nothing. I reckon she knows, and is glad 'cos I keeps 'im off 'er!'

'Surely not!'

'You don't know what 'e's like. You don't understand. Oh Amy, swear you ain't going to tell no one. Please!'

'I can't,' protested Amy. 'There must be something I can do, someone who'll help—'

'Swear to me! Swear you won't tell no one! I couldn't bear no one else to know about 'im and me. Don't shame me. Please! Please! Swear you won't tell!'

In her agitation Daisy's grip had tightened until it was agonizing. But it was the terror and the desperation in her eyes rather than the

pain that made Amy say quietly, 'All right, I swear I won't tell anyone.'
She knew she had not made the right decision.

That night she lay awake, haunted by Daisy's confession. Poor, poor
Daisy, to have suffered so in silence for all this time. No wonder she
looked ill and unhappy. Amy bitterly regretted the promise she had
been forced to give. If she had been able to talk to someone… Jed, for
example. He was a good person to confide in, always full of common
sense, and one who could hold his tongue… If she had been able to
talk to him, between them they might have been able to find a way to
help Daisy. As it was she racked her brains for hour after hour without
success. The only possible solution would be to help her to run away,
and even as the thought entered her head she knew it would be useless.
To make her escape successfully Daisy would need money and good
health, and she had neither. She was not equipped to survive in the
world alone…

'I'll do for 'im!'

The words echoed in Amy's head, and a terrible dread churned at
her insides. What if Daisy did something awful? Poor soul, she had
sounded desperate enough. Too late Amy wished she had been more
comforting, more supportive. She felt she had done so little. Yet what
could she have done or said that would have helped in a nightmarish
situation like that? 'Poor Daisy. Poor, poor Daisy.' Again and again she
whispered the words. Of all the people in the world such a thing had
to happen to Daisy. She was so vulnerable, the person least able to
cope with Floyd's sort. It was the overwhelming sense of helplessness
that caused Amy dreadful anguish. Her friend was in trouble and she
could do nothing! Nothing! Nothing! If only she had not made that
stupid promise… But she had, and there was no going back.

Todd noticed she was weary and heavy-eyed as she went about her
work next day.

'My, you'm a ray of sunshine on a grey morning,' he grinned. 'We'll
have to make you sign the pledge if you can't hold your liquor no better
than that.'

For once Amy could not respond to his joking. 'I've got things on
my mind,' she said.

Todd grew serious. 'That friend of youm?' he said.

For a moment Amy was startled. How could he know?

Then he went on, 'I'm not surprised. Poor maid looks real sickly. The Floyds should get her to Dr Searle and quick if they've any Christian charity.'

Amy nearly laughed aloud. Christian charity? The Floyds? With an effort she controlled herself and said, 'I agree. That's what I said, but Daisy's scared of doctors.'

'Well, there's no forcing her if she be scared, so there's an end of it. Is that my vittals?'

'Yes.' She handed him the food for his day's fishing. 'Is it enough?'

He grinned. 'I should hope so. We'm only going off Start Bay, you know, not round Cape Horn.'

When he had left the house Amy returned to her work, trying not to think of Daisy trapped in the house with the disgusting Floyd. Angrily she rubbed at the windowsills in an effort to obliterate the bad dream, then by chance she happened to glance out to sea. Dawn was brightening the horizon and the early light caught the white flash of topsails. For one thoughtless minute her heart soared at the sight, then plummeted to new depths of misery. It was too far for a definite identification, but she knew which ship it was. It was the *Balmoral*. Daniel was coming home, and she would have to break the news to him that their love affair was at an end.

Chapter Six

Normally Amy would have had great difficulty curbing her impatience to see Daniel. But on this occasion she dreaded their reunion. Eventually she managed to slip away for an hour one afternoon. There was no sign of Daniel among the bare elderbushes, but she found a note pushed in under the roots.

'My own darling,' it began.

> I am desolate because you are not here. I am desperate to take you in my arms again, yet I am afraid I must wait longer for that wonderful moment. My mother has invited vast numbers of guests to stay, and I must be a good boy and play the welcoming host in my father's absence. I will be free again on Sunday, then we can be together at last. Somehow we must manage to exist until then.
>
> My love is yours for always.
> D.

Amy clutched the note to her, not certain whether she was glad or sorry. She still had the prospect of seeing him once more. After that she would never see him again.

The rest of the week passed like a tormented dream, and she shed many anguished tears in the seclusion of her attic. Knowing that what she was about to do was right did not make it hurt any the less.

When Sunday came she approached their rendezvous with trepidation. She had intended to be cool and rational. She would greet Daniel calmly, preparing him for what was to come. Yet the minute she saw him her plans went for naught. Before she could stop them her arms went out to him. In a trice she was in his embrace, returning his kisses with all the hunger of long separation.

'I've missed you,' he whispered. 'I've been desperate for everyone to leave. You've no idea how delighted I was to push the last guest into the railway carriage.'

'Poor you, having to be nice to so many people,' she answered sympathetically. 'Can't you tell your mother how much you dislike it?'

'Not really. She would be terribly hurt. Dear Mama, she only does it for my sake. She's always worried I'll be bored when I'm home from sea. If she only knew!'

His voice took on a special tone when he spoke of his mother. Amy had never been in any doubt that he was an adored and adoring son.

He gave a contented sigh, and settled her more comfortably in his arms. 'And what have you been up to while I've been away?' he asked.

This was her opportunity. 'I visited your house,' she said.

He held her at arm's length and looked at her.

'You did what!' he asked incredulously.

'I visited your house.' Somehow a bitter edge entered her tone as she added, 'By the servants' entrance, naturally. I took a letter from Mr Prout to your father.'

'You met my father? Did he realize…? Did you say anything about…?'

'About us? No, of course not!'

The sudden tension went from him. In spite of his protestations he was clearly as nervous about their love affair being known as she was. The knowledge gave strength to Amy's wavering resolve.

Daniel drew her close again. 'What did you think of him?' he asked.

'He was very nice to me, and kind. You look awfully like him.'

'So everyone says, though I believe I get my temperament from my mother. I wish you could have met her too. You'd have seen how truly wonderful she is.'

'I did meet her, briefly. She's a very elegant lady, isn't she?' Amy added hurriedly, afraid in case she had betrayed what she really thought of Mrs Newton.

'Indeed she is. She has superb taste.' Love and devotion sounded in Daniel's every word. 'Do you know, when we had the house refurbished she supervised everything herself. There was none of this getting a man down from Exeter or London to plan the colours. Mama chose it all.'

Amy swallowed hard. She had been wondering how to begin what she wanted to say. This was the opening she needed.

'You have a beautiful house,' she said. 'I don't suppose there are many better in the whole of Brixham. I never realized you lived anywhere so grand.'

'I wouldn't call it grand exactly.'

'I would. It must cost an awful lot of money to have a house like that, with such beautiful furniture, and so many servants. Why did you never tell me you were rich?'

'We're not rich. We're comfortably off, certainly, but a handful of servants, and one carriage – that's not rich. Not in my estimation.'

If Amy had had any doubts about parting from Daniel, the sincerity of his remarks drove them swiftly away. He lived in greater luxury than she had ever imagined, yet to him it was merely being 'comfortably off'. She needed no more proof of the great division between their two worlds.

'Daniel,' she said. 'I'm not going to see you any more.'

'What?' Shock and disbelief registered in his green eyes.

'We've got to finish, you and me. There's no future for us. It's better we break up now.'

'What's brought this on?' he demanded. 'Has someone said something? Did either of my parents—?'

'No, it's nothing to do with them, not entirely. Look, you're from a grand house, used to mixing with grand people. I'm a servant, brought up in a workhouse. There's no place for us in this world together. We're too far apart.'

'You've gone back to that old tune, have you?' he said, more calmly. 'How many times do I have to tell you that such things don't matter to us? You still love me, don't you?'

'Yes, you know I do.'

'And I still love you. Nothing else is important. Different worlds and such nonsense can be ignored.'

'No, they can't. Someone, somewhere, at some time decided that folks should be divided up into different levels, and that those levels should not mix. I'm not saying that it's right or fair; I'm saying that is how things are, and we can't change them.'

'Of course we can! If we love each other enough we can do anything we like. Who made up these stupid rules, anyway? Not you or me – they're nothing to do with us. We'll live our lives together the way we want. I agree that at the moment we have to be careful, but that's only because we aren't independent yet. In a few years, when I get promotion, things will be very different. We'll be married and we'll live happily ever after, as it says in the storybooks, because we love each other. The fact that we were born in different circumstances won't matter that much!' And he snapped his fingers.

Amy gave a sigh of distress. Why did he close his eyes to what was obvious?

'Have you thought about your career?' she asked. 'Having a wife who was once a servant would be a terrible drawback. It would ruin your chances of promotion.'

'No it wouldn't!' He laughed fondly. 'The only thing that would ruin my chances would be if I failed my exams. My mariners' tickets, they're what I need to get on, not a wife who is all airs and graces.'

He went to take her in his arms again. She backed away, knowing that once she was close to him, once she felt the warm security of his body against hers, she would be lost.

'There's more than one experienced man with his captain's ticket in Brixham who never gets a chance to sail a decent vessel,' she said.

'That's because they have other things against them in their backgrounds. A fondness for the drink or being unreliable or something serious like that. It's nothing to do with who they married.'

'Are you sure? How many times do you tell me about the entertaining your parents do, wining and dining agents and importers and exporters? Would your father have succeeded the way he has with a company like the South Devon Line if your mother had not been such a suitable hostess? I doubt it. If your mama had once been a servant or come from a workhouse my guess is that the best your father could have hoped for would be to be skipper on some grubby coaster, going from port to port begging for cargoes. I couldn't do that to you. I would hate myself for dragging you down, and in time you would begin to hate me too. You do see that, don't you?'

'No!' said Daniel flatly. 'If you're bothered about the social niceties and etiquette and whatnot we could soon find someone to teach you. I believe there are plenty of books on the subject. You'd pick it up in no time.'

She noticed that he did not suggest that his mother should teach her.

'No,' she said, equally decisively. 'I don't think I could. Once workhouse, always workhouse.'

'What complete nonsense! If you take that attitude then we're certain to have problems!' He calmed down a little then added, 'All right, if the social side of things ashore bothers you, then you can sail with me. There are still a few captains who have their wives living aboard. We could sail the world together. How would you like that, eh?'

'I think I might like it very much. I'm not so sure about you, though.'

Daniel gave a sigh of exasperation and exclaimed, 'You're determined to put objections in the way, aren't you? It doesn't matter what I suggest, it won't work. You don't want to marry me, that's the root of it, isn't it?'

'No!' she cried in distress. 'I love you very much, and in other circumstances being your wife is the most wonderful thing I could imagine. It's not my happiness I'm considering, it's yours.'

'Then let's agree to marry, because it's the only way to make me truly happy!' His angry tone sounded far removed from a declaration of love.

'We can't! We can't!'

Why could he not see the problems the way she could? He seemed to believe that everything would be all right simply because it was what he wanted. But then presumably Daniel had always got what he wanted. Money, a quick brain, education, and loving parents had ensured that nothing had been denied him. As far as he was concerned his unsuitable choice of wife could present no problems. Amy's heart ached with tenderness for him. Despite his advantages he was extraordinarily naive. If she had loved him less she could have taken advantage of such social innocence. As it was, she had to protect him from himself.

'Since you feel strongly on the matter, why don't you introduce me to your mother?' she said.

Daniel was taken aback.

'You've already met,' he said.

'We weren't introduced. I want to meet her properly.'

'So you shall.' He was hesitant. 'Not yet, though.'

'When?'

'Once we're of age. I've told you—'

'Will she approve? Will she fling her arms about me and say how happy she'd be to have me as a daughter-in-law?'

'She— she'll take to you at once, for your own sake, and because I love you.'

'Oh, Daniel, Daniel, Daniel, you know she will do no such thing! On the one occasion when I met her all she did was to make a terrible fuss about my dirty boots on her carpet. That was how much I impressed her.'

'Well she's… she's very house-proud.'

'She's son-proud too. She'd never accept me as your wife. Your father was kind to me, and considerate. There's some hope with him, but not with your mother. If she ever suspected how things are between us she would move heaven and earth to break us up.'

'You seem to have formed a poor opinion of my mother in a very short time,' he snapped.

'I haven't. I'm merely facing facts, facts which you persist in ignoring. How could I marry you when it would cause trouble between you and your family?'

'You don't mean my family, you mean my mother, don't you?' He spoke swiftly and angrily. 'I don't know why you are so prejudiced against her. You attack her, condemn her out of hand, yet she's done you no wrong.'

'I didn't attack her, or condemn her!' Amy cried.

The last thing she had wanted was for them to quarrel in such a way. 'Then you did a passable imitation.' His voice had grown low with suppressed anger.

'I am only trying to point out to you the difficulties which lie ahead. Difficulties we can't overcome,' Amy cried desperately.

Daniel gave an impatient snort. 'I thought you loved me as much as I loved you,' he said. 'Clearly I was wrong. You can't do, not when you persist in seeing such obstacles to our future, and especially since you evidently consider my mother to be the greatest obstacle of all.'

'She will never accept me! Never!'

'So you say. Perhaps you are right. I think you and my mother could be friends.' His words were cold and brusque. 'But such a friendship is impossible while you persist with such an unreasonable attitude. However, if you are right about this one thing no doubt you are right about others, too. The fact that we have no future together, for example. Since you are so determined on it then you shall have your wish. We'll part now, for ever. We'll never see each other again.'

He turned and strode away from her with long swift strides. Pain and disappointment and anger were etched in every line and sinew of him.

'Daniel! Daniel!' she cried after him. This was not how she had wanted their parting to be, not with bitterness and quarrelling. 'Daniel, wait!'

Already he was nearly at the top of the slope. She ran after him a little way then stopped. What would catching up with him achieve? Only the opportunity to prolong the agony. They had parted, and that had been her intention, hadn't it? Far better to let him go.

'Daniel, I love you,' she called after him. But her voice was barely audible through her tears, and her words were swept away on the wind.

Amy stayed in the grove of elderbushes for a long time, nursing her unhappiness. When she could weep no more she stood up and took one last look round. This secluded place had meant much to her and Daniel and held so many memories she felt their love must be imprinted on the smooth trunks and the bare branches. She would never come here again, she decided. She would abandon it to the poignant ghosts of what might have been.

–

When the *Balmoral* sailed from the harbour Amy felt as if her life had ended. She could see nothing ahead of her but darkness. Each morning she awoke feeling dragged down with misery, each evening she fell asleep to tears and a great sense of emptiness. This was life without Daniel, and although she knew it was right she did not know how she could bear it.

'I don't know what's the matter with you these days,' declared Jessie. 'You're fading before my eyes and you go moping about the place like a wet wash-day. Go on like this and before you know it you'll have the consumption or wasting disease or some such, and then where will we be?'

'It's just the winter weather, missus,' protested Amy. 'I've never liked the cold. I'll be fine once the spring comes.'

'Hm!' Jessie gave a snort. 'Always supposing you last that long!'

Under normal circumstances Amy would have smiled at Mrs Prout's doom-laden remark. Today she saw nothing funny in it. Winter or spring, it made no difference to her. One season was as bleak and meaningless now as another.

–

The town was preparing for Christmas but Amy felt she had little to rejoice about. She felt incapable of responding to the brightly decorated shops, or the hectic preparations for the coming festivities. All she wanted to do these days was to remain at home, shutting out the world with one of Todd's books whenever she could.

One evening her solitary misery was interrupted by a knock at the bottom door. When she opened it, there stood Jed.

'Hullo,' she said, standing aside to let him enter. 'What a surprise. I thought this was your night-school evening.'

'It is,' said Jed. 'We finished early on account of it being the last class before Christmas. I thought I'd come up and see how you're getting on.'

'No Seth?'

'No Seth.' Jed's features eased into a smile. 'Mr Burton found out he's been playing hookey instead of coming to night-school with me. Young Seth's doing his learning under the skipper's eagle eye now, and somehow I don't think his class will finish early for Christmas.'

'There's just the two of us, then. Sit yourself down while I go and tell the missus you're here, then we'll do a bit of toast, eh? The fire's nice and red.'

It was a mere formality for Amy to ask permission for Jed to stay now. Jessie would make some sharp remark about her kitchen being treated like the station waiting-room, or some similar comment, but she never refused. Amy was back in the kitchen almost immediately.

'Here, you get started on this. The toasting fork's by your side,' she said, cutting a slice of bread and handing it to him. 'I'll make us a pot of tea.'

For a while they were content to feast upon hot buttered toast and to talk about things in general. She had grown used to being alone with her dark moods, and had no inclination for her solitude to be interrupted. Jed was different, though. With him she had a link, a sympathy. They came from the same roots. He was like family.

'Things are going well with you?' he asked.

'Yes, fine, thanks.'

'Glad to hear it,' he said. He looked as though he did not believe her. 'I saw you in Fore Street the other day. I thought you looked a bit down.' She shrugged. 'Just the winter miseries.'

'How's Daisy?'

'Not too good. She looks as if a puff of wind would blow her away.'

'She's having a bad time, isn't she? Those people aren't treating her properly.'

'What makes you say that?' Amy asked sharply.

'My own eyes, and putting two and two together.'

'Yes, you're right, of course. Poor soul, she's desperately unhappy, and that isn't saying the half of it.'

'What's been going on?'

'I can't tell you. It's enough to say that she's got to get away from there. But how?' Amy knew she was on dangerous ground, but she was desperate. With each week that passed Daisy was growing more haggard and distressed. 'I wish I could help her find somewhere else but...' She shrugged helplessly.

'Exactly.' He nodded in agreement. 'Where? Who do we know who would employ her? No, if it's as bad as you think then we've got to get someone to stand up for her. We're no good. We need someone with a bit of authority. I suppose we could write to the Guardians at Lambeth.'

'Even if they did take any notice, they'd only fetch her back to the Union; and look at the way she was treated last time.'

'That's true. It's got to be someone here. How about your Mr Prout? Everyone says he's a decent man, and you trust him.'

'That's what I suggested to Daisy. Mr Prout would speak up for her if he felt she was being... being badly treated.' Amy had almost said 'misused', but that was too near the truth for comfort. 'Daisy wouldn't have it, though. What's worse is that she made me swear I wouldn't speak out for her. I've said far too much to you already.'

'You haven't told me anything I hadn't guessed for myself. It's a tricky situation... There's nothing for it, you'll just have to persuade Daisy to talk to someone – the vicar or the doctor, someone like that, who might help her get another situation. You'd go with her, wouldn't you?'

'Of course,' said Amy, 'I'm not sure she'd go.'

'Do your best. It's her only chance. Anyone can see she's dying on her feet. If I can help I will, but you'd do a much better job of it.'

'She should have someone more important than me to stand by her. She should have someone of her own. That's the trouble with being from a workhouse; you're never given a chance. Still, if you think I can persuade her... It'll take some doing, but if I keep on at her...'

'You'll do it if anyone can. You and Daisy have always been close.' Jed's words made her feel quite heartened. Here was something she *could* do for Daisy. In the weeks and months ahead she could give her friend her undivided attention now that Daniel was no longer a part of her life. One way or another she would talk her into seeking help.

'Thanks,' she said. 'Talking to you has helped. I should have done it ages ago.'

'Advice is cheap,' he said almost brusquely, but he looked pleased. 'And being a workhouse kid doesn't mean you've got to be the dregs all your life, you know. Some folks manage to rise above it.'

'I don't know anyone who's done it.'

'Yes, you do. George Beale!'

'What, Mr Beale who owns the *Faith*, the *FI ope* and the *Charity*?'

'Didn't you know he was once a workhouse boy? From Acton I think he said.'

'You're joking.'

'No, I'm not.'

'But he owns those smacks. And he has a decent house up Mount Pleasant. I've seen it. And Mrs Beale dresses very well. Their children don't go to the National School, they go up to Mr Bovey's and that costs money...'

'I know that.' Jed grinned at her incredulity. 'It doesn't change anything. Skipper Beale was sent down as an apprentice from the workhouse, just like Seth and me. He told me so himself, and how he worked his way up.'

'When did he tell you this?'

'During the summer, in Tenby.'

'This last summer?'

'No. When we first came here.'

'You kept very quiet about it. You didn't tell me!' Amy was quite indignant.

Jed did not reply immediately.

'Perhaps I should have done,' he said eventually. 'It was just that he— he gave me plenty to think about.'

'That's a long time to think, even for you.'

'He gave me advice, you see. He said— he said that he thought I could do what he'd done.'

'What, become a trawler owner?'

'Yes.'

'And is that what you want?'

'Yes.'

Amy looked at him. His eyes were bright, and his face, flushed by the warmth of the fire, had an animation she had never seen before.

'I want to get on, you see,' he continued. 'To build something up for myself by my own efforts. It's no use relying on other people, they only let you down. I've learned that time and again. That's why I'm determined to do it for myself. That's why I go to night-school. I'm going to get my certificates. I'm going to learn everything Skipper Burton can teach me, and more. I'm going to be a darned good seaman, so that when I get my own boat – and I'll get it, supposing I have to build it plank by plank myself – it'll be the finest fishing smack in the harbour. I'll stand at the helm of my own boat and I'll be my own master. I don't care that it'll take years of hard work. I can't think of anything better in the whole world. To be my own master!'

Amy had never heard him deliver such a long speech, nor to be so impassioned by anything. He meant every word, with an intensity she found surprising. She sensed that this was the first time he had put his dream into words. She was so impressed by his ideas and stirred by his ambitions that, when he had finished, she could not help clapping her hands enthusiastically.

'You'll do it!' she cried. 'I know you will! And when you launch your boat I'll come and wave and cheer.'

Jed looked awkward. 'I've been spouting a load of rubbish. I'm sorry,' he said.

'It wasn't rubbish. Don't you let me catch you saying such a thing ever again, Jediah Greenway,' she retorted fiercely. 'To be skipper of your own boat would be a wonderful thing. And you must never stop working for it, do you hear? Never!'

'I don't suppose I dare now. Not when you call me Jediah like that.' He grinned sheepishly.

'You'll get that boat, or I'll call you a lot worse than Jediah!' Amy declared.

Then suddenly they both burst out laughing.

Jed had made no mention of Lucy Burton. She was still offering her attractions, both her undeniably voluptuous flesh and her desirable dowry, the *Our Violet*. He suffered the normal lusts of any healthy young male, and in addition the equally strong yearning for a boat of his own. Sometimes the temptation was almost overpowering. Yet he held back. He would have to render an incredibly high price for the *Our Violet*. He was not convinced he could pay it.

'I'd best be going. It's getting late.' He rose, cap in hand. 'I've enjoyed tonight.'

Amy picked up the lamp to light him to the bottom door. 'So have I,' she said. 'We don't often get a chance for a good chat.'

He paused at the door.

'We talked about Daisy, and Seth, and about me,' he said. 'The only person we didn't talk about was you. How are things really? Are you still seeing that Newton fellow?'

Amy gasped. 'How did you know about him?' she demanded. Not waiting for his answer she continued, 'That was over ages ago.'

Jed said nothing. He could see from her face that it was not.

–

The first intimation Amy had that Daniel was home was at the Christmas concert. Todd had given her a ticket.

'Yer,' he had said. ''Tis an early Christmas present. Go and enjoy yourself, you could do with a bit of amusement. 'Tis for a good cause too, the Mission to Seamen.'

Amy had not been certain she wanted to go, especially not alone. She did try to persuade Daisy to come, without success. Once she found herself filing into the new Market Hall with the crowd she felt the novelty of the situation begin to have its effect. On the way in she met up with a couple of other maidservants she knew, and they sat together on a bench at the back, chatting in happy anticipation. Soon she was totally absorbed in the activities on the stage. If there were any imperfections in this amateur production, Amy was not aware of them. To her eyes it was wonderful.

So absorbed was she by the performances that it was not until near the end that she saw Daniel. In the flickering gaslight she caught sight of fox-red hair. It was only the briefest of glimpses, but she recognized him immediately. He was at the front in the most expensive seats.

Her eyes focused hungrily on the back of Daniel's head. If only he would turn so that she could see his beloved face again. Though if he did he might catch sight of her – the hall was not large – and that would be terrible. She crouched as low on the bench as she could without obscuring her view. Her gaze never left him for a second.

When finally the conceit ended and the audience rose, Amy was faced with a problem. What if she and Daniel met up on the way out? Already she could see him escorting his party towards the exit. Ahead of him went his mother and an elderly lady she did not know. It was the young girl by his side who held Amy's gaze. Expensively dressed in green velvet, she clung to him, demanding his undivided attention. A tearing pain went through Amy at the sight, a pain she reluctantly recognized as jealousy, envy – and love. Then the group moved into the brighter illumination cast by one of the gas brackets. For the first time Amy saw the girl properly. She noted the fine features, the swift deft movements – and the mane of red hair covered by the fashionable hat. The resemblance was striking. This was Daniel's sister.

Amy sat down again sharply.

'What's the matter?' asked her companions. 'You thinking of staying yer for Christmas?'

She searched for an excuse.

'I—I've dropped my glove,' she said.

'Right, we'll help you look.'

'Thanks.' She was grateful for a chance to recover, and also to remain concealed until Daniel and his family had left the hall.

'It idn't lost!' declared one of the girls with a chuckle. ''Tis on your hand. You'm wearing it, you daft pudden.'

By the time they left the hall there was no sign of Daniel or his family, for which Amy was very thankful.

Long into the night she lay in bed thinking of him. The love she felt for him and the hurt of losing him came rushing back with a greater intensity than ever. She had thought she was getting over Daniel, but she had been fooling herself.

The next time that Jessie let her have an hour off Amy found herself wandering towards the woods at Fishcombe. She did not mean to. It was as if her feet were beyond her control, taking her along the cliff-top, then down the path which skirted the cove. It was damp in the little clearing that had been their special place, and cold. Amy noticed no discomfort as she sat there, reliving every loving moment she had spent with Daniel. The harsh words that had been exchanged when they parted were firmly pushed to the back of her mind. All she wanted now was happy memories, tender memories, of the days when she loved and was loved. The tears ran down her cheeks unchecked as she remembered.

Eventually she could weep no more. Taking out her handkerchief she dried her eyes, then stood up, wincing as the blood rushed back into frozen limbs. Slowly she began the walk back, her head down in case anyone she met should notice that she had been crying. She did not see the figure ahead of her, not until they collided.

'Amy? Amy? Is it really you?' Daniel's arms were about her in an instant, crushing her in a fierce embrace. 'Amy, my darling, you've no idea how terrible it's been without you.'

'Yes I have!' she cried, her arms encircling his chest. 'It's been like a horrible nightmare. Everything's been dark gloom, there was no light or happiness anywhere.'

'You felt like that too?' he looked down at her as if he still could not believe she was in his arms.

'I did!' She laid her head against his chest. 'I know I sent you away, but I suffered for it most dreadfully.'

'You did it for the best. I saw that afterwards, and I was bitterly sorry for my quick temper. You did it for me, didn't you?' He smiled at her. 'Darling Amy, when will you stop trying to look after me?'

'Never,' she said. 'Not while I've got breath in my body.'

He bent to kiss her. The unhappy hours melted away at die touch of his lips on hers, and with them went all of Amy's resolutions that they should part. Any thought of attempting to send him away a second time was useless. She was not strong enough.

For a long, long time they clung together without speaking. Words were unnecessary. It was sufficient for them to be together again.

Daniel broke the silence. 'I've had a whole sea voyage in which to think over some of the things you said. About you having problems being accepted by society and things like that. You were right, of course.'

'I always am,' said Amy.

'Don't be saucy!' he rebuked her fondly. 'No, I mean it. You were right. It was stupid of me to close my eyes to reality. The way things are in this country we'd have a hard time of it together, and I'm not having you snubbed. I couldn't stand by and let that happen. I love you far too much.'

'What do you suggest then? That we set up home on board ship?'

Daniel gave a chuckle. 'That was one of my dafter ideas, wasn't it? Oh, it would be grand to have you come with me on a trip – captains often take their wives with them – but as a permanent way of life it has little to recommend it. When we marry we'll have a proper home in a proper house. You deserve it.'

'How is this to happen?' She was bewildered. 'Life here would still be full of problems for both of us.'

'Life here, yes. But we don't have to stay in this country, do we? We could go anywhere in the whole wide world – America, Canada, Australia – they're places where decent people aren't put down just because they don't happen to have money or were born in the wrong place. We'd have a chance to be happy in one of those countries. And it would be an adventure too. What do you say? Would you like to go?'

'Yes,' said Amy, her eyes shining. 'Oh yes!'

'That's the answer I knew you'd give.'

In his delight he swung her off her feet. Struggling to regain their balance brought them closer to one another, their bodies entwined. Sharp need, and a surge of nameless emotions shot through Amy, making her blood race, and the whole of her yearn for Daniel. He, too, was affected by their closeness as his kisses became more urgent, his caresses more intimate.

Large drops of rain spattering through the bare branches brought them back to reality. With a great effort Daniel gently pushed her away from him.

'Not yet,' he said, his voice unsteady. 'That's something we'll save for the future.'

And Amy, who had thought she already loved him to distraction, found she loved him even more.

Discarding caution, they walked back towards the cliff-top path with arms about each other. Only when they drew near to the houses did they decide to part.

'Can you meet me tomorrow afternoon?' asked Daniel.

'Yes,' said Amy, with no hint of uncertainty. She would manage it somehow.

'Good.' He kissed her on the nose. 'And when I do go back to sea you'll have something to occupy you now.'

'What?'

'Looking up those countries and seeing which one sounds the best. Knowing how much you like geography you should enjoy that.'

He was teasing, she knew. Nevertheless, the idea fired her imagination. It would be planning for their future. To Amy, as she ran light-footed back to the Prouts', it seemed as if a miracle had happened.

–

When the *Balmoral* sailed again after Christmas, taking Daniel away, Amy spent her spare time poring over her atlas and the couple of battered geography books she possessed, trying to choose which country should be their future home. She was so absorbed by her new occupation that Todd remarked, 'And what's old *Ivanhoe* done, then?'

'Done?' Amy was puzzled.

'Yes, poor soul, you'm neglecting him something chronic these days. I've had him all to myself of late – he'll be wondering what's happening.'

Amy grinned. 'A bit of neglect won't do him any harm,' she said. 'I thought I'd improve my mind for a spell, instead of wasting time with novels.'

'Wasting time? So that's how you thinks of my books!'

'Not really,' Amy said contritely. She thought she detected a note of genuine hurt beneath his mock indignation. 'You know how much I value them, and how grateful I am to you for letting me borrow them.'

'That's all right, then. For a nasty minute I thought you'd gone off un. You go on helping yourself to what you want. You don't have to ask.'

'Thank you.'

Amy's gratitude was heartfelt. Life without recourse to Todd's bookcase would have been empty indeed. And not only for her. She would recount what she had read to Daisy when they met during their time off. These days such stories seemed to be the only things which would divert Daisy's attention from her misery.

Remembering the conversation with Jed, Amy attempted to wear down Daisy's resistance to seeking help. Intermingled with the adventures of Ivanhoe and Mr Pickwick and the rest she would gently try to persuade her friend to see someone in authority. It was no use. Daisy would simply close her ears to every entreaty, and say, 'Tell us what happened next.' She never again mentioned what went on in the Floyd household, which only added to Amy's anxiety.

After breakfast one morning, Amy was doing the washing-up when Jessie came into the kitchen, some letters in her hand.

'That man would forget his own head if it wasn't screwed on,' she announced. 'Mr Prout was most particular he wanted these sent off early and he's left them behind. Leave what you're doing and run down to the post with them.'

Amy dried her hands willingly and fetched her coat. The winter was finishing in a welcome burst of mild weather, and although it was barely light there was a promise of spring in the air. It was so pleasant that after her errand was completed she decided to go home the long way round, past the harbour. It was then she noticed a commotion further along the Quay. The fish-market was still busy, but that did not account for the crowd of people gathered at the harbour side. Curious, she hurried forward.

'What's happened?' she asked, recognizing one of the fishwives.

The woman turned to her, and a look of concern crossed her weatherbeaten face.

''Tidn't nothing for you, my lover,' she said. 'You'd best be off home.'

A sense of unease gripped Amy.

'What's happened?' she demanded. 'Has there been an accident?'

She tried to move forward but the fishwife caught hold of her. 'There idn't naught you can do. Best go home,' she said kindly.

Amy pressed against the restraint, her disquiet growing with every second. Although she could not see properly she gathered there was a boat alongside. Men were lifting something wrapped in canvas and carrying it up the steps, their faces grave. Vaguely she became aware of comments in the crowd.

'Old Bert found 'er, coming back from checking 'is moorings. Swears 'er weren't there on 'is way out.'

'Then 'er can't 'ave been in the water long.'

'Long enough for what 'er wanted to do, poor soul.'

A terrible sense of foreboding swept over Amy. She had to know what was going on. Wrenching away from the fishwife's grip, she pushed her way into the crowd – to come face to face with Jed. He looked ashen.

'Go away! Go away!'

His voice was almost a snarl in his distress. He grasped her and tried to push her back. Amy resisted with all her strength, looking past him to see what was happening as she did so. The men had reached the top of the steps. That it was a body they were carrying was only too evident. From the end of the improvised shroud there escaped a cascade of hair. Pale, silver-gold hair that when dry would have been as light and fine as dandelion fluff.

'No!' said Amy, in little more than a whisper. 'No! No! No!'

The men gently placed their burden on the ground, and inadvertently allowed the canvas to fall back. A faint sigh, like a breeze in rigging, went round the crowd. Daisy lay there, white and fragile-looking, as if fashioned from alabaster. The wet nightgown clinging to her slight body emphasized the full rounded belly.

'Poor little sprat, six months gone if 'er were a day,' said a woman in the crowd, as one of the fishermen gently replaced the canvas.

The words and the action cut through Amy's initial shock.

'Daisy!' she screamed. 'Oh no, not that! Not that!'

Struggling like a thing possessed she tried to escape Jed's hold, shouting and crying as she did so. He was too strong for her. Suddenly Todd was there as well. She had not noticed that he had been one of Daisy's pallbearers.

'Daisy…! Let me go to her,' sobbed Amy, still beating against Jed with her fists.

Todd's arms went round her too.

'Her'm past helping now, my maid,' he said with sympathy. 'There idn't naught you can do. 'Tis best if you go home. You'll take her, will you, boy?'

Jed nodded. 'Come on, Amy,' he said, trying to draw her away.

She refused to move.

'I've got to stay with her,' she protested. 'I've got to look after her. I've always looked after her.' The men were lifting their burden again. 'Where are they going? Where are they taking her?' Amy's panic-stricken cry was like that of a trapped animal.

'We'm taking her to the Seamen's Rooms.' Todd's jerk of the head indicated a building further along the Quay. 'Dr Searle's been sent for, and Constable Gill. They'll look after her properly, never fear. Go on home, maid. I'll come up presently and tell you what happens. This idn't no place for you.'

He took up his station with the other men and they moved away. They seemed far too large and numerous for the slight burden they carried on their shoulders. Sobbing uncontrollably Amy tried to follow, fighting against Jed's hold. Other bystanders came to his aid, encircling her with their arms. The intervention was kindly meant, and her captors spoke to her gently and with sympathy, but all Amy wanted was to be with Daisy. She fought them every step of the way.

Somehow, she did not know how, she found herself alone with Jed in the kitchen of the Prouts' house. He tried to persuade her to sit down but she could not. She had to move, to pace agitatedly back and forth, trying to give vent to the terrible anguish within her yet not knowing how.

'I could have prevented it,' she kept saying over and over again. 'I knew, you see. I knew what that animal was doing to her. I was the only one who knew.'

'What animal? Who do you mean?'

'Who do I mean?' Her grief made her unreasonable and she was indignant at such ignorance. 'Don't you know? Can't you guess?'

'You mean Floyd?'

'Of course I mean Floyd! Oh, why is he still alive? How can he go on breathing when poor Daisy's cold and dead? What did she ever do to deserve such treatment? What harm did she ever do him? He never let her alone. From the very first night we arrived he was at her. Poor, poor Daisy, what could she do against the likes of him? I should've stopped it. I should've done something.'

'I guessed something of the sort was going on. I didn't realize it was so bad, though.' Jed looked both shaken and angry. He had given up trying to get her to rest and was now pacing with her, his arm consolingly about her shoulders. 'You tried to persuade her to talk to the vicar or the doctor, you know you did. And she refused. You couldn't very well have dragged her there by force.'

'No, but I could have gone myself. If I had she'd be alive now.' The words came out in a wail of anguish. 'She made me promise not to say anything. Oh, I was a fool to keep that promise. I was more than a fool! I was weak and wicked and stupid.'

'No you weren't. You weren't, do you hear!' Jed halted their pacing as he shook her sharply. 'You kept your word, you can't be blamed for that. And supposing you'd gone to see Dr Searle or someone by yourself, what would have been the good of that? Daisy wouldn't have backed you up. No one would have believed you.'

Amy did not want to hear his reassuring words. She was too busy condemning herself. This tragedy could have been averted if only she had acted. She was almost as much to blame for Daisy's death as the vile Floyd. In agitation she resumed her pacing.

Todd came back just before noon, looking very solemn.

'There's to be an inquest,' he said. 'Probably at the end of the week.'

'Where – where is she?' Amy asked.

'Joseph Dawe, the undertaker, has taken charge. Him and Dr Searle together. They'll do everything that's proper, don't you fret.'

Amy wanted to believe him. She could not bear to think of Daisy lying alone in some bare, barn-like room. Poor Daisy had never liked being alone, she had always been afraid. The combination of grief, shock, and the brandy administered by Jessie began to have its effect on Amy, causing her to feel as if she were enveloped in fog. She was hardly aware of Seth coming in. He had only just come back from fishing, and the news had stunned him. He held on to her hand tightly, for once bereft of speech.

When he and Jed eventually left she was barely conscious of their going. Only Jed's parting words, whispered in her ear, made any impression. He said, 'You're not to blame yourself, do you hear? It was Floyd's fault.'

She thought he added, 'And he'll pay for it,' but she was not sure.

Amy certainly wanted Floyd to be punished. She was sorely tempted to stand in Fore Street and yell to the passing townspeople exactly what sort of a creature he really was. Only respect for Daisy's memory held her back.

As it happened she had no need to take such action. No sooner had word of Daisy's tragic death got about the streets than other rumours began to circulate. The Floyds had come to Brixham from up Barnstaple way, and whispers spread of a scandal there involving the draper and a servant girl, and a similar incident at Okehampton where they had lived before that.

'I've never liked that man,' stated Jessie. 'Far too oily to my way of thinking. I'd never deal with him willingly. There was only that time I wanted waxed ribbon most particularly, and, my, what he wanted to charge me for it… No, I always go to Decent's, up the road. Mind, that Floyd's got something of his just rewards. Apparently he fell downstairs the night before last. They were talking about it at the Sewing Guild last night. Can hardly put one foot in front of the other, they say.'

Amy said nothing. Her regret was that the stairs were not higher and the ground at the bottom harder. No matter how much she blamed Floyd she was still left with a terrible guilt, like a festering wound within her.

One more scandal was to rock Brixham. Before dawn on the day of Daisy's inquest, the fishwives and porters heading for work at the fishmarket noted that the Floyds' shop was empty. The draper and his family had done a flit.

–

The room at the Market Hall where the inquest was to be held was soon filled to capacity. Amy found herself wedged between Jed and Seth. She was thankful for their presence. The three of them had to stick together, they needed each other. John and Todd Prout were there, too, sitting in the row behind. The buzz of conversation died as the coroner, a dignified gentleman in a high winged-collar, took his seat. He looked about the room through gold-rimmed pince-nez, his gaze finally alighting on the constable who was acting as usher.

'What's been done about identifying the body?' he demanded. 'Normally the deceased's employer would be required to perform the office, but I understand he is – er – not available.'

'No, sir,' said the constable.

'I believe the deceased came with a group from the Lambeth Union. Perhaps one of the others… a particular friend…?'

Amy's stomach contracted painfully. Surely she was not going to be asked to play a part in this inquest? It was bad enough the way the coroner kept referring to 'the deceased' and 'the body'.

'That's been taken care of, sir.' The constable approached the table where the coroner sat and spoke to him in a tone so low that only snatches could be heard. 'Maidservant… Mr Prout… already very upset… reliable young fellow… Jediah Greenway.'

The coroner nodded. 'Very well. Call Jediah Greenway.'

Jed rose. He had given no hint that he was to be called. Amy realized that he must have gone alone, unbeknown to her or Seth, to identify the pale dead creature that had once been Daisy. It should have been her duty, since she was Daisy's closest friend. She guessed he had done it to save her further distress. How typical of Jed not to say anything. As he started to edge his way along the row of spectators she took his hand and gave it a grateful squeeze. He did not look down at her, but his fingers tightened briefly about hers.

The inquest was brisk and formal, the verdict a foregone conclusion – death was by drowning, and Daisy Simms had taken her own life while the balance of her mind was disturbed. The coroner did have some sharp things to say about employers who misused their responsibilities towards the people in their charge. He was wasting his time, though. The man at whom his words were aimed was miles away.

When it was all over Jed and Seth had to get back to work. Their farewells were brief and rather awkward, neither of them could find the right words to express their feelings.

'We'll come see you as soon as we can, won't we, Seth?' said Jed.

'Of course we will. And you're to keep your pecker up, do you 'ear?'

Somehow Amy managed a little smile. 'I'll do my best,' she said. In her heart she felt it would be almost impossible.

When it was time to go home there was no sign of Todd, so Amy and John Prout set off alone. They had not gone far before Todd came hurrying after them.

'Well, is it all fixed up?' asked John.

'There was no need.' Todd put something in his brother's hand, and Amy heard the chink of coins. Seeing her curious look he said, 'It didn't right, that poor li'l maid having a pauper's burial, so John and I thought... Anyway, it wasn't necessary. I had a word with Joe Dawe and he says it have been taken care of. It seems that Floyd had at least one decent bone in his body. He paid handsomely for the funeral before he ran off. He sent the money with young Jed.'

Amy walked home in silence, her throat choked with tears that were not for Daisy alone. The kindness of the Prout brothers touched her. She thought of Jed, too. Jed, who had taken Floyd's sovereigns to the undertaker, and whose knuckles, as he had sat beside her that morning, had been cut and bruised. Maybe Floyd's fall downstairs had been less of an accident than it seemed.

Oh Jed, she thought, you took such risks, and you took them alone.

She did not like the idea of Floyd's money paying for Daisy's burial. Nothing he did would ever pay for his wickedness. But Jed had done what he could to exact retribution, she would never forget that. And Daisy, who had never had anything in her entire life, would at least have a decent funeral.

Chapter Seven

The warm sun had not yet dried up the lush growth of early summer. Devon pride – the rose-pink valerian – sprouted from old stone walls, along with wiry rock daisies and festoons of tiny purple toadflax. Amy had taken the trouble to learn the names of most of the wild flowers she passed on her way. She had never forgotten the occasion long ago when she and Daniel had climbed the cliff path above Fishcombe and found the grass starred with flowers. He had been so knowledgeable about such things that she had been determined to learn as well. Of course, Daisy had been with them then. The thought of her friend cast a dark shadow over Amy. It made no difference that it was more than a year since Daisy's tragic death, a terrible sadness still held Amy in its grip. Her sense of guilt remained with her like an unwanted burden.

However, this was not a time for mourning or gloomy thoughts. She had the rare luxury of a whole day off. Even more wonderful, Daniel was home and they were going to spend it together. He was waiting for her at their special place.

Rising to greet her, he grasped her round the waist and rained kisses down on her.

'You're crushing my ribs!' she protested, breathless with laughter and the force of his embrace.

'It's no more than you deserve for keeping me waiting,' he complained, half seriously. 'Why am I always the first to arrive?'

'Because you don't have to keep Jessie Prout sweet in order to get away,' Amy smiled.

'I thought she'd given you the day off. Aren't the Prouts visiting their aunt in Newton Abbot or something?'

'She did, and they are. Then there was breakfast to clear away, the kitchen to scrub out, beds to make, rooms to dust, and a few minor chores like that.'

'You sound as though you've done a day's work already. Are you sure you want to go walking? We could have the picnic here.'

'No, we couldn't,' Amy said firmly. 'I've never had a whole day off before, and I want to go somewhere different.'

'Then that's what we shall do,' said Daniel. 'I've got everything we need in here.' He patted the haversack over his shoulder.

'Didn't anyone ask who you were going with, or awkward questions like that?'

'Why should they? I said I was going on an expedition and asked Cook for a little something to keep me going. That was enough to put her on her mettle.' He pretended to sag under the weight.

'Perhaps we'd better stay here if you're too weak to go on,' said Amy gravely.

'I think I can manage to stagger along for a while.' Daniel slumped against her as if in urgent need of support. Taken by surprise Amy overbalanced and, in fits of laughter, the pair of them fell over.

'Help me up!' exclaimed Amy. 'My new dress is getting ruined.'

'No it's not,' said Daniel, suddenly serious. He made no attempt to move, but gazed at her intently.

'Why are you looking at me like that?' she asked uncertainly. 'Have I got a smut on my nose?'

'No, I'm trying to decide if your eyes are more green than brown or more brown than green.' He paused, continuing to look at her. 'You are beautiful, do you know that? When I'm at sea I think of you the whole time. I imagine your face, and your hair streaked gold and brown, the colour of pulled toffee, and I think, she can't really be as lovely as I remember. Then when I get home I find my memory has played tricks on me because you are much, much lovelier.'

With one finger he traced the line of her brow, her cheek, her jaw. When he reached her chin he gently tilted up her face to his, and he kissed her. Amy's arms went about his neck as she responded. Never had she felt so happy. It was intoxicating, knowing that they belonged together. Their love had moved a long way from the days of youthful flirtation. Need for each other, combined with the seclusion and the fragrant warmth of the summer morning was a heady mixture. Too heady for Amy's peace of mind. She moved away slightly.

Daniel smiled wryly. 'Maybe you're right,' he admitted with reluctance. 'If we're going to have this picnic we'd better get moving.'

He helped her to her feet.

'Where are you taking me?' she asked, as they turned their backs on the sea and struck inland along a narrow track.

'Wait and see,' was the only answer he would give.

They walked on, taking deserted country paths, where they met no one. Hand in hand, content with his company, Amy hardly noticed the distance until hunger began to make itself felt.

'I've never been this far before,' she said. 'I've never had the time. Won't you tell me where we're going?'

'No,' said Daniel, 'because we're almost at the first place I want to show you.'

'The first? You mean there's more than one?'

'Yes, for girls who aren't impatient—'

'And whose bellies aren't stuck to their backbones with hunger?' she finished.

He laughed. 'If you're in such a state then it's just as well we're there,' he said. 'Just over this bit...'

They had been climbing steadily for a while and now they emerged on to a hilltop. The path was thickly edged with white clustered heads of yarrow, and the field at either side was green with unripe barley; but that was not why Amy gave a gasp of pleasure. From such a high vantage point the surrounding countryside was laid out all round her. In one direction a river flowed between rolling hills dappled with fields and woodlands; in another she could see the curve of Torbay with the blue Channel beyond; while in the far distance an even higher range of hills showed as a smoky-blue smudge against the horizon.

'That's Dartmoor,' Daniel said, noting the direction of her gaze. 'And the river is the Dart, if you haven't guessed.'

'Oh,' said Amy, enchanted by all she saw.

'I thought we'd have our picnic here, if it suits you.'

'If it suits me!' Amy looked round again, her eyes wide with wonder. 'How could we have anywhere better? We can see so far... It's as if we'd got the whole world spread out for us to look at...'

'It is special, isn't it?' He put his arm about her shoulders and the pair of them stood drinking in the scene. 'The best view in England, in my estimation... and I dare say it will look even better once we've had something to eat, eh?'

'It certainly won't look worse,' Amy agreed.

They found a spot beneath a wind-gnarled hawthorn, then, comfortably ensconced to enable them to appreciate the view, Daniel unpacked the contents of his haversack. Amy's eyes widened as he took out ham sandwiches, a pork pie, hard-boiled eggs and wedges of cheese, fruit cake and apples, and finally a bottle of ginger beer.

'That was intended just for you?' she asked in amazement.

'It was!' He chuckled. 'Cook considers it her personal duty to build me up into a fine strong lad.'

'She has certainly succeeded.' Amy leaned across and kissed him. 'You can tell her that her efforts have been worthwhile.'

'I certainly shall. Now what was the message again? It was the bit in the middle I can't quite remember.'

Laughing, Amy obliged and kissed him again.

'That was wonderful,' he said approvingly, 'And as a reward...' He proffered the opened packet of sandwiches. '...Or if madam would prefer...' He held out the sliced pork pie.

Amy felt her first experience of a picnic to be perfection. It was some time before they had eaten their fill. She brushed the crumbs from her skirt.

'Your new dress is awfully pretty,' said Daniel.

'Do you think so?' she said with some relief. He had made no mention of it before, and she had been afraid he had not noticed it or, worse still, did not like it. 'I made it myself,' she added casually. The few words gave no hint of the weeks of effort and torment that producing the dress had provoked. Honesty forced her to add, 'Mrs. Prout helped me. She's good like that. Her tongue can be sharp at times but what she says and what she does are two different things.' She ran a hand over the white-spotted apricot poplin, whose choice had caused her much anxious pondering as well as months of careful saving. 'Do you really like it?' she asked, diffidently.

'Of course I do. I'm sorely tempted to take you somewhere crowded with people, to show you off.'

Amy gave a sigh of pleasure. 'What a day of firsts this is for me,' she said. 'As well as everything else, this is the first pretty dress I've ever had.'

'Once we're married I'll buy you as many pretty dresses as you want – not that you need them. Whatever you wear you look lovely to me.'

Reassured, she again sighed contentedly. Once we are married – those were the words that filled her with happiness, not his promise of fine clothes.

'Once we are married!' She repeated the words aloud.

'Yes.' Daniel slid his arm comfortably about her, and they leaned back against the grassy bank. 'When you are Mrs. Daniel Newton you shall be the best-dressed woman in— in wherever we decide to settle. Have you made up your mind where that should be?'

'I've been giving it a lot of thought while you were at sea,' she said. 'I think I like the sound of New Zealand best. It sounds a bit like here, but more exciting with those geysers and things. Though I'm not sure I understand how hot water suddenly shoots up into the air for no apparent reason. Have you ever seen a geyser?'

'No,' admitted Daniel. 'That's something we shall have to discover together, and maybe we'll find out why they behave in such an eccentric way.'

'You approve of New Zealand as a place to live, then?'

'Indeed I do. In fact, there is one more point in its favour that you overlooked. It is exactly the sort of place where sea captains flourish! Are you sure you won't mind having a hot sunny Christmas and a chilly June?'

'I would get used to it.' She snuggled closer to him, convinced that she could get used to anything.

'I fancy we could do very well there. But it will be a while before we can think about marriage. I'd have to be a third officer at the very least.'

'That doesn't matter. The important thing is that we will get married one day. I can stand anything as long as I know we have a future.' She spoke urgently and with such sincerity that he drew her closer to him.

'It won't be for a moment longer than necessary, I promise you,' he said softly.

For a while everything receded, even the joy of planning for the future, as their need to caress and embrace each other blotted out the world. They were both aware that it was becoming more and more difficult to restrain the growing passion which consumed them when they were together. In calmer moments Amy was conscious of how easily their feelings could sweep away all caution. Daniel was aware of it also, and he pushed her from him with a groan.

'You're tempting me too much,' he said unsteadily. 'We'd better start walking again.'

Together they rose, faces flushed, eyes bright with thwarted passion. Daniel looked so handsome as he swung the haversack over his shoulder that Amy could not hold back just one more embrace.

'I love you,' she said, her arms tight about him. 'I keep thinking I love you as much as is possible, then I see you again and I find I love you even more. No matter what happens I'll never stop loving you. I'd wait for an eternity to be your wife.'

'Oh, Amy, that wait will be worthwhile, never doubt it for a moment. We're going to be happy together – very, very happy...'

Their arms entwined about each other, they continued on their way, blissfully discussing their prospects and their plans as they went.

'Where are you taking me?' demanded Amy suddenly.

'Ah,' said Daniel, his eyes sparkling. 'This is the second surprise of the day – or it may be the second and third. I'm not sure. Five minutes and you'll see.'

Their downhill path became progressively steeper as they joined the road. Before long Amy could see water through the trees, and passing boats.

'We're coming to the river!' she cried excitedly.

Another few yards and they reached a small quay. The Dart seemed vast from their viewpoint, almost like a lake, for high hills masked its route.

'Where's that?' Amy waved a hand towards the large village on the opposite shore.

'That's Dittisham. There's a cottage down on the riverside which does delicious shrimp and cockle teas. Shall we go and sample them?'

'Do you mean it?' Her face lit up with delight. 'You mean we're going out to tea?'

'Don't tell me! It'll be the first time you've ever been out to tea!'

'It will! Properly out to tea, that is! Once or twice I've had a cup with Mrs Craig's Ivy, up the road from us, but that's all.'

She had been about to ask how they were to cross the river when a thick-set man emerged from a thatched cottage nearby. 'You'm wanting to cross?' he asked. 'I 'opes you 'aven't been waiting long. I didn't know you was 'ere. Should've rung the bell! That would've fetched me.'

As he talked he led the way down some steps to a boat which was moored at the bottom. He climbed in, then helped Amy. He would have offered a helping hand to Daniel, but he had already leapt aboard.

'You done that afore, I can see!' The boatman grinned approvingly as he pushed them away from the small jetty.

Effortlessly he pulled on the oars, making nothing of the distance, nor the strong current which caught them in midstream. Amy sat silently, her eyes fixed upon the approaching village. It was not that she was afraid to be on the water, it was because of the sense of sorrow which unexpectedly beset her. The lapping waves, the translucent green depths on every side – how had Daisy felt as she had sunk down into the cold, cold water?

'Are you all right?' Daniel asked.

'Yes, of course I am.' She managed a smile.

He did not look convinced. He was still regarding her with concern after the boatman had deposited them on the beach and pocketed his pence.

'Something is wrong. Come on, tell me what's upset you.' Daniel persisted.

'It's nothing… It's just that being on the river – the water and everything – I was remembering Daisy.'

'That was ages ago. You must stop getting emotional about it. I know she was your friend, but life goes on.'

'Perhaps you're right, only I still feel guilty. I could have done something—'

'No you couldn't,' he cut in, the concern in his voice replaced by a sharper note. 'If the silly girl was set upon killing herself there was no way you could have prevented it.'

'You don't understand—' she began, then stopped. How could he understand? He had no comprehension of despair or dread or hopelessness. He had never experienced any of them. 'You're right. I should make an effort to get over it.' She summoned up another smile. 'There, I'm better now. We can't let anything spoil today, can we?'

'That's my girl.' He put his arm about her shoulders and gave her a hug. 'And when you have had some tea you'll feel better.'

For Amy this first experience of going out to tea far exceeded her expectations. From what she had seen at Jessie Prout's, tea-parties had always seemed uncomfortably formal occasions, full of opportunities for making social blunders. This was quite different. They ate in a cottage garden, shaded by some of the plum trees for which the village was famous. The plates came piled high with shrimps and cockles, accompanied by home-made bread, local farm butter, and quantities of good strong tea. They ate and drank, laughed and talked, until the sun began to dip in the sky, warning them it was time to leave.

The thought of the return trip across the river caused Amy some qualms, but this time she was prepared. They reached the other side without Daniel having any suspicion of what a desolate effect the green water had on her. Together they trudged back, steeped in sunshine, weary yet happy.

'Have you enjoyed your outing, with all its firsts?' Daniel asked, as they neared home.

'Enjoyed it?' Amy considered the words. They were far too inadequate to express what she felt. 'This has been the most beautiful, wonderful, exciting day in the whole of my life. I'll always remember it. If I live to be a hundred and ten, I'll remember it!'

'By the time you're a hundred and ten you'll have lots more other wonderful days to remember with it,' said Daniel, as they kissed before parting. 'Every day of our marriage is going to be wonderful and special because you will belong to me, and I will belong to you.'

Belonging to Daniel! Amy savoured the thought. She treasured it all the way home and for a long, long time afterwards. Belonging to Daniel! It sounded like heaven!

–

In the summer sunshine the enclosed yard behind the Burtons' house radiated warmth. Jed and Seth lounged on the steps leading up to the cabin, their shirt collars open at the neck, their sleeves rolled up, luxuriating in the heat and in the brief spell of leisure.

'This is the life, ain't it?' murmured Seth, stretching himself comfortably. 'When I'm rich I'll do this every day, just laze about and do nothing.'

'By the time you're rich you'll be so old that's all you'll be able to do,' replied Jed, without opening his eyes.

'You don't believe me, do you? Well, just you wait and see.'

'How do you intend getting this money? Playing pitch-and-toss with men like Cy Heath?'

'Nah, of course not. I mean to find myself a rich widow. I do,' he insisted at Jed's sceptical snort. 'I've got a way with women, older ones especially. They want to mother me.'

This was true enough. Jed had observed that middle-aged women tended to make a fuss of Seth. Perhaps it had something to do with the fact that in spite of the plain solidity of Mrs. Burton's cooking he still looked underfed. There was something else about him that Jed could not quite fathom, a sort of little boy vulnerability. Whatever it was it had mature women flocking to him in droves. There were exceptions, though.

'Ma Burton doesn't want to mother you, for one,' he observed.

'Maybe not, but then a lifetime spent with the skipper's enough to knock the mothering out of anyone. No, I'm looking for someone who'll take care of me and coddle me in the way that I deserve. Someone cuddly and comfortable.'

'With a cuddly and comfortable amount in the bank, I suppose,' said Jed with a grin. It was impossible not to smile at Seth, he never seemed to take anything seriously.

'Oh yes, 'ow else would she be able to buy me smart suits, posh shirts and the gold watches that I fancy? Of course the old girl'd 'ave to 'ave money.'

'What be all this 'bout soft old girls with money, then?' demanded a voice, and Lucy descended on them, rustling her striped cotton skirt. Unknown to them she must have been in the privy out at the back and heard their conversation.

Seth was not one bit abashed. 'Just men's talk,' he said. 'Nothin' for your girlish ears.'

'Men's talk, eh? I can guess what that were about! You should be ashamed, the pair of 'ee.' She lowered her eyelashes seductively and pretended to pout. As a display of outraged maidenly modesty it was a total failure. 'I idn't going to stand 'ere and listen to you two talking dirty,' she added, making to push past them.

In doing so her skirts deliberately swept over Jed. She pretended to stumble and put a hand on to his shoulder to steady herself. But it was Seth who, sitting up, caught hold of her and pulled her on to his lap.

'You don't want to throw yourself at old Jed,' he said, bouncing her up and down. ''E's only interested in boats and 'is silly old maths books. Why don't you throw yourself at me? It'd be a lot more fun.'

'I wouldn't waste no time on 'ee,' replied Lucy, making no attempt to move. ''Ee idn't never going to 'mount to nothing.'

'Oh yes? And who says so?' demanded Seth with amiable indignation.

'Pa. 'E says so. 'E'm never wrong 'bout things like that. 'E reckons as it's Jed as 'as the makings.' She beamed invitingly at Jed, who merely glowered at the ground in front of him.

'The makings of what?' Seth wanted to know.

'Ah, that'd be telling.' Lucy freed herself from his grasp and stood up. 'Jed knows, don't 'ee, boy?'

She ran a caressing hand along his bare arm, causing Jed to shift uncomfortably. Knowing full well the disturbing effect she was provoking she chuckled and went into the house.

Watching her go, Seth grinned and dug a sharp elbow into Jed's ribs. 'My!' he chortled. 'You're going to be all right, my lad, and no mistake. Lucy's got 'er eye on you, and 'er 'ands too given 'alf a chance. I 'ope you're up to the challenge. Lucy could be quite a 'andful in more ways than one.'

'Oh, shut up,' snapped Jed.

Seth was undismayed. 'Not that I envy you,' he went on. ''Aving the skipper as your pa-in-law! I can't say I'd fancy that. Still, I've known all along that you're the skipper's pet. I'm not jealous, 'onest. I'm looking forward to dancing at your wedding, and I wish you luck. You're going to need it, with Lucy if not with 'er old man.'

'Will you shut your mouth?' roared Jed.

He launched himself at a laughing, protesting Seth, and they rolled about in mock combat until a deep voice from the house bellowed, 'Stop that racket, you two, afore I comes out and makes 'ee! Can't a body get no peace?'

They stopped their wrestling immediately, and exchanged chastened grimaces.

'There, you've upset your daddy,' taunted Seth.

'I'll upset you if you don't give over,' answered Jed, aiming a half-hearted blow at him. 'Now sit down and shut up. It's too hot to fight, anyway.'

They collapsed back on to the steps and resumed their sunbathing. As he sat with eyes closed and face raised to the sun Jed was soon absorbed in thought. The encounter with Lucy was only one of many incidents that were bringing his situation into sharper and sharper focus.

There was no denying that Matthew Burton was favouring him more openly these days, as was the voluptuous Lucy. Jobs ashore and afloat beyond the usual responsibilities of an apprentice were being handed over to him. The other men noticed this favouritism and taunted him with it, not always good-naturedly. Jed took no notice of the jibes; what troubled him most was the way he was being pushed more and more into the Burton family and towards Lucy. If he were not careful he would end up marrying her whether he wanted to or not.

He should have been on his guard. He should have been aware that Lucy's pursuit of him was growing more intense, but he was not. Not until he returned to the cabin after night-school one evening. As he went to light the lamp, Lucy's voice addressed him out of the darkness.

'Don't 'ee turn un up too 'igh,' she said. 'Us don't need much light, do us?'

Far from turning up the lamp Jed almost dropped it in his surprise. 'What the devil are you doing here?' he demanded.

When he turned round he formed a pretty good idea. Lucy was leaning against the wall in a manner that could only be called provocative. She was wearing a calf-length chemise in white cambric. It was her sole garment, a fact that was all too evident in the soft glow of the oil-lamp. Her abundant brown hair, strewn loose across her shoulders, did nothing to hide the fact that her low neckline was exposing a disturbing amount of her equally abundant bosom.

'Are you mad?' demanded a startled Jed. 'Your ma and pa—'

''Ave gone to a Bible-study meeting. They won't be back for a good hour. As for Seth, I don't know where 'e'm to but 'e don't signify. That leaves 'ee and me, Jed Greenway.'

'No, it doesn't. It just leaves me. Out you go!' Jed felt panic sweep over him. He did not share Lucy's faith in the length of the Bible-study meeting, and whereas Matthew Burton might look on him approvingly as a prospective son-in-law he was not married to Lucy yet. To have Skipper Burton discover them in such a compromising situation would really put the cat among the pigeons.

'Oh, I be going, be I?' asked Lucy coyly. 'You'm going to make me?'

'Yes,' said Jed firmly, and he caught hold of her by the waist. This was a tactical error. Far from resisting, Lucy squirmed closer to him, pressing her full breasts against him. He was uncomfortably aware of the softness of her body through the thin cotton.

''Ee don't really wants to send me away, do 'ee?' Lucy whispered seductively, her head on his shoulder.

'Yes, I do!' In spite of himself his voice wavered uncertainly.

'What'd 'ee want to do a thing like that for?' Lucy snuggled closer, her fingers creeping up the back of his neck and into his hair. 'Us could 'ave such a nice time yer together.'

To prove it she drew his head towards her and kissed him, her mouth devouring his.

'Will— you— stop— fooling— about!' Jed's protests were punctuated by her lips making speech impossible.

'There,' she breathed eventually. ''Ee enjoyed that, don't pretend 'ee didn't.'

He tried to deny it, with little success. Her closeness was having its effect, making his body respond to hers. Without him realizing it his hands slid down to caress the plump curves of her buttocks as he drew her more tightly against him. By accident or design the shoulder of her chemise had slipped down, exposing one rounded white breast. He could not tear his eyes away from the sight. It filled him with an unbearable excitement. His mouth began to take a frenzied path down her throat towards the soft swell of its contours. Lucy arched against him, her soft whimpers of desire driving him on to greater and greater passion. Somehow they were now lying on his narrow bed. Feeling Lucy supine beneath him Jed knew he had to have her. He could not help himself.

Even as he pulled at her flimsy chemise the words rang out in the recesses of his brain. He was not in control, either of himself or of the situation. He, Jed Greenway, who prided himself on his independence and restraint, was on the point of succumbing to Lucy's conniving. From the very beginning she had been manipulating him to get what she wanted, and he was close to giving into her. Disgust at himself and at the animal lust that had taken possession of him cooled his ardour swifter than any douche of cold water. He rolled away from Lucy and stood up.

'Get out!' he said.

She stared up at him, not comprehending.

'What?' she asked.

In her bewilderment, and with her chemise rucked up round her waist she looked grotesque.

'You heard!' he snapped. 'Get out! Now!'

'Why?' she demanded. 'What've I done?' Then, as she realized he meant what he said, her puzzled expression was replaced by anger. She pulled down her chemise and leaped off the bed.

''Ee can't do it, is that what's the matter?' she taunted, her face distorted with fury. ''Ee bain't man enough, eh? You work'ouse lot are all the same. 'Ee likes to think 'ee can play the stallion but when it comes to it you'm no use. No use at all. Don't think I'd ever come to 'ee again. I idn't that desperate. I prefers a proper man, not a load of rubbish like ee.

'Go away,' said Jed wearily.

'I'm going, don't 'ee worry,' Lucy paused long enough in the doorway to spit back. 'And don't think 'ee've got a 'ope of getting the *Our Violet*. 'Ee've spoiled your chances good and proper there, boy! Good and proper!'

After she had gone Jed sank on to his bed and buried his head in his hands. Out of the turmoil of his thoughts and emotions one thing was clear. He had no regrets that he had not lain with Lucy. Even to himself he chose the word 'lain' with care. 'Made love to' would have been too far from the truth. Carnal attraction had been the one thing which had drawn him to Lucy, and he knew now that it would never have been enough to endure a lifetime with her.

Against his will he thought of Amy. He did not want to. After what had nearly happened it seemed wrong to bring her into his thoughts; but she came just the same. She was back with the Newton fellow again. He had not seen them together, but he could tell by the joyous light in her face and the sheer happiness which shone from her eyes. Jed knew she would never look like that because of him. No one would. Emotions such as love and tenderness had no place in his life, they never had and they never would. At the thought the emptiness in him deepened and, though he fought hard to quell it, the nameless ache he so often experienced grew more intense. He did not recognize it as loneliness.

–

In the summer Brixham shed some of the workaday atmosphere which shrouded it during the other seasons, and took on a more lively, light-hearted air. Each year the railway brought more and more visitors who flocked to the growing number of guest-houses that were opening. A smattering of artists and photographers made for the picturesque harbour', setting up their paraphernalia, and attracting crowds of small boys. More interesting to Jed were the sleek yachts which appeared with the summer swallows. They made Torbay or Dartmouth their home ports from which they could sail the Western Channel, drawn by the string of regattas which took place along the south coast.

One such yacht was entering the harbour as Jed was walking along the New Pier. It was brand new, judging by the gleaming paintwork and the pristine sails. He stopped to watch. The wind was difficult that day, with long spells of dead calm interspersed with sudden gusts which seemed to come from nowhere. When it came the breeze was freakish and sharp. The helmsman was caught unawares. The yacht was carrying too much canvas, and there was no time to rectify matters.

People began to gather with interest, for the course the yacht was taking was sending her into the stem of one of the fishing smacks moored at the pier.

'Cor, 'tis a darned shame! Lovely boat like that!' declared someone.

As the helmsman struggled to avoid disaster, Jed saw a cart nearby piled high with supplies to provision one of the schooners. Those provisions included a couple of sacks of oatmeal. Without thinking he seized one, and with it on his shoulder he leapt down on to the fishing boat. He just had time to get the improvised fender over the side before the two vessels collided. Much to the delight of the crowd the impact caused the sack to disintegrate violently. Oatmeal went shooting everywhere, particularly over Jed. But it had done the trick. By the time he had brushed oats out of his hair, eyes and mouth, the yacht was under control, edging towards its moorings. He could see anxious figures leaning over the side, although he could not see how much damage had been done. Nor did he have time to find out. An irate figure, the owner of the sack of oats, was rushing along the pier.

'Yer!' he exclaimed breathlessly when he reached Jed. 'I saw that! What do you think you'm up to? Who said you could sling my property into the water like that?'

'I'm sorry,' said Jed. 'I just grabbed the first thing I saw.'

'First thing you saw? Couldn't you have found something else? Why did it have to be good food, and my good food into the bargain?'

'I didn't have time,' Jed exclaimed. 'I had to act fast.'

'And are you going to pay fast, that's what I want to know?'

'That's not fair,' Jed protested, his heart sinking. 'Anyway, I haven't any money.'

'Should have thought of that afore you made free with other people's property. I want's paying, that's what I want—'

Jed was about to explain that he really did not have the money when a well-bred voice cut into the altercation.

'Don't worry, my man, you'll get paid!'

The crowd, who had been watching the drama with great interest, fell back to let the man through. He was tall and fair-haired, and he wore the well-cut flannels and brass-buttoned blazer that were the uniform of wealthy yachtsmen.

He dropped some coins into the grocer's outstretched palm.

'Here, take your money and be off with you,' he said brusquely. Then he turned to Jed and his expression changed to a smile. 'I don't have any difficulty identifying you, young man,' he said.

Jed was very conscious that he was still covered in oatmeal.

'Is your yacht all right, sir?' he asked.

'Thanks to you she is. Some superficial damage, a bit of paintwork gone, nothing major. But for your quick action it might have been a very different story. What's your name, my friend?'

'Jediah Greenway, sir.'

'Well, Jediah Greenway, that was quite a feat you achieved a few minutes ago. It can have been no easy task, leaping about like that with a sack of oats on your shoulder. How on earth did you do it?'

'I don't know, sir, it just sort of happened.' Now he looked back on the incident Jed was quite amazed himself.

'Thank goodness it did happen, say I. I've had to wait long enough for the *Silhouette* to be completed, I don't want great holes smashed in her during her first season. You work at the fishing?'

'Yes, sir.'

'Then how would you like a change of occupation for the summer? I'm a crewman short, and you're just the sort of fellow I need for racing – strong, agile and, above all, quick thinking.'

Jed drew in his breath. A number of Brixham fishermen did serve as crews on yachts during the summer, but somehow he had never considered such a course for himself. Perhaps his thoughts had been too set upon fishing as a way of life. Crewing a yacht was not a permanent job, except for a small minority, but as a diversion for the summer...

'I'd like to accept, sir, but I can't,' he said with regret. 'I'm still apprenticed, you see.'

'Now that is a pity. How much longer of your time must you serve?'

'One more year, sir.'

'Then you would be free next summer? If you are, then get in touch with either my skipper or with me. I'm planning to winter the *Silhouette* in the Dart, you'll find her easily enough. Here's my card.' He handed Jed a slip of pasteboard on which was engraved, 'J.H. Hudson', and an address in Berkeley Square. 'And since you can't crew for me just yet here's something for your trouble.'

Five golden sovereigns dropped into Jed's hand. He looked at them in stupefaction.

'I can't take these, sir,' he said, trying to give them back. 'I did nothing and, besides, you had the oatmeal to pay for.'

'Your quick action saved me from having to pay out a deal more than a paltry sack of oatmeal,' said the yachtsman, pushing away the proffered coins. 'But more important than the money, you saved me time. I've had little enough opportunity to try out the *Silhouette's* paces as it is. Any more time spent on major repairs and I could say goodbye to the entire racing season. No, Jediah Greenway, you keep your sovereigns. You've earned them.'

Before Jed could argue further or utter his thanks, Mr Hudson had shaken him by the hand and departed. After he had gone, Jed continued to gaze down at the sovereigns.

'Now you'm into money, how about lending us a quid, eh, boy?' demanded one of the bystanders.

'You'll have to stand in line, Stan,' Jed replied to the fisherman. 'I'll let you know when it's your turn.'

'What'm you going to spend it on?' asked Stan.

'High living and low women,' Jed answered.

Already he was striding along the pier. He knew exactly what he was going to do with his unexpected windfall. Purposefully he hurried along Fore Street, his hands covering Mr. Hudson's visiting card in one pocket and the sovereigns in the other. Into the post office he went. There, still spattered with oatmeal, he deposited his five pounds. On his way back to the Burton house he marvelled at the fact that he, Jediah Greenway, late of Lambeth Union, now had a savings account. He had no need to rely on Lucy. He had begun his own boat fund.

News had a way of travelling fast in Brixham. He had no sooner sat down to dinner than Matthew Burton fixed him with a stem eye and said, 'Jediah, you'm come into money, so I hears. I hopes you don't intend to be profligate with it. The possession of gold is a great responsibility and has led many from the path of righteousness. I suggest you give me your money for safekeeping.'

'There's no need, thanks, Skipper,' said Jed, jabbing his fork into a portion of fried whiting. 'I've put it in the post office.'

'The post office, you say?' Matthew Burton's eyebrows rose approvingly. 'Where it can be earning interest. A very wise move, my boy. You'm a sensible lad.'

'Too mean to spend it,' snapped Lucy spitefully. ''Ee wouldn't know 'ow.'

Her parents looked puzzled. They had not yet got to grips with her changed attitude towards Jed. He felt sure they soon would.

Lucy sniffed hard and wrinkled her face in disgust. 'There's an awful smell in yer,' she complained. 'Just like the work'ouse. Fair turns me up, it does.'

And she looked pointedly at Jed.

Her father followed her gaze and his eyebrows, ever the barometer of his temper, registered suspicion and doubt. Jed's face remained impassive, but he steeled himself for what was to come. Lucy was going to make trouble for him. He might have known he would have to pay for spurning her. His days as Skipper Burton's favoured apprentice were numbered.

Chapter Eight

The laden basket seemed to grow heavier as Amy plodded up the hill. When its weight was suddenly relieved from her grasp she spun round in startled surprise. She found herself staring into Seth's beaming face.

'Carry your shopping for you, miss? Very reasonable terms, only a florin,' he whined, touching his forelock with great frequency.

'Two shillings for that short distance? It's a bit steep isn't it?' she said with a grin.

'So's this 'ill, miss, and don't forget I'll have to come down again. That's wear and tear on good boot-leather, not to mention me legs, and—'

'Would you settle for a cup of tea and a bit of lardy cake instead?'

Seth pretended to give the matter grave consideration.

'You drive an 'ard bargain, miss, but you've a kind face, and this wind's decidedly parky… Right-oh, I agree.'

Laughing, they struck hands to seal the agreement. In fact, while they had been arguing they had already reached the Prouts' house.

'What are you doing in town at this time of day?' asked Amy as she opened the bottom door. 'You are on the *Our Violet* these days, aren't you? I could have sworn I saw her go out first thing this morning.'

'You did, and if you'd been watching you'd 'ave seen 'er come back in again just before noon. 'It something under the water as we were outward bound. A whale, we reckoned. Coulda' done for us if we 'adn't managed to free ourselves quick.' Seth settled himself in a chair by the range.

'Did this collision do any damage?' asked Amy, mentally substituting a submerged log for Seth's imaginary whale.

'It caught the rdder an 'efty whack. That's why we came back into port. It should be fixed by tomorrow.'

'Then, you're a free man for an hour or two.'

'That's right. A gentleman of leisure, that's me!' Seth stretched himself nonchalantly, his hands behind his head and his feet on the fender.

There was something over-bright in his manner that caused Amy to regard him uneasily.

'I'm surprised Mr. Burton didn't find you something to do,' she said. 'It's unusual for him to give you time off.'

'We can't do much until the tide drops a bit more and John Prout's men can get at the rudder. Besides, Jed's got all the 'ard work to do. Skipper decided 'e could clean the bottom while the *Our Violet* is out of the water.'

'Not a pleasant job on a chilly day like this.' Amy wondered at the change in situation. Usually it was Seth who was given the unpleasant tasks.

He must have read her thoughts, for he grinned. 'Bit of a change round, ain't it, me being the favourite and Jed doing the dirty jobs? Used to be the golden boy, did old Jed. Now 'e can't do a thing right.'

'That's not like Jed. He's usually so conscientious.'

'I don't reckon 'e's changed, it's the Burtons. They've gone off him.'

'But why? He must have done something…'

'If 'e did then I don't know what. You know Jed, 'e never lets things slip. My guess is that it's something to do with Lucy. At one time she was all over 'im. Not one to be backward in coming forward, is our Lucy, and she made no bones about the fact she meant to 'ave 'im. Can you imagine it? Staid old Jed, who likes to keep 'imself to 'imself, and Lucy… Well, you know Lucy Burton, don't you?'

'Yes, I know her,' said Amy. She had to admit they were an unlikely couple.

'Whoever marries Lucy'll be very comfortable, in more ways than one.' Seth accepted the tea offered to him. 'But give Jed 'is due, I never saw 'im make up to Lucy. She did all the running, and even 'er ma and pa joined in. Cor, talk about your slippers warming by the fire!

The skipper did everything bar call Jed "Son". Not any more, though. Now all 'e does is bawl at 'im and quote long streams of scripture at 'im – the bits about folks who came to a bad end. If there's a dirty job or a nasty watch then Jed gets it these days. Whatever 'e's done, 'e's blotted 'is copybook and no mistake.'

Amy was puzzled. Jed being Jed, he had given no hint of it whenever she had met him recently. She guessed Seth was right when he laid the blame at Lucy's door. What little she knew of Miss Burton spelled trouble. It was a shame that such a baggage should be making Jed's life miserable. She feared he must be having a difficult time with the Burtons ashore and afloat.

'That leaves the way clear for you with Lucy, since you're so impressed,' she said.

'What, me and Lucy? No, I'm not up to Lucy's weight, nowhere near. She'd make an old man of me long before my time – and don't ask 'ow, because I won't tell you!'

'In that case I'll save my breath,' Amy smiled.

'Besides, I can't see the skipper liking the idea of me as a son-in-law. This spell of being the favourite is only because 'e's already used up all of 'is bits of 'ell-fire scripture on me. It won't last.' He took a bite of lardy cake, coating his mouth with sugar in the process. 'Don't you usually 'ave to tell Ma Prout when you've got gentlemen callers? This lardy's good and I don't want to be turned out before I've finished it.'

'I haven't got any gentlemen callers – only you,' Amy grinned. 'Even if I had there'd be no need to worry because Mrs Prout's not in. She's gone out to tea and won't be back for a couple of hours.'

'I'll ignore your rude remark, my girl, because I'm nice and comfy.' He paused. 'I'm glad I don't 'ave to rush off.'

The tone of his voice changed so abruptly that Amy looked at him with concern. He sounded depressed, almost anxious. Something was definitely troubling him. She was tempted to ask questions, to find out what it was, but she thought better of it. If he wanted to tell her he would do so when he was good and ready.

She said briskly, 'You can stay another quarter of an hour, no more. You may be the idle rich but I've got the ironing to do.'

'A quarter of an hour'll 'ave to do then. Would there be another cup of tea in the pot? By the way, did you 'ear 'ow the crew of the *Vigilant* caught a mermaid?'

'No,' said Amy, pouring the tea.

'You don't believe me, do you? I'm surprised Todd didn't tell you. Someone – and I'd bet it was Todd 'imself – found the top part of an old doll and decided to put a fishtail on it. There it was, dolly at the top, cod at the bottom, with a bit of seaweed decoration for decency's sake. It looked just the job. You'd be surprised 'ow many people were taken in by it. They rang the bell at the fish market for the auctioneer to come, just as if they'd brought a proper catch in. 'E was a real sport, started the sale all straight faced like, and some folks were daft enough to make a bid. The *Vigilant*'s lot couldn't stand up for laughing.'

'It does sound like something Todd would think up,' chuckled Amy. 'No doubt he'll tell me about it first chance he gets.'

'And some of the lads played a grand joke on old Luke. They'd 'ad a few, mind. You know old Luke, who lives in that wooden shack at Shoalstone? Well...'

Seth could tell a good story. Often his tales were embroidered by his rich imagination, but Amy did not mind, she was used to him. She enjoyed his yarns, which became more ridiculous as he went on. He was on form that afternoon, making her laugh until her ribs ached. Yet, while she was helpless with mirth, she could still sense that something was bothering him. She had felt it throughout the afternoon. He was talking more than usual, and at great speed, like someone trying to blot out an unpleasant truth. His smile was too wide, his laughter too frequent, yet the humour never reached his eyes. They remained bleak and troubled. Something was definitely wrong.

The teapot was empty and not one crumb or grain of sugar was left on the plate. Seth heaved a great sigh and said, 'It's ever so nice 'ere. I wish I could stay.' His voice held all the pleading of a desperately unhappy small boy.

'You can call again soon, you know that,' said Amy. 'Mrs Prout isn't too keen on more than once a week, but you know I'm always glad to see you.'

'I wish I could come again next week,' he cried.

Amy was quite startled by his sudden vehemence. Then she remembered.

'You're off round land, aren't you?' she said.

'Yes,' was the stark reply. 'This time next week we'll be in the Bristol Channel.'

She did not blame him for being unhappy about having to face the autumn winds as they navigated Land's End. Summer was the usual 'round land' season, but a long spell of poor catches was forcing some boats to risk the treacherous journey late in the year.

'Todd's going too, on the *Vigilant*,' Amy said. She did not add that even he, who was seldom bothered by anything, had admitted he was not looking forward to the next few weeks. She went on, 'He says that if the fish had any consideration they'd winter somewhere a bit more pleasant. Though I suppose it's too much to expect consideration from a fish.'

She paused, hoping for a joking reply, but her attempt at light-hearted chatter did not succeed. Seth continued to stare into the fire, his face grim. She tried again. 'I hear Bristol's a fine place. Lucky you, to get to a grand city like that. I wonder if the Bristol girls know that you lot are coming. Poor souls, someone should warn them.' Still there was no response. She said reassuringly, 'The time'll go quickly. You'll be back for Christmas before you know it.'

Seth turned to her. Suddenly his face had gone white, and his eyes seemed over-large, their expression fearful.

'Ame,' he said in a quiet voice. 'Ame, I'm scared.'

'Scared?' she replied in surprise. 'What of?'

'Of 'aving to sail that long way. Of being out there so far from land. Of the sea. Oh Amy... I'm terrible afraid of the sea!'

'How can you be?' She could not comprehend. 'You go out on the sea every day. You earn your living there.'

'And I'm afraid! Don't you understand?' His cry was one of desperation. 'Every time I goes out I'm scared. I always 'ave been, from the very first trip. I thought I'd get over it, but I 'aven't. It's just got worse. I dread it. Being on the water, with it all round me, deep and— and dead... It's an awful cold dead thing, is the sea, and it frightens me...'

Amy listened with mounting distress. Never for one moment had she suspected what torment poor Seth had been suffering. Her respect for him grew. How had he stood it for four long years? Going out day after day, living with fear all the time. A fear that was continually growing. It was horrifying.

'What am I going to do? I can't go on like this no more. I can't, but I don't know what to do.' His eyes were pleading, begging her to give comfort, to find a solution.

To Amy this was Daisy all over again, and the realization struck fear in her heart. With the fear came a grim determination. Seth needed help and she would not fail him as she had failed Daisy. Never again would she hate herself for not having done enough for a friend. She put her arms about him.

'You aren't alone,' she said. 'You have Jed with you. He'll always help, you know that.'

'Jed's not afraid of nothing. 'E'd not know what I was on about.'

'You'd be surprised. Jed understands a great deal. You could go to him. He'd never let you down.'

''E can't take the sea away, can 'e? The emptiness! Jed can't do nothing about that! The thought of going down in all that water – not being able to breathe – that's what scares me...'

Seth pressed his face against her in panic. As she held him she could feel his body shivering with terror. Desperately she searched her mind for anything which might give him confidence.

'It'll be the last time you'll have to go round land,' she pointed out. 'You haven't much longer until the end of your apprenticeship. Not even a whole year, only a few more months. After that you need never go to sea again. Isn't that a grand thought? You could find yourself work on land. Do you know what I reckon would suit you? A job at the railway station. Have you ever thought of that?'

She had his attention now. Her gentle words were cutting through his terror, his trembling was lessening.

'D—do you think I could?' he asked uncertainly.

'Of course I do! I can just see you in that smart brown uniform, wheeling barrows and carrying suitcases for folks on holiday – I hear you can get good tips doing that. You'd have money to burn.'

'It— it sounds grand.' His interest had been caught – but only briefly. 'What's the good of dreaming about a job on the railway when I go off round land tomorrow?' he demanded. 'It's tomorrow I've got to face the sea, and the day after, and the day after. Another whole year of being scared. Another year of dreading waking up each morning. I can't take no more, I tell you. I just can't take no more.'

To her distress Amy could not think of anything else to take away his fears. The only way she could give him comfort was to hold him closer, and hope that her encircling arms would give him the solace he so desperately needed.

At what point the mood changed she did not know. Perhaps it was a combination of their close contact, Seth's craving for reassurance and her own longing to give consolation. Whatever the reason she became aware of a change in Seth's breathing, then his fingers began to caress her breasts.

She tried to ease away from him, but he whispered, 'Please, Amy, please. We're sailing tomorrow. I may never see you again. Please let me.'

A few caresses! It seemed such a little sacrifice to make, especially when it could drive away his nightmarish fears. She did not mean it to go further, but Seth's demands grew more urgent.

'No,' she protested, pushing away his importunate hand.

Seth's response was to cry, 'Let me love you, Amy. I've only got you. There's no one else who cares. Love me just this once.'

She could have resisted anything but an appeal for love. And she did love Seth. It was a very different emotion from the one Daniel engendered in her. It was more a response to Seth's terrible hunger for affection. She had a longing to give, and he had no one else, only her. She felt the ghost of Daisy was haunting her, reminding her how she had once been found wanting. Knowing that it was within her power to help Seth what else could she do? She let him love her in the way he needed. All the time she knew it should have been Daniel's body crushing down on her's, not Seth's. It should have been Daniel to whom she was giving herself, not this frightened boy. Minute-by-minute she felt regret creeping up on her, a regret she knew would be with her for the rest of her fife, yet she could not send Seth away uncomforted. She would have regretted that just as much. It was a cruel dilemma, and tears ran down her face at the unfairness of it; but it was too late for tears now. She had made her decision.

His passion spent, Seth rolled away from her.

'I didn't hurt you, did I?' he asked awkwardly.

'No,' she replied, not entirely truthfully.

'You— you ain't angry with me?'

'No.' This time she could answer honestly. He had come to her in desperate need. How could she be angry with him for that?

'Amy, I'll always remember this, truly I will. You're a grand girl. The grandest in the whole country.' He leaned across and kissed her, not with ardour but with gratitude.

After he had left the house her tears returned in earnest. She wept because she had betrayed Daniel. How could she tell him? He would not forgive her, she knew, because he would not understand. Of course there was no need for him to find out what had happened – but this was a thought which stayed with her for barely a moment. She was too honest and too deeply in love to deceive him as well as betray him. Her honesty was likely to drive him away for ever, yet she did not know what else to do. But strangely enough, even as bitter sobs born of misery racked her body, the sense of guilt which had burdened her since Daisy's death seemed to fall away.

–

The late autumn and early winter that year was a time marked by the absence of men. Daniel was crossing the Atlantic to Florida, while Seth and Jed were away in the Bristol Channel with the fishing fleet. Todd Prout was with the fleet, too, on the *Vigilant*. It was surprising how quiet the household was without him. Even Jessie remarked upon it.

One minute she would exclaim, 'It's astonishing how easy it is to keep this place tidy without that great lump cluttering it up.' Then the next she would sigh, 'How I hate these long dark evenings, with nothing to cheer us up.' Once or twice she went as far as saying, 'I'll be glad when the boats get back. It'll give this place a bit of life.'

Amy, too, was anticipating the return of the fishing boats with greater and greater urgency. For her the weeks before Christmas were grey and unbearably prolonged. A growing dread was making her desperate for the *Our Violet* to come back. If it had been possible she would have joined the women who trudged to the best vantage points at the breakwater or Berry Head to catch the first glimpse of red sails on the horizon. Not that such efforts were necessary. The news that the fleet was at last in sight spread about town with the rapidity of a forest fire.

Sick with relief, Amy tried to watch the boats sailing into the harbour, but Jessie had other ideas.

'Get the copper lit and put the tin bath out,' she instructed. 'When you've done that be sure Mr Todd's clean clothes are set to air in front of the range, with a couple of towels. Not my good ones, mind! There's a fresh bar of soap in the cupboard. He'll be in an awful state after these many weeks away, and I'm not having him set one foot up those stairs until he's properly clean.'

If Jessie had wanted the place enlivened then she certainly got it with the arrival of Todd. Amy wondered if any of the other households in town were made as chaotic by the return of the menfolk. They probably were. There was cheerful shouting through the scullery door as Todd divested himself of his filthy clothes. Then there was much carrying of hot water to fill the hip-bath, followed by a discreet withdrawal to allow him to soak away the grime of weeks without washing in the warm privacy of the kitchen.

At last Todd called out in a coy falsetto, 'You can come in now. I be all decent and proper.'

Amy went into a kitchen filled with steam and the smell of carbolic. Todd was pulling a comb through his tangle of wet hair.

'There, that's better,' he said appreciatively. 'I reckon I'm a good stone lighter after that scrub.'

'Did you have a good trip?' she asked, then followed it with the question that had been scorching her tongue ever since he arrived.

'And is the *Our Violet* back safely?'

'Yes, to your first question, and yes and no to the second. Don't worry, the *Our Violet's* fine, she's just a day or so behind us.'

'Behind you?' Amy looked at him in surprise. 'But Mr. Burton's always one of the first back. He prides himself on it.'

'Well, his pride came before a fall this time. He had to wait because he was a crewman short. That young fool Seth ran off.'

Amy, who had been about to drag the bath out to empty it, let go her grasp of the handle so suddenly that water slopped over the kitchen floor.

'He did what?' she gasped.

'Ran off. Went ashore and never came back... Yer, maid, be you all right? You'm proper pale.' Swiftly Todd caught her and sat her in a chair. 'There, I'm sorry,' he said contritely. 'I should have remembered he were a special friend of youm and not spoken out so blunt. I'll call Jessie, eh?'

'No!' said Amy hurriedly. 'No, thank you. I'm fine, really. It was just such a shock.'

'Not half as big a shock as that Seth'll get if Matthew Burton ever catches up with him.' Todd chuckled, then he continued more seriously. 'That was a downright dangerous thing to do. A couple of years back he could've been sent to prison for running away, him not being out of his apprenticeship. And I reckon he'd deserve it, leaving his boat to come home short-handed at this time of year.'

'Does— does anyone know why he did it?' Amy asked.

Todd shook his head. 'He wouldn't be the first as didn't fancy sailing back round the Lizard in December, and that's a fact.'

'Y—you're sure he's gone for good?' she asked hesitantly.

'Sure as I can be 'bout anything. Us had a good search round for him, in case of an accident or summat like that. An old woman selling hot pies on the quayside was the last to see him. He bought four off her, seemingly, and when she remarked on what a good customer he was he said not to get her hopes up 'cos he was leaving and wadn't likely to be that way ever again, not if he had any say in the matter.'

Not likely ever to be that way again. It sounded terribly final. Cold panic gripped Amy.

'Perhaps the old woman was mistaken, and it was someone else...' she said desperately. Her voice trailed away at this unlikely event. Old women noticed Seth and, besides, the reply was typical of him, she could almost hear him saying it. 'He may come back eventually,' she said, anxiously grasping at straws.

'Would you come back to face Matthew Burton after you'd left him in the lurch? No? Nor would I, maid.'

At this point Jessie came in, bustling as ever.

'What on earth are you thinking about, girl, keeping Mr Todd talking when he must be desperate for something to eat?' she demanded.

Guiltily Amy leapt to her feet. 'Sorry, missus,' she said.

'So I should think! And I don't suppose you've set his clothes to soak yet, either, have you? You'd best get started straight away. She turned to her brother-in-law. 'As for you, go on upstairs. There's some stew keeping hot in the oven. I'll bring it up to you – if this idiot girl hasn't let it dry up to nothing!'

Amy was already on her way to the scullery. Todd's dirty clothes were piled up on the floor, and as she bent to collect them up the rank smell of fish and sweat that impregnated them caught in her throat, making her retch. Afraid she was going to be sick she clapped a hand across her mouth until the feeling died down. Clenching her teeth, she was about to tackle the clothes again when she became aware of Todd standing in the doorway. He was watching her with concern.

'I left my baccy pouch in among that lot somewhere,' he said. 'Let me get un out afore it's spoiled by soap-suds. I'll give 'ee a hand shifting this lot while I'm at it, eh?'

'No you won't!' said Amy, gritting her teeth firmly. She handed him his tobacco pouch and gently began pushing him out of the scullery. 'Here you are, smelling like a May morning after your bath, and you want to rummage about in that fishy lot again. Off you go to your dinner and let me get on with my work.'

'Gawd, what it is to be bossed by women.' Although Todd joked as he retreated he was looking at her gravely.

Conquering her nausea, Amy got on with the task of sorting and soaking – the real washing would begin next day when the copper had had a chance to heat up again. She worked automatically, barely conscious of the grimy state of the clothes, nor the thick coating of fish and scales which still clung to them. She had far more serious things on her mind. For the last few weeks she had suspected the awful truth. She had hoped and prayed that her monthly courses would start again. Nothing had happened. She had to face reality: Seth was not coming back – and she was pregnant!

Her life lay in ruins. The dream of a golden future with Daniel had crumbled into dust. She had something more than mere betrayal to confess to him now. The prospect of his eyes looking at her with disgust and pain filled her with dread. For once she was thankful that he was at the other side of the world, and would not be home for weeks.

More immediate problems occupied her. How was she going to manage? She was alone in the world and pregnant. Where was she going to go? Memories of Lambeth Union shot through her like shards of glass. The horrifying vision of having to return to a workhouse made her tremble. She had no illusions of how unmarried girls who got pregnant were treated there. And Jessie Prout would dismiss her instantly, of that there was no doubt. Then what would happen to her?

In truth, even if Seth had returned, she was not sure how much difference he would have made. He would probably have married her, of course, and given respectability to her and to the unborn child. What else he could have done she did not know. He was certainly not ready for the responsibilities of either marriage or fatherhood. She could not imagine any sort of a stable future with him. But she would have had someone to whom she could have unburdened herself. Being forced to keep her secret alone compounded the pain.

Jed was her only friend now. He had always said she could go to him in trouble. The realization that he was the only one left in whom she could confide made her look with renewed eagerness for the return of the *Our Violet*. Again her hopes were dashed. A few days later the gossip along the harbour-side was that the *Our Violet* was not expected home until well into the New Year. Gale-force winds had blown her against the stone quay at Newlyn, where she had been sheltering, causing extensive damage. Skipper Burton had written to his wife saying that, since he could not now get home for Christmas, once his boat was repaired and seaworthy again he would stay at Newlyn for a while longer and fish from there.

If only it had been Daniel's baby! Amy felt she could have withstood anything in those circumstances; out of the ruins of her love and hopes, she would have had something left. Instead she was to bear a child conceived out of pity and consolation, and a very different sort of love. Despite the mess she was in, Amy still did not entirely regret that one act of compassion. What was the point? What was done could not be undone. And although the baby was not Daniel's it was hers! Hers alone! And already she was beginning to feel a fierce protectiveness towards the child growing inside her. It had no one else to love and care for it, only her. She owed it to the poor blameless little creature to do her best for it, and she would! She was absolutely determined about that... But how?

'You look as though you'm carrying the troubles of the world on they shoulders of youm.'

Todd's voice made her jump. She had not heard him come into the kitchen.

'I'm just a bit tired,' she said, getting to her feet. 'Can I get you something? A cup of tea? Cocoa?'

'I can tell you what you can do, maid. You can sit back down again and tell me what's the matter. 'Cos something is!'

'No, there isn't—' Amy tried to protest but Todd caught her by the wrist and pulled her gently into the chair again.

'You'm in trouble.' It was a statement, not a question. 'You'm in trouble. You might as well tell me, afore it becomes so obvious that Jessie notices.'

'How – how did you know?' She stared at him in astonishment.

'Amy, chile, I may be a fool but I bain't stupid! I can put two and two together and make four. Or should it be one and one and make three?' There was no reproof in his voice, simply such a great kindness and concern that Amy burst into tears. The whole sad story came tumbling out.

'What else could I do?' she finished, sobbing. 'He was very frightened and desperate, just like poor Daisy... Only I didn't do anything to help her...'

'Maidie, maidie!' Todd shook his head regretfully. 'You can't cure everyone's woes, you know. Not by yourself.'

'I know,' wept Amy. 'But I had to do something.'

'That you did. And young Seth's solved his own woes and left you in a pretty pickle.'

'He didn't know. I'm sure he never thought... I didn't think you could get caught first time.'

'You knows better on that score now, don't you?' Todd said dryly. 'I suppose you haven't some fond sweetheart as'd take care of you?'

'No!' replied Amy, a shade too quickly. 'Are— are you going to tell Mrs Prout?'

'What do you think I am?' He sounded indignant. 'More to the point, what do you propose doing?'

'I don't know.'

Amy wiped her eyes on her apron. Having someone to share her worries with had helped. She tried to think positively. 'Mrs Prout won't keep me on, I know that. I'll just have to find somewhere to five, and get some work until the baby's born—'

'And pigs might fly!' Todd was disparaging. 'What do you think you'd find round here with no character and your condition beginning to show more and more? A bit of fish curing or packing while you were still up to it, which wouldn't be long. 'Tis heavy work. And then where would you be? Up to the workhouse on Baker's Hill.'

'No! Never there!' Her reply was emphatic.

'What, then?'

'I don't know! I don't know...'

'In that case, how about if you was to wed me?'

Amy stared at him, speechless, not believing her ears. 'Wed you?' she uttered at last. 'You don't mean it!'

'Ah, but I do! Us could have the banns read for the first time this Sunday, and be married in the New Year. What do you say?'

'I couldn't marry you!' cried Amy, appalled.

'Don't be so hasty. You think on un,' Todd insisted. 'I know I idn't much of a catch – I wouldn't even make stocker-bait on the marriage market by most women's reckoning – but there idn't naught wrong with the name Prout. And it'd stop the babe getting called things a darned sight worse.'

'I didn't mean it that way.' Amy was full of remorse that he should have misinterpreted her objection. 'It's not you who isn't good enough to marry – it's me. I couldn't saddle you with someone else's child to bring up. I couldn't make you a laughing-stock like that, you're far too good and kind.'

'I've bin a laughing-stock all my life. It wouldn't be no great novelty. But who's to know I idn't the father, if us don't tell no one... ? To be honest, I be powerful fond of little uns. Jessie says I've never grown up, maybe that accounts for it. Anyway, I've always wanted childer, but no woman's ever been daft enough or desperate enough to wed me.' He looked suddenly shamefaced. 'I've got to confess I've sowed a few wild oats in my time, but no one's ever placed no crying bundle on my doorstep afterwards, so it don't seem likely I'm ever going to have no family tree of my own following after. Here's me wanting a youngster, and there's your babe needing a pa. It seems daft us not getting together.' Tears were streaming down Amy's cheeks, but this time there was no sorrow in them.

'Oh, Todd,' she said. 'You're one in a thousand, you really are.'

'My old dad used to say that.' Todd gave a self-conscious grin. 'He always finished with "Thank goodness!".'

'Don't be forever putting yourself down.' retorted Amy indignantly. 'By one in a thousand I meant that there can't be many men as kind and generous as you. I appreciate your offer, you've no idea how much. But I can't let you make such a sacrifice just to help me. It wouldn't be fair.'

'Why wouldn't it be fair? And what sacrifice?' he demanded. 'I'd be getting to be master of my own fireside, though it wouldn't be as grand as this. I know John makes a big thing of this being my home, but it idn't always easy. Jessie's good enough to me in her way but her don't approve of me and never has. Her'd as soon have my room as my company. Well, you knows my daft antics by now. Sometimes I takes a drop too much, and money seems to go through my fingers like water in a leaky bucket. You'd have your work cut out nagging me to change my ways. Somehow, though, I don't think your tongue'd ever be as sharp as Jessie's. I'd treat you right, I promise you that. And I'd be real proud to call your babe my own... What do you say?'

But Amy was too choked with sobs to reply.

'Mercy, girl, I idn't that bad a prospect!' he said with a quick smile. He covered her hand with his. 'I've took you by surprise, I can see that. You'll want a bit of time to think about it, I dare say.'

Still unable to speak, Amy nodded.

'Right, then, you consider the pros and cons—' Todd gave an unexpected grin. 'I were going to say take your time, but upon consideration that wouldn't be sensible... You think about it, all the same, and give me your answer when you'm ready.'

After he had left the kitchen, Amy sat there in stunned disbelief.

Marriage to Todd. Such a way out of her predicament had not occurred to her. It was a tempting prospect: marriage, security, a name for the baby...

I can't do it, she decided after long and careful thought. It would be unfair to Todd. Doubtless he had offered on the spur of the moment. He was probably having regrets already.

In the days which followed, Todd did not look as though he were regretting anything. He did not pester her by repeating his offer, but his eyes held an expression of unmistakable hope whenever they lit upon her. Amy knew it would be up to her to mention the subject again.

'Todd,' she said, 'a few days ago you did me the honour of asking me to be your wife. I have given the matter careful consideration and, while I am most deeply grateful to you, I must decline. Under the circumstances I am convinced that such a marriage wouldn't benefit either of us, particularly you.'

Todd regarded her steadily for a moment.

'I haven't heard such a fancy speech since the parish supper,' he said. 'How long did it take you to make it up?'

'I didn't – I mean, naturally, I've thought about it carefully,' she stammered.

'Are you sure? That bit about the marriage not being a benefit to either of us – now that don't sound right. What are you going to do if you don't wed me?'

'I've got my plans,' Amy said airily. 'I'll manage.'

'And what plans be they? Go on, you can tell me.'

'They're just – just plans.'

'Have you somewhere else to go? Another job? Anyone who'll look after you when the babe comes?' he persisted gently.

Amy tried to say yes, but the lie stuck in her throat.

Todd continued to regard her kindly. 'You idn't no good at untruths, maid, that's your trouble. Seems to me you've got a choice between me and the workhouse... Dang me! I've got to be a better option than that...!'

She felt the tears begin to trickle down her cheeks. 'You don't think I'd keep you to that offer, do you?' she cried. 'You were being kind. You spoke without thinking. Now you've had more time I'm sure you wished you'd kept silent.'

'No, I don't,' said Todd unrepentantly. 'The more I think on it the more I like the idea. I'm going to be some disappointed if you turn me down now. I were just getting nicely used to the idea of being a pa.'

'Oh, Todd...' said Amy tearfully. Then because she could not think of the right words to say she repeated, 'Oh, Todd!'

'Does that mean yes?' he asked hopefully.

'Yes,' she whispered. 'Yes – and thank you.'

'That's proper grand, it really is. And you don't need to thank me. You idn't never going to regret accepting me.' He took her hand, his face beaming. 'Now us had better sort out our first real problem. Which of us be going to tell Jessie? You or me?'

'We'll go together.' Amy managed a smile, while wiping away her tears yet again.

'Together! I like that! We'm a partnership, eh?' Todd rose and offered her his arm with a courtly bow.

Amy made to take it, then paused.

'Todd,' she said. 'I told you a lie a while ago. I shouldn't have done it. There is someone I was – still am – fond of.'

Such an understatement! To dismiss Daniel and all he meant to her in so few words! But she had to be practical – and honest.

'I thought there might be. Jed Greenway, I suppose.'

'Jed...? No.' Amy was surprised at the suggestion. 'Why did you think of him?'

'I dunno, just an idea. Not that it matters. It idn't none of my business.'

'Yes, it is, if we are to marry. You've promised you'll treat me well. In turn I'll never deceive you or play you false, I swear it.'

She could make promises for her mind and her body, she was less confident about her heart.

'That'll do me fine.' He smiled down at her. 'Now, if I idn't being too bold, I suggests as maybe you should wash your face afore us tackles them upstairs. John idn't no problem, but Jessie won't be pleased, having a future sister-in-law with a red nose and weepy eyes.'

It was a good suggestion. Amy felt she needed something to restore her. Cold water and a quick use of the hairbrush did at least make her feel better. She did contemplate putting on a clean apron, but upon consideration she took her apron off altogether. She was going to confront Jessie Prout as a member of the family, not as a maidservant. She did not relish the prospect.

If Amy and Todd had anticipated a dramatic reaction to their news they were not disappointed. John Prout listened to what they had to say calmly, without comment. Jessie more than made up for him. She listened at first in stunned silence, then let flow a stream of angry disapproval and reproach which reached flood proportions until it swept on into full-blown hysteria.

'Well,' said John Prout, when his wife had finally been put to bed, a cold flannel on her brow, the *sal volatile* within reach. 'This is a bit of a how–do–ye–do and no mistake. You'd best get yourselves off to see the vicar first thing in the morning, since the matter's urgent like.'

'Is that all you'm saying?' asked Todd.

'Nothing I say'd make no difference, would it? 'Cepting I wishes you both the best of luck.'

'Thank you, Mr Prout,' said Amy gratefully.

His composed acceptance of their marriage brought much relief to her. John Prout was an easy-going man, but she had feared hearing that Todd was going to marry a maidservant might have been too much even for his equanimity. To have been the cause of conflict between the brothers would have caused her great distress.

'You'm going to have to get used to calling me John,' he said with a smile.

Amy gave it a moment's thought. 'Not until after the wedding,' she said. 'It wouldn't be proper otherwise.'

'Whatever suits you.' His smile widened. 'Have you thought where you'm going to live, the pair of you? There's plenty of room yer, if you've a mind, and you'm welcome to it.'

Amy and Todd exchanged furtive glances. 'That's good of you, John,' Todd replied. 'But maybe us'd be better off on our own, like.' And he raised his eyes upwards to where Jessie lay prostrate with anger and mortification.

'Maybe you will at that,' John agreed. 'Well, there's one thing I've still to do and that's kiss the bride. I suppose that's all right, me being the prospective brother-in-law.'

He did not wait for an answer, but bent down and planted a smacking kiss on Amy's cheek. It occurred to her that Todd had not kissed her yet. In fact, he had barely touched her. For a couple about to be married they had had remarkably little physical contact. It was an aspect of wedded life they had still to work out. In the meantime, she was aware of an overwhelming sense of gratitude to Todd, and enormous relief that the future was assured for both her and the baby. She dared not think of Daniel and all that she had lost.

The next Sunday the banns were read out for the first time at All Saints'. A shocked silence greeted the announcement from the pulpit, followed by a suppressed excitement which hung over the congregation for the rest of the service. Amy feared Jessie might leap from her seat and cry out when the vicar declared: 'If any of you know cause, or just impediment, why these two persons should not be joined together in holy matrimony...' Fortunately Jessie Prout was a strong believer in family solidarity. She remained silent in the pew, staring rigidly ahead, a grim expression on her plump features.

Amy wished she could be as impassive. From all round the church she could feel eyes boring into her neck. Not used to being the centre of attention, hot colour flooded into her face. Then surreptitiously Todd took hold of her hand and gave it a squeeze. His grip was as rough and coarse as granite, and just as solid and dependable. Automatically her fingers curled round his, and remained there until the end of the service.

Amy and Todd were married in mid-January. It was a very quiet wedding. Jessie and John were the only guests. Amy had no one she wanted there except Jed, and he was still fishing off Cornwall. It was one of those bright, sunny winter days in Devon that give a happy foretaste of the spring to come. Amy hoped that it was a good omen. She had her misgivings about her marriage. Todd was a good man – but she did not love him. None the less she would try to be a good wife to him; she owed him that much.

After the wedding they returned to the house at Furzeham for refreshments. It was a difficult occasion. There was no disguising Jessie's disapproval of the whole affair. She maintained a stony silence throughout, which was far harder to bear than any outburst of recriminations. It was a relief to both Amy and Todd when they could decently say their farewells and leave.

They had managed to rent a small house in the centre of town, in the rabbit-warren of alleys, courts and buildings which huddled in the hollow between Middle Street and busy Fore Street. It was not much of a dwelling, but all they could find at short notice. The best thing about it was its address – Paradise Place. It was a two-up, two-down, damp from the Mill Tye at the back, and too close to both the gasworks and the brewery for comfort.

Todd put the key in the lock and turned it. As he pushed open the door a musty damp smell came to meet them, although he had already whitewashed the inside walls and Amy had scrubbed the place through thoroughly.

'It idn't much, but it'll do for a start. Yer, where do you think you'm going?' he demanded as Amy made to enter. 'Us be doing things proper in this household.'

To her intense embarrassment he swept her off her feet and carried her indoors.

'You fool! You're mazed!' she cried, uncertain whether to laugh or be angry.

'That's right,' he agreed, setting her on her feet again. 'If you didn't know that by now 'tis high time you did!'

Then unexpectedly he bent and kissed her. It was a swift gesture that took her unawares. She did not know how to respond. He, too, stood uncomfortably, as if uncertain what to do or say next.

'Us can be on the look-out for something better. Somewhere with a decent view for you and a bit of garden for the babe,' Todd said to hide his awkwardness. Suddenly he grinned mischievously. 'In the meantime this place has definite advantages. I'm within striking distance of the Globe, the London, the Manor, and the Buller's Arms, and if I fancy going all la-do-da, the Bolton's no long walk. Talk about being spoiled for choice!'

'Well, whichever one you choose, if you stay too long or drink too much I'll be waiting here at the ready.' Amy struck a stem attitude, her hands on her hips.

'Curse it, I forgot for a moment as I'm a married man!' Todd struck his brow melodramatically. 'I suppose such treats'll be things of the past now.'

'If you do as you're told I might let you off the leash once or twice a year, say at Christmas and on trawler-race day.'

'Lor! what've I let myself in for?'

'Are you regretting it already?' Amy meant to continue with the joking, but somehow the words escaped with an earnest sound.

'No, I idn't regretting it now, and I idn't going to, not ever.'

The humour had gone from Todd's expression, leaving him looking unusually serious and grave. Then, as so often happened when the situation between them threatened to get too personal, they were both smitten by embarrassment.

Amy gave an exaggerated shiver. 'I don't know why we're standing in the cold like this,' she said. 'I'll get a bit of fire going, and the place'll be as snug as can be in no time.'

She was as good as her word. Soon the flames were crackling in the grate, the kettle was singing on the hob, and she realized with awe that at last she had a home of her own. Not since the Hatfield Street days, when she had been no more than two or three, had she lived in a proper house. After Hatfield Street she and Ma – and occasionally Pa – had lived in a succession of tenements and garrets along with countless others. Each lodging had been progressively worse than the last, until the ultimate degradation of the workhouse. Not any more. Now she had a house to herself, one she need only share with Todd and the baby. She had a proper home.

The delight of being mistress of her own hearth swept over her in such a wave of pleasure she had to go round the tiny cottage and examine every corner and crevice to assure herself it was real.

The furnishings were rudimentary but adequate, bought in great haste with a gift of twenty pounds from Jessie and John. At the time Amy had thought it a fortune, but the money disappeared with alarming speed when spent upon such trifles as buckets and wash-tubs, linen and crockery. In the end much of their furniture had to be bought secondhand. Remembering the devices Jessie used to make her home pleasing, Amy had already covered the scratched table with a cloth of red chenille, giving the room a warm, cosy air. Now she looked for other ways of improving the house. The battered chairs would look decidedly better for a coat of varnish. Muslin curtains at the windows would be fresh and clean and not cost much. And maybe some twigs of evergreen in one of her china jugs would make the place look pretty.

Her wanderings took her up the narrow stairs to the bedroom. The new brass bedstead, with its plump feather mattress, was the only furnishing, apart from a battered sea-trunk of Todd's. The bed loomed uncomfortably large in the bare room, reminding Amy sharply that there was more to marriage than furniture and muslin curtains. She was Todd's wife now, with all that it entailed, and while she did not dread it she certainly faced the prospect with unease.

Todd's feet sounded on the stairs.

'This is where you'm to,' he said, his eyes also drawn to the bed.

'Yes, I was wondering whether I could make a hooked rug to go at the side, it would take the bareness off the boards. I've never tried one, mind, but I've watched Jessie doing them often enough...' On and on she rattled in her nervousness, not certain what she was saying, and not caring. Then Todd took a step forward and put an aim comfortably about her shoulders.

'There's a thing or two us needs to get sorted out,' he said. 'I should've spoken out sooner but somehow there never seemed the right moment. Well, us've got the right moment now. You idn't to worry yourself about tonight, if you knows what I mean. Nor the nights to come. 'Twouldn't be right, I'd be afeared of harming you or the babe. I'd sooner wait a spell, then us'll see how things go, eh?'

'I—I don't know what to say,' said Amy, greatly moved by his consideration, yet conscious of a strong sense of relief. 'You must be the kindest man who ever walked this earth, Todd Prout.'

Impulsively she took his face in her hands and, drawing it down towards her, planted a kiss on his mouth.

'There, that's enough of that caper,' he said, looking pleased. 'Now how about trying out some of they new pots and pans and cooking me a bite to eat? What with one thing and another my belly don't know if it's coming or going.'

Not a day passed but Amy felt grateful to Todd for rescuing her from her predicament. Yet Daniel still haunted her. Although she did her best it was impossible to keep him from her thoughts entirely. The pain of losing him was always there, hidden inside her. That was something she could not dispel, no matter how hard she tried. He was on the *Osborne* now, one of the larger fruit schooners that was on the trans-Atlantic run to Florida, and she knew he would be home soon. What would she do then? How could she explain what had happened in a way which would give him the least hurt, yet would not betray Todd?

-

It turned out that her first explanations were to Jed, not Daniel. She answered a knock at the door to find him standing there, looking grim.

'I didn't expect this,' he said without preamble.

'I don't suppose you did,' she answered. She did not know what else to say. For the first time that she could remember she felt uncomfortable in his presence. Silently she opened the door wider to let him enter. Without hesitation he strode straight into the parlour. He made no attempt to sit down.

'Todd Prout home?' he demanded.

'No, he's at sea.'

'Right, then you can tell me the truth. Was it like Daisy?'

'Daisy?' For a moment she was not sure what he meant.

He caught hold of her arms. 'Amy, you can tell me. I must know. Did Todd Prout force himself on you? If so I'll—'

'No! He certainly did not!' Amy cried, horrified. 'Todd wouldn't do a thing like that.'

'You don't have to be afraid. If he's harmed you in any way, tell me.'

'Of course he hasn't harmed me! I don't need any protection! Todd's a good decent man who wouldn't hurt anyone!' It had never occurred to her that Jed would think that history had repeated itself. The great difference between her situation and Daisy's made her tone sharper than she had intended. She continued more gently, 'Look, I don't know what ideas you've got in your head, but I swear to you that Todd has never been anything other than good and kind to me. I presume you heard about it round the harbour. I wish I could've been the one to tell you, then you wouldn't have got the wrong impression. I promise you, I'm married to a good man and I'm looking forward to the baby.'

'I don't believe you,' he said flatly. 'He must have forced himself on you. I refuse to believe that you were willing... He'd have plenty of opportunity... Wait until I get my hands on the rotten—'

'I won't have you talking that way about Todd!' cried Amy. 'You aren't to say a thing against him. He's a fine man and I couldn't have a better husband.'

Jed paused, looking at her in puzzlement. 'You mean that, don't you?'

'Yes.'

He continued to look at her, but questioningly this time, as though he were thinking out some problem.

'Maybe I have got things wrong,' he said. 'Maybe Todd wasn't the cause of your trouble… Maybe it was Seth.'

'What – what do you mean by that?' she cried, disconcerted by the suddenness of his statement.

He ran a hand through his hair. 'I should have guessed… Did Seth come to see you before we sailed for the Bristol Channel?'

'What if he did?'

'Answer me. Did you see him?'

'Yes.' Her reply was little more than a whisper.

He gave a groan. 'I might have known it was something like that. He wasn't looking forward to the trip out, that was certain. I think he ran away sooner than face the voyage back. If only I'd been sharper… The night before he left he told me some long rigmarole about seeking his fortune and looking for gold, but I didn't take much notice. I thought it was just one of his stories – you know what he's like. He kept on saying, "Take care of Amy", but I thought it was part of his daft tales. There was more to it than that, though, wasn't there? He knew you might be in trouble, because he was the one who caused it. That's it, isn't it?'

'I don't know what you're on about.' Amy's protest was far from convincing.

'Don't keep beating about the bush. The baby's Seth's, isn't it? I know it is. There's no point in denying it.'

'Don't keep on, Jed,' Amy begged, on the verge of tears. For Todd's sake, she was determined not to admit openly the baby's true father. 'Don't say any more. What's done's done, and now I'm a married woman.'

'All right, I won't bully you any more.' He spoke quietly. 'But you didn't have to go to Todd, you know. I'd have helped if only I'd known.' Amy gazed at him, surprised and uncertain. Was he saying that he would have married her?

'You were in Cornwall,' she said. 'I didn't know when you'd be back. It wasn't the sort of message I fancied putting in a letter or telegram.'

'I suppose not.' He sounded dispirited. 'He really does treat you well?'

'Yes.'

'That's good, then.' His smile was brief and forced. 'I suppose I'd better be going. I just wanted to know that you're all right.'

'I'm fine,' said Amy. 'Everything's fine.'

As she was about to open the door to let Jed out, Todd came in. The two of them faced each other in the tiny passage, and she was surprised to sense hostility between them.

'I didn't know the *Our Violet* was back,' said Todd.

'Got back two or three hours ago.' Jed faced up to him.

'Jed came to wish us luck on our marriage,' Amy said hastily.

'That's good of you.' Todd's expression did not relax.

'Least I could do, Amy being such an old friend.' Jed moved closer to the door. 'I'll be on my way. 'Bye.'

'What did he really want?' demanded Todd once the door was closed.

'Just to make sure I was all right and that I had a good husband.'

'Oh, and what did you say to that?'

'I told the truth. I said I had the best husband in the world,' said Amy. For the first time Todd relaxed. A smile of pleasure spread over his face.

'And they say *I'm* daft!' he grinned.

Chapter Nine

The marriage of Amy and Todd was a nine-day wonder in the town, soon forgotten as some other piece of gossip took everyone's imagination. Few people questioned the need for such a speedy wedding, they rightly assumed that the reason would make itself evident in the coming months.

'Got caught, did 'ee?' Lizzie Drew, who lived next door, was sympathetic. 'Just like I did. Had a drop too much scrumpy one regatta night. He took me up behind Mr Varwell's ropeworks and that was that. He were off to the east coast soon after. Come back to find my old dad waiting for him on the pier, and me the size of a house! I still laughs when I remembers the look on his face. He hasn't learnt yet! One a year regular. 'Tis the only thing he'm good at!'

Amy had to smile. It was impossible not to like the good-natured, slatternly Lizzie, with her overcrowded cottage filled with happy-go-lucky unwashed children. The contrast between the two homes could not have been greater, for Amy took a great pride in keeping everything in her house spotless.

'Wait till the babes come. 'Ee won't be so keen,' observed Lizzie, watching her scrubbing the front step. It was many years since Lizzie's doorstep had seen soap and water.

'I may as well keep at it while I can,' Amy said. 'And Todd likes to see the place looking nice.'

'Mine don't notice no more,' said Lizzie. 'Just as well, really.' And she wandered back into her own house leaving Amy to get on with her scrubbing.

Todd was indeed very appreciative of Amy's efforts. 'Us could eat our dinner off they floors,' he would remark proudly when he came home.

'Don't tempt providence,' was Amy's stock reply. 'We may have to one day.'

Despite having worked for Jessie all that time she had never managed to conquer her early clumsiness where china was concerned, and the frequent accidents to the crockery were now a standing joke between them.

'As long as you didn't sling it at me I idn't complaining,' Todd would say as she picked up the shards of yet another smashed plate or bowl.

Amy could not imagine ever being angry enough with Todd to throw things at him. Sometimes she felt he was too good to her. His kindness and consideration greatly troubled her conscience; she felt she gave so little in return.

The one-sidedness of their marriage did not appear to bother Todd. He seemed extremely content to have her, their home together, and his beloved books. And he was looking forward to the arrival of the child; Amy was astonished at how much. If he had been the baby's natural father he could not have cared more.

'Make the most of un,' remarked Lizzie's voice of experience. 'The novelty don't half wear off quick.'

Amy had smiled and not believed her. There was something about Todd's happy anticipation she knew would not fade. Already she had discovered a great dependability in him which would have astonished those who knew him only as the fool of the Prout family. He could be surprisingly serious, too, as she often discovered when they discussed the books they were reading. Todd, at home with her, was a very different character to the public Todd, laughing and fooling about with his fisherman friends.

As her waistline thickened, Amy took a greater and greater delight in the coming child. The early days of her pregnancy had been like a nightmare in their fear and uncertainty. Now she was secure and comfortable. She dutifully counted her blessings. But she was not truly happy. Happiness was inseparable from Daniel. He still stalked her thoughts and occupied her heart. She told herself that she must drive him from her mind, that she owed her complete loyalty to Todd. It was no use. Visions of Daniel would come to her in her dreams, his red hair glowing in the sun, his green eyes filled with such love for her that they shone... And she would wake to find her pillow wet with tears.

It was the end of March when the *Osborne* returned to Brixham. Down in Paradise Place, Amy could not see the traffic in the harbour. The first she knew of the schooner's arrival was when she saw the vessel moored at the pier. During these last months she had agonized over how she would tell Daniel of her marriage. She could put the moment off no longer.

The letter she wrote to him cost her a whole morning, most of a writing-pad, and more bitter tears than she had ever dreamed possible. At last she finished it. She was far from satisfied with the end result; it seemed too brusque. It betrayed none of the anguish she had suffered during the last few weeks. Nevertheless, she could think of no way of improving it. Sealing the envelope, she took the well-known path to Fishcombe and slipped it under the roots of the elderbush.

When Todd came home he asked, 'You all right, maid? You'm looking peaky.'

She did not want to keep the truth from him. He deserved her honesty.

'Todd,' she said, 'do you recall I told you that there was someone I was very fond of? Well, today I wrote to him. I told him I was married and that everything between us is over.'

Todd patted her hand. 'You did the right thing. 'Tis only proper he should know,' he said.

Would Daniel accept that everything between them was over, and that they must never meet again? She feared that the answer would be no. Her great dread was that he would come hammering at the door, demanding to see her. Every rap on the door knocker brought her heart to her mouth. The risk that they might meet by chance was equally great. Each time she went out she was poised ready to dash down an alley or into a shop if she should glimpse the familiar red hair. When she did meet him there was no chance of evasion.

Amy was beginning to discover the joys of having leisure, of being her own mistress. The house was neat and tidy, Todd's dinner was ready for the oven, the fire was banked up – and a fine bright March afternoon beckoned. Eager for sharp clear air and wide vistas after the cramped conditions of Paradise Place, Amy set out for the limestone cliffs of Berry Head. As well as the enjoyment and the freedom of her walk, she would be able to keep a look-out for the *Vigilant* and would be able to get back in plenty of time for Todd's homecoming.

Her route led along the familiar road past John Prout's boatyard. Instead of keeping to the lane, Amy took a footpath which wound upwards through the trees. Thickly spiked furze bushes, speckled with yellow blossom, began to fringe the track, impeding her view. She was not aware of the oncoming figure until they were almost face to face. There was no way of avoiding one another in the narrow green alley. They both stopped abruptly. A fulmar wheeled overhead on straight wings, a rabbit scuttled in the undergrowth, rustling the dried leaves. Amy did not notice them. Her eyes were only for Daniel.

'How – how are you?' she asked at last.

'There is no need to ask how you are!' His voice was hostile. 'Your condition is pretty obvious.'

Her heart sank at his tone, yet what else had she expected?

'Yes,' she admitted.

'Pregnant and married – have got that in the right order I presume? My, you were busy while I was away. Thank goodness I was on the Florida run. If I'd only been going to the Mediterranean I'd have come back too soon, which would have spoiled your little escapade.' There was more than animosity in his voice now, there was sarcasm, there was anger, there was bitterness.

'Daniel, I'm sorry.' Her words sounded woefully inadequate.

'*You're* sorry? That's rich!'

'Did you get my letter…? I did try to explain.'

'I got your letter. At first I didn't believe it. I thought you were having one of your "I'm not good enough for you" spells again, trying to send me away. I was ready to come and find you, to persuade you that such ideas were nonsense. I should have realized that claiming to be married and expecting a child was a bit much, even for you. Imagine how I felt when our gardener told me the sordid details of how John Prout's brother had gone up the skirts of their servant girl and been fool enough to marry her afterwards. What a charming tale. It quite brought tears to my eyes.'

There were tears in Amy's eyes at his stinging rebuke and she fought to control them. 'You've every right to be angry,' she said quietly. 'I can only repeat that I'm sorry.'

'Is that all you can say? No excuses? No explanations?'

Amy shook her head. What excuses or explanations could she give?

'Not even "Please, I couldn't help it. He was the master's brother. He forced me to do it"?' he cried, his voice a cruel imitation of a woman's.

Amy did not respond, and her silence seemed to infuriate him more.

'You mean you lay with Todd Prout willingly, is that it?' He was almost beside himself with rage and pain. 'You claimed to love me yet you could go with another man? You – you slut!' He raised his hand to strike her, then froze, as if appalled at what he intended to do.

His arm fell to his side. 'I loved you,' he said very quietly, 'and you betrayed me!'

He pushed past her and hurried off down the path.

Amy stood immobile. She had not flinched at his intended blow. Nor did she look after him as he went away. She simply stood there, dry-eyed, numb with pain and grief. Not until long after the sound of his footsteps had faded did she turn slowly and retrace her way back down through the wood. The encounter had ensured one thing: there was no fear that Daniel would try to rekindle the love between them. He had gone from her life for ever.

–

Two more weeks and Jed would be out of his apprenticeship. This milestone in his life shone like a beacon for him. He would be bound to no man, neither Matthew Burton nor anyone else. The yachting season was in full swing, and he often saw the *Silhouette* in the bay.

The sight of her slim lines tantalized him. To be part of her crew was his immediate ambition, and it was agony to have to wait. Ever since the previous summer and the incident with the bag of oatmeal he had looked forward to the time when he would join the yacht's crew. It had made the discomfort of life with the Burtons bearable. Skipper Burton would probably expect him to stay on — some masters did consider it customary for their apprentices to remain for another year at least — but Jed did not think he could tolerate twelve more months in his present situation.

It was extraordinary the way the entire Burton family had turned vindictive towards him. Lucy was the main instigator. She never lost an opportunity to make his life miserable, usually by accusing him of some slight or misdemeanour. It was no use Jed protesting his innocence. The elder Burtons were completely under Lucy's influence; she was their youngest, their ewe-lamb. Matthew Burton, who was ruthless in seeking out the weaknesses of others, could see no fault in her. He accepted any charges made by his daughter without question, and acted upon them. In spite of his religion, Matthew was not one to leave retribution to the Lord. He preferred to deal out his own punishment.

Strangely enough it was not the cuffs and the beatings which made Jed's life a misery, it was continuing day after day without ever doing anything right. He did not want the skipper's approval for its own sake. Improving his seamanship was what he was set on and he wanted to know he was doing a job well for his own satisfaction.

It was late in the season for him to be applying for a berth on board the *Silhouette*, but he had had no chance before. It had taken a funeral in the Burton family to keep the *Our Violet* in port and give him a few hours off. Officially he had been left enough tasks on board to keep him busy until dusk. Unofficially he was going to walk the four miles to Dartmouth to seek out the *Silhouette*. He had been careful to keep the card which Mr Hudson, the owner, had given him.

Opening the tin box in which he kept his possessions he paused, frowning. He was meticulous about the order of his things. His few papers of any importance he kept at one side, along with his books from night-school. At the other were his clean clothes. Something seemed wrong: he was not quite sure what. Yet everything was there when he checked, even Mr Hudson's card. This was not the first time he had had the feeling that someone had been through his belongings.

The obvious culprit was the new apprentice, Albert Chapman, the replacement for Seth, who was stretched out on the opposite cot.

'Have you been in my box for anything?' Jed demanded.

'No, Jed, honest.' Albert sat upright.

'Because if I ever catch you at it I'll belt you one, do you understand?'

'I never touch your things, I swear it.' The boy looked so anxious that Jed relented.

'All right, I believe you,' he said untruthfully. He was still convinced that Albert was guilty, and he understood his motives clearly enough.

Against all the odds, Skipper Burton had gone to a workhouse again for an apprentice. Not Lambeth. 'That place be filled with the spawn of the devil!' he had declared. This time he had applied to the Poplar and Whitechapel Union, who had duly provided him with Albert, aged fourteen, predictably undersized, yet with a cheerful manner and an eagerness to please that reminded Jed of Seth.

Knowing Albert's background, Jed could sympathize with the boy's interest in his tin box. When you owned nothing of your own it was easy to be intrigued by other people's possessions, however modest.

'Ain't you got a lot of books?' Albert observed, regarding the contents of the box curiously. 'What d'you want them for?'

'There aren't that many, just what I need at night-school.'

'What d'you go to night-school for?'

'To learn things,' said Jed patiently, then to forestall the question he knew would follow he added, 'I want to get my seamanship tickets, then I can be a skipper one day.'

'You want to keep on at the fishing?' Albert regarded him incredulously. 'You must be barmy. I ain't staying one minute longer than I have to. I ain't being walloped and bawled at for years. I don't know why you don't fetch Old Man Burton a fourpenny one, honest I don't.'

'I feel like it at times,' admitted Jed. 'It wouldn't do any good, though. I've stood it this far, another fortnight won't hurt.'

'It's 'cos Lucy don't like you, ain't it? That's why you get all the stick.'

'What makes you say that?'

'I've got eyes in my head and ears sticking out of it. What's she got against you? You seem a decent enough bloke to me.'

'Thanks. If I ever need a character I'll come to you. As for Lucy, who's to know how her mind works?'

'Why're you putting on a clean shirt? Going somewhere?'

'Don't you ever stop asking questions?' demanded Jed in exasperation, emerging from the folds of the shirt. 'To answer you, yes I am going somewhere. And if you tell the skipper I'll tie that long nose of yours into a knot to stop it poking in other people's business.' Albert obviously did not take the threat seriously. He fell back on the bed with a chuckle.

'You're off to see your sweetheart on the sly,' he said, putting his arms comfortably behind his head. 'Now I know why Lucy's got it in for you. You've jilted her for someone else.'

'You shouldn't know about such things at your age,' said Jed.

'Gam,' replied Albert rudely. 'Give her a kiss from me. A big smacker.'

By way of a reply Jed threw his pillow at the boy, and hurriedly left the cabin before he could retaliate.

Almost the first person he saw as he stepped out into the street was Amy. Her face lit up with pleasure at the sight of him.

'Hullo, stranger,' she said. 'I haven't seen you in ages.'

'Things have kept me busy,' said Jed.

'I've missed you. Why do you never come to see me?'

Jed shrugged. 'I don't like to intrude,' he said. 'Especially when your husband is home.'

'You aren't always at sea when he is. Come when he's away.'

'I couldn't do that!' Jed looked slightly shocked. 'People would talk.'

'What, with me this size?' Amy laughed and patted her swollen stomach.

Jed wanted to ask her how she was. He searched awkwardly for the right words.

'Much longer to go?' he asked brusquely.

'Only another fortnight, hopefully.'

Two weeks! Amy's baby and his own freedom would arrive together.

'And how are you keeping?'

'Never better.'

He knew she was telling the truth. Her eyes were sparkling, there was a rich gloss to her hair and a glow on her cheeks which spoke of perfect health.

'And – and…' He wanted to ask her if she was happy, but he was afraid the question might sound impertinent. Now she was married he feared he no longer had the right to ask her personal questions. 'Everything's still all right?' he asked eventually.

'Everything's still fine. Todd's a good man, and he looks after me very well.'

'Good.' Then in a rush of concern about her he said, 'Should you be standing about like this? Here, give me your shopping. I'll carry it for you.'

Laughing, she held the basket out of his reach.

'You can't be seen walking through the town carrying a shopping basket,' she laughed. 'What would the lads down at the harbour say? Anyway, I'm not an invalid, you know. But perhaps I'd better be on my way.' Her smile widened. 'Not because I'm afraid of swooning away at your feet, but because I've some baking to do.'

'If you insist.'

'You will come and visit sometime, won't you? Come one Sunday, and we'll have tea all posh and proper with the best china and everything.'

'Right, I'll come. Perhaps I'd better leave it until after…'

'Yes, perhaps you're right. Babes are unpredictable things. Mine should arrive in a fortnight, but I've been warned it might come any day now.'

'I can use the time practising how to drink tea with my little finger sticking out.' Jed smiled. 'Take care of yourself until then.'

'I will. There's no need to worry about me, you know. I'm fine.'

No need to worry! Her words stayed with him as he began to walk away from the town. Although she sounded confident, he could not dispel the unease inside him. Women died in childbirth. His own mother had, along with the baby sister who had never drawn breath. Although he had been a very small child at the time he could still remember the feeling of desolation. What if it should happen to Amy? He could not bear to think about it. It was better to imagine her with the babe safely arrived, cradled in her arms. He did not think he would visit the house in Paradise Place, much as he wanted to see her again. He could picture it all too clearly. Amy by her own fireside, nursing her child, her husband standing by. It would make a fine scene, but there would be no place in it for him.

He wondered about Todd Prout. What sort of a man would willingly father some other fellow's unborn child? Jed knew the answer to that one. It was someone who was in love with Amy.

He had had a hard climb out of the town. When he reached the brow of the long hill he was hot and perspiring. He took off his jacket but did not slacken his pace. The beauty of his surroundings barely registered with him. He did notice the river winding its way through the valley below simply because it was his destination. He started downhill, and was glad to increase his pace in his eagerness to reach it.

Jed knew the estuary of the River Dart pretty well. He had often sought shelter there during a storm or when conditions made it difficult for the *Our Violet* to get her catch round Mansands and Berry Head to Brixham. When he reached the riverside he looked for the familiar lines of the *Silhouette*. There was no sign of her.

'In the Dart,' Mr Hudson had said vaguely. Jed prayed he did not mean right up near Dittisham. He hadn't enough time as it was. A small crabber was being unloaded at the jetty. In desperation he asked he man on board.

'Mr Hudson's yacht?' said the man. ''Er'rn up to Sandquay, bain't 'er, Henry?'

Jed found the *Silhouette* easily enough, on the other side of the river, a little way upstream. Finding her owner or her skipper was a very different matter. Mr Hudson, he learned, was visiting friends and was not expected back on board until late evening. More time wasted. Eventually Jed ran the skipper to earth at the Ship-in-Dock, where he was enjoying a leisurely pint.

'I remember you. You're the fellow with the sack of oatmeal,' observed the skipper. 'You did a good job that day, although we were clearing up soggy meal for days afterwards. You're a bit late coming here, aren't you?'

'I couldn't come before, sir. I won't be out of my apprenticeship for another fortnight.'

'That's more than a fortnight too late as far as I'm concerned.' The skipper gave an uninterested shrug. 'If you want to crew on a yacht you need to speak up early, lad, not leave it until half-way through the season.'

'Then you won't take me on?'

'Not won't! Can't! We've our full complement.'

'But Mr Hudson said to come to him this year when I was free.'

'I dare say he did. But he'd say a lot more than that to me if I took on one hand more than was necessary.'

'He said I was to come,' insisted Jed. 'He gave me his card and everything.' He laid the piece of pasteboard in front of the skipper.

The man gave a patient sigh. 'I'm not calling you a liar, lad. I'd best explain, for it's clear you've a lot to learn about gentlemen like Mr Hudson. He'll make no bones about spending a fortune on a stylish yacht complete with fancy trimmings. But when it comes to paying out the wages for the men who sail her, then suddenly his purse-strings go tight. He expects the best from them, mind. Only first-rate seamen are taken on to crew this boat, for they're the ones who'll win his races for him. But he'd take great exception to me hiring an extra hand, especially one who isn't absolutely necessary. That the man might have done him a service doesn't enter into it, nor the fact that the man's wages would come to less than the cost of the fancy wines and spirits he has on board to entertain his friends. Don't ask me why he's like that, he just is.'

Jed stood there impassively, not allowing one muscle to betray how much of a blow this was to him. For a full year he had dreamed of sailing on the *Silhouette*. Now that dream faded like sea mist.

'I'm sorry I wasted your time,' he said brusquely.

'It was your time you wasted, son, not mine,' replied the man. 'Try asking in the town. You might be lucky if someone's had a man fall sick or something. My advice is to start applying early next year.'

Thanking the man, Jed went back through Dartmouth. Although he made plenty of inquiries the answer was always the same:

'You're too late, we've all the men we need.' The four-mile walk back to Brixham seemed far longer and more arduous than the journey coming.

'You ain't had much luck with your new lady friend, by the looks of you,' remarked Albert when Jed returned to the cabin. 'You'd best go back to Lucy, if she'll have you.'

Jed was too tired to respond. He flung himself down on his bed. He had been a fool to have set such store by the yacht job. When would he ever learn that it was stupid to put faith in other people? The only person he could rely upon was himself. He closed his eyes, more to discourage Albert's incessant curiosity than because he wanted to sleep. He had a lot of thinking to do; he had to reshape his plans.

By the time the end of the fortnight came his hope of freedom had lost its significance. What did it matter if he was out of his apprenticeship? He was still stuck with Skipper Burton. He did try looking for another job, but with much of the fleet away fishing in other waters there was nothing going. When Matthew Burton heard he was looking for a new place he lashed out with his fist and with his tongue. Jed dodged the fist with an ease born of long practice. The stream of vehemence was harder to avoid. He was continuously bombarded with long sermons until his ears throbbed.

Albert was full of sympathy. 'It ain't fair,' he complained. 'You ain't done nothing wrong. You shouldn't have to put up with his jawing day-in day-out.'

'I won't,' Jed assured him. 'As soon as I find something suitable I'll be off.'

'It ain't fair,' repeated Albert. 'I don't suppose you was asked if you wanted to be a rotten old fisherman. I weren't! I ain't much gone on the sea, neither. I'd swap every blooming drop to be down Whitechapel on a Saturday night. And as for eating fish, there ain't one as can match a plate of jellied eels for being tasty.'

Jed let Albert chatter on unhindered. The boy's quick speech and sharp accent brought to mind a part of his life that was rapidly receding from his memory. Had life in London really been better than down here in Devon? Parts of it he recalled with nostalgia. Like Albert he had enjoyed crowded streets where there was always something of interest or someone of note. That had been before his workhouse days, of course. There was no doubt in his mind that anywhere was better than being incarcerated in Lambeth Union. His present situation might be unpleasant, but it was only temporary. In the meantime, since he had no wish to be unemployed, he would have to tolerate the conditions.

Life at the fishing went on as usual. The only difference was that now if Jed saw the *Silhouette* in the bay he would turn away, not wanting to look at the cause of such disappointment. His post office savings book was an important spur towards his ambitions. The five pounds given to him by Mr Hudson had made a fine start, and ever since then he had done his best to put something in each week. He could never afford much, but he argued with himself that not much was better than nothing at all, especially when he began to understand the intricacies of compound interest. With a carefully hoarded shilling in his pocket he went to his box one day to get the precious book. As soon as he raised the lid he knew someone had been among his things. The box's contents were neat and tidy, yet he knew someone had been prying.

He took out his savings book. Outwardly it looked normal, but it felt odd. It was too thin. He opened it and groaned. There was nothing inside. The book consisted of only the cover, the pages had been ripped out.

His immediate reaction was a feeling of dismay. Then anger swept over him and he rushed from the cabin with a roar of rage. He collided with Albert in the doorway and, grasping him by the arms, began to shake him.

'Ow, stop it!' yelled the boy. 'You're hurting! Have you gone barmy or something? Ow!' Jed did not release his grip.

'I haven't even started hurting you yet. Why did you do it? Tell me what you did with them before I rattle every tooth out of your thieving head.'

'Do what? What are you talking about? I ain't touched nothing—!' Albert's protests were punctuated by cries of pain.

'You tore the pages out of my savings book! Tell me what you did with them,' said Jed, still shaking him. 'I'll keep this up until you do.'

'Leave off— for pity's sake— before I'm sick!' wailed Albert. 'I ain't touched nothing, I keeps telling you… What the hell's a savings book, anyway?'

Jed suddenly stopped shaking him. Albert did not know what a savings book was. He released his grip and looked thoughtfully at the boy, who was whimpering and rubbing his bruised arms. Whoever had damaged his book had known its significance and its value. Albert, straight from the workhouse, was ignorant of things like post office savings accounts.

'Sorry, mate,' he said awkwardly. 'I shouldn't have gone for you like that. I see now it wasn't you. I was stupid to think it was. I'm really sorry.'

'I should think so,' said Albert aggrieved. Then his curiosity got the better of him. 'What's it all about then? Someone torn one of your precious books?'

'Yes, only it wasn't any old book. It was special.' Jed showed the boy the mutilated cover and briefly explained its importance.

Albert was impressed to learn that Jed had savings. He was also sympathetic at their loss.

'Cor, no wonder you went off your head,' he said. 'It— it's like someone tearing up your money, ain't it? Have you lost it all, do you reckon?'

'I'm not sure. I'll have to find out.'

'Who'd want to do something like that? Pinching your money's one thing, I can understand that, but there ain't no sense in tearing up a few bits of paper. And who'd go to your box, anyway…?' His voice tailed away.

'What is it?' demanded Jed.

'It ain't nothing,' Albert said hastily.

'Tell me!'

'I don't want to make no trouble for no one… Oh, all right,' conceded the boy as Jed began to look threatening again. 'Maybe it ain't nothing… Maybe she was doing what she said… It's just that this morning I come in and found Lucy bending over your box. She said she'd just brought the clean washing back.'

Lucy! Of course! Why had he not thought of her first? Who else would have had the opportunity? Who else would be so vindictive?

'Was the box open?'

'Dunno, I couldn't see. She was in the way. She didn't half jump when she saw me, though.'

'Wait until I get my hands on her!' Jed spoke in a low whisper, but Albert heard him.

'You won't tell her it was me as let on, will you?' he pleaded.

'I won't,' promised Jed. 'And I owe you a favour for having gone for you like that. Would some toffee make it up to you?'

'There ain't no need for that, honest. You're my mate. What's a shaking or two between mates?' Despite his protestations, Albert's eyes sparkled at the prospect of the sweets.

'I owe you something. I always pay my debts.'

'In that case, Jed, could you make it stickjaw, please?'

'Stickjaw it'll be. It might even stop you chattering for a spell, in which case it'll be doubly worth the money.' Jed grinned at the boy.

He felt far from smiling. Lucy Burton had a lot to answer for, and he had every intention of confronting her. Not when she was by herself, though. He was always careful not to be alone with her, it was too risky. No, he would accuse her in front of her father. It would not be an easy matter, taking on two Burtons together, but he was tired of being the butt of their animosity. It was high time everything was brought out into the open and Skipper Burton learned a few home truths about his precious daughter.

His opportunity came that evening. He went into the parlour where Matthew was reading the Bible. The older man looked at him questioningly over his steel-rimmed glasses.

'You'm wanting something, boy?' he demanded.

'Yes, Skipper, I want a word with Lucy, and I want to say it in your hearing.'

'A word with Lucy, you say?' The fierce eyebrows lowered threateningly. 'Let me tell you here and now if you'm thinking of asking her to wed you the answer's no!'

'I have no wish to wed her,' said Jed fervently.

'Then what's it about, eh? Ah, yer comes Lucy now. Put they plates on the dresser, maid, and come yer.'

'Pooh, there bain't 'alf a terrible smell in yer. If I didn't know better I'd say they drains was blocked again.' Lucy held her nose between forefinger and thumb and pointedly turned away from Jed.

'You may as well save your breath,' retorted Jed. 'I want to talk to you.'

'I don't want to talk to the likes of you. I don't 'ave to, do I, Pa?'

'It is very important,' said Jed.

The grimness in his voice caused Matthew to look at him curiously.

'If 'tis that serious it don't do no harm to listen,' he declared. 'What's this about, boy?'

Jed laid his mutilated savings book on the table.

'I want to know why you tore the pages out, and what you did with them.' His gaze never left Lucy as he spoke.

'What you'm on about? Pa, what's 'e on about?' Lucy's tone was defiant, but her eyes flickered uneasily.

'That's what I wants to know!' said Matthew sternly. 'I hopes I didn't get your drift proper, my lad. For a moment I thought you was accusing my maid yer of something.'

'I am!' Jed met his glare without flinching. 'I'm accusing Lucy of ripping up my book.'

'What?' Matthew leapt to his feet. 'You dares to accuse her in front of me?'

'Did you ever 'ear such a pack of lies? You knows what these work'ouse lot are like, Pa. Trouble-makers all of them. To say such things of me—'

'Yes, Skipper, I do dare to accuse her in front of you.' Jed cut into Lucy's flow of words. 'I want you to hear everything I've got to say, clear and above board. You've a reputation as a fair man. All I ask is for you to hear me out.'

Matthew sank back into his chair, almost appeased. He was proud of his standing in the community.

'Very well, speak your piece,' he said.

'You idn't going to sit there and listen to 'is dirty lies, be you, Pa?' demanded Lucy.

'Quiet, girl! Us'll listen!' ordered her father. 'Now, boy, you tell your tale from the beginning.'

'This afternoon I took my savings book out of my box and found the pages had been ripped out. It's my belief that Lucy did it.'

'Of all the lying 'ounds…!' cried the girl.

'And why do you believe my Lucy did this?' asked her father with studied calm. 'Why not someone else? Young Albert for instance.'

'Albert had no idea what a savings book was, for another he had no reason to cause such mischief.'

'And I 'ave, I suppose!' cried Lucy. 'And what reason would that be, pray?'

'Because you don't like me. You've made that pretty clear these last few months.'

'My, don't you fancy yourself?' mocked Lucy. 'You don't think I gives you a moment's thought, do you? Why should I?'

'We both know why you've taken such a dislike to me.'

'I'm the only one in ignorance, seemingly.' Matthew looked from one to the other. 'I idn't accustomed to being kept in the dark, not in my own house.'

'I didn't touch they stupid pages.' Lucy was still defiant, but her unease had increased. 'Don't listen to 'im, Pa. I didn't do it!'

'Then who did?' demanded Jed. 'Who else comes into the cabin? No, Lucy, it was you, right enough. You'd do anything to spite me. Admit you tore the book. Tell me what you did with the pages and this whole business ends here.'

'Daughter, this is a grave thing. Did you destroy the book?'

''Course I didn't, Pa. 'E'm adding mischief-making to 'is lies. Don't believe a word of it.'

'You tore up my book, you know you did!'

'I didn't!'

'I means to get to the bottom of this!' Matthew banged his fist on the table. 'You, boy! Give me some straight answers. Why should my girl do a thing like that to you?'

'Because I wouldn't lie with her.'

There was a sudden silence, broken only by the steady tick of the clock.

'What did you say?' Matthew Burton's voice was little more than a whisper.

'Lucy came to the cabin one night when you and Mrs Burton were out. She was dressed only in her shift. She wanted me to go to bed with her. I refused.'

'You dare to say that? You dare to call my daughter a wanton in front of my face?'

'I do, Skipper, because it's no more than the truth.'

'You foul-mouthed devil!' Matthew leapt to his feet, too incensed to remain calm any longer. 'I idn't standing by and listening to this filth! You idn't calling my chile a strumpet and a whore and getting away with it! First I'm going to give you the thrashing of your life, then you'm going down on your knees to beg the Lord's pardon for telling such base lies.'

'That's it, Pa! You give 'im a good 'iding,' shrieked Lucy. ''E were the one as was always on at me to do wicked things. I wadn't having none of it. That's why 'e'm saying these dreadful things 'bout me!'

Already Matthew had unbuckled his heavy leather belt and was wrapping the end round his hand as he advanced menacingly on Jed. But Jed did not retreat. He faced the skipper squarely and removed his own belt.

'I'm not going to be thrashed like a dog,' he said grimly. 'Not now I'm a grown man. And especially not for telling the truth.'

Matthew's features went florid with increased anger. No one had ever questioned his authority with such determination before.

'I idn't going to be defied in my own house!' he roared. 'I shall be a scourge for the Lord!'

His belt whistled through the air. Jed neatly avoided it.

'I won't strike first, Skipper,' he cautioned. 'But I warn you, fetch me just one blow and I'll give you as good as I get.'

Matthew came to an abrupt halt, a look of acute astonishment on histhat might have seemed funny in other circumstances. Swallowing hard to regain his composure, Matthew resettled his grip on his belt and faced up to Jed, his shoulders hunched, his feet apart, ready to spring. Jed did the same.

'You can't beat me when the fancy takes you any more. I'm not a boy any longer,' said Jed.

This was true. Although Jed was not as tall as Matthew Burton, he was compact and well-muscled, particularly about the shoulders. He was agile too, able to move and dodge with an ease the older man could no longer equal. Above all, he was young, whereas his opponent was way past middle-age and in indifferent health.

For the first time Matthew Burton was forced to confront his own weaknesses. The leather belt hung limply at his side.

'Get out of this house,' he said shakily. 'I don't want to see that face of youm ever again.'

Jed did not move. He had not got the satisfaction he had come for. Lucy had not admitted her guilt.

'Go on, run off with your tail a-tween your legs!' taunted Lucy. 'All this fuss about a blummin' savings book. Anyone'd think you 'ad a fortune in there instead of a measly seven pounds ten shillings.'

For the second time that evening a tense silence filled the room.

'What was that you said, girl?' demanded Matthew slowly.

Realizing her blunder, Lucy looked frightened, as Matthew turned to face Jed.

'How much did you have in there, boy?' he asked.

'Seven pounds, ten shillings and sixpence,' Jed replied.

'How did you know the exact amount as was in the book? Answer me!'

'It— it were a guess, Pa! A lucky guess.' Lucy was looking terrified now.

'No,' roared Matthew. 'For you 'twere an unlucky guess. You tore the book, didn't you? You'm a liar, and you'm malicious, just as he said you were. Now, I wants to know if the rest be true. Be you'm a wanton too?'

He towered over Lucy in his fury, his belt once more raised. The girl gave a shriek and cowered in a corner, her arms over her head for protection.

'Don't 'it me, Pa! Please don't 'it me,' she wailed as her father advanced towards her.

He looked so beside himself with anger that Jed moved forward to intercept the blows that were surely to rain down on Lucy. Those blows never came. Matthew's anger subsided as swiftly as it had arisen. He sank into his chair, his face ashen.

'I–I can't do it,' he said brokenly. 'I–I can't beat you, chile. I knows you deserve it but I can't raise my hand to you. Get to your room till your ma gets back. Her'll have to deal with you.'

Sobbing bitterly Lucy rushed out, pushing her way past Jed as if he did not exist. He waited for Matthew to speak, but the skipper was slumped in his armchair, his head in his hands. He seemed oblivious of Jed's presence. Without a word Jed left the parlour, closing the door behind him. He had got what he came for – Lucy's admission of guilt. There was no point in staying, he no longer had any future with the Burtons.

He went over to the cabin and packed up his belongings quietly, trying not to disturb the sleeping Albert. With his box on his shoulder he walked away from the house and headed for the harbour.

That night he slept on board one of the trawlers, then at dawn he did the rounds of the boats which were preparing to put to sea, in the hope that one of them might need an extra hand. He was out of luck. The advice given to him was always the same: 'Wait till the boats come back from Tenby, boy. There's bound to be summat then.'

Disappointed, but not surprised at his lack of success, Jed strode back up Fore Street to the post office. There was still the matter of his savings book to attend to.

Mr Cranford, the postmaster, opened the cover of the book gingerly between finger and thumb, and regarded Jed over the top of his spectacles.

'An accident, you say?' he said. 'It must have been an extraordinary accident to have demolished every page.'

'It was,' Jed assured him shortly. 'The important thing is, have I lost my money?'

'No,' was the reply. 'You have other identification with you? Then it should be a simple matter to replace the book.'

At this Jed felt an overwhelming sense of relief. It was short-lived. Mr Cranford looked down at the inside cover.

'Ah, you are still under twenty-one, I presume? I see Mr Burton, as your employer, signed for you last time. I'm afraid we'll have to trouble him again for his signature.'

'Is that necessary?' asked Jed.

'It is. As a minor you must have someone to stand as your guarantor.' Mr Cranford looked at him across the counter. 'What's wrong? Is it that Mr Burton would be unlikely to sign for you a second time?'

'I wouldn't ask him,' replied Jed abruptly.

The postmaster pursed his lips. He had not believed Jed's story about an accident ruining the book. There was not much that went on in Brixham he did not know about. He had heard rumours of the rift between Matthew Burton and the once-favoured apprentice from the workhouse. He could guess the cause, too. To have young fellows under same roof as that Lucy Burton was asking for trouble in his opinion. However, he prudently kept his views to himself.

'I suppose there is no hope of retrieving the missing pages?' he asked.

'None,' replied Jed. If he knew Lucy she would have consigned them to the kitchen fire.

'The cover is intact,' Mr Cranford said thoughtfully. 'The signatures, both yours and Mr Burton's, have not been defaced in any way. Perhaps they can still stand for your new book. I will have to consult my superiors.' As Jed thanked him he added, 'I'm afraid this means you can't make any withdrawals until the matter is sorted out.'

'That's all right, I can manage,' said Jed, though his heart sank.

Being out of work and with nowhere to live, it would have been reassuring to have had his savings to fall back on. Then he thought again and was glad. Those savings were for his boat. Since he could not touch his money he would just have to survive with what was in his pocket. It was little enough – a couple of shillings and a few pennies, out of which he had to buy the stickjaw for Albert, not to mention feed himself. But sleeping accommodation was not too much of a problem during the summer. There were numerous sheds and net stores in which he could find shelter, or friendly skippers who would let him spend a night on board their boats.

He found work for a few hours that day, shifting sacks of grain at the brewery in the centre of town. It was not much, but it added a welcome shilling or so to his funds. He spent the night uncomfortably in a dilapidated shed, among crab-pots and old fish-baskets. It was quite a relief when dawn came and he could go down to the harbour once more in search of work. As he was rounding the corner towards the Quay a familiar figure came in view.

'Well, then, boy,' Harry Preston greeted him. 'What's this yer 'bout 'ee having a bust up with the skipper?'

'Let's just say we parted company,' said Jed.

'That's the way of un, eh? And what you'm doing now, then?'

'Casual stuff. I'm managing.'

'Hm!' Harry did not look convinced. 'I tells 'ee this, boy. If yesterday's trip was aught to go by, the skipper'll have 'ee back in no time. My, talk about a straggle! Trying to get the trawl up with just Cy, who'm brawny enough but cussed with un, and young Albert who'm useless, and the Skipper who idn't the man he was! Believe me, it wadn't no picnic. Bide your time and 'ee'll be back on the *Our Violet* in a trice.'

'No,' stated Jed decisively. 'I won't.'

'Well, 'tis your business. 'Ee knows un best,' said Harry wisely. 'Where'm 'ee lodging?'

'Where I can,' Jed admitted.

''Ee looks un, too, boy,' grinned Harry. 'Tell 'ee what! Come along home with me. My old woman'll find 'ee somewhere in with our brood. 'Twon't be much but it'll be better'n naught.'

It was on the tip of Jed's tongue to refuse the kind offer, then he reconsidered. There was no point in sleeping rough if it could be avoided. He had enough money for a night's lodgings – just! It was better for it to go to Harry's family than to someone else.

'Thanks,' he said. 'If you're sure it's all right. I'll have to get my things from Ma Griggs.'

Ma Griggs sold shrimps, which she boiled in a large copper at the back of her minute cottage near the beach. She also acted as depository of goods and messages for the seagoing men, and was reputed to deal in illicit spirits. Jed fetched his belongings, paid his dues, and returned to where Harry was waiting for him. As he approached he saw that Harry was talking to someone. He stiffened slightly at the sight of Todd Prout; he never felt comfortable in that man's presence. Todd evidently felt the same, for he nodded briefly to Jed as he approached.

'I were just going to ask ol' Todd yer if he'm a daddy yet,' said Harry.

Jed felt the tension in him increase as he, too, looked inquiringly towards Amy's husband.

Todd's face split into a beaming smile.

'A li'l maid! Yesterday morning! Pretty as a picture. Bright as a button, too, and with lungs as'd deafen a donkey,' he said proudly. 'Amy's all for calling her Euphemia, after her mother. I reckons that's too big for such a babe, so that's to be her Sunday-going-to-meeting name. Rest of the time her'll be just Effie.'

'And Amy? How's Amy?' demanded Jed, irritated at all the talk of the baby and none of the mother.

'Oh, her'm fine. Come through it as good as gold, thank God. Her'm talking of getting up already! It's a good job our John's wife's with her. Won't stand no nonsense will Jessie!'

Jed's sigh of relief went unnoticed as Harry slapped Todd on the back.

'There now, if that idn't good news!' he declared. 'Us'll be down the Buller's tonight to wet the baby's head.'

'Best leave it until tomorrow,' said Todd. 'I reckon I ought to stay home tonight and be on cradle watch if I don't want the womenfolk jawing my ears off.'

'Tomorrow it is! Us can wait that long, eh Jed?'

'Yes, we can wait. And will you tell Amy I— I'm very pleased for her.' How stilted that sounded, but he could not find the words to say what he felt. He never could.

'There's one man as idn't disappointed 'cos the babe's a maid and not a boy,' said Harry, as Todd made his way towards Paradise Place. 'Come on, let's see what my Sally can give us for breakfast.'

If Harry's wife had any objections to having another man to look after, she did not voice them.

''Tidn't much,' she said, showing Jed what was really no more than a curtained-off section of the landing. 'But you'll be a bit more private yer than in with the childer.'

Jed regarded his new accommodation with approval. It may have been makeshift, but it was warmer, more comfortable and cleaner than the cabin. The fact that Sally Preston proved to be a far better cook then Violet Burton was an added bonus. When Jed quietly put some money on the kitchen table after breakfast, Sally pushed it back at him.

'There idn't no need for that,' she said. 'You'm a friend of Harry's.'

'Friend or not, I pay my way,' insisted Jed, dropping the coins into her apron pocket.

The grateful look that flickered in her eyes told him how much she appreciated the extra money.

During the rest of the summer he became a permanent lodger with the Prestons. Because he was strong, hard-working, and did not care what he did, he usually managed to find casual work. Somehow he always earned enough money to pay for his lodgings each week.

'You'm a good lad, Jed,' Sally would say appreciatively. 'But I knows you'm running yourself short. I don't mind waiting a bit for the money; it don't worry me none.'

'Take it while I've got it,' was Jed's habitual answer. 'I'll sponge off you quickly enough when it's gone.' And they would both laugh.

He found it surprisingly easy to joke these days. The Preston household was a cheery, if noisy, one, and some of its light-heartedness seemed to rub off on him.

"Course we'm poor,' was Harry's answer when he questioned how they could be so happy on so little. 'Poor as church mice, that's us. Luckily we'm too stupid to notice it!'

It had been many years since Jed had lived as part of a family and even then he had been a resented outsider. At first he had been surprised and embarrassed at the kisses and hugs that Harry and Sally openly showered on each other and on the children. Hany astounded him in particular, often taking one of the younger children on his lap. Jed had always known that women nursed children. It came as a surprise to learn that men did too. He thought of Amy and her baby. Did Todd nurse their little one the way Harry did with his youngest? Jed wondered what it must be like to be able to show one's affections so easily. Probably very nice, he decided, especially when that love was returned openly, as it was between Sally and Harry. Then he would deliberately turn his mind to something else. Such easy emotions were fine for the Prestons, but they had nothing to do with him.

With the approach of autumn the fishing fleet arrived home from the Welsh coast. Jed watched them return in anticipation. He had survived the summer on casual work. Although his post office savings book had eventually been restored to him, he had got by without withdrawing a single penny, despite the hardships. Now, with luck, he would get a proper job.

But when he began approaching skippers for work, his optimism soon began to dim. The story was the same from everyone. There had been a glut of fish. Everywhere there had been heavy catches, and the east coast fishermen had been competing with the Brixham men for their traditional markets. Transport costs had gone up, market prices had plummeted, until fish could not be given away free. Everywhere it was a tale of woe. Far from taking on new hands, some skippers were talking of laying up their boats and looking elsewhere for work themselves.

Jed listened to the sad stories with a sense of despondency. He did not want to be a casual labourer all his life – he had worked too hard for that – yet there seemed to be nothing for him in the fishing fleet.

'Cheer up, boy! If all else fails there's always the *Muck* Pot' Harry clapped him cheerily on the back.

'Abe Skinner's boat? You mean she's actually got home?'

'Yes, 'gainst all the odds. The devil looks after his own, that's certain.'

'Where is she? In the inner harbour? Or should I go to Abe Skinner's house do you think?' Jed leapt to his feet.

'Lor', I weren't serious!' protested Harry.

'I am! If there's one man who'll need an extra hand it's Abe Skinner.'

'No one with any sense sails with 'e! 'E'm drunk more times than 'e'm sober, and as for his boat... ! Jed boy, that idn't a proper craft, 'tis a load of flotsam looking for a beach to be washed up on! 'Tis a laughing stock! 'Ee can't sail on her.'

'She's still afloat, isn't she?'

'Yes, only just!'

'Then I'm going after a job on her.'

Jed hurried off, Harry's objections still echoing in his ears.

Abe Skinner's boat was easy to find. Officially, and incongruously, called the *Swan*, it was by far the scruffiest, most dilapidated craft in the harbour. It was a floating mass of rust, splintered timbers, peeling paint, and frayed ropes. By some miracle she kept going, limping from port to port, disaster to disaster, until she had become a bad joke the whole length of the Devon coast and beyond.

Jed found her skipper easily enough. He was still aboard, for the simple reason that he was too drunk to get himself ashore. The stench in the cramped cabin was enough to take anyone's breath away, but Jed did not flinch.

'You'll be wanting an extra hand,' he said. He made it a statement, not a question, confident that Abe Skinner was always in need of an extra hand!

'Yesh, I be!' was the slurred reply.

'In that case I'll be aboard first thing Monday morning,' said Jed.

And that was how he became part of the crew of the *Swan*, better known to all Brixham as the *Muck Pot*.

Chapter Ten

To say that the *Swan* limped into harbour was an exaggeration. She barely crawled in. As she tried to round the New Pier her mainsail, ripped from top to bottom, gave up the unequal struggle. It emptied of what little wind it contained, and hung lifeless, bringing the smack to a virtual halt. Fortunately she was close enough in for willing helpers to manhandle her round the pier end to a mooring. Harry was one of those who helped her in.

'There now, Jed, you'm a sight for sore eyes,' he said. 'Us thought 'ee'd gone this time.'

'I thought so myself once or twice,' Jed admitted wearily. 'That was a stiffish breeze, wasn't it?'

''Ee never said a truer word. I knowd the *Swan* was astern of us when us started to run for home, and that was the last I seed of 'ee. Us was some worried and no mistake.' Harry looked at the smack. 'This old girl wadn't never no beauty, but now her'm in a real sorry state. 'Tis a miracle 'ee managed to bring her in. Howd 'ee do un?'

'I got out and pushed,' replied Jed, somehow summoning up the energy to smile.

He could not remember when he had last been to sleep. He had spent hour after interminable hour clinging to the helm through the worst storm he had ever experienced. His whole body was one massive ache of fatigue: his fingers were rigid with stiffness, his eyelashes encrusted with salt, and his eyes so red and inflamed he could hardly see.

The other trawlers had cut their losses and run for shelter. But Abe had been full of the obstinacy of the half-drunk.

'Load of damned li'l maids, afeared of a bit of a breeze,' he had chortled. ''Tis the real men as'll stay out and get the good catches.'

Jed had done his utmost to persuade him to change his mind, but it was no use.

It had been more than a bit of a breeze. The wind had freshened into one of the worse gales in years. By the time the danger of their situation penetrated Abe's alcoholic bravado it was almost too late. The *Swan* was in no shape to make a speedy dash for safety, she had been forced to ride out the storm as best she could. By then Abe had been well and truly drunk and it had been Jed who had brought them safely into harbour.

'You get yourselves home,' said Harry. 'I'll get some of the lads to unload for 'ee.'

'Thanks.' Jed was grateful for the offer. 'I'll hang on for a bit, but you two go.' He nodded to the hands who had shared the ordeal with him. At a guess they would not be aboard the *Swan* when she set sail again.

'What about Abe?' asked Harry.

'Best leave him,' Jed replied.

'Sleeping it off, eh? I don't know how you stand un, I really don't.' Harry shook his head in disbelief.

Jed waited until the meagre catch had been unloaded and transported to the fish-market, then he turned his attention to the sleeping Abe.

'Leave un there,' advised Harry.

But Jed would not. 'He had a hard time of it like the rest of us and he's no youngster. We'll take him home.'

He was so exhausted his own words were as slurred as any drunk's. As he made to step ashore his legs refused to obey him. He would have fallen if strong hands had not caught him. 'Steady as you go,' Todd Prout's voice said. 'Amy'll be that relieved to hear you'm all right. Her were mortal worried about you.'

Jed could do no more than twitch his face into the semblance of a smile. Someone had been concerned about him. That was nice. In fact, he was surprised at the many hands that clapped him on the shoulder and the voices that murmured, 'Glad to see you back safe, boy.'

'If you'm dead set on getting Abe to his home we'm going to have to carry him,' said Harry from the deck.

'Best take him in a barrow,' said Todd. 'Hang on a minute and I'll give you a hand.'

The three of them trundled the skipper to his house. Or rather, Harry and Todd did the trundling. It was as much as Jed could do to put one foot in front of the other.

'Sling un on the floor. Over there, where I can't fall over him,' was Mrs Skinner's unemotional reaction to the return of her husband. An untidy, fat slummack of a woman, she seemed to have had the feeling knocked out of her long ago, but when Jed handed her the wholesaler's receipt for the fish she bit her lip before replying, 'You'm a good man, Jed Greenway. It was a lucky day for Abe when 'ee stepped his way. He'd not've come out of this by himself, not the way he is these days.' Then she spoiled the tender moment by adding sharply, 'The drunken old sot!'

'I don't envy poor Abe tomorrow,' chuckled Harry. 'Come on then, boy, let me give 'ee a hand.'

'Can manage!' slurred Jed in protest.

'I dare say, but 'ee'll manage twice as quick if I helps a bit.' Refusing to be discouraged, Harry supported him the rest of the way home.

Jed remembered the children running to meet him, and Sally laughing and crying at the same time and wiping her face on her apron. After that there was a blur, then nothing. He woke up to find himself in bed in the makeshift room on the landing. For a while he lay dozing, trying to get his wits together. His mouth was dry, the skin on his face and hands was sore where the salt wind had burned him, and he was ravenously hungry. Apart from that he felt fine. Judging by the sun it was early evening; he must have slept for several hours. Rather stiffly he rose, washed and dressed, then went downstairs. Sally was peeling potatoes. She looked up as he entered, and beamed.

'My, you'm back in the land of the living!' she exclaimed.

'Only just.' Jed gave a huge yawn. 'That was a rare sleep I had. How long have I been out? Nine – ten hours?'

'You'm way adrift,' laughed Sally. 'A whole day out in your reckoning. 'Twas Tuesday when you went to sleep. 'Tis Wednesday now.'

'It can't be!' He was astounded, then he grinned. 'No wonder I'm starving and could drink the well dry.'

'You sit yourself down, and your dinner'll be ready in no time. Or do I mean breakfast?'

'I'll eat it whatever it's called,' Jed assured her.

They did not talk much until he had cleared his plate and downed four cups of tea.

Sally tidied away the dishes and sat down opposite him, an unusually grave expression on her face. 'I think us should have a serious talk.'

'Why, what have I done?' asked Jed in alarm.

''Tidn't what 'ee've done, 'tis what you'm going to do! You'm going to leave Abe Skinner and find a decent boat to sail on! 'Twas touch and go with 'ee out there. Don't expect to be so lucky in the next storm. That old pile of rubbish can't stand no more, and neither can my nerves. Harry's sure Old Man Burton'd have 'ee back like a shot now his temper's cooled.'

'No!' said Jed firmly. 'I'll never go back to him.'

'Then what about some other boat? I don't know what's kept 'ee so long on the *Muck Pot*.'

'Old Abe's not that bad. He lets me have an extra share of the catch sometimes, especially when we're short-handed.'

That was not the only reason. With Abe often drunk and with a crew which changed from one week to the next, Jed usually had charge of the boat. He was the skipper in all but name. Also, improvised repairs were a way of life on board the *Swan*, such was her dilapidated state. Through sheer necessity Jed had learned how to mend just about anything, from torn sails and parted rigging, to more serious matters such as sprung planking and a leaking hull. One way and another he felt he had squeezed half a lifetime's experience into the last two years, and he appreciated it.

'I should think Abe Skinner does pay 'ee over the odds,' said Sally indignantly. 'Everyone knows that 'ee've doubled his catches. You'm getting him more drinking money. No wonder he'm grateful. 'Ee should be looking to better yourself, Jed. Else why've you bothered to get your skipper's certificate?'

'I'll make a move soon.'

'See 'ee do! And while you'm about it 'ee can start looking for a nice girl. You'm a good man wasted, Jed Greenway! 'Tis high time 'ee was courting.'

'I'd be wasting my time,' grinned Jed. 'All the best women are taken.'

'Go on with 'ee,' chuckled Sally delightedly. 'There, 'ee habn't had your sleep out yet,' she said, as Jed stifled another yawn. 'Just 'ee bide there and rest some more.'

When Jed went down to the harbour next morning he met with a depressing sight. The *Swan* was decidedly low in the water. The ancient timbers of her hull had been unequal to the battering they had received. She was leaking like a sieve. He left her to go and report to Abe.

Abe Skinner was sitting morosely at his kitchen table, a blanket round his shoulders, when Jed arrived.

'Her won't let me out,' he said, jerking his head in the direction of Mrs Skinner. 'Her says I've took a chill and've got to stay in house. And you don't looks as if you've good news, neither.'

'I haven't,' said Jed. 'The *Swan* is in a pretty bad way. I pumped her out as best I could, but she's still taking in water. She'll have to be beached and have some proper repairs done. Shall I have her towed round to John Prout's if she'll make it?'

'Bad as that, eh? You sure it idn't nothing you can fix? Ah, well, in that case John Prout had best take a look at her. Though where the money's to come from I don't know.'

'Talking of money…' Jed prompted.

'Eh… ? Ah, yes. Your share be on the mantelpiece, in the cloam dish.'

Jed pocketed his money. 'I'll see about getting her to the boatyard straight away,' he said. 'The sooner the better, the state she's in.'

He regarded Abe with concern. The skipper was shivering, despite the warmth of the kitchen and his blanket, and his face looked more haggard than usual.

'Your wife's right,' Jed said. 'You don't look good. You'll be better off staying at home. I'll see to what's necessary.'

'Then keep they pumps going – and be sure to go steady when they'm towing her.'

'Don't worry, I won't let her sink.'

'No, I don't suppose you will... And Jed, thanks a lot for everything!'

Jed gave a brief grin, then, raising his hand in farewell, left the Skinners' house.

Getting the *Swan* to Prout's boatyard was no easy task. It took some hectic pumping to keep her afloat.

'I'll go over her soon as I can, and let you know what's to be done,' said John Prout.

'If you wants my honest opinion I think kindling wood's all she'm fit for,' Charlie Bowden, the foreman shipwright said grimly.

'Let's not look on the black side till us sees what's got to be done,' retorted John.

John's verdict, when he delivered it, covered two whole sheets from his notebook.

'He'm making work for hisself,' said Abe, pushing the list away. 'Us could do most of it ourselves.'

Mrs Skinner picked up the list and read it.

'John Prout's an honest man. Leastways, I habn't never heard no different,' she said. 'What's your opinion, Jed? Be he trying to make his fortune out of us?'

Jed shook his head. 'Some of the repairs we could do ourselves, certainly, but an awful lot of it needs a shipwright. There are some major timbers to be replaced, and whole sections of planking – that's craftsmen's work.'

'And we'm only talking about the hull yer,' said Mrs Skinner. 'Us haven't even mentioned nothing about rigging or sails, let alone the gear.'

'Oh, the sails'll be no problem!' Abe waved an airy hand. 'A bit of work patching up, then I'll take un to the barking-yard for a good soak. That'll do for they.'

'No, it won't,' said Jed firmly. 'The mainsail's ripped completely in two, and as for the others, they're so worn there's nothing left to hold the patches. We need a new suit.'

'New sails on the *Swan*?' Abe laughed at the idea. 'They'd pull the heart out of her.'

'One thing's for sure. Us've plenty to think about.' Mrs Skinner waved the list. 'And us idn't doing nothing hasty. You idn't fit for it, and neither's the boat.'

'Don't take no notice of her,' said Abe. 'I'll be along to Prout's Yard presently. I'll have the old *Swan* back fishing in no time, see if I don't.'

'You idn't going nowhere until that chill's off you,' said Mrs Skinner, in a voice that brooked no argument. 'As for the boat, us'll have to see. 'Tidn't a matter of ramming a few rags in a leak and doing a bit of caulking this time. Even I can see that. Jed, boy, us'll let you know what us decides as soon as I can talk some sense into this old fool. There idn't no contending with both the sea and the bottle, not at his age. He'll have to give up one or t'other, and since he don't seem able to give up the bottle, there idn't much alternative. Can you manage for a bit, do you think?'

'I can manage,' Jed assured her, and got a grateful smile in return.

He went back to the harbour with a feeling that history was repeating itself. Here he was, looking for work once more, albeit perhaps temporarily. For once luck was on his side. The owner of a crabber took Jed on while his partner recovered from a broken arm. He would be kept on for a few weeks. From what he had seen, the broken arm would be mended long before the *Swan* was fit to go to sea again – if she ever was.

When he called at the Skinners' house a week later, he was shocked at the deterioration in the skipper in such a short time. He seemed to have shrunk, and his flesh hung loose about him. In front of him, on the scrubbed table, was the inevitable glass and bottle of spirits. He pushed the bottle invitingly towards Jed, who declined it.

'Us've come to a decision,' said Mrs Skinner. 'Any road, us've had the decision made for us. Doctor says his fishing days are over, and no arguing.'

'Bloody doctor! What do he know?' grumbled Abe.

'He knows what's good for you, which is more'n can be said for you, you daft old fool,' replied his wife. 'In a way it's made things easier, for now there idn't no point in us scratting and scraping trying to get enough money together to put the boat back in the water. Jed, you'd best look for a permanent job somewheres else. Us be grateful for all you've done these last two years, and we'm rare sorry to lose you, but there idn't no help for it.'

'I'll be sorry to leave you,' said Jed honestly. 'But it hasn't exactly come as a surprise. Don't worry about me, I'll soon find something else. What abut the *Swan!* What's going to happen to her?'

'We'm going to sell her, if us can find a buyer.' Mrs Skinner had established herself as spokeswoman. 'Not that us can sell her as a floating concern, so to speak. John Prout reckons us'll only get the price of her timber.'

'John Prout's a damned idiot,' Abe growled.

'No he idn't,' retorted Mrs Skinner. 'I sent my cousin Elsie's husband, as served his time as a shipwright down to Upham's, to have a look at her, and he says the same: ""Twould take a deal of money, a lot of time and a danged idiot to try and get her afloat again." They was his very words.'

Abe did not reply. He seemed to shrink into the heavy folds of his blanket. Jed felt sorry for him. He was a decent man spoilt by alcohol, was Abraham Skinner.

Since he had an hour or so to spare before it was time to set the crab-pots, Jed decided to walk out to the boatyard to take one last look at the *Swan*. She was a pathetic sight, hauled up on the beach, the signs of her final battle with the elements all too evident. It made him sad to see her like that. Shabby, dilapidated, and a laughing stock she may have been, but she had somehow managed to keep going. There had to be a strong heart in her somewhere.

The crunch of feet on the beach pebbles sounded behind him. He turned round to see John Prout approaching.

'It looks as though the old girl's had it at last,' John said.

'I can't say I'm looking forward to seeing her broken up,' sighed Jed.

'No, indeed.' John sighed too and gave the weed-covered timbers a fond pat. 'She were a grand li'l craft in her day, you know, and still would have been if Abe had spent the boat's share on her instead of the booze. My missus's dad built her in his hey-day, and my, did he know what he was about then. A real master-craftsman. Only the very best timber for him, each bit seasoned a good ten years. And it paid off. Look at that!' He jabbed with his pipe stem. 'I went along every inch of that keel, and it's still absolutely sound. Finest elm, matured proper, that's why.'

While John Prout had been talking, Jed had been conscious of the hairs at the back of his neck standing up.

'Mr. Prout,' he said. 'Someone said it'd take a deal of money, a lot of time, and a danged idiot to try to get her afloat again. Do you agree with that?'

John thought for a long time before he replied.

'Yes,' he said at length. 'I do.'

'You mean you think she could be repaired?' Jed's voice betrayed none of the excitement that had suddenly gripped him.

'She could be repaired,' agreed John. He looked at Jed shrewdly. 'But if you'm thinking of making an offer, friend, I'd advise you walk round Berry Head a few times to clear your brain. 'Tisn't summat to be taken on lightly. Her idn't much more than a wreck as her stands there.'

'I know that. And to be honest I haven't a lot of money. But I do have plenty of time. I'm prepared to work and wait, and I'm certainly idiot enough to try to refloat her.'

'Well, I suppose there idn't no one knows her better than you,' admitted John. 'And you've a list of everything as needs doing; you can't have no illusions.'

'I haven't,' said Jed. He could have admitted that he did have dreams. 'There are two things I need to know before I really get down to thinking about this. First, could I leave her here, near your yard?'

'Yes, you'm free to leave her here; I don't own the beach. I'd prefer it if her were a bit out of sight, mind,' John added with a grin. 'Her don't exactly give the place a good name.'

'I couldn't afford to have all the repairs done at once. Some I can do myself, but the skilled stuff – would you be prepared to do them a bit at a time? When I've got the money together?'

'Certainly. Us'll do anything you'm prepared to pay for, specially when us hasn't got no boat on the stocks. Anything else I can tell you?'

Jed shook his head. He had more than enough to occupy his mind for the present.

'You wants to buy the Swan?' Abe stared at him in amazement.

'Yes, what's left of her,' Jed replied. 'I'm offering you every penny I've got, which should be a shade more than you'd get for her timbers alone.'

'Her'm youm!' Mrs Skinner spoke up before her husband had time to open his mouth. 'I think you'm touched in the head, but that be your affair.'

'Wait a minute, woman!' objected Abe. 'Don't be so hasty. I reckon her'm worth a deal more than he'm offering.'

Jed's heart sank.

'Well, you'm in a fool's paradise there,' retorted Abe's wife disparagingly. 'Jed's given a firm offer. He can't pay no more. Hasn't he just said so? I'd rather have his money to hand than have to wait for someone as might or might not want to buy her timbers. Us can't afford to be choosy.'

Abe snorted and snuffled, his blanket drawn up tightly about him, every line of his muffled body expressing doubt and disagreement. Jed watched him, hardly daring to breathe.

'You'm to pay John Prout's fee for towing her round to the yard and beaching her, mind,' Abe said suddenly.

'All right,' agreed Jed with intense relief. He was not certain how he could afford the extra amount, he just knew he would manage it somehow.

'Then 'tis a bargain.' Abe stuck out a considerably shrunken hand. 'You'm now the owner of the Swan.'

Jed went away from the Skinners' house feeling that he was floating above the ground. It had been far easier than he had anticipated. The Swan was his! He owned a fishing boat – at least, she would be a fishing boat again by the time he had finished with her. A rare need to share his excitement came over him, and he found his feet leading him to Paradise Place.

'You're a stranger these days,' Amy greeted him when she saw him on the doorstep. 'A very welcome one, though. Come in.'

He followed her into the kitchen then came to an abrupt halt. Effie was sitting on the floor banging on an old saucepan with a wooden spoon. As Jed entered she paused in her noisy game and looked up. He caught his breath. Her light-blue eyes, anxious at his intrusion, were exactly like Seth's. Then she cried, 'Up. Up,' and held out her arms to her mother. Amy scooped her up and held her close. Jed's breathing returned to its normal rhythm. Now he looked at the child again, her colouring and the shape of her face made her resemblance to Amy more striking. It was only in her eyes. And maybe he was the only one to note the similarity.

'What's your good news?' Amy asked, after Jed had refused any refreshments.

'How did you know?'

'It's written on your face. It must be something pretty special, because you don't usually give much away. Come on, tell me.'

Jed hesitated. He had no doubts about what he had done, but if Amy should disapprove or laugh or call him a fool then he knew the pleasure he felt at that moment would dissipate.

'Jed, if you don't tell me what this is about instantly I'll – I'll crown you with Effie's saucepan!' cried Amy.

'I've bought the *Swan*.' He waited tensely for her reaction.

'You haven't!' She was incredulous. Then, when he did not deny it, a wide smile spread across her face. 'Your boat! You've got your boat! I always knew you would.'

'It's not much at the moment. More of a wreck, really.'

'You can work on her. Where is she?'

'On the beach by Prout's Yard.'

'And what does John say?'

'He thinks she can be repaired.'

'Well, John wouldn't say that if he wasn't sure.'

'There's a lot to be done.'

'You can take your time. You aren't planning to sail her immediately, I don't suppose.'

'Oh, no. I think it'll take me a good three years, what with the work and getting the money together to do the job.'

'Three years!' Amy's smile widened as she considered it. 'And if it takes longer, four years say, it's not long to wait if you know you'll be sailing your own smack at the end of it. Skipper Greenway. Doesn't it sound grand? How can you sit there so calmly? In your shoes I'd be bursting with excitement.'

'You approve, then?'

'Of course I approve. Did you ever doubt it?'

Jed shook his head. 'Not really,' he admitted.

'I must go and see her. Do you mind if I take Effie up this afternoon?'

'Of course not. She's nothing to look at.'

'I won't notice that. I'll be seeing her as she will be when you've got her smart and seaworthy again. I'll come to see her refloated. I'll buy a swanky hat specially for the occasion.'

'You've plenty of time to save up for one, at any rate.' Jed rose to his feet.

'You aren't leaving already?' Amy looked dismayed.

'I must, I'm afraid.' He smiled at her. 'Us boat owners have things to do.'

'You still haven't come on a visit. A proper visit, I mean.' She looked at him reproachfully.

'I will,' he assured her. 'One day.'

Sally and Harry thought he had taken leave of his senses. Most of the fishermen round the harbour told him he was completely daft. Even Mr Cranford at the post office, on the day he withdrew his savings to pay Abe Skinner, looked at him over his spectacles and said, 'A big step, Mr Greenway. I do hope you have not been imprudent.'

Jed did not feel imprudent. Nor did he care what anyone said. He owned a boat, and Amy approved of what he had done. As far as he was concerned, nothing else mattered.

As she closed the door behind him, Amy reflected that it was the first time she had ever seen Jed really happy. She wished he would look that way more often; he was far too serious. Sometimes she worried about him. He was on his own too much. He was comfortable with the Prestons, and they were good, kindly folk, but he was still only a lodger. She wished he would find someone of his own and settle down.

'You idn't never going to guess what that friend of youm's been and done,' announced Todd when he returned at midday.

'Which friend? Jed? Let me see if I can guess.' Amy pretended to ponder. 'I know. He's eloped with Ma Griggs?'

'No. Even dafter than that.'

'In that case, there's only one thing left. He's bought the *Swan*.'

'You knowd, you wretch, and you had me on a piece of string.' Todd made a mock attack at her.

'He came to tell me, not long since.'

'I hope you told him he should sign up for the asylum.'

'No, I didn't. He's made his mind up to get the boat back in the water, and I'm sure he'll do it. He's a very determined character, is Jed.'

'I dare say he is. Determination only goes so far, though. He'll be an old man afore that wreck floats again.'

'Your John thinks she can be saved.'

'You know our John. He can't bear to see an old boat broke up. Is that where the *Swan* is? Over to John's?'

'Yes. I thought Effie and I could have a walk over to look at her this afternoon, if you don't mind.'

'Why should I mind, my lover? I think I'd better go up and have forty winks after dinner while I've got the chance, else I'd have come too.'

'What time are you sailing tonight?'

'About six o'clock.'

'I'll be back long before then to get you your tea.'

'One word of warning. I don't want you two climbing over that wreck. I don't reckon her'm safe.'

'We won't do anything foolish, I promise, you old fusspot,' smiled Amy. 'Besides, John'll be on hand to keep us out of mischief.'

'So he will. I was forgetting. It's just that my two girls is precious to me.'

He often said things like that, and she was never certain how to respond. She took refuge in brisk practicality. 'By the time you get washed your dinner will be on the table, then afterwards it's to bed for you, and for Effie,' she said.

'Just the two of us?' Hope was in his voice as his hands slid about her waist, caressing her for a moment. Then he let her go. 'Perhaps not,' he said regretfully. 'Us'll leave such things for when us has more time.'

He had kept to his word and not made love to her until after Effie was born. He was still considerate and not over-demanding, coming to her as if she were bestowing some great privilege upon him instead of granting him his marriage rights.

'When we have more time for pleasure,' Amy agreed, quelling the faint feeling of relief within her.

Then she felt ashamed. Few men would have asked so little of her, and it was one way in which she could redress the unequal balance of their marriage. It was one thing she had to give him.

Later that afternoon, Amy and Effie set out to see Jed's boat 'Who's this, come to see her Uncle John then?' John Prout held out his hands to take Effie from Amy's weary arms. 'Why 'tis my favourite li'l maid.' And he tossed a delighted Effie in the air.

'How's Jessie?' Amy asked.

'Fine. Her were asking only the other day when this scamp was coming up to see us again.' And he tossed Effie once more, making her laugh.

'I'll bring her up soon,' Amy promised. 'Tomorrow, perhaps. It depends when Todd gets back.'

'Jessie'll like that,' said John approvingly.

She knew that Jessie's enjoyment would be selective. On the surface the relationship between the two sisters–in–law seemed amicable enough. Amy realized how far Jessie was from forgiving her for besmirching the Prout name by marrying Todd. But Jessie's determination to uphold family solidarity was as strong as ever: any misgivings she might hold in private were never allowed to show beyond the family boundaries. When Amy had expressed her gratitude and surprise at Jessie's willingness to look after her when Effie was born, her sister-in-law's reply had been blunt and unequivocal: 'I'm doing it because you're family now. No one's ever going to say I don't know where my duty lies.'

Where Effie was concerned, however, Jessie's sense of family obligation mellowed into devotion. She loved the little girl with every inch of her child-hungry heart, until Amy began to sense that she was tolerated by John's wife because she was Effie's mother.

No one ever doubted that Effie was Todd's child, although Jessie had once declared, 'The maid reminds me of someone about the eyes, though for the life of me I can't think who. She certainly didn't get them from her father or mother.'

Amy's heart had been in her mouth, afraid her sister-in-law would pursue the subject further in her determined way. It had been John who had come to the rescue.

'Grandma Prout!' he had said with conviction. 'The babe's got her great-grandma's eyes. Her's the spitting image.'

Amy had had to bend down to keep her face hidden, in case her relief had shown too clearly.

'I suppose you'm come to see Jed Greenway's boat.' John's voice broke into Amy's thoughts. 'What a carry on that is, eh?'

Swinging Effie on to his shoulders, he began to stride across the pebbles with Amy at his side.

When she saw the *Swan* out of the water, supported by strong timbers, Amy's heart sank. Minus masts and rigging, and with long fringes of green weed hanging to her splintered timbers, the vessel had a defeated air about her.

'Will she really float again?' she asked.

'Her'll float,' said John, 'if young Jed idn't too impatient. There's a few years' work there, I reckon.'

He sounded so confident that Amy's spirits rose again. Jed was on his way to realizing his ambition, and she was very happy for him.

After that, she often took Effie out to Breakwater Beach to see what progress Jed had made on his boat. Occasionally he would be there working.

'Not much to show for my efforts so far,' he would say. 'I'm still paying off the towing bill,' or, 'I'm cleaning her down. It's a nice cheap job while I save up for some good, seasoned timber.'

Enjoyable as it was watching the *Swan* slowly regaining something resembling a hull, Amy found just as much to interest her as she walked through the boatyard. There was always something going on; a new boat being constructed, an older craft in for repairs. Most of the men were well-known to her from the time when she had brought John his dinner every day, and they would always spare a minute to chat to her. The sweet smell of freshly-cut wood evoked in her an unexpected pang of nostalgia. There were few things she missed about her time as a servant, but visiting the boatyard regularly was one.

Memories of her earlier servant days made her grateful for her present way of life, but marriage to Todd was not all plain sailing. As a father he was ideal, as a husband he was kind and considerate, but where finances were concerned he was as incompetent as ever. Amy tried to make allowances. Sometimes, though, her temper snapped. Todd drank far less than in his bachelor days, but the occasions when he was enticed into the George or the Buller's Arms by his cronies were frequent enough to cause a sizeable hole in their meagre income. And he still could not resist spending money on useless toys and jokes, particularly now he had the excuse of keeping Effie amused.

''Twas only summat to make the babe smile,' he protested when Amy complained about his latest purchase, a clockwork monkey which banged a tin drum when wound up.

'You're always buying her things we can't afford!' exclaimed Amy in exasperation. 'How much did it cost? A shilling? One and six? That money could have gone towards the rent. Goodness knows, it's going to be hard enough to get it together this week with you at home!'

'You don't begrudge the li'l maid some amusement, surely?'

'I don't begrudge it We can't afford it. You don't seem able to understand the fact.' Amy knew her voice was sharp with anger, but she was tired and hot, and the light airs of the last few weeks had made fishing poor and money short 'If Effie wants to make a noise she can bang a saucepan with a spoon, like she usually does. She'll go back to it, anyway. It's her favourite toy.'

''Tidn't my fault there idn't no fishing at the moment,' Todd retorted. 'I'd be out there like a shot if there were the least breeze. What's it you'm wanting me to do? Row the danged trawl along?'

'It would stop you throwing money away,' Amy snapped.

'Right, I'm going out!' retorted Todd, but before he reached the door a loud wailing scream from Effie brought him to a halt.

'Now see what you've done,' cried Amy, gathering the child into her arms. 'She's cut herself on that wretched gewgaw you bought!'

Todd rushed back, lull of contrition.

'Poor mite! Oh, look, her poor li'l finger's bleeding. If I idn't the daftest fool there is. Not the sense to make sure there weren't no sharp edges on the blasted thing afore I gived it to her.'

He was so upset by his omission and the pain it had caused Effie that Amy's heart softened. 'It's not bad,' she said, uncertain whether she was comforting the child or the man. 'Just a cut. We'll give it a wash, then tie a bit of rag round it, eh?'

Once cleaned, the wound was out of all proportion to the noise it had provoked, but Effie was inordinately proud of her bandaged finger, especially since the two ends of the white rag had been left long. That had been Todd's idea.

'They'm bunny's ears,' he had assured the child. 'That's a li'l old bunny you'm got on your finger.'

The idea had so intrigued Effie that she had forgotten her tears. 'Yer, I'll take her out of your road for a bit' He picked up the child. 'Us'll go and sit on the doorstep in the sunshine for a spell and see what that there bunny gets up to, shall us?'

Amy watched them go, completely absorbed in each other. She felt sorry for the sharp words she had spoken to Todd. His inability to handle money was his one true failing; he was very good in other respects. It was unreasonable of her to expect him to be perfect.

Because of the heat, the doors and windows stood wide open and, as she sorted out the ironing that had been set to air, Amy could hear Todd's voice telling Effie a story. It seemed to consist of the bandage rabbit having a variety of adventures which involved loud animal noises. Listening to Effie's chuckles Amy wondered, not for the first time, at the power of Todd's imagination. He seemed able to think up an endless supply of tales that inevitably held Effie's rapt attention.

'You'm mazed, Todd Prout. You knows that, don't 'ee?' said a voice.

Glancing through the window, Amy saw the stout form of Mrs Cobb, who lived two doors down. A solid figure, in her too-tight buttoned boots, Betsy Cobb was always called in for deathbeds, layings-out, and similar emergencies. It was a gloomy calling that had affected her temper. Mrs Cobb was quick to criticize and almost never gave praise, so Amy was not surprised at the sour note in her voice.

'Yes, you'm mazed as they come. A grown man sitting there making daft noises to a chile,' the old woman went on, then added unexpectedly, 'but maybe 'tis a pity there aren't more like 'ee. There'd be fewer crying childer, that's for sure.'

Her words stung Amy's uncomfortable conscience. She should not have lost her temper with Todd. For the thousandth time she told herself what a good man he was and how much she owed him. The one thing she wished she could give him was a child of his own: Effie was growing away, and was steady on her feet; now would be a good time. But there were no signs of another pregnancy.

Her arms filled with clean clothes, Amy went upstairs to put the things away. The bedroom, once starkly furnished with only a double bed, now contained a large cupboard and Effie's cot. She began stacking Todd's clean clothes in the cupboard. His shirts and underwear soon adorned the shelves in neat piles, but his socks were another matter entirely, particularly the long thick sea-boot stockings she had laboriously knitted for him from oiled wool. When the same pair had refused to stay put for the third time, Amy lost her patience and rammed them in place. She used more force than she intended and sent the contents of the shelf tumbling to the floor, including Todd's box.

Amy had always regarded the box as Todd's private province.

'There idn't naught in it you can't see,' he had protested when they were first married.

Amy had been adamant. After her years in the workhouse she knew only too well the value of having somewhere private.

'A man's got to have somewhere of his own,' she had insisted. 'Otherwise where are you going to keep the love-letters from your other women?'

They had joked about it, although Amy had been serious in her intention never to pry. And now, through a moment's carelessness, she had sent the box's contents flying. Speedily she picked them up.

They were an innocent enough collection – his apprenticeship indentures, a blurred sepia photograph of his parents, Sunday school certificates, and a collection of old school exercise books. One of these books looked newer than the rest, and it did not have his name on the cover. A shameful curiosity overcame her and she opened it.

Inside, penned in Todd's scrawling copperplate, was a collection of poems. They were simple poems about simple everyday things – the changing seasons, the sea, the sky – yet expressed beautifully. Amy was not surprised Todd had chosen to copy them down. She could not help reading on, wondering where he had found these verses. They had not come from any of his books as far as she could recall.

She had to turn just one more page. It was then she saw her name, 'Amy'. Beneath it was a love poem, full of tenderness and adoration. There was also an underlying note of sadness, for it was a plea from the poet to be loved in return. Amy read it over again and again. It took three readings before her suspicions were confirmed. The poem had not been copied from a book. None of them had. Todd had written them, every one. And the Amy of the title was her!

Todd was a poet, and a good one. She should have been astounded, but she was not. Her mind was too absorbed by another, more shattering discovery. Todd loved her. She had suspected it for some time; now she knew for certain. A terrible sadness swept over her, along with self-reproach. She did not love Todd in the way he longed to be loved, and he knew it. The moving yearning in the poem had betrayed that all too clearly. He deserved her love, so why couldn't she love him?

Full of remorse, Amy put her head down on her knees and wept. I'll try harder to love you, she sobbed silently. I'll try, I really will.

It would have been easier if she had not known the passion, the wonder, the ever-hungry emotion that love of Daniel had engendered in her. She was painfully aware how hard it would be to fan the affectionate feelings she had for her husband into something resembling that experience. But she would try. She would try!

Her brief storm of weeping over, she scrubbed her eyes hurriedly with a corner of her apron. Gathering the books and papers together she put them into the box and returned them to the privacy of the cupboard.

—

That autumn the skipper of the *Vigilant* took Jed on as second hand. Amy was delighted. With Todd and him sailing together it broke down the uneasy near-hostility that had existed between them. Jed was less reluctant to call upon her, although he never became a frequent visitor. These more amicable relations also meant that Amy was kept up to date with the progress of rebuilding the *Swan*. If Jed himself did not tell her of the latest developments, then Todd passed on the news on his behalf. Amy found herself becoming increasingly interested and involved in the boat's restoration. When the *Vigilant* was spending the summer off the Welsh coast, it was to her that Jed appealed if he needed anything.

Reading his latest letter she was forced to smile. It was an innocent enough request for her to order him some pine planking for when he returned. Following the insistence that it should be one-and-a-half inches thick was the phrase, 'I showed this letter to Todd, and he agrees it is the most suitable thickness.' Amy gave a chuckle. Jed's letters always included a sentence like that. He was letting her know he was writing to her with her husband's full knowledge and approval. Dear Jed, he was so meticulous about everything. She was glad he and Todd had become friends, for she cared about them both very much.

Since the day she had read his poetry Amy had worked hard at loving Todd. She had become conscientious in all the little intimate gestures that lovers exchange – the swift kisses in passing, the embraces for no reason, the smiles, the soft words. Sometimes she feared she was making scant impression on her own emotions, but at least Todd was happy.

The winter that year was remarkable for the biting cold. The wind blew unceasingly from the east, bringing with it iron-hard frosts rarely known along the South Devon coast. It was particularly arduous for the fishermen, struggling against temperatures so severe that even their clothes froze. After each trip they returned to port exhausted. Todd was no exception.

Now as Amy waited for him to come home she made extra sure that the kitchen was cosy and welcoming. The fire was banked up; it just needed a touch with the poker to bring it into life. A meat and potato pie was keeping hot in the oven, its savoury smell adding to the comfortable ambience. Lamplight filled the small room with a golden glow. She did not like the long dark nights, and now that it was January she was already looking forward to the brighter evenings. Everything was peaceful. The wind had dropped, no longer whistling down Paradise Place, but it was raining hard. Satisfied that everything was ready she sat down by the fire with her knitting. He would not be long now.

The sound of footsteps echoing along the narrow alley made her wake with a start. Todd was home! Thrusting her knitting-needles back into their basket she hurriedly mended the fire. In spite of her careful preparations she had let it die low. She glanced up at the clock on the befringed mantelpiece. It was nearly midnight.

A heavy knock on the door caught her unawares. Todd would not knock. She hurried to open it, the lamp held high in her hand. Illuminated on the doorstep was Jed, his hair plastered down with the wet, his face pale against the dark sheen of his oilskins.

'Can I come in?' he asked quietly.

She knew why he was there.

'Todd?' she said.

Jed stepped into the passage, closing the door behind him.

'Yes,' he said.

Todd was dead. The look on Jed's face spoke more clearly than any words. The oil-lamp in her hand wavered alarmingly, sending bizarre shadows leaping across the wall. Jed took it from her and steered her to a chair in the kitchen. He remained standing, the water from his oilskins trickling into puddles on the floor.

'They're bringing him home,' he said. 'Skipper sent me on ahead of them.'

'What happened?' she asked eventually, the words sticking in her throat.

'He tried to save the ship's boy. You know young Tommy Webb? He lives — lived — up near the church with his mother and sister. He was on the bowsprit, repairing the jib tack, when he fell. Todd went in after him. He didn't think twice, just dived straight over the side. He got hold of him, too, but when we reached them they were both… It was bitter cold out there. I think that was what did it, not drowning.'

For some reason Amy remembered Seth and his fear of being covered by the water, unable to breathe. She was glad that had not happened to Todd.

'The skipper's gone up to Tommy's family. He was Tommy's uncle, you see. I said I'd come to you. I didn't want you to hear it from anyone else.'

'John! He'll have to know!'

'One of the other lads has already gone.'

Jed's plain recital of the facts helped. Flowery expressions of condolence would have confused her, muddled her thoughts. Todd was dead. The knowledge was too new for her to grasp. She could not cope with it. Jed's simple statements enabled a part of her mind to accept that she must stir herself. The other half of her was as cold and as numb as if she, too, had been in the icy water.

'I have things to do,' she said, getting up from the chair.

'Can I help?' Again there was no fussing from Jed.

She looked at the grate. Her poking had made hardly any improvement.

'The fire,' she said. 'Would you blaze it up?'

Like an automaton she went upstairs, stripped the bed and remade it with fresh linen like an automaton she came downstairs again and set Todd's clean nightshirt to air in front of the rejuvenated fire. It was stupid, she knew. An unaired nightshirt could not affect him now, but she could not help herself. All the time she was listening for the sounds of Todd being brought home. Outside, there was silence. She refilled the kettle, fetched clean towels, had the big bedroom jug ready to take upstairs… And still they did not bring Todd home.

She could bear it no longer. Snatching a shawl from behind the door, she put it over her head.

'Where are you going? You'll get wet,' said Jed.

'I'm going to watch out for them coming.' What did it matter if she got wet?

Jed did nothing to hold her back. He followed behind her, keeping his distance, yet letting his presence be a comfort.

Paradise Place should have been in darkness. Instead there was movement everywhere, a rustling of clothes as people hurriedly began dressing, a rattling of coal buckets as fires were relit, a sudden resurgence of light as lamps and candles burst into life. By some aged, well-worn instinct, Brixham knew there had been another tragedy out at sea and was preparing to mourn.

Asthmatic puffing and tottering footsteps announced the arrival of Mrs Cobb, a sixth sense having told her that her services would be needed. She had a folded piece of clean canvas in her hand.

'You'll be needing this for the bed,' she said.

Amy looked at her uncomprehendingly.

'I've just changed the bed,' she said. 'Clean sheets!'

Mrs Cobb's expression was unexpectedly kind.

'He'll be wet, my lover,' she said gently.

This simple realization struck Amy more forcibly than anything else had done, and she drew in a sharp breath.

From the direction of the beach came a new sound, the regular tread of feet stepping in unison. They came into view, dwarfed by the high stone walls of the sail lofts at either side, their way lit by hurricane-lamps swinging beside them. A sombre procession of fishermen carrying a form on a stretcher. Despite the rain they were bareheaded out of respect for the dead. The only sound was the crunch of their boots and the stiff rustle of their oilskins as they walked. As if at some prearranged signal the doors of Paradise Place opened, and folks stood on their doorsteps in varying stages of undress, silent and respectful as the improvised cortege passed by.

Amy stood aside to let the fishermen enter the house. Mrs Cobb, well used to such affairs, had gone ahead, and stood at the top of the stairs holding a lamp to light the way. It was difficult getting the stretcher with its canvas-shrouded burden up the stairs. Following in their wake, Amy noticed with disinterest that the streaming oilskins were leaving wet trails along the whitewashed walls like snail tracks. Then the men left, muttering awkward words of sympathy to her, till only Mrs Cobb and Jed were left.

'I'll stay,' Jed said, 'until the Prouts arrive. Then I expect you'll want to be left alone.'

Amy did not know what she wanted. She did not know anything any more.

'I'd best go and help Mrs Cobb,' she said.

With surprising gentleness Mrs Cobb removed the canvas covering the body. This isn't Todd! was Amy's first reaction. Not this cold, white, sea-wet creature they had brought home to her. Todd was always so warm, so alive. So alive! What a stupid thing to think. She was glad she had not said the words aloud. She noticed that his fingers were roughly bandaged, and went to undo them.

Jed shot out a hand to stop her.

'Please don't,' he said. 'He had a tight grip on Tommy. A very tight grip.' They had had to break his fingers to part him from the boy. How close he must have come to saving him. How pitifully close... 'Is there anything I can do?'

'Fetch us some warm water, there's a good lad,' said Mrs Cobb. 'Then leave us alone. This is woman's work.'

Amy worked with Mrs Cobb, stripping Todd of his wet clothes; then they washed him and put on him the clean nightshirt so incongruously aired by Amy. Mrs Cobb was wheezing with the effort by the time they had finished. They had barely drawn the clean sheet over Todd when John and Jessie arrived. They came hurrying up the stairs.

'This be terrible,' said John. His face had taken on a pinched look. 'Our Todd! This be terrible!'

He put his arms about Amy in a gesture of sympathy, although his eyes were constantly drawn to the still figure in the bed.

Mrs Cobb drew back the sheet. 'There, he looks proper handsome, don't he?' she said with satisfaction.

Jessie burst into tears, and a muffled sob came from John. Amy remained unmoved. The figure on the bed did look handsome, like one of the stone effigies in the churchyard, but she could still not believe it was Todd.

'Us could all do with a hot cup of tea,' said Mrs Cobb authoritatively. 'With a drop of summat strong in it, as well. I come prepared.' She rummaged in the basket she had brought, and produced a bottle of brandy.

'I'll go down and make sure the kettle's boiling,' said Jessie, dabbing at her eyes with a handkerchief. 'It's a miracle Effie's slept through all this, bless her. You're not to worry about her when she wakes up, Amy. I'll see to her. But first I'll make that tea.'

'You go on down with Jessie.' John gave Amy's hand a gently squeeze. 'I'll come down presently and have a word with Jed. I presume he were there when it happened? For the moment I'll stay yer...'

Amy understood. He wanted to be alone with his brother. She squeezed his hand in return, then obediently followed Jessie downstairs. While her sister-in-law bustled about, vying with Mrs Cobb for control of the situation, Amy allowed herself to be guided into a chair once more and plied with tea laced with spirits. She was glad to see Jed still there. He was a great source of strength to her although he said little.

Quite by chance she glanced at the clock. It said half-past two. Then the irony if it struck her. She gave a strangled noise that was part laugh, part sob. When the others looked at her with concern she could not explain. How could she tell them she had just realized what day it was? It was her wedding anniversary. She and Todd would have been married three years exactly.

Chapter Eleven

The funeral procession moved slowly up the hill, following the hearse drawn by black-plumed horses. For Amy everything had assumed a dream-like quality. No, that was not the right word – nightmarish would be more appropriate. She had a sense of not being involved, of merely observing this scene of grief, like a bird flying high overhead. She could not believe that Todd was dead. She had a feeling that there had been a mistake, and that the sorrowing around her was unnecessary.

The cortege came to a halt at the church gates, the horses' hooves slipping slightly on the damp cobbles. The oak coffin was slid from the hearse on to waiting shoulders. They were all Prouts who bore it towards the church: John, two cousins from Newton Abbot, the brother from up-country who somehow looked like Todd yet did not, and a couple of his sturdy sons, young and over-awed in their black suits. Only Joseph, the brother in America, was missing. Still Amy did not feel that this panoply of mourning had anything to do with her. The coffin was a wooden box, nothing more. She paid close attention to the graveside service, accepted the murmured condolences politely – and felt nothing.

There was no change in the days which followed the funeral. Her brain knew that Todd was dead, but her heart was unable to grieve. Her life continued in its old pattern, even to her spending the evenings knitting the most recent pair of sea-boot stockings she had started for Todd. Why shouldn't she? She was waiting for him to come home. At any minute Todd would come striding along the alley as usual, easing off his boots the instant he was inside the door, slinging his stocker-bait into the stone sink as he always did.

To maintain her old daily routine, that was what she strove for. There were some differences, naturally. Not a day passed when she was without company. Either Jessie, John or Jed would drop by to see that she was 'all right'. She was not all right, of course, but she did not know what to do about it.

Effie was restless and distressed. As well as missing Todd she was disturbed by the unaccustomed comings and goings. Yet even as she tried to comfort the child Amy felt nothing.

The bleak east wind continued to blow sharply. It was biting enough to cause pride and fashion to be abandoned as hats were discarded in favour of much warmer shawls. The female population of Brixham was so muffled up as to be almost unrecognizable. Thus wrapped against the cold, Amy set out to do her shopping one morning, glad that Jessie had taken Effie up to her house for the day. It was far too inclement to trail a child about the shops. In spite of the weather there was a fair number of people about, and when she went to buy vegetables at the market house she had to wait to be served. Nearby a group of fishermen was sorting out nets ready to be mended, chatting to each other as they did so. Amy took no notice until Todd's name caught her attention.

'I hear Lennie Pollard's on the *Vigilant* now,' said one man. 'Been took on in Todd Prout's place.'

'That were a sad thing, that were,' replied the second, 'for Todd and young Tommy Webb to go together.'

'Trust old Todd,' the first speaker snorted scornfully, oblivious to the fact that Todd's widow was within earshot. 'Always were a fool. Couldn't never get naught right. You could bet he'd make a mess of things.'

Amy listened in disbelief. How could anyone say such cruel things about Todd? She knew she should fly at the man and demand an apology, but the apathy that had gripped her since Todd's death slowed her responses. Before she could consider what to do, a girl shot out from somewhere up ahead, and launched herself at the fisherman, pummelling him with her fists. Her shawl fell back, and Amy recognized her as Maggie Webb, the sister of the drowned boy. Usually she was a quiet, mouse-like creature, but now she lashed at the man with all the effort her slight frame could muster.

'How dare 'ee say such things, Dave Tozer?' she cried. 'Saying such things about Todd Prout! You idn't fit to utter his name, that you idn't. But for he our Tommy'd be lost out in the cold sea, like Pa and our Freddie. Because of Todd us could lay him in the churchyard, decent like. He give his life to save our Tommy. 'Tis Ma's only comfort. "Todd Prout give his life," her says, "Us can't ask more'n that." He were a fine man, was Todd, and a proper hero. And 'ee calls him a fool? Where was 'ee when my brother went overboard, Dave Tozer? Answer me that. 'Ee didn't do naught to help him, did 'ee?'

As suddenly as it had begun, the girl's onslaught ceased, and she collapsed sobbing into the arms of a motherly bystander.

'There, there, my lover, don't fret,' soothed the woman gently, then in a far sharper voice she addressed the fisherman. 'See what 'ee've done, Dave Tozer, with that gurt mouth of youm?' she demanded. 'I hope you'm proud of yourself.'

Dave Tozer looked shamefaced. 'I be real sorry, Maggie, my maid,' he said contritely. 'I were out of order there, and no mistake. I shouldn't have said they things about Todd. 'Twere a rare thing he done. I wadn't close enough to help when it happened, though if 'ee wants the honest truth I idn't sure I'd have had the courage to go in the sea after anyone, me not being able to swim.'

No more could Todd, thought Amy, yet it hadn't stopped him. No one had recognized her, shrouded in her shawl, and she pulled it closer about her, shielding her face as she crept away. She should have been the one to defend Todd's memory, not Maggie Webb, yet she had done nothing. The shame of her inaction made her hate herself as blind instinct caused her to dash for home. Almost outside her front door she cannoned into someone.

'Amy, maid, what be the matter?' demanded a voice.

Looking up she saw the kindly features of her brother-in-law.

'Oh John! Oh John!' she cried in her distress.

Without further preamble he took the key from her unprotesting fingers, unlocked the door and helped her in.

'Now then, tell me what've been going on,' he said.

'Down by the market— one of the men— he called Todd a fool and— Oh, John, I did nothing! I kept silent and let Maggie Webb speak up for him. He was my husband, as good a man as ever was. I didn't value him properly when he was alive; I didn't love him enough; and I couldn't defend his memory now he's dead. That's the sort of wife your brother had. Oh, John, I didn't love him as he should have been loved – as he deserved to be loved... He should have married someone better.'

Amy leaned her head against John's waistcoat as her narrative ended in a storm of weeping. The emptiness inside her had vanished, filled at last by a surge of grief.

'He did just fine in the wife he chose. You was the one he set his heart on. He were happier with you and the li'l maid than at any time I can remember—' John's voice suddenly broke and became unsteady. 'And— and don't you blame yourself if you didn't always give him his due. You idn't alone. None of us did, even me. Ever since he were a li'l tacker us didn't have no expectations of Todd. He were always a bit different, no good at the things the rest of us was good at. Us never looked to see what he could do... Us never thought he'd end up a hero like one of they fellows in the books he was so mad about... Always with his head in a book, he was, and us laughed at him. Us shouldn't have done that. Us should've given un a chance—'

For a moment they stood there, sharing their sorrow, unable to speak.

Then Amy, her cheeks wet with tears, said hesitantly, 'He wrote poetry, did you know that? Real poems, not just silly verses.'

'Our Todd did?' John was astonished.

'Yes, would you like to read them?'

'I would, maid. Indeed I would.'

Amy fetched the exercise book. But first she tore out the one called 'Amy' and put it in her apron pocket.

'That one's personal,' she explained.

John nodded in understanding, then settled himself at the kitchen table. Amy watched as he turned the pages, seeing disbelief, then wonder and pride cross his face as he did so.

'Our Todd wrote these, you say?' he asked incredulously. 'They'm fine pieces. Better'n a lot of the stuff they learned us at school. I idn't a great one for such things, but even I can tell they'm good. The one about the sea when the sun have just gone down, that's exactly how it is in the dimpsey, at twilight time. And he described it real beautiful, I could fair see it. And our Todd wrote all they?'

Amy nodded. 'If you like I'll copy them down for you,' she said.

'That would be grand, if it idn't too much trouble.'

'To be honest I'd be glad of something to do.'

'How'm you'm managing, girl?' John asked kindly. 'That's what I came to find out. I had to go down the bank so I thought I'd drop by while I had a minute.'

'I'm glad you did,' said Amy honestly.

'You'm getting by well enough?'

'Yes, so far, thanks. Everyone's been very kind, you and Jessie especially.'

''Tidn't naught kind about it. You'm family, you and the chile. And you idn't to worry about the future, do you hear?'

Amy nodded, although she was not quite sure what he meant. 'Well, I suppose I must be going.' John rose to his feet 'There idn't no point telling you not to grieve, I knows, but there idn't naught for you'm to reproach yourself with. You was a good wife to our Todd, and you made un very happy. They's the things which matters.'

Amy sat quietly for a while after John had left, thinking how silent the house was. While she had been in her numbed state she had not noticed. She was beginning to realize now that she had many things to cope with, things like sadness and loss and loneliness.

Eventually she forced herself to stir. Jessie would be arriving soon, bringing Effie back. As she rose she noticed four half-crowns on the corner of the dresser. They had not been there earlier. It was not the first time since Todd's death that John had left money behind for her. He was good to her, as was his wife. Jessie's basket always contained welcome additions to the larder such as a packet of tea, rashers of bacon, a pound of butter. Jed, too, kept a benign eye on her. Often he brought her his share of the stocker, and the discarded splintered timbers of the *Swan* were added to her firewood stack.

'You shouldn't bring this to me,' Amy had protested at receiving a sackful of wood already chopped. 'Sally Preston could do with it.'

'There's more than enough coming off old *Swan* for the pair of you,' Jed had pointed out.

Everyone was very kind, making sure she was not in want, but nothing could make up for the loss of Todd. Sometimes the pain of missing him was so keen she almost wished she could be back in her numb state of limbo once more. She could not, of course. Somehow she had to go on with her life.

For the first time she began to look to the future – through necessity not through optimism. How was she going to make a living for herself and Effie now that Todd was gone? They had no savings. A sum had come from the Friendly Society, and there had been a subscription in town for her and for Tommy's mother, but together they had not come to much. No matter how prudently she managed her finances, she would be forced to seek work soon.

The next time John called she had the copies of Todd's poems ready for him.

'Thanks, they'm something I'll always value,' he said when she gave them to him. He turned the neatly written pages admiringly. 'You'm certainly got a neat hand. I takes my hat off to anyone as is good at handwriting. Can't abide it myself, although I gets to do plenty. Give me a decent adze or a chisel and I knows where I'm to, but a pen…!'

'I enjoyed doing it,' Amy admitted. 'I always got top marks for penmanship at school. But I don't do much these days.'

'Ah, you saying you don't do much these days reminds me. I've a bone to pick with you, my girl.'

'You have? What've I done?'

'You'm been asking about town for work, that's what you'm done.'

Amy smiled. 'Is it possible to do anything in Brixham without everyone knowing?' she asked.

'Not much. Is it true?'

'Yes, of course it is. I must find work, otherwise how will I support myself and Effie? Rely on the quartern loaf and shilling a week I'd get from parish relief?'

'There idn't no need for you to go out to work, neither. Jessie and me, us means to see you'm both comfortable. It won't be as much as we'd like, but 'twill mean you won't have to leave the li'l maid and go off scrubbing floors and whatnot.'

'I can't let you do that,' said Amy abruptly. 'It's kind of you and Jessie – no, it's more than that. It's wonderful of you to want to do this. But I can't accept.'

'Why not?'

'Because I can't. It wouldn't be right.'

'I don't see why. You wouldn't be running us short nor nothing. 'Sides, 'tis only right and decent for me to take care of my brother's family. He'd have done the same for me.'

'I can't accept,' said Amy with increasing distress.

'I still don't understand why. 'Tis fine for you to have your pride, but think about Effie. Be you'm going to leave her while you'm to work when it idn't necessary? Poor li'l soul, her've lost her pa, her'll want her ma more'n ever.'

'I know! I know!' Amy cried. John's gentle insistence was driving her close to panic. 'It isn't anything to do with pride. There are reasons, good reasons why I can't accept your kind offer.'

'If 'twere only you, girl, then I'd say "Fair enough" and hold my peace. But 'tis the li'l maid I'm thinking of. What reason's strong enough to turn down help offered for her sake?'

John Prout could be obstinate when he chose, and Amy saw that he was not readily going to take no for an answer. Yet she knew she could not accept. It would be neither fair nor honest. Her only course was to tell him the truth.

'You don't have any obligation towards us,' she said. 'You owe us nothing. Effie isn't Todd's child.'

She tensed herself for the explosion of amazement, anger and disgust. 'The offer still stands,' said John without surprise.

'You knew!' Amy exclaimed.

'I've knowd from the beginning. Todd told me hisself.'

'Does Jessie—?'

'No, nor will she unless you chooses to tell her.'

With an effort Amy collected her thoughts. John had known all the time and never once betrayed that knowledge. No, that was not quite accurate. She remembered with gratitude the occasion when he had insisted upon Effie's resemblance to Grandma Prout. Dear John, he was a good man. As good as his brother. But, owing him so much already, she did not see how she could put herself further in his debt.

'You understand now why I can't take the money you offer,' she said quietly.

'No, I don't. If Todd were happy to accept Effie as his, then that's good enough for me. Please let us help. You'm going to put me in a terrible pickle with Jessie if you says no,' he added, with an expression of comical dismay. 'For I'd be proper stumped to find a reason that'd satisfy her.'

Amy came to a sudden decision.

'Very well, I accept your offer with many thanks and upon one condition: I'll work for you.'

John looked rather startled.

'I don't know about that,' he said. 'Us don't need no more help in the house now we'm got one of Bessie Milton's brood. Driving Jessie mazed her is, her'm that stupid, but her works well enough.'

'I didn't mean work for Jessie. I meant work for you.'

'Me? You intend coming to serve your time as a shipwright or summat?' John grinned.

'I would if I didn't think it would cause too many raised eyebrows.' Amy managed to smile. 'No, I was thinking of doing your office work. You've just admitted you hate writing letters and things. You'd have to show me what to do, but I'd soon pick it up.'

'There isn't no need...'

'Yes, there is. I work for the money or I don't accept it.'

'Of all the pig-headed females... Oh, very well, I suppose I don't have no choice.'

'I'll come twice a week to start with. I wonder if Jessie would have Effie, then? You could deduct some money to cover it if she will, I'd have to pay someone else to look after her.'

'What, pay Jessie to look after the li'l maid?' John chortled at the idea. 'Bless you, her'd pay you good money to get the chile to herself regular.'

'Then it's agreed?'

'Yes, 'tis agreed. I don't have no option, do I?'

From then on, two mornings a week, Amy went out to the boatyard to work in the stone-built shed which served as an office. At first there was a certain amount of leg-pulling from the men.

'I sees we'm getting some of they 'mancipated women down yer now,' remarked Charlie Bowden on her first morning. 'I didn't expect them to take over boat-building though.'

'Don't blame me. 'Tweren't my idea,' said John.

'You've nothing to worry about for the moment, Charlie,' said Amy. 'I'm only starting in the office for now. It'll be a week or two before I get round to your lot. It'll give you time to get your work up to scratch.'

'Up to scratch? Did 'ee yer that?' demanded Charlie in mock indignation. 'I can sees us having to mind our Ps and Qs and no mistake. Us'll be wallpapering the fish-rooms next and doing cut rugs to go in the cabins.'

'Just 'cos I'm employing one woman don't mean we'm starting to hold mothers' meetings,' said John pointedly. 'Us idn't getting no work done while you'm jawing.'

Still grinning, the men dispersed.

Not all the workers approved of having Amy in their midst. One in particular, Sid Dendy, was especially vocal on the subject. She was hurt and surprised, for in her servant days Sid had always been friendly.

'You never objected when I used to bring Mr Prout his dinner every day,' she protested, when his comments had been more barbed than usual.

'That were different. You was just visiting. A boatyard's no place for a woman permanent.'

'Why not? I'm doing a good job. There haven't been any complaints so far.'

'That's as maybe, but where's us going to be if women starts taking the place of men and putting them out of work?'

'I didn't take anyone's place!' retorted Amy, angry at his attitude. 'John Prout was doing the clerking himself until I took over. No one's lost his job because of me.'

'That don't alter things,' snapped Sid belligerently. 'You'm taking away work from a good man.'

Amy took a deep breath.

'It's because I lost a good man that I need the work,' she said quietly.

'Oh…!' Sid had the grace to look ashamed. He turned away without another word.

His was not the only opposition that Amy encountered, but gradually the grumblings and the mutterings faded as the men grew accustomed to her presence. Within a few weeks it was as if she had always worked there.

Amy found herself thoroughly enjoying her work. She learned how to cope with the letters, the bills, the invoices, and the order-books easily enough. Coping with John's erratic filing was a different matter, and it took some effort before she finally evolved a simpler, more efficient method. The primitive office left a lot to be desired by way of comfort, but she was usually too busy to notice.

'Hullo, I didn't expect to see you here.' A voice from the doorway interrupted her one morning. Amy looked up from her work to see Jed standing in the doorway.

'I'm the new clerk, didn't you know?' she smiled.

'No. When I heard John Prout saying he'd got a better way of dealing with his letters, I though he had bought one of these modern typing machines.'

The idea of such advanced technology in that cramped old shed made Amy chuckle.

'No, just me,' she said. 'Not as up to the minute, but just as efficient. And I can make tea!'

'With qualifications like that I can't see you ever being replaced.'

'Have you come to work on the *Swan* or do you want to see John?'

'Neither, really. I came to see how Charlie and his men are getting on.'

'Very well, I hear. They're working on the deck beams at the moment.'

She looked at him curiously. Now she was working at the boatyard she knew how much the boat was costing Jed. It was a pretty penny. 'The *Swan* must be taking everything you've got,' she said. 'Do you never spend anything on yourself?'

'Not often.' Jed held out the ragged sleeve of his jacket. 'Sally says I should hire myself out as a scarecrow to make a bit extra.'

'I met her yesterday,' Amy said. 'She's worried about you. She thinks it's time you got married.'

'Sally's dying to play matchmaker, that's her trouble.'

'Why don't you let her? I'm sure she'd find you someone very nice.'

Jed grimaced. 'I can't be bothered with things like that at the moment,' he said. 'What would I be doing with a wife when I'm up to my ears in debt?'

'Are you having regrets?' Amy asked, suddenly anxious.

'About buying the *Swan*.' He looked at her incredulously. 'Certainly not! It was the best thing I've ever done.'

'Even though you're burdened with debt?'

'It's only temporary. When she's afloat I'll pay off everything I owe in no time.'

Amy relaxed. Lack of determination was not one of Jed's failings. If that was all it took to succeed then he was destined to be triumphant However, she fancied that it also required a share of luck, and she fervently hoped he would have that too.

Jed said goodbye and went off to look at his beloved *Swan*, leaving Amy to get on with her work. She had not been busy for long before she had a second interruption. A slight, balding man stood in the doorway.

'Why, Mr Rogers, I didn't think you would be in today,' she said.

Cedric Rogers was an accounts clerk, and a good one. Unfortunately weak lungs forced him to eke out an inadequate living doing the books part-time for one or two small businesses such as Prout's.

'Oh, Mrs Prout, I quite forgot that today was one of your days,' he said. 'How foolish of me.'

'Can I do something for you?'

'No, thank you. I'll come another time. Yesterday was my usual day for bringing Mr Prout's accounts up to date, but I was ill. I meant to make up time today, forgetting that you would be here. Please tell Mr Prout I'll be in tomorrow without fail.' He tipped his hat to her and would have gone away if Amy had not called him back.

'You don't look well,' she said. 'This place is far too small for us both to work at the same time, but why don't you sit down and have a rest?'

She pushed a chair towards him, and Mr Rogers sank into it thankfully, closing his eyes. He did indeed look ill. His complexion was grey, and perspiration beaded his face although the day was not warm.

'Is there anything I can get you?' she asked. 'Some water? A cup of tea?'

'No, thank you. If I might just sit here for a few minutes... ?'

Amy returned to her work, leaving him to sit quietly as he had requested. After a while she was relieved to see him with his eyes open, looking rather better.

'You should not have come today, you know,' she chided him gently. 'The place for you is in bed.'

'That is what my wife said.' Mr Rogers smiled his gentle smile. 'But I do hate letting Mr Prout down, and I am already one day late in seeing to his books.'

'I am sure being two days late won't make too much difference.'

'It might. Besides, when people are kind enough to employ me and rely upon me I feel it is my duty to keep up to date with their accounts.'

'Is there nothing I can do?' asked Amy. 'If you showed me something of what is required, couldn't I do it for you? I could bring the accounts to your house tomorrow for you to check. I'm sure Mr Prout wouldn't object under the circumstances.'

'Would you? Could you? Such kindness...' Looking hopeful Mr Rogers rose to his feet, but swayed ominously and had to sit down quickly again. 'Perhaps if I showed you some of the elementary principles?' he said when he had recovered. 'That way I would not be so far behind. If we start with the ledger...'

249

It was accountancy at its most basic. Not much more than cross-referencing bills and receipts, and entering the details in the ledger. By the time Mr Rogers departed, somewhat unsteadily, Amy had enough work to fill in one long, lonely evening.

''Course I don't mind,' John said, when she explained to him. 'Poor soul, he'm not going to be able to work much longer. A shame for him, and for me. I'll have to look about for someone else.'

Mr Rogers was of the same opinion when Amy took the books to his house some time later. He regarded her work and nodded his head approvingly.

'Excellent. This has saved me a lot of work.' He looked at her gravely. 'Mrs Prout, I fear I'm going to have to retire very soon. This is getting too much for me.' He waved a thin hand at the ledger. 'Competent accounts clerics are scarce in this town. I would hate to leave your brother-in-law in the lurch, and it has occurred to me that I should train a successor to carry on after me.'

'That seems a good idea, if you feel up to it,' said Amy. 'Have you anyone in mind?'

'Indeed I have, dear Mrs Prout. You!'

'Me?' Amy was astounded. 'Oh, I couldn't! I haven't got the schooling.'

'Please forgive me if I contradict you. I think you are quite capable of taking over from me, after some training, of course. You have a sharp intellect – Mr Prout has sung your praises to me many times – and you have proved that you are quick to learn. Any inadequacies in your education can be overcome without too much trouble I am sure, if you have the will.'

'I have the will,' Amy replied immediately. The challenge of the project was already exciting, but one thing surprised her. 'I don't think I've ever heard of a female accounts cleric before. You've no qualms about suggesting a woman for the job?'

'None at all. I believe you ladies to be capable of achieving anything you set your heart on. My dear wife is an excellent example.'

Amy understood what he meant. Because of her husband's ill-health, Mrs Rogers was the true bread-winner of the family.

Somehow she managed to combine teaching music with running a home, nursing a semi-invalid, and rearing a large brood of children.

'Besides, you already work as a cleric in the boatyard.' Mr Rogers gave a smile. 'I understand that in London it is becoming quite the thing for young ladies to do office work. Don't you think it would be nice to show that here in Brixham we can be as go-ahead as in the capital?'

'I do indeed,' said Amy. 'And if my brother-in-law is agreeable then I will certainly accept your offer.'

Mr Rogers was looking tired now, and still very far from well. She rose to her feet.

'I must be on my way,' she said.

'Then I will await Mr Prout's decision with great interest. In the meantime, perhaps this book might be of some use to you.' He passed her a small, well-thumbed volume called *Elementary Bookkeeping*. 'I suggest you do not try to absorb too much at once. The first two chapters should suffice to begin with.' Again he managed to smile his gentle, weary smile. 'I do not intend to relinquish my post to you too soon.'

Amy hurried home, the book clutched in her hand, her head in a whirl. That such an opportunity should come her way was incredible. Usually one had to pay for such instruction, yet here was Mr Rogers offering to teach her for nothing. If only John would agree…

John scratched his head when she put the matter to him.

'I don't see why not, I suppose,' he said. 'The way poor Mr Rogers looks these days 'tis plain I'll have to find someone else soon. If he thinks you can cope, then that's fine by me. One thing, though. When you take on his work you'm to take on his pay as well, and no arguments… No arguments!' he repeated as Amy opened her mouth to protest. Then he grinned. 'I don't hold with not paying workers. They'm harder to sack if they'm idn't no good.'

'Sack me if you dare, John Prout,' she retorted, laughing. 'I'll be so good at my job you'll wonder how you managed without me.'

Admittedly those days were some time coming. It took a while for Amy, working under the patient guidance of Mr Rogers, to learn enough about debit and credit, compound interest, and double-entry bookkeeping to feel confident of doing the job alone. At night, when Effie was asleep, she would study the book Mr Rogers had given her, often cursing the basic nature of her own education. At the workhouse school, what she had studied had not even been graced with the title of mathematics; it had simply been called arithmetic.

She went on missing Todd. Her life continued to consist of a hollow emptiness. That was why she was grateful for her job at the boatyard and for the extra study required by her bookkeeping. For a few hours they did block out the awful void. In spite of John's comforting reassurances she went on feeling remorseful. She had underestimated Todd, she had not loved him enough, and it was too late to do anything about it: this was retribution with a vengeance.

In the autumn two major events happened in Amy's life. One was that Cedric Rogers' health finally forced him to take to his bed permanently. Ready or not, she was in sole charge of the boatyard finances.

The other thing was that she met Daniel.

It was early morning. She had just taken Effie up to Jessie's and was on her way to work. As she was hurrying along the road towards the boatyard she came face to face with him. It was extraordinary. He seemed just as young and boyish, his eyes had that same quick intelligence about them that had always delighted her. He was perhaps a little more weather-beaten now, but that was all. In his dark-blue uniform he looked extremely handsome. Amy was half inclined to hurry past him. So much had happened to her in the last few years that she felt she must be unrecognizable.

'Amy, can it be you?' He stopped, blocking her path, removing any chance of her pretending to ignore him.

'Good morning, Daniel,' she said, hoping she sounded calm. 'How are you?'

'Extremely fit, thanks. And you?'

'Very well, thank you.'

They were being so civilized. Two polite acquaintances meeting on the road.

'I was sorry to hear news of your husband. His was a very brave action, I've been told. Such a pity it cost him his life.'

'He died a hero,' she said simply.

'Your child will grow up being proud of its father.'

There was something different about him. A greater maturity, no doubt born of his years as an officer. Authority and responsibility had left their mark.

Then, unexpectedly, his composure seemed to desert him. 'Amy, we met like this once before. Head on, on a pathway.' He spoke with a sudden urgency, his voice unsteady with emotion. 'I said some terrible things to you that day. I've regretted them ever since. I was in no position to judge you, I see that. My only excuse is that I was deeply unhappy. Will you forgive me?'

Amy drew in a sharp breath. 'There is nothing to forgive,' she said. 'I know how it must have seemed to you. There were circumstances that I couldn't – can't explain, even now. I minded very much that I had hurt you. I tried hard not to, but I never blamed you for what you said to me. I felt that much of it was justified.'

'That is a far more generous answer than I deserve, though I suppose I should have expected such a response from you, knowing you and lo… knowing you as I do.'

He had been going to say 'loving'. Amy was glad he had stopped himself in time. Already her heart was thumping in her breast, for she was finding this encounter as difficult to cope with in its way as their last had been. Then Daniel had been all pain and anger, and she had expected nothing less. Now that he was being regretful and apologetic she did not know how to respond. She had almost forgotten the strength of his appeal to her, but the moment she had set eyes on him she had felt it again, tugging at her forcefully.

'Would it be impolite to ask where you are off to at this early hour?' He had got his feelings under control again, and had returned to being the concerned acquaintance. But his green eyes continued to glow with emotion.

'I'm off to work. I'm clerk to my brother-in-law, John Prout.'

'At his boatyard?' Daniel looked at her with surprise, then he gave a chuckle. 'How like you to have found yourself such unusual

253

employment! And I'm sure you're making a great success of it. Didn't I always know you had ten times more spirit than any other girl!'

'I'm not a girl any more,' she smiled.

'No, you are right. You are a woman now, and a very beaut…' Again he stopped, then rallied himself. 'We can't carry on a conversation like this in the middle of the road. Can we meet again sometime?'

'Yes, we can.' The words were out before Amy could stop them.

'Good.' His whole face lit up, as if illumined from inside. 'Where? Our old place?'

'No.' Once more her response was instinctive. Then she said more gently, 'Not there. Too many ghosts.'

'Perhaps you are right.' He smiled at her. 'I know, I'll call upon you. It's permitted now, you know,' he said, laughing at the startled expression on her face. 'We are both adult. We have no need of secrecy and crawling about behind elderberry bushes.'

'Maybe not but…' Amy thought of him, in his smart blue uniform, coming through the narrow grimy alleys to Paradise Place.

He sensed her hesitancy. 'Would you object to me coming to your house?'

'No…'

'Then it is no one else's business; and there's no reason why I can't come. Would tomorrow evening be convenient?'

'Yes…'

'Good. Please forgive me if I dash off. I should have been at the shipping agent's a quarter of an hour ago. Until tomorrow then.' For a brief second he swayed, as if about to kiss her, then he saluted her instead and hurried away.

Amy turned her steps towards the boatyard, her mind in a turmoil. Daniel was going to call upon her tomorrow! She could not believe it. Quite how it had come about, and how she had come to give her consent, she was not sure. But Daniel had been insistent, and his quick impatience at being denied anything was as strong as ever.

Her work that morning was disastrous. She found she could concentrate upon nothing. Daniel had entered her life again to the exclusion of everything else, including writing letters.

'You'm idn't sickening for something?' asked John anxiously as she ripped up yet another rejected letter. ''Tidn't like you to make mistakes.'

'I'm fine, thanks. I've just got a head full of sheep's wool this morning.'

'Ah,' John teased, 'you'm going to have to take more water with un in future.'

'I'll remember your advice,' said Amy, summoning up a smile. 'Anything to eke out the gin.'

It was no good, joking did not help. Her nerves remained in such a state of ferment she almost regretted having met Daniel again. That's what she tried to tell herself. Her more honest soul knew that she could not wait for him to come.

Amy was a mass of uncertainty when it came to preparing for his visit. To put on a full meal might seem pretentious, not to say expensive at such short notice, yet she wanted to offer him refreshment of some kind. In the end she laid out some of her precious housekeeping money on a bottle of wine, nuts and raisins, as if it were Christmas, and baked a batch of crisp, almond-flavoured biscuits. The small house was scrubbed and polished until it could stand scrubbing and polishing no more.

With Effie settled down to sleep, Amy finally got herself ready. Her choice of dress was restricted, not just because of economy but because she was in full mourning. In the end she wore a skirt of barathea, and her best blouse of *crepe de chine* ornamented with pin-tucks, its high collar and tight cuffs edged with narrow lace. The starkness of unrelieved black suited her, accentuating the soft-tinted warmth of her complexion and the rich honey-glow of her hair which, no matter what she did to it, inevitably escaped its confines in a mass of gleaming waves. Her only ornament, apart from her wedding-ring, was a silver and jet mourning brooch, a gift sent from Todd's brother in America.

In spite of her careful preparation, Amy remained uncertain about this visit. Her nerves were so on edge that when the knock came at the front door she started violently, sending the nuts she was putting into a glass dish cascading to the floor.

Hurriedly she began picking them up until a second knock reminded her of Daniel's lack of patience. Abandoning the nuts she hurried to the door. As she opened it she knew how much curiosity the handsome figure on her doorstep was attracting. She could feel the inquisitive eyes, and the twitching of lace curtains among those houses in Paradise Place which boasted such luxuries.

'Do I have to stand here? Aren't I allowed inside?' he asked with a grin.

'I'm just letting my neighbours get a good look at you,' Amy replied, holding the door wide for him.

'Ah, the whole of Brixham will know that the beautiful Widow Prout has had a gentleman visitor.' His voice went low and conspiratorial. 'I should have remembered the efficiency of the local telegraph system and crept here at dead of night.'

'It would take more than darkness and a later hour to defeat the gossips hereabouts,' Amy replied. She knew he had been joking and the word 'beautiful' had slipped by her unmarked, but to hear herself called the Widow Prout had stung. She did not feel like Todd's widow, she still felt like his wife. Perhaps that was the cause of her disquiet.

'Ah, well, there's my reputation gone the way of all flesh.'

'Will coming here cause you trouble?' she asked in alarm. 'Will anyone object?'

He laughed. 'You mean will my mother object?' he said. 'No, she realizes that I'm a big boy now and she lets me visit anyone I please. I was only joking, you know.'

'Oh.' She was relieved and a little surprised to find that old habits died so hard.

'This is charming.' Daniel looked round the tiny kitchen-cum-parlour. 'How cosy you've made it.'

A sudden recollection of the rich elegance of the Newtons' house came back to Amy, increasing her unease. That aspect of things had not changed. Their worlds were as far apart as ever.

'I do my best,' she said. 'Won't you sit down?'

'How very kind. Thank you.'

They had become stiffly formal again. Amy had an uncomfortable vision of the next hour or so, spent in rigidly polite conversation. It was a daunting prospect, one she longed to disperse, if she could think of a way.

'No, please take the rocking-chair,' she insisted as he courteously made for one of the less comfortable seats. Determined to be the perfect hostess she added, 'And can I get you some—'

She never got as far as offering him some wine, for as Daniel crossed from one chair to another, his feet shot from under him and he sat down on the floor.

'Oh!' Amy's hands flew to her mouth in horror. 'Whatever happened?' she asked as she helped him up.

'I don't know. I trod on something round and—'

'Nuts!' exclaimed Amy.

'I beg your pardon?'

'Nuts! I dropped some on the floor just as you arrived and I haven't had time to pick them up.'

'I see...'

They stared at each other awkwardly, then the farcical situation got the better of them. They collapsed with laughter, until a fretful wail from upstairs told them they had woken the child.

'That's Effie. I must go up to her. I won't be long.' Amy headed for the stairs.

Daniel shot out a hand and took her elbow.

'For heaven's sake be careful where you tread! This place has been booby-trapped against invaders,' he warned.

The touch of his hand burned through the thin silk of her blouse, driving away any humorous response to his joking. She could feel the imprint of his fingers clearly on her flesh as she went up to comfort Effie.

It did not take her long to get the child back to sleep.

'It's all clear, the traps and snares are gone,' Daniel greeted her as she re-entered the room. 'I've gathered up the nuts, and very good they are, too.' He indicated a pile of nutshells on the plate in front of him. 'In your absence I've made myself at home. I hope you don't mind.' He did indeed look completely at his ease, lounging in the rocking-chair, a cushion behind his head. He had opened the wine and a full glass stood on the table.

'Of course I don't mind.' Amy went to help herself to wine but, before she could grasp it, he poured her a glass with the casual ease of the master of the house.

'Your little girl— It is a little girl you've got? Has she gone back to sleep?'

'Yes. She's very good and soon settles down.'

'And how old is she?'

'Three, and very forward for her age. She's a dreadful chatterbox, her tongue is never still...' She stopped, aware that he was not really interested in Effie. Why should he be? 'But what of you?' she said. 'What exciting voyages have you been on lately?'

Like most seagoing men he was a good raconteur, and Amy listened with rapt attention – and sometimes incredulity – to his tales. It had been a long time since she had laughed so much; she could not remember the last occasion when she had felt so light-hearted. Since Todd's death the hours after dark dragged for her, but that evening fled by.

Daniel looked at his gold pocket-watch and heaved a regretful sigh.

'I'm afraid I had better be leaving,' he said. 'I think I've stayed long enough to set the neighbourhood by the ears.'

'You've probably earned their undying gratitude for livening things up,' smiled Amy.

'And what about you? Have I livened things up for you?'

'Very much.'

'Good, I'm glad. It's been almost like old times, hasn't it? Almost?'

'Almost,' said Amy.

Throughout the evening he had made no reference to how things once were between them, and she was grateful. She was not sure she wanted to be reminded of those days too forcefully. The memories remained close enough to cause pain.

'I've enjoyed being with you very much. Am I allowed to come again, or would that put too great a strain on the nerves of your neighbours?'

She nodded. 'Come by all means, my neighbours thrive on having their nerves strained.'

'Fine. I'm home for a whole month, maybe more, while my ship is in for a refit. We could see each other often in that time.' He rose and, reaching out, raised her to her feet, holding her hand in both of his. 'You've no idea how happy I am that we're only saying *au revoir*,' he said softly. And he bent and pressed his lips to the hand he held captive.

That night, after he had gone, Amy lay awake for a long time going over the events of the evening. Incredible as it seemed, Daniel was back in her life again. Was she glad or not? Her emotions were in too great a turmoil for her to tell.

Daniel called frequently after that. Not frequently enough to cause a scandal, but enough to set tongues wagging.

'You're seeing that Newton fellow again,' Jed said one day. He had come with a sack of firewood for her, which he had stacked with his usual neatness in the shippen at the back.

'And do you object?'

'It isn't up to me to approve or object. It's your business.'

'Then why did you mention it?'

'Because he might be the one doing the objecting.'

'What on earth about?'

'He may not like me coming here. I don't want to cause you any trouble.'

Amy laughed at the idea. 'Don't be so silly. You'd never cause me trouble. And don't you dare even think of not coming here, Jed Greenway. It took me long enough to persuade you to come in the first place.'

'But if you're walking out… ?'

'We aren't walking out! The town gossips have got way ahead of themselves. We're old friends who meet from time to time. He comes here because… Well, where else could we go at this time of year to chat and pass the time? The bar parlour of the Buller's? Have you got anything else to say on the matter?'

'No.'

'Right, in that case sit down and have a cup of tea, and let's hear no more barmy ideas.'

He grinned at the echo of their old Lambeth days in her speech and obediently sat down. Amy poured him his tea and cut him a slice of home-made currant cake. Both the tea and the cake had been on the table ready for when he had come in but, with his natural reticence, it would never have occurred to him to help himself. As she pushed the sugar towards him she reflected that Daniel was not so backward in coming forward.

'Your guttering over the back door's blocked,' Jed observed. 'I'll come and clear it tomorrow.'

'You've enough to do on the *Swan* without taking on my odd jobs too. I'll tackle it myself or get someone else to do it.'

'He doesn't mind getting his hands dirty sometimes, then?'

'Who?'

'The Newton fellow. That's who you meant, wasn't it?'

'No, it wasn't.' The idea of Daniel cleaning gutters was so ludicrous it made her laugh again.

'In that case, I'll do it tomorrow. And don't let me find you've had a go yourself.'

'No, Jed.' Amy pretended to sound demure.

At this point Effie, who had been quietly playing tea-parties in the corner, rose and presented Jed with an empty saucer.

'This is for you,' she said.

'Thanks. What is it?'

'Cake. You're to eat it up.'

Under Effie's wide-eyed gaze, Jed obligingly ate his imaginary cake. 'That was grand,' he said. 'I've never tasted better. It was even nicer than your ma's.'

'Have some more?'

'No, thanks. I'm full.'

'You can have it tomorrow.' Effie took his saucer and happily returned to feeding her family of rag dolls.

Jed watched her with interest. Amy had noticed how fascinated he was by the child's games, particularly the strength of her imagination. She guessed that such fantasy was a new world to him, for play had not been a part of his own childhood. He never sought to intrude, which was probably why Effie, who disliked grown-ups who thrust their attentions upon her, was happy to include him in her games. Sometimes Amy suspected that Jed was rather bemused by the roles he was expected to undertake; he had hardly any experience of such things. But she could tell he was pleased to be commandeered.

When it was time for Jed to leave, Amy said to the child, 'Uncle Jed's going now. Have you got a kiss for him?'

'Yes, I've got one left.' Effie raised her face to him and held out her arms.

This, too, was new territory for him, Amy suspected. Effie was the only one who could ignore his barrier of reserve and show him such open affection. And the child was the only one to whom Jed responded.

''Bye, Effie,' he said, happily accepting her embrace. 'Save me a kiss for tomorrow.'

He was learning.

After he had gone Amy wondered if she had been quite truthful with him on the subject of Daniel. Just saying they were old friends had not been accurate. She and Daniel had been far more than that, and although when they met the conversation never strayed beyond the bounds of mere friendship, the memory of those years of passionate loving hung over them. Neither of them mentioned it, but it was there, so strong it was almost tangible. Amy sensed it would not take much to fan the cold embers of that old love into flame again. Did she want it? That was what bothered her. Two or three years ago she would have said yes without any hesitation. Now she was not sure. Then she shrugged off her uncertainties. It was far too soon to think of things like emotions and relationships yet. She was still bound to Todd's memory.

A few evenings later Daniel called unexpectedly. Her pleasure at the sight of him was tempered slightly by her consciousness of her disarrayed hair and workaday clothes.

'This is a surprise!' she exclaimed.

'A pleasant one, I hope,' he smiled with the confidence of a man assured of his welcome.

'Of course. Come in,' she replied, smiling too. Hurriedly she discarded her apron and the aged woollen shawl she had been wearing. 'To what do I owe the pleasure of this visit?'

'To the fact that I missed you,' he said. 'And to the fact that I was desperate to see you again.'

Amy drew in her breath. It was the first time he had said anything like that to her in years. Her heart resumed its familiar racing.

Daniel stopped abruptly in the kitchen doorway.

'But I'm disturbing you,' he said. 'You're working hard.'

'You aren't disturbing me,' she assured him, somewhat untruthfully. She began to clear the books and papers which littered the table. 'The men get paid tomorrow. I'm making sure the books are straight for the week, then I can make up the pay-packets as soon as I get to the yard in the morning.'

'Why do you do it? Haven't you got enough to do with a house and child to look after?'

'Because it's necessary. We've got to live,' she said. 'No, that's not quite fair. My brother-in-law would happily support us, but I couldn't let him do that, not unless I could do something in return.'

'You haven't changed, have you?' He shook his head in fond disbelief. 'The same old Amy, full of pride and a sense of obligation. You're no different from the girl who used to meet me behind the elderberry bushes and worry herself silly because she thought she was ruining my life.'

'That was a long time ago,' said Amy hurriedly.

'Was it? Was it really?' It was there in his voice, a note of tender longing that she remembered so well from those faraway days.

'Yes, it was. Things are different – we are different now.'

'I'm not.' He spoke with a vibrant urgency. 'Amy, I feel the same way about you that I felt then. These last three or four years I tried to tell myself that I no longer loved you but it wasn't true. I had only to meet you that one time on your way to work and I wanted you as much as ever.'

She tried to speak, only to find herself swept into his arms, his lips seeking hers. In an instant the intervening years might never have happened. A hunger she had all but forgotten welled up in her, sweeping away restraint as she responded to his caresses.

'Daniel! Daniel! Daniel!' Was she crying his name aloud or was it in her head? Her dreams, her bitter-sweet memories were overtaking her in a wave of passion.

'Amy! My sweet, my lovely Amy.'

How wonderful it was to hear the sound of his voice, trembling with love, just as it used to do. Her response was to take his face in her hands, the better to cover it with hot kisses. She could feel his heart pounding against hers, a swift tattoo of passion that sent the blood throbbing through her veins.

'I love you, Amy.' His voice was no more than a moan as his mouth sensuously followed the line of her throat. 'I've been very self-controlled each time I've come. I've been good, haven't I? And all the time I've been desperate for you. We've been apart long enough, Amy. We've wasted too much time.'

She wanted him with a hunger borne of the long years without him. She knew she did, yet when he began to lower her to the floor in front of the fire, his fingers searching for the tiny buttons on her blouse, something inside her froze.

'Please,' she said. 'Please, no—'

'There's nothing to worry about.' He spoke soothingly. 'We love each other, we always have. We belong together.'

'No,' she said with greater determination.

'We'll be married soon,' he said. 'That was what I really came to tell you, until the sight of you made me want you so terribly that everything was driven out of my head. The ship's refit is complete. We've to take her out on trials next week, then I've another fortnight's leave. We can get married and you can sail with me. A voyage to the Mediterranean, an ideal honeymoon.'

'Marriage? Honeymoon?' She was bewildered.

'Yes. Of course we're getting married.' It was his turn to be bemused. 'What else did you think I had in mind?'

She was not sure. She was conscious that she, Todd Prout's widow, had come close to allowing another man to make love to her here, in Todd's own home. A sense of shame swept over her.

'It's… it's too soon to speak of marriage,' she said.

'How can you say that? We've loved each other for nine years, nearly ten.'

'I can't just rush off and marry you like that. I've obligations.'

'If you're talking about the work you do for your brother-in-law, he'll soon find someone else. Clerks are ten a penny. As for the child, it can go to your sister-in-law. She seems to have it for most of the time, anyway.'

Shock at this cold dismissal of her precious Effie took her breath away. For the first time she realized that Daniel rarely referred to her child by name or sex, only as 'it'.

'I couldn't leave Effie like that,' she said firmly. 'And I repeat, it's too soon for me to think of marriage. I'm still in mourning.'

'For Todd Prout?' The scorn in his voice seared her.

'Yes, for Todd Prout! He was a good man and a brave one. His memory deserves respect.'

'Respect it as much as you like.' Daniel's tone now became conciliatory. 'But don't let him come between us any longer. You've worn your widow's weeds for long enough. Forget about him, he's in the past. Marry me.'

'You think that of me?' she demanded with growing anger. 'You think I could cast off the memory of such a fine man as if it were an old coat, of no more use to me?'

'For pity's sake! It's not as if you loved him!'

'I did!' she protested in anguish. 'I did!' And she knew it was true.

'That's nonsense. You love me, you always have done. Look, if it makes you any happier we'll call our first son Todd. How will that be?'

Such insensitivity stunned her. She had found his tactless persistence upsetting, but now he had gone too far. It was as if she were seeing another Daniel, one far different from the idealized being who had inhabited her dreams. One who was impatient, and determined to get his own way, seeing only his own point of view and ignoring hers. A man of any real feelings would have understood and given her more time, respecting her reluctance.

'Please understand, I will not marry you,' she said. 'Now kindly go.'

He could not believe it.

'Amy, if I've upset you… I'll come again tomorrow, we'll talk things over properly—'

'I have no intention of changing my mind. There's no point in you coming tomorrow or any other day. Please leave. I want you out of my house.'

Angry and confused, he snatched up his hat from the table and stalked towards the door.

'I'll never ask you to marry me again,' he cried petulantly. 'Never!'

And he slammed the door behind him, letting the whole of Paradise Place know that he had left for good.

Chapter Twelve

After Daniel's departure, Amy expected to be overcome by regret or sadness or even annoyance. To her surprise she felt a strange sense of freedom, as if some area of her heart which had been restrained had suddenly burst free of its bondage. It seemed odd that there was no longer any Daniel in her life, either in person or as an unfulfilled love that was forever haunting her. He had been a part of her for so long that for a while she felt quite adrift. Never once, though, was she sorry she had rejected him, which was, perhaps, the oddest thing of all.

Gradually she began to look towards the future with new eyes. She realized that, deep down, she had always considered Daniel to be her future. Despite her marriage and everything else that had happened to her, he had always been there on the far horizon. Not any more. Now she was responsible for her own destiny, and Effie's.

Not everyone could understand her contentment. Lizzie Drew from next door for one.

'Now you'm almost out of mourning 'ee can soon start looking about for another man,' she observed. 'Shouldn't be too hard. You'm young and hard-working and still got your looks. 'Ee won't have no difficulty getting some man to take 'ee on.'

'I don't want some man to "take me on" as you call it,' protested Amy laughing.

'That's what you'm saying now.'

'It's true. I've had one good husband, I'm not looking for another. I've got Effie, I've a decent job, and I've my independence. What more could I want?'

'Independence don't keep 'ee warm in bed of a night.'

'No, but look where keeping warm's got you,' Amy pointed out, for Lizzie was expanding yet again.

'You'm right there, girl, I suppose.' Lizzie gave an envious sigh. 'Your waist idn't one inch bigger from having your Effie, but me – I don't recall what my waist's like. 'Tidn't there long enough for me to get a good look at un.'

'And you're egging me on to get married again?' grinned Amy.

'I still says I'm right 'Tidn't natural for a woman to be without a man. Apart from aught else, your chile needs a pa.'

'She's not short of male company. She sees plenty of her Uncle John and Jed.'

'There's an idea. Why don't 'ee set your cap at Jed Greenway? You've knowd him long enough.'

Amy laughed out loud. 'I don't think Jed would notice if I did,' she chuckled.

'Perhaps you'm right. Any road, he'm got too much on his plate with that old wreck of his to think of marrying. No, 'ee'll have to look round a bit.' Lizzie was not going to be deterred.

Amy, in turn, was determined not to marry again. These days she was standing on her own two feet. Such freedom was heady indeed, and she had no intention of giving it up lightly.

John Prout was one who had misgivings about her self-reliance, particularly when her domestic arrangements did not go too smoothly.

'Jessie's not well at the moment, is she?' Amy said when she arrived late for work one morning. 'I didn't want to leave Effie with her, she was looking so poorly, but she was insistent. I could have taken Effie to Mrs Cobb.'

'That idea met with a brave answer, I'll be bound,' chortled John. 'Don't you fret none. Poor Jess don't seem able to throw off that bout of winter colic her had a while back, and her's a bit down. Having the li'l maid'll cheer her up more than anything else.'

'Are you sure? I feel guilty at leaving Jessie to cope when she's ill. Effie's my child, after all.'

'It can't be easy, rearing a young un alone and working yer into the bargain. If you'm finding it too much you'm only to tell me. The offer I made when our Todd died still stands, I'd see you was all right.'

'I know, and it's very kind of you.' Amy was touched. 'I'd be happier working here – unless you are trying to get rid of me tactfully.'

'I wouldn't have to be tactful about it,' grinned John. 'I'd just say "Out", and that'd be it. Seriously, if you'm set upon earning your bread, you could make things easier for yourself. There idn't no need for you to keep living down Paradise. There's room up to our house for you and the maid. It'd save you rent and housekeeping.'

Amy held out her hands in a gesture of helplessness. How could she explain that the thought of giving up her modest cottage made her heart sink? 'It's such an extremely generous offer it embarrasses me to refuse, but I must. Things will be a lot easier soon when Effie starts school. Until then I can manage. Besides, have you thought what trouble two women in one kitchen would cause?'

'You managed well enough not so long since.'

'Circumstances were different then.'

'I suppose you'm right, but the offer's there.'

'I'll remember,' promised Amy.

She had a fair bit of work to catch up that morning. When she had finished she looked with satisfaction at the neatly-penned letters awaiting John's signature, and at the carefully filed invoices and bills, faithfully recorded in the relevant ledgers. Remembering the hesitant start to her clerking career she was surprised to realize how much she had learned in a very short time. And there was much more to learn. That was what made the job interesting.

As she left the boatyard her way took her past the *Swan*. 'No need to stand there idle. I'll soon find you a job.' Jed's voice made her start. Then she saw him looking down at her over *Swan's* stem.

'Sorry, I left my hammer at home,' she called back.

'That's no excuse. Wait there. I'm coming down.' With practised ease he hurried down the rickety ladder, leaping the last few feet to the beach. Together they looked at the hull rising above them.

'If you'd known what you were taking on when you started, would you have bought her just the same?' asked Amy.

'Probably not,' said Jed. 'But I'd have regretted it for the rest of my life.'

'There's certainly been plenty of work done on her already,' said Amy, looking at the many new planks that had been fitted in the vessel.

'And there's a deal more to do before she's fit for sea,' replied Jed.

'You look as though you've been busy, at any rate,' she said, for he was liberally covered in sawdust. 'What are you doing now?'

'Just finishing off bits here and there.'

With so much major work to be done there could only be one reason for him spending time on small jobs. Lack of money!

'What are you saving up for now?' she asked.

'The caulking. And the money is saved, I'll have you know. I'm just waiting for a chance to get started.'

'The caulking? She'll be weatherproof! You'll have a proper hull! That's marvellous progress!' Amy found herself beaming proudly at the prospect, almost as if the *Swan* were her boat. 'What's next on your list? You said something a while back about a new pump. Won't the old one do?'

Jed shook his head and grinned. 'You wouldn't ask that question if you'd spent as much time and effort as I have trying to get the old girl dry. No, I'm afraid it's past redemption. Joe Brooking's got a new one waiting for me down at his workshop.'

'You mean you've ordered a pump and you didn't tell me?' said Amy indignantly.

'I didn't think you'd be interested. You must be bored with me going on about my boat week-in week-out.'

'Bored? Honestly, Jed, there are times when I wonder about you! I could never be bored with the *Swan*. Watching you bring her back to life is fascinating. It's like something from a storybook. And yet you don't bother to tell me about something important, like ordering the pump.'

In spite of her scolding he looked pleased and surprised. Jed never expected people to be concerned about him or interested in his activities. His grin widened.

'I'll have an announcement put in the *Chronicle*, shall I? "Mr Jediah Greenway is happy to announce that he's just bought a pump." Folk'll think I'm ready for the asylum, but if it's what you want then I'll do it.'

'Good, I'll read about it in next week's edition,' Amy grinned.

'Make the most of it. It's going to be a while before I'll be able to afford anything else worth shouting about.'

'I'll be patient. I'd better go now and fetch Effie. She will be thinking I've got lost.' As she hurried away, Amy glanced back over her shoulder. Jed was already back on the *Swan*, not wasting a minute.

Up at Furzeham, Jessie looked no better. Amy glanced from her sister-in-law's pale face to the sofa, where the piled cushions and hastily discarded rug told their own tale. Jessie Prout lying down during the morning? It was unheard of!

'I shouldn't have left Effie with you today,' she said remorsefully.

'Oh, yes you should!' Jessie responded quickly. 'She's been a great help.'

'I have, Ma!' Effie insisted. 'I've been looking after Auntie Jessie, haven't I, Auntie? I made her hanky all wet with lavender water and put it on her head. And when she went to sleep I played very quietly so's not to wake her up.'

'I don't know how I'd have managed without you this morning,' Jessie informed the child. 'Just having you here's made me feel much better.'

Effie beamed with delight.

Amy was not convinced. 'You should see the doctor,' she said. 'You've not been feeling well for a while.'

'I've seen him,' Jessie said, then she looked significantly at Effie. 'Didn't I say you could have an apple to take home, my love?' she said. 'You go down to the kitchen and ask Millie to get you one. The biggest, rosiest one there.'

Amy felt uneasy. There was a tension about Jessie she could not understand. Once Effie had left the room she looked inquiringly at her sister-in-law.

'I'm expecting,' said Jessie simply.

For a moment Amy just stared at her.

'Expecting!' she said in astonishment. In the years she had known Jessie there had never been the least sign of a pregnancy. 'That's wonderful news… ! But what's wrong?' she asked, the smile fading.

'It is wonderful,' agreed Jessie, her hands clenched tightly. 'It's what I've always longed for, a child of my own. Oh, Amy, I'm so afraid things will go wrong again. I'm thirty-eight! I couldn't keep a babe full-term when I was young. What chance have I now? I can't bear the thought of the unhappiness and disappointment And poor John—'

'Now wait a minute!' Amy put in briskly. 'What does the doctor say?'

'He says everything should be fine if I'm careful.'

'And what did he say those other times?'

'I didn't go to him then – there didn't seem any need – until it was too late. Money was a bit scarce, you see, with John building the business back up...'

'Well, then, if the doctor is confident, you should be happy. Just follow his advice. And thirty-eight's no great age. Plenty of women have their first baby much older. When these early months are over and you're more comfortable, you'll feel a lot more cheerful and optimistic, you'll see.'

'You think so?'

'I certainly do. And what about John? The wretch, he didn't let on anything about it.'

The glimmer of a smile crossed Jessie's face.

'He's thrilled to bits, but worried.'

'Fathers always are,' grinned Amy, thinking of Todd's anxiety when Effie was bom. For a moment she had forgotten that Todd was not the child's natural father. The recollection brought her up with a jolt. Then she knew she had been right first time. Todd had truly been Effie's father, in everything but the begetting.

'Is something wrong?' asked Jessie.

'I was thinking about Todd,' Amy replied.

The sound of small feet laboriously ascending the stairs warned them of Effie's return.

'One thing I didn't ask,' said Amy hurriedly before they were interrupted. 'When is the baby due?'

'In June. It will be a summer babe,' said Jessie. For the first time a look of happy anticipation lit her features.

The news of the coming child made Amy more certain then ever that she should not leave Effie with her aunt so frequently. Jessie was equally adamant that she could cope. In the end, Amy appealed to John for support, certain she would find an ally. She was wrong.

'Jessie needs rest, she shouldn't be coping with a lively four-year-old,' she insisted.

'And supposing you takes the li'l maid to someone else? What'd happen then?' asked John. 'Can you see my Jess lying down on the sofa with a book or a bit of knitting? I can't! Her'd be turning out this and scrubbing out that! I knows her! But when her's got Effie with her, her's got to slow down a bit. Her takes the child on walks, don't her, and reads her stories, and plays snap with her to keep her amused? 'Sides, the chile idn't no trouble, her'm a good li'l soul.' John paused, and when he spoke again his anxiety showed through his normal calm. 'To tell the truth I'm convinced Jess'll get more rest looking after Effie than her will left to her own devices. I reckon that was part of the trouble they other times. Her did too much. I'd be obliged if you'd go on letting her have the li'l maid.'

There was such appeal in his voice that Amy did not have the heart to say no.

'I know your wife, too, don't forget!' she said. 'And while she may take things easy playing snap, when the child's gone I'll bet she's up and dashing about trying to catch up on her housework. I'll tell you what we'll do. On the three mornings a week that I work here, Jessie can have Effie, and those three afternoons I'll go up and do her housework for her. How's that?'

John made no attempt to protest. Proof, if any were needed, of how worried he was. 'That'd be grand,' he said with a relieved smile. 'It'd mean her resting three days a week. And the company wouldn't do her no harm, neither. That maidservant us've got at the moment, young Millie, her'm a fair worker, but her'm that stupid 'tis hard to believe. Jess needs better conversation than her'n just now.'

Amy knew what he meant. Millie Milton combined lack of intelligence with a remarkable memory for disasters. She was quite capable of regaling Jessie with stories of tragic pregnancies, complete with graphic and gruesome details.

'In that case, I'll make a point of calling on Jessie every day while you're at work,' she said.

'That's real good of you,' said John gratefully. 'I'm hard put to it to know how to say thank you.'

'There's no need,' said Amy gently. 'I'm only paying back a fraction of what you and Jessie have done for me. I'd never have managed without you.'

'Yes, you would,' said John firmly. 'Our Todd knew what he were doing when he married you. He couldn't have done better.'

Remembering the anxieties and problems of the last few years, Amy was greatly moved.

-

The next few months were full of activity for Amy. What with helping Jessie as much as she could, encouraging Jed with his working on the *Swan*, and seeing to her own affairs, she felt as if she never had a moment to spare. But although her formal mourning for Todd finally came to an end and she set aside her widow's black, whenever she had a moment to think, she felt just as bound to him as ever.

Throughout her pregnancy, poor Jessie remained far from well. It was evident that, as well as her persistent sickness, her fear of another miscarriage was proving a strain.

'That's another month safely past,' she would say with intense relief. 'Four months! I've never gone so long.'

Then it was: 'Five months, and the babe is growing splendidly, the doctor says.'

And: 'Six months! Surely all must be well this time?'

During this difficult period, Amy felt the last barriers between her and Jessie begin to crumble. No longer was she tolerated simply for being Effie's mother, but for herself. It was a good feeling, this growing warmth between them. It fostered in Amy a happy sense of belonging she had not experienced since her early childhood. Now when Jessie said, 'You're family', Amy felt she meant it.

Jed's life, too, had become a series of minor triumphs. Each new improvement to the *Swan* became a cause for celebration, no matter how trivial; the fixing of a new stove-pipe in the galley was greeted with as much rejoicing as the fitting of the new rudder and tiller.

On a fine spring day the *Swan* returned to the water. Amy was there with Effie to see the vessel refloated, both of them dressed in their Sunday best. Lack of funds would not allow her to buy the smart hat she had promised for the launching of Jed's boat but she had compromised by retrimming an old one with swirls of veiling and a bunch of artificial violets. Effie's bonnet boasted new pink ribbons and the pair of them felt very festive.

'It isn't a proper launching, you know,' said Jed, looking first at them and then at Sally Preston and her brood, who had also come to watch the fun.

'It'll do until a proper one comes along, won't it, Sally?' said Amy.

'Remembering what 'ee started with, it won't be far short,' agreed Sally.

'You shouldn't have gone to this bother.' Jed switched his attention to the baskets of food and drink which Amy and Sally had brought with them. 'It really isn't like a launch, no matter what you say. I'm not certain she's seaworthy. It might go wrong.'

'Cor, listen to the boy!' protested Sally. 'You'm a proper li'l ray of sunshine, bain't 'ee?'

Amy noted the deep furrow of anxiety between his dark brows and the air of tension about his whole being. This was a very important moment for him; his whole future hinged upon it. No wonder he was looking careworn.

'You've nothing to worry about. Everything will go splendidly,' she said with complete assurance.

Her confidence was less absolute when the *Swan* began to move. It was an anxious time for everyone, as the workmen scurried about checking tow-ropes, removing the chocks from beneath the keel, and making the innumerable adjustments that were necessary for the boat to enter the water safely. The ropes tightened, took the strain, then slowly the *Swan* began to slide down the well-greased, makeshift slipway. Amy held her breath. A protesting cry from Effie made her realize she was clutching the child's hand too tightly. Easing her hold, she turned her attention back to the scene on the beach.

John was there supervising, of course, along with Jed, who seemed to be everywhere at once. There was an agonizing moment as the vessel gained momentum. Then suddenly the *Swan* entered the sea with a whoosh, displacing a great wave of water which surged up the beach, wetting the feet of unwary bystanders. For a brief, terrible instant it seemed as if she would never rise out of the water, but miraculously she bobbed up again, rocked perilously, then held steady. The *Swan* was proudly floating on the tide.

It may not have been a proper launching, but the men from the boatyard cheered as if it were, waving their hats in the air, and sending the alarmed seagulls soaring and screaming. Amy found herself cheering with delight, while Effie jumped up and down in her excitement.

Jed had followed the *Swan* into the water, oblivious of the danger if she should keel over or capsize. He stood immobile, not seeming to notice he was thigh-deep in the sea. With a hand shielding his eyes against the reflected glare, he continued to stare at his boat as if he could not get enough of her. Suddenly he turned and ran up the beach towards Amy, streaming sea-water as he came. When he reached her he flung his arms about her and whirled her round, his face alive and lit up in a way she had never seen before.

'She floats!' he cried. 'Just look at her! She floats! Isn't it marvellous?'

The realization of what this meant seemed to strike him without warning. As swiftly as it had arisen, his euphoria faded, and the excitement drained from his face.

'She floats,' he repeated, very quietly.

He still had his arms about Amy, and suddenly he pulled her close and held her tightly, his face buried in her shoulder. The water from his clothes was soaking her, but Amy did not notice. For once in his life Jed needed someone else. Relief and the strength of his happiness had taken him unawares and overwhelmed him. He had to have someone to cling to. Amy was glad she was there.

'Uncle Jed, you're making Ma all wet.' Effie's piping voice cut through everything.

With a start Jed released Amy and stood back, looking with horror and embarrassment at the damage he had caused. The sea-water from his clothes had soaked the front of her jacket and skirt, staining the light-green wool a much darker hue.

'I'm sorry,' he gasped. 'I didn't think!'

'Ma will be cross with you,' warned Effie. She had been watching what was going on with disquiet, her fingers in her mouth. Abruptly she rushed forward and flung her arms about Amy, pressing herself against the damp skirt. Fond as she was of her Uncle Jed, he had no right to cuddle her ma. That was her prerogative.

'No, I won't,' said Amy, gently stroking the child's hair. 'My skirt will soon dry and, anyway, today is far too special and nice to be spoiled by anyone being cross.'

She looked at Jed and smiled. He smiled back, but it was an expression heavily tinged with awkwardness. Whether his unease was because of the ruined skirt or the fact that he had let his feelings get the better of him, Amy could not tell.

'I think we should eat, don't you, Sally?' she suggested, her voice suddenly brisk.

Sally did not appear to hear her. She, too, had been watching the scene, and had been bemused by what had been going on.

'Well I never!' she exclaimed softly to herself. 'If that don't beat everything!' Then she realized she was being addressed and came to with a jump. 'Eat, my handsome? Yes, I reckon 'tis time us tucked into this food.'

'I'm sorry, I haven't the time.' Jed started to back away. 'There's a lot to do.'

'Lor' bless 'ee!' declared Sally hotly. 'That precious boat of youm's safely afloat. Her idn't going to sink just because 'ee takes ten minutes off. You'm allowed to enjoy yourself now and then, Jed Greenway. There idn't no law as says 'ee has to work every blessed hour God gives.' Then she added more gently, ''Sides, Amy and me, us've gone to a lot of trouble over this bun-fight. 'Tis in your honour, 'ee can't run off now!'

'If you turn your nose up at our picnic you will never get another bit of saffron cake from me!' declared Amy in mock indignation.

'In that case I'd better come and eat.' Jed remained ill at ease, despite his smile.

'Don't you want to get changed?' Amy suggested. 'John keeps a spare pair of working trousers handy. I'm sure you could borrow those.'

'Change?' Jed looked down at himself with some surprise. He had forgotten he was wet. 'No, I don't think so, thanks. I'll only get soaked again later. First, I'd better go and share out the cider I brought for the men, and have a drink with them.' He set off across the beach towards where John and his workmen had gathered.

Amy and Sally selected a site among the pebbles and spread the blanket that Sally had brought. Then they began unpacking the baskets.

''Ee knows,' said Sally, pausing thoughtfully, a home-made dough-cake in her hands. 'After all the time that Jed have bided with us I thought I knowed him like I knows my own boys. But I be real mistaken.'

'He's always kept himself to himself,' Amy said. 'Even when he was a youngster. No one knows what he's really thinking.'

'There's some as knows more'n others about him though,' answered Sally cryptically.

When Amy looked at her questioningly she was busy preventing her children from making an early attack on the food and did not reply.

Jed soon returned, and settled himself down to join the picnic.

'Isn't John coming over?' Amy asked.

'He sends his apologies. He says Jessie's already given him enough to feed the starving of the parish. If he has two lots he won't be able to work any more today.'

'Never mind. I don't suppose there'll be much wasted.'

'Waste? With my lot about there idn't no such word,' grinned Sally.

And they settled down to eat. It was a simple enough meal, with pasties, bread and cheese, buttered doughcake and saffron cake, cider and ginger-beer. There was hardly any conversation, for eating took precedence. Amy noticed that Effie was much engrossed with feeding Jed small portions of saffron cake from her slice, as if to make amends for her earlier resentment of him.

Out on the sea, just beyond the beach, the *Swan* bobbed serenely, minus her masts and rigging, but looking very trim nevertheless.

'No one will call her the *Muck Pot* now,' observed Amy.

'I should hope not, the hours I've spent painting her,' said Jed. 'She'll need doing again before she's finished, of course.'

'How much more have you to do on her?'

'Enough. It's not the work, it's getting the money, as usual. My next priority is the capstan boiler. The old one's serviceable, thank goodness, but needs a good overhaul. With luck I'll be able to afford to have it done before summer. After that, we're talking about the big stuff. A new mast for certain, and new rigging, followed by a suit of sails – and we haven't begun to think of the gear...'

The list was uncomfortably long, and for a moment the hull rocking gently on the waves did not seem such a momentous achievement. But Amy refused to be daunted.

'You're more than half-way!' she declared. 'And you've done it in less time than anyone thought possible. You'll get the rest of the repairs and refitting done eventually, you'll see.'

'I'll get them done,' said Jed with complete conviction. 'I don't know when, but I'll get them done. I'll be making good money this summer with any luck.'

'You will? Where are you going? The Bristol Channel?'

'Better than that. I've got a place crewing a yacht for the season. The *Curlew*. Have you heard of her?'

Amy shook her head. 'I'm afraid I don't move much in yachting circles these days,' she said.

'A pity, otherwise you'd know that the *Curlew* is one of the top racers. She's in the same class as *Galatea* and *White Heather*, I stand to get a decent wage. Some good prize money, too.'

'That's splendid! Don't go spending it all on champagne,' Amy said, thinking how quiet the summer would be without him. She focused once more on the *Swan*. 'You know, there's just one thing spoiling your handiwork out there,' she said.

'Oh?' replied Jed defensively. 'And what's that?'

'Why does she have to have that Dartmouth registration mark? She's a Brixham boat, born, bred, and renovated. She should be registered here.'

'Complain to the Board of Trade,' smiled Jed. 'In the meantime, I'll keep a pot of white paint handy to change the DH to a BM.'

The food had been eaten and the children, including Effie, were getting boisterous.

'I suppose us'd better get these young turks to home afore they start getting under John Prout's feet,' stated Sally.

'And I'd better get back to work,' added Jed. He looked at the pair of them. 'Thanks,' he said. 'It would have been a special day anyway, but you being here and all this' – he gestured towards the remnants of the feast '– this has made it extra special. I'm sorry Harry was away at sea and couldn't be with us. You both went to a lot of trouble, and I want you to know how much I appreciate it.'

To the astonishment of the two women he bent and kissed each of them on the cheek, then hurried off to row himself out to the *Swan* in a borrowed punt.

'What did I say?' declared Sally in amazement. 'I don't know 'e at all.' She collected her basket and straightened up. 'Mind, I must confess I never thought to see this day. I was sure the old *Swan* would never float again.'

'Then you certainly don't know Jed,' said Amy. 'Because I never had a minute's serious doubt.'

Amy saw rather less of Jed in the weeks which followed because, as the days lengthened, he worked more and more on his boat. He continued to call regularly to provide her with firewood and attend to any odd jobs which needed doing, but he rarely had time to stay for long. She did not mind. She understood the compunction that drove him on. Besides, her sister-in-law was occupying more of her time.

By her seventh month Jessie was growing more hopeful and confident with each passing day. It was not an easy pregnancy, but she surprised everyone by consenting to rest frequently and following the doctor's instructions to the letter. It looked as if at last there was going to be a happy outcome to her years of longing.

The bright April sunshine made Amy think in terms of spring cleaning. She was about to take down the curtains in the kitchen, ready to begin whitewashing the ceiling, when there was a frenzied knocking at the door. Hurrying to open it she found Millie, Jessie's maidservant, standing there. Her face was crimson and perspiring, her cap askew.

'The missus have started. Can you come?' she panted.

'Started?' For a moment Amy did not understand what she meant.

'Yes. The babe!'

'So soon?' Alarmed, Amy was already hurrying into the kitchen to collect Effie. 'Have you called the midwife? Who's with her now?'

'Why, no one!' Millie's round dull eyes stared blankly. 'Her didn't tell me to call no one, only you.'

'Couldn't you have got Mrs Craig or one of the other neighbours—?' Amy stopped in exasperation. What was the point? Hoping that Millie might have used her initiative was expecting too much. 'Get back up to the house quickly,' she said. 'Tell Mrs Prout I'll be up the minute I've found someone to look after Effie. And stay beside her until I come, do you hear?'

Millie nodded, and set off at a run again, boots slithering, skirts flying.

'I've got to go up to see Auntie Jessie, she's not well,' Amy told Effie. 'Collect up some of your toys and we'll see if you can stay with Mrs Cobb until I come back. I may be late so I want you to be a good girl.'

Fortunately Mrs Cobb was happy to oblige – her somewhat sour disposition did not extend to anyone under the age of seven. As Amy was leaving her cottage she almost bumped into one of Lizzie Drew's brood.

'Sammy,' she said, 'here's tuppence. Get over to Nurse Thorpe's as fast as you can and ask her to go to Mrs Prout's in North Furzeham.'

Pocketing his two pence Sammy Drew was off like the wind.

Amy did not bother to knock when she reached her sister-in-law's house. She rushed straight up to the bedroom, discarding her hat and coat as she went. A white and frightened-looking Jessie lay in the big bed, her hands nervously clutching at the sheets.

'Oh Amy!' she said. 'Thank goodness!'

Amy went over to her and gently smoothed her hair back from a forehead that was already damp with perspiration.

'I'm here,' she said reassuringly. 'You've got nothing to worry about now.' It was a silly statement. They both knew there was a great deal to worry about. However, Jessie seemed comforted and clutched at her hand. 'I've sent for Nurse Thorpe, she'll be here any minute. Have you been having your pains long?'

'Since about five o'clock, though I've been uncomfortable all night. I didn't say anything to John—' Jessie's face suddenly contorted with pain and her grip on Amy's fingers tightened, then as the contraction faded she relaxed and lay limp. '...I didn't say anything to John,' she continued weakly, 'I didn't want to worry him. He's better off at work.'

Amy took up a towel from the washstand and wiped her face for her, then she turned her attention to Millie, who was standing uselessly at the foot of the bed.

'Go downstairs and make sure there's a good fire in the range,' she said. 'Is the cistern full? Good, then fill both the kettles and the biggest saucepan with water and get them boiling.'

They were a long way from needing boiling water, she knew, but it was as well to be prepared.

'And keep an ear open for Nurse Thorpe,' she called after the departing maid. 'It's too much to hope that Millie got your bed ready for you, I suppose,' she said to Jessie. 'Never mind, I'll see to it. Where are the draw-sheets and everything?'

'The big drawer at the bottom of the tallboy. Oh Amy, I'm so glad you came!' A tear trickled down Jessie's face.

'Of course I came. Did you think I'd do anything else?' Amy gave her a hug. 'I'll just get you nice and comfortable before the nurse gets here.'

Her preparations were disturbed as Jessie was racked by another contraction, making Amy wish the midwife would hurry up. From her own limited experience, and from what she had heard from other women, these pains seemed severe for so early in the labour.

'It's too soon. My baby's coming too soon,' protested Jessie tearfully from the bed.

'It's the seventh month. There are plenty of strapping folks walking about who were seven-month babies.' Amy was determined to be confident. 'Sally Preston's eldest came two months early, so she says, and look at him now. Built like a young bull and eating them out of house and home.'

Jessie managed a smile. 'I know young Billy Preston,' she said. 'I wouldn't mind having one like him.'

'Imagine the cooking you could do, and not a crumb of it wasted,' said Amy, glad to encourage her thoughts along such positive lines.

'That would be really lovely, and John would be happy to have a son like that.'

'Son or daughter, it won't make a scrap of difference to your John. He'll spoil it, whatever it is.'

The arrival of Nurse Thorpe came as a relief. A thin ramrod of a woman, she brought with her a feeling of confidence along with an aura of starch and carbolic.

'Are you likely to faint?' she demanded crisply of Amy as they climbed the stairs. 'If so, stay out of the way. We'll be better off without you.'

'I won't faint,' Amy promised.

'Good. And how's Effie, the little lamb?'

Nurse Thorpe maintained an interest in every child she had delivered. She had a sharp way with relatives and would-be assistants, standing no nonsense. With her patients, however, she was a model of kindness and understanding, as Amy remembered well from her own confinement.

'There now,' Nurse Thorpe beamed at Jessie as soon as she entered the room. 'Isn't it typical? There you've been waiting all these years for Baby Prout, and now he's that impatient to arrive he can't wait his full term.'

'It's a boy then is it?' asked Jessie.

'Boy, girl, it doesn't matter.' The midwife set down her bag on a chair. 'Whatever it is it's an impatient little tyke, that's something we know for certain. We'll find out the other details before too long, I'm thinking.'

But as the day wore on, Nurse Thorpe's confident manner did not last beyond the bedroom door.

'She's not making any progress, poor soul,' she confided to Amy on the landing. 'Normally it'd be a bit early to be calling Dr Searle, but knowing Mrs Prout's history, I think we'd better send for him.'

'I'll find someone to take the message.'

'Does Mr Prout know the baby's started?'

'Yes, I wrote him a note and Millie took it with his dinner. I decided it was the best course, though I was in two minds whether to save him the worry.'

'Never does the husbands any harm to worry a bit,' declared the nurse acidly. 'Why shouldn't they pay for their pleasures?'

'I think poor John's been worried the whole way through with this one,' said Amy. 'I told him to stay at work, there was no need for him to dash home.'

The doctor came promptly, and at his first visit seemed optimistic. John was home when he came again, an anxious John, who may have been kept occupied at the boatyard but who had not been saved any worry. He looked white and haggard.

'My girl'm going to be all right, idn't her?' he asked pleadingly as the doctor came downstairs.

'It would be foolish to pretend that everything is as we would like it,' Dr Searle said gently. 'I can only promise that we will do everything humanly possible for your wife and baby.' He could offer no more comfort than that.

He came back at midnight at Nurse Thorpe's urgent summons – and stayed.

Amy shared her time between fetching and carrying for the sickroom and comforting John. It was the longest night she had ever known, even more harrowing than the night when Todd had died. Then she had known the worst, and that Todd was no longer suffering. The same could not be said for poor Jessie, who was by now past crying out, past screaming. Long, low animal moans echoed through the house, causing John to bury his head in his hands in anguish.

'Can't you do summat to help her?' he cried to the doctor. 'Her don't have to go through such suffering in this day and age. Can't her have chloroform? Us can afford it.'

Dr Searle shook his head. 'It's not a question of money,' he said kindly. 'Excellent though chloroform is, it does put strains on the body, particularly the heart. In my opinion neither Mrs Prout nor the baby are strong enough.'

'Then if 'tis a matter of saving one or the other, save my Jess,' cried John in desperation. 'God forgive me for saying so, for my girl never will, but for pity's sake save her!'

Dr Searle patted him on the shoulder. 'I'll try,' he said in a quiet voice.

'I don't often say this, but it's a pity Mr Prout's not a drinking man,' whispered Nurse Thorpe in passing. 'Drinking or praying are his only comforts just now, I'm afraid.'

'I can't even get him to take a glass of brandy,' said Amy. 'As for praying, we've neither of us stopped.'

Dawn streaked the sky and brightened into morning, with no end to Jessie's torment – or John's.

'Her can't take much more, poor maid,' he kept whispering.

Amy tried to make comforting remarks, though she was of the same opinion. Surely no one could go through so much and survive. Already she had given up hope for the baby. Only once had she seen anyone suffer in travail like this. It had been back in Lambeth, when she and Ma had rented a garret not far from Kennington Road. The girl on the floor below had gone into just such a difficult labour. Amy could not remember her name now, only that the unfortunate creature had struggled alone until Ma had taken pity on her. There being no one else, she, Amy, had clambered up and down the rickety stairs with water and slop-pails and been witness to all that went on. The awful groans had only ended when the girl died. But she had been too poor to afford a doctor or a midwife. Jessie was well tended. She had the best medical attention the modern world could provide. Jessie would not die. She must not!

Suddenly a new note sounded through the house. A thin wail as newborn lungs took their first breath. John sat up sharply and clutched Amy's hands across the table.

'You hear that?' he demanded in disbelief.

Amy nodded. She had heard it, though she was afraid to believe her own ears.

The doctor came in eventually, looking weary.

'You have a son, Mr Prout,' he said. 'But I fear the child is very frail. I beg you not to be too hopeful.'

'And Jessie?' demanded John.

The doctor's expression did not alter.

'You do not need me to tell you she has had a bad time. The next twenty-four hours will be crucial for both of them.'

John did not wait. He got to his feet and stumbled up the stairs.

'Poor fellow, I wish I could have told him something more cheering.' The doctor began rolling down his sleeves. 'I must go now and attend to my other patients. I'll be back at noon, but before that I'll send up another nurse to relieve Nurse Thorpe. Until then Mr Prout may as well sit with his wife, if that's what he wants. His presence can only encourage her. You will be staying?'

'Yes,' said Amy. 'I must go and see to my little girl first.'

Several times during that unnaturally long day Amy had slipped down to see how Effie fared.

'Her'm missing her ma, but her'm being a good li'l maid,' Betsy Cobb informed her, then lowered her voice significantly. 'Her'm welcome to stay on, since I gather you'm sore needed up to Furzeham.'

'I am. My sister-in-law is very ill indeed.'

'Then don't you fret none. The chile's safe with me.'

Amy's words of thanks sounded inadequate. News of Jessie's plight had already spread about town. On her way back up the hill Amy was stopped half a dozen times by people inquiring about 'poor Mrs Prout'. When she eventually reached the house again she feared what she might find. She encountered a tired Nurse Thorpe preparing to leave.

'Nurse Hicks is upstairs,' she informed her.

'And Jessie and the baby?'

'Sleeping for the moment, praise be. Hicks is very competent. They're in good hands.'

When she had satisfied herself that her services were not required, Amy sank into a chair. The next thing she knew it was midday and the doctor had called again. Ashamed that she had fallen asleep she was relieved when he said, 'Well, they're still holding their own, the pair of them.'

Jessie lay unconscious with exhaustion, but thankfully she continued to show no trace of the fever which so often struck after childbirth. The baby was a tiny skinned-rabbit of a creature who, against all the odds, showed no inclination to continue sleeping like his mother. As his fretful crying was likely to disturb Jessie, Amy took charge of him.

'See what you can do for him,' said Nurse Hicks as she handed the child to Amy. 'But I'm afraid we can't hope for too much from the poor little fellow.'

Amy had other ideas. She abandoned the house to Millie's tender mercies and concentrated upon her nephew full time. Carefully she cleared his tiny nose of the mucus which constantly threatened to choke him, gently she anointed his tender skin with olive oil and made sure he was kept warm. Most of all she tried to get him to take nourishment, encouraging milk into him drop by drop.

As she rocked the frail infant in her arms she compared him with her recollections of the new-born Effie. From the first her little girl had felt sturdy and compact, smooth skinned and sweet smelling. This child was fragile skin and bone, with a raw, unfinished look about him. Yet nestling him close to her breast she felt a passionate tenderness for the poor scrap of humanity, and a rush of regret that she was unlikely now to have another child of her own. It made her all the more determined that he would survive.

When night fell mother and son, if no stronger, were no weaker. An exhausted John consented to get some sleep himself, while Amy went down and fetched Effie from Mrs Cobb's.

Another day came and went with Jessie and her baby both weak but surviving. It was becoming increasingly evident that running the house was too much for Millie. With John's willing consent Amy brought in Aggie Preston, a relation of Harry's, a cheerful, capable widow with four sons of her own, who was happy to come in daily. The house settled down to a routine centred on the sickroom and the baby.

Somehow a week slid by. John felt he could occasionally tear himself away from his loved ones for an hour or two to attend to his business. Jessie was still terribly frail, but she was sleeping more naturally and taking more interest. Her first words upon waking were invariably, 'My baby, where is he?' as if she feared he might be a figment of her imagination.

'Isn't it about time you gave this poor lad a name?' suggested Amy as she put the child in his mother's arms.

'Us've got a name picked out right enough, haven't us, Jess?' said John. 'But us wants your consent.'

'My consent?' Amy was surprised.

'Yes. Us thinks you should be consulted because us'd like to call the boy Todd.'

'Oh…' Amy was taken aback. 'Oh, yes, I'd like that very much,' she said, greatly touched.

'Are you sure?' said Jessie huskily. 'If it upsets you then we'll call him something else.'

'No, I think it's lovely to call him Todd,' Amy replied with growing delight.

'That's grand.' John beamed happily. Some of the strain was fading from his face. 'If he'd been a maid us'd have chosen Amy. Oh yes,' he insisted as Amy began to protest. 'Us knows us idn't out of the wood yet, and us'm going to have to take special care of young Todd here, him being such a li'l tacker. But the fact that we'm got him this far be due to you. If us hadn't got you to tend un I daren't think what might have happened. I'm thankful to the doctor and the nurses for saving my Jess, but it were you as saved the boy. To say we'm grateful's a powerful understatement, idn't it, Jessie?'

Jessie did not reply but she took hold of Amy's hand and tears ran down her pallid face. Amy's own cheeks grew wet, and she found herself thinking how good it would have been if she could have given her Todd a son. That could never be now, but she knew he would have approved of his tiny namesake. If she had been instrumental in helping this second Todd to survive then it was the next best thing to bearing a child herself, and, through her tears, she felt very happy.

Chapter Thirteen

Although Jessie recovered from her ordeal she never regained her former bustling energy. However, she considered less robust health a small price to pay for her baby.

'I'm not bothered about the odd cobweb here and there these days,' she would say. 'I've got far more important things to think about.' And she would hold her child close to her and rock him gently.

Needless to say there were no more cobwebs in the house now than there had ever been. Aggie Preston saw to that. The brisk, capable woman had stayed on after the child's birth. It was a good thing she did, for in the first weeks of little Todd's life there was emergency after emergency. Undersized and frail, he proved vulnerable to every childhood ailment, and frequently he caused those who loved him to be frantic with worry.

'I bless the day you found Aggie for me,' Jessie said frequently to Amy, usually after the baby's health had caused yet another crisis. 'She's so calm and sensible. Sometimes I wonder how I would have fared if I'd been left to cope with just Millie on hand. The thought of it makes me go cold.'

'She's a good soul,' agreed Amy. 'And I know she's grateful for the work.'

She, too, was glad of Aggie's presence in the Prout household; it meant she felt able to spend less time with her sister-in-law. Not that she begrudged going to Jessie's, but with Aggie there she was more at liberty to go about her own affairs with a clear conscience. Her chief concern was the need to be with Effie.

Although the child had been very good during the anxious time since Todd was born, it was evident that she was beginning to feel pushed out of things. Used to being the bright star with her uncle and aunt, she realized that she had been superseded. Strangely she could accept Jessie's preoccupation with the new baby, but not her uncle John's. If he was set upon admiring this noisy wrinkled interloper then she would devote her favours to the one man she knew would give her his undivided attention – her uncle Jed. Jed was somewhat bemused by this sudden popularity, but he took it well.

'What have I done to deserve this?' he asked, when Effie suddenly flung her amis about his neck for no apparent reason.

'It's 'cos you're my bestest uncle and I love you lots,' was the reply, delivered with a kiss.

Jed's arms tightened round the little girl, and Amy saw that he was very moved by the childish pronouncement. Judging by the sudden emotion in his face – emotion he was swift to suppress – she suspected it might have been the first time anyone had said they loved him.

He said abruptly, 'I join the *Curlew* at the end of the month.'

'Are you looking forward to it?' asked Amy, accepting the sudden change in conversation.

'Yes and no. The sailing side should be good. It's something different and I'm sure I'll enjoy the racing.'

'Then what's the problem?'

'I don't fancy being dressed up like a dog's dinner.' He scowled, drawing his dark brows together. 'It seems the crew are rigged out in navy jerseys with *Curlew* embroidered on them, white duck trousers and cheese-cutter caps. If anyone down the Seamen's Rooms sees me in that lot they'll split their sides laughing.'

'Don't be silly, it's no more than plenty of other Brixham men have had to wear,' chuckled Amy. 'It's the penalty for mixing with the gentry. Besides, you'll look very handsome, and you know it. It'll be the girls you'll have to worry about, not your friends from the Seamen's Rooms. They'll be after you in droves.'

'They won't catch me, then, because I've got my girl here.' And he swung a delighted Effie into the air.

'You'll be sure to come and see us in your nice yachting rig before you go, won't you?' Amy said.

Jed glowered at her with such disgust that she burst out laughing.

He did come to say goodbye on the night before he joined the *Curlew*, but he was not wearing his new uniform. Never for one moment had Amy imagined he would. Effie cried bitterly at learning she would not see him for a while.

'I'll come and see you when I can,' he promised. 'We'll be back for the regatta; I'll try and come then. And you can stand on Berry Head or up on Furze Field and cheer me on when I'm racing. How about that?'

'Which will be your yacht?' asked Effie, somewhat mollified.

'The best one, of course,' was the reply.

After Jed left, life suddenly became quiet and rather empty for Amy. She missed his company, and the stimulus of following the *Swan's* progress. The better weather had also brought an improvement in Todd's health, so Amy was no longer needed at Furzeham so often. There had been times during the previous few months when she had longed for a lessening of the demands on her. Now she was beginning to feel at a loose end. Working at the boatyard three mornings a week, keeping her house clean, and taking Effie out for walks seemed the sum total of her days. After the hectic activity of the winter and spring she found it hard to grow accustomed to such relative idleness.

'I suppose you saw Jed the other day,' remarked Sally when they met by the harbour. 'He looked a rare treat, didn't he?'

'Jed?' replied Amy, quite dismayed. 'He was here in Brixham? No, I didn't see him.'

'I thought he might have called.' Sally looked at her keenly. 'No doubt he didn't have time. He were down to the Strand getting provisions for the yacht, that's where I seed him. My, he looked brave and no mistake. A fine figure of a man he'm turning into, and I idn't the only one as thinks it. You should've seed the girls giving him the eye.'

'To think he was here and I didn't see him.' Amy did not want to be told about how attractive Jed was to the opposite sex; she was too upset that she had missed him.

'I dare say he was in a rush,' Sally said kindly. 'Some of they yacht owners can be proper tartars where their crew's concerned, 'specially during the season. Rest assured, if Jed could've managed it he'd have come calling.'

But he had not. Amy felt absurdly hurt.

'How's he getting on?' she asked, swallowing her rancour.

'Getting on fine, he says. Good bunch of men he'm with, and he'm taken to the racing real proper. Only complaint be the food. 'Tis all bully beef. He reckons he'll look like a tin soon. He says he dreams of a nice thick bit of fresh ray with a decent pile of fried tiddies alongside. There, you knows what to feed him on when he gets home.'

'You'll be the one feeding him, not me,' pointed out Amy, rather more sharply than she had intended. Then she felt ashamed of letting her resentment show quite so plainly. She added more gently, 'I don't envy you. He's got a keen appetite at the best of times. What he'll be like after weeks of poor food, goodness knows! Is the *Curlew* winning lots of races?'

'He didn't say. He didn't have time, really. He were busy shifting gurt baskets of groceries from the shop to the launch as was waiting.' Sally grinned. 'Not everyone on board's living on bully beef, seemingly.'

Amy continued on her way, knowing it was silly to get upset because he had not called. Nevertheless, she could not shake off her feeling of disappointment.

Brixham Regatta was held in August. In the *Dartmouth & Brixham Chronicle* Amy saw that the *Curlew* was entered for several races. Jed would be back in Brixham again. She made sure she had a decent ham – keeping fresh ray on hand in case he called was not practical in the warm weather – and some good cider. Also, she baked one of the saffron cakes that he liked. She was all prepared now for Jed's homecoming. But he did not come.

The regatta was the big event of the year in Brixham, a time when exiles returned and families were reunited. The town was in a cheerful holiday mood, its inhabitants clad in their Sunday best, determined to enjoy themselves. Tall elegant yachts, dressed overall, arrived and anchored offshore, their slim lines contrasting with the sturdier hulls of the fishing boats.

'Which one of those yachts is Uncle Jed's?' demanded Effie, jigging up and down excitedly.

'I don't know,' was Amy's honest reply. 'The one in the front, I expect.'

'Uncle Jed said he'd come and see me at regatta,' said Effie.

'He said he would try,' amended her mother. Until that moment she herself had forgotten Jed's uncertainty. Perhaps he would not come after all.

Throughout the next day, the second of the regatta, she felt fidgety and unable to settle. She found the carefree atmosphere around her irritating, though she went through the motions of enjoying herself for Effie's sake. As she watched, her daughter's hand clutched in hers, she was conscious of an odd feeling of loneliness. Around her were families enjoying the display. As far as she could see she was the only woman alone with a child. Perhaps this was the reason for her feeling of isolation.

Long after she had returned home and put Effie to bed, Amy was conscious that she was waiting for something. For footsteps coming along Paradise? They came in plenty, but did not stop outside her door. Although it was late she could still hear music and laughter echoing in the streets. Uncomfortably aware of being excluded from the celebrations, she eventually went to bed herself, unable to think of anything else to do.

Next morning she awoke heavy-eyed, the feeling of dissatisfaction remaining with her. As she sat at breakfast with Effie there came a knocking at the door. Opening it she found Jed on the doorstep, an extremely handsome Jed, smartly dressed in his navy jersey and white duck trousers.

'Oh, you've come at last, have you?' she said acidly.

The smile faded from his face and he looked perplexed.

'I couldn't come sooner,' he said.

'You'd better come in.' The invitation was less than gracious.

Jed hesitated on the doorstep. 'If it's an awkward time...'

'Oh, come in!' said Amy in exasperation.

If her welcome had seemed cool, then Effie's more than made up for it.

'Uncle Jed!' She flung herself into his arms.

'I'm glad someone's pleased to see me,' he remarked, regarding Amy over the child's head.

She pretended not to notice, busying herself with setting another place at the table.

'Were you at the regatta?' asked Effie. 'Ma said you were on one of the big yachts but I couldn't see you.'

'I was there, sure enough. I expect I was too far away for you to make me out.' As he spoke, Jed kept glancing in puzzlement towards Amy, who was frying him some bacon and making a lot of noise about it.

'You missed the fireworks,' said Effie. 'I wanted you to come. Then you could've lifted me on your shoulders like you did last year so's I could see everything.'

'I'm sorry about that. Perhaps this'll make it up to you.' He handed the child a brown-paper parcel.

Excitedly Effie tore off the wrapping to reveal a rag sailor-doll.

'He's dressed like you,' she cried delightedly. 'Look, he's got white trousers on like yours, and a blue jersey with red writing on, just like yours as well.'

'And the letters are the same,' Jed informed her. 'They say *Curlew*. That's the name of the yacht I'm on. He's a spare member of the crew. I've brought him home to play with you.'

'He isn't really,' Effie giggled at his nonsense. 'He's a dolly!' And she hugged the rag doll to her.

'Have you said thank you for the nice present?' demanded Amy, then when the child had obliged she added, 'There's no need for you to keep bringing her things, you know.'

'I don't keep bringing her things,' protested Jed. 'One of the crew made a sailor-doll for his own girl in his spare time. I thought Effie would like one so I asked him to make another, that's all. It's a good thing I did. It means I'm in one person's good books in this house.' Then he said more anxiously, 'Have I done something to upset you?'

'No, of course you haven't,' Amy retorted. 'How could you? I haven't seen you in weeks. Here you are! Eat this!' She slammed the plate of bacon and eggs down in front of him. When he made no move to pick up his knife and fork she snapped, 'Oh for goodness' sake eat! You can't waste good food.'

With evident reluctance Jed turned his attention to his plate, but not before she had seen the expression of hurt bewilderment in his eyes. Immediately she regretted her ill-temper.

'I'm sorry. I didn't mean to snap at you,' she said. 'I don't know what's got into me. It must be the weather.'

'That's all right,' said Jed politely.

Amy did not blame him for responding coolly, especially since he had done nothing wrong. With an effort she calmed herself, seeking to find a happier topic of conversation. 'What sort of a season is the *Curlew* having?' she asked.

'Pretty good. We did extremely well at Cowes against some stiff opposition.'

'I hope that means you are getting plenty of money.'

'It certainly pays better than fishing – if you win. What with the start money and the bonuses for being placed, I'm doing nicely. I have to earn it, mind. You can't do well against the sort of competition we've got unless you work darned hard, but it's worth it.'

For the rest of his visit they concentrated upon yachting, but the talk was stilted and artificial, quite unlike their normal chatter. When Jed finally left he said goodbye and walked away swiftly, never once looking back. Amy felt he was eager to get away from her – and she could hardly blame him. She felt ashamed and remorseful. Why had she behaved in such a silly way? Because she had not had his company at the regatta when she had expected it? How she wished she could call him back and make things right again. She was Jed's oldest and closest friend and she knew her petty irritability would wound him deeply.

By now the *Curlew* would be heading for the next regatta, which was at Dartmouth. There was nothing for it, she would have to write a letter. If she addressed it c/o *Curlew* and sent it to Dartmouth Post Office, hopefully he would get it.

Amy wrote many business letters these days for John, but it had been a long time since she had written anything personal. Not since the summers when Todd had gone round land to fish off the Welsh coast. Writing to him had been easy. She had filled the pages with Effie's activities and bits of local news and gossip. This letter to Jed was more difficult, for it was to a friend, not a husband. In the end she let Effie have free rein on the last page. The resulting drawing of the *Curlew*, the scribble in lieu of a signature, and the row of kisses along the bottom added just the right touch of informality.

A couple of days later Jed's reply arrived in the shape of two postcards. Amy's bore a picture of the twin castles at the mouth of the Dart. 'I don't know what the fuss is about,' he had written. 'But thanks very much for writing. I appreciate getting letters. The season is nearly over, and I will be back in Brixham again soon.'

Amy smiled to herself, partly with relief that things were back to normal between her and Jed, and partly because the message was so typical of him, seeming to brush off her bad temper as though it were of no importance. He had clearly been pleased to get her letter. Who else was there to write to him? Only the Prestons, and letter-writing was not much in their line. In the past her letters to him had been very practical affairs, concerning the *Swan*. In future she would write to him regularly.

'Please, Ma! Please read mine now!' An impatient Effie had been frantically tugging at her apron for some time.

'Very well. Look, Uncle Jed's sent you a picture of a yacht. Isn't it lovely? He says, "Dear Effie, thank you for the beautiful drawing of the yacht. The one in this picture is not half as good as yours, but it was the best I could find. I am looking forward to seeing you again, your loving uncle Jed." And he sends you some nice big kisses.'

'I could read those for myself,' said Effie proudly, as she took her postcard and put it on the dresser – the most prominent place she could find. 'That's mine,' she announced. 'That's my very own postcard from Uncle Jed. The postman brought it specially for me.'

Seeing the child's delight, Amy wondered if Jed had any idea how much pleasure he had given Effie by sending her a card of her own. She was touched by his thoughtfulness.

In a few short weeks Brixham changed from a summer resort back into a workaday port again as the visitors departed and the men who had been on the yachts or fishing elsewhere came back. Jed called upon Amy almost as soon as he returned home. He looked bronzed and fit, and was unusually expansive about his adventures at the numerous regattas along the coast.

'You're really glad you joined the yacht crew?' asked Amy, though she knew his reply.

'Very glad. It was a real experience. Not that I'd like to be on yachts permanently. I prefer a bit more independence. But for a few months it was grand, and the money was even grander.'

'I thought the money would come into it somewhere,' Amy smiled. 'I suppose you've already been to have a look at the *Swan*?'

'Of course! She's come through splendidly. Dry as a bone. Harry says he's hardly had to use the pump on her all summer.'

'And what's your next purchase?'

'I'm going to have a word with John Prout tomorrow about getting the riggers to her.'

'Tomorrow? You certainly aren't wasting any time.'

'Why hang about? She'll look a proper boat again with her masts stepped and the rigging up. I can't wait to see her.'

'And have you got any work to be going on with to pay for things like food and lodgings?'

'I have. Don't worry. Sally won't be turning me out on to the street just yet.' He gave a quick grin. 'I met George Beale when I was down looking over the *Swan*. I told him if I hadn't come across his example I would never have thought of burdening myself with a half-wrecked hulk. He laughed, then said, "Seeing's I've got so much to answer for, the least I can do is offer you a job. There's a place going on the *Charity* if you want it." Naturally I said yes.'

'That's good news.' Amy was delighted. 'She's a lovely boat. How could she be anything else seeing she was built at Prout's yard?'

'As long as she floats, that's all I ask,' he said gravely.

'Oh you!' Amy gave him a playful thump.

Remembering fire strange awkwardness there had been between them on their last meeting she could only wonder at her own silliness. Jed made no mention of it until he was leaving, then he said, 'I haven't thanked you for writing to me.'

'I should have written more.'

'The letters you did write were fine.'

'Next time you go away I'll write to you regularly,' she promised. 'Proper letters, not just news of the arrival of a new anchor chain for the *Swan*, or how much two fifty-fathom warps are going to cost.'

'Good. I'd like that.' He meant it, too.

Not that Jed is likely to go away for a while, she thought contentedly. Not until the better weather next year brings the 'round land' season again.

'Her'm looking proper vitty now her'm fully rigged,' said Harry Preston approvingly, as they regarded the *Swan* together one day.

'She does look splendid, doesn't she?' agreed Amy proudly. 'I suppose the next step is a suit of sails.'

'And a pretty penny that's going to cost!' Harry winced at the prospect. 'I only hopes Jed idn't going to have to get deeper in debt to pay for they.'

Harry's worries proved unfounded for, one day, Jed came hammering on Amy's door, his face alight with excitement.

'I've got them!' he declared. 'I've got the sails!'

'You have?' Amy was astonished. 'I didn't know you had spoken for any.'

'I hadn't. These are made already.'

'They're second-hand? That's unusual, isn't it? What's wrong with them?'

'Nothing's wrong with them. They're some George Beale had. They're cross-thread sails he tried a while back, but he didn't get on with them. He was going to cut them up for boat covers and the like, until I made him an offer.'

Amy was uneasy. 'It isn't like George Beale, or any other boat owner for that matter, to lash out on sails and then discard them. They cost far too much. What's being cross-thread to do with it?'

'They're a new type of sail that came in a few years back. Instead of having the weave of the canvas up and down, they are cut with the threads across. It makes them much stronger. They're growing quite popular on the east coast.'

'But not with George Beale,' said Amy. 'What's he got against them?'

Jed shrugged. 'Like anything else they've got things for and against. Some reckon they're a bit too strong and don't give; if a sea breaks into the belly of the mainsail, instead of ripping and letting the water out like the old sort, it'd be more likely to capsize the boat.'

'That sounds downright dangerous.'

Again Jed shrugged. 'The answer is to know what you're doing and not catch a big sea. I reckon you'd be very unlucky to have it happen. The east-coast men seem to manage well enough.'

'Oh, Jed, do you think you were wise?'

'To be honest I'd prefer the ordinary sails I'm used to – and George wasn't too keen to sell them to me – but beggars can't be choosers.' He looked at Amy's anxious face and smiled reassuringly. 'Having them means I can start fishing earlier – and earning money. You know I'm always careful, I won't take risks. I'll use them for a while until I can afford some ordinary sails. Believe me, I've no intention of risking the *Swan*, not after the hard work I've put in.'

With that she had to be content, though she was not easy in her mind.

Interest in the *Swan's* progress continued unabated among the habitues of the harbour.

'Her'll be fishing by Easter,' was one prediction.

'Never! Jed Greenway won't be landing nothing this side of regatta, you mark my words!' was a more gloomy verdict.

'What do you say, Mizz Prout? You knows more about un than most?'

Amy would never be drawn into the arguments.

'Jed will go when he's ready, and not a moment sooner,' was her stock answer.

Before the *Swan* could begin fishing, her new sails had to be adjusted to fit and tried out. With her heart in her mouth, Amy watched the smack being put through her paces out in the bay. From where she and Effie stood, everything seemed to be going splendidly, and the longer the boat was at sea the greater grew her confidence.

Eventually the *Swan* sailed back into the lee of the breakwater and made for the harbour.

'There, wasn't the *Swan* splendid?' Amy demanded of Effie.

'Her went a fair treat,' agreed an old fisherman nearby, thinking she was addressing him. 'That were a danged good trial. What do you say, Arthur?'

Arthur, equally old and weather-beaten, was less enthusiastic.

'Cross-threads!' he said dourly. 'He'm going to regret they!'

Amy closed her ears to his grim pronouncement. The *Swan* had proved herself to be as good as she had been in her heyday; she was sure there was no more cause for concern.

Jed went to Wales that summer. He felt he owed it to George Beale to take the *Charity* round land for him one more time.

While he was away Amy kept her promise and wrote to him regularly, letters which he meticulously answered. She found she enjoyed both sending and receiving, and the postman's regular delivery became the high spot of her week.

When Jed returned to Brixham the final stages of the fitting out of the *Swan* provided plenty of excitement. Then came the taking on of the crew, the last stage before the boat eventually returned to her place in the fishing fleet.

One disappointment for Jed was that Harry would not sail with him.

'Maybe he doesn't like the idea of serving under a younger skipper,' Amy suggested.

'I thought that, too,' said Jed. 'But he says no. Matthew Burton is the reason he won't come. The old man's beginning to look really ill, and Harry hasn't the heart to leave him, not after sailing with him for so many years.'

'How like Harry,' Amy said.

'Yes. It's a pity, but it can't be helped. However, he's recommended some of his relatives.'

'You'll certainly have plenty of choice.' She chuckled, for Harry's family were a prolific lot.

Jed finished up with one of Harry's brothers-in-law, a cousin by marriage and, oddly enough, a boy who was no relation.

'Slipped up there, didn't you?' commented Amy with a grin.

'I took him on to even things up a bit,' explained Jed. 'In case the Prestons mutiny. Seriously, they're both good men. Not as good as Harry, but experienced seamen, all the same. Talking of Harry, have you heard his news? Old Man Burton's finally given up the sea, and he's made Harry skipper of the *Our Violet*.'

'That's wonderful! No one deserves it more.'

'I agree. I'm glad Harry didn't come in with me now. I could never have offered him anything like that. He's like a dog with two tails.' Jed gave a sudden snort of laughter.

'What are you sniggering at?' demanded Amy.

'Well, everyone used to think that whoever took on the *Our Violet* had to take on Lucy Burton too. I was just wondering what Sally would do if Lucy so much as laid a finger on Harry.'

'There'd be blood from here to the turnpike,' chuckled Amy. 'As for Lucy, there's a rumour she's going to marry that fellow who works in the chemists's.'

'What, the skinny one?' Jed laughed again. 'He'll need a drop of something to build him up if that's the case.'

'Your name was linked with Lucy Burton once,' Amy reminded him.

'I escaped, thank heavens! Her type doesn't appeal to me.'

'What type does appeal to you, then?'

'Not Lucy Burton, that's the truth! I'm grateful to her, though. If she hadn't turned nasty I wouldn't have the *Swan*. I might have been skipper of the *Our Violet* instead of Harry, but I'd have been shackled to that wench for life. It doesn't bear thinking of.' And he shuddered.

'Why did she turn against you in such a way? You never did explain.'

'Nor will I,' declared Jed, a rare spark of mischief in his eyes. 'Not until you're an old woman long past being shocked.'

'I don't shock easily now,' protested Amy. She was wasting her time. Jed refused to say any more.

'If Lucy Burton's not your type, tell me who is!' she persisted.

'Very well, since it interests you.' He closed Ms eyes and pretended to think. 'My type is... ketch-rigged, weighs about twenty-five tons, about seventy feet long overall, with a nine-foot draught and... Ooh, stop hitting me! Ow!'

Their mock battle ended in laughter. But after Jed had gone Amy was still curious: what had happened between him and Lucy? She also wondered what sort of a girl really appealed to Jed. It was something she would have dearly liked to know.

The first Amy knew about the *Swan* sailing with the fishing fleet was when she walked along the Quay and saw the moorings were empty.

'Sailed on the tide with the others, as fine as you please,' she was informed by an aged fisherman who was mending nets on the quayside.

Minutes later she encountered Sally.

'Did you know he meant to go fishing today?' Amy demanded.

'No, he didn't say a word,' said Sally. 'He were that quiet and brooding I knowd something was up. Since he swore nothing was wrong it could only have been one thing, couldn't it? He were off to the fishing with the *Swan*.'

'Why didn't he tell me?' Amy protested.

'Why didn't he tell anyone?' replied Sally. 'But idn't that typical of Jed? Either he didn't want no fuss, or he didn't think no one'd be interested. 'Ee knows what 'e'm like.'

'It's about time he realized his friends are interested in what he does!' said Amy crossly. 'For goodness' sake, he's twenty-four! How much longer is it going to take him to appreciate that he has got friends, and good ones at that?'

'Well, you'm the best one to bring it home to un,' said Sally. 'Give un a good piece of your mind for sneaking off and doing things on the quiet when there's folks as is concerned about un.'

'I think I will,' declared Amy. 'I have known him longer than anyone else.'

'That wadn't what I meant,' said Sally. Then seeing the perplexed expression on Amy's face she went on, 'Never mind, maid, 'ee'll get round to un eventually, I 'spects.'

'Round to what?' asked Amy.

In reply Sally merely laughed and hurried off.

Amy did not rush over to East Quay when news of the *Swan's* arrival came. If Jed had not told her he was going out fishing then no doubt he had his reasons. The last thing she wanted was for him to think she was spying on him, but she could not miss the landing of the *Swan's* first catch. The harbour was so crammed with trawlers that the *Swan* had to moor up to one of the central buoys and transfer her catch ashore by punt.

In the jostling and confusion of small boats trying to land, Amy almost lost sight of the one carrying the *Swan's* fish. Her curiosity would not be quelled and she edged forward, eager to see how many baskets it carried. Her view was not clear enough to count them, but there seemed to be a respectable number. She waited until she finally saw the punt head off towards another smack, proof that the catch from the *Swan* had been unloaded. Then, passing the fish market on her way home, she tried unsuccessfully to find the baskets bearing Jed's marker.

Suddenly a canvas bag full of fish appeared over her shoulder from behind, and a familiar voice said, 'Can you use these?'

Turning round she found herself facing Jed. 'I can use them all right.' She felt embarrassed, fearing he would resent her curiosity.

'What are you doing here?' he asked. 'You're out and about early, aren't you?'

Amy's diffidence faded. 'Did you think I wouldn't come along to see your first catch landed?' she retorted. 'Why didn't you tell me you were going out?'

'I didn't—'

'And don't you dare say you didn't think I'd be interested, Jed Greenway,' she interrupted. 'Or I'll box your ears, here in front of everyone!'

'Then I won't,' he said, and grinned.

'And was your first catch a good one?' Amy asked, more calmly.

'Pretty fair.'

'What does that mean? Really, you are the most aggravating man!'

'It means we took about seventy baskets...'

'But that's very good!' She beamed with delight.

'...And if you want to know what Sally gave me for my vittals, it was bread and cheese and pickle.'

'Oh.' She was suddenly chastened. Here she had been grumbling at him for not telling her things, and really she had no right to expect it. It was nothing to do with her. 'I'm sorry,' she said. 'I was being nosy. You should tell me to mind my own business.'

'Would it do any good?'

'Probably not,' she admitted. 'But you should tell me, anyway. I've no call to interfere in your affairs, and I'm sorry.'

'Don't be sorry. I've got used to you interfering, as you call it. I'd miss it if you stopped.'

She looked up at him sharply, not certain how to take his remarks. His face was serious, as usual, then his lips began to twitch.

'Oh you... !' snorted Amy. She was relieved to see him smile, but then when had he ever been angry with her? Strangely enough she could not remember one single occasion.

'I've got to go,' she said.

'I'll come and tell you how much the catch fetches.'

'There's no need,' Amy said quickly.

'You'd only find out from someone else.' He tried to sound resigned, but again he was grinning.

—

The *Swan* soon became such a customary part of the fishing fleet that people stopped remarking on her or her history; her days as the *Muck Pot* were forgotten. As if to continue her good fortune the weather held fine and the catches were good. Amy was pleased to note the furrow of worry between Jed's brows lessening as he began to pay off his debts.

'How things change,' remarked Jessie contentedly to Amy one afternoon. 'A mere two years ago I'd never have believed this could happen.' And she flung out a hand to indicate her parlour. No longer was it neat and tidy. The floor was given over to Todd, who sat in the middle, surrounded by playthings. But not for long.

'He's off again,' Amy warned, laughing, as the child made a dash for the sideboard. He had recently discovered the secret of opening the doors, and much preferred emptying the cupboards to playing with boring wooden bricks or rag animals.

'I don't know where he gets the energy from,' declared his proud mother, going after him and returning him to his toys.

'He's certainly active,' agreed Amy as he set off again.

'There's nothing breakable he can reach,' said Jessie, giving up the unequal struggle and sinking into her chair. 'It's good to see him bonny and energetic, after some of the scares he's given us. At times I get quite frightened because everything is going so well, not just with Todd, but with John and the business. I've got everything I've ever wanted and it's frightening. Is that silly?'

'No,' replied Amy gently. 'I know exactly what you mean. I feel the same way when I step through my front door. At one time I never thought I'd have a proper home of my own, you see, and sometimes even now I can't believe it. I have to touch something – the teapot, the rocking chair, the china dog on the mantelshelf – anything to prove to myself that it's real.'

'You had a harsh upbringing,' Jessie's voice was very quiet. 'And I'm afraid that at first I didn't do much to make things easier.'

'I found your place a definite improvement on the workhouse, if that's what's bothering you,' grinned Amy. 'And I'd never been so well fed in my life. In fact, if it hadn't been for those wretched potatoes I would've managed fine. Those potatoes!' she repeated, spluttering at the memory.

'T-they were everywhere...' Jessie joined in her laughter. 'And— and I was absolutely furious because John wouldn't stop laughing—'

Hilarity overwhelmed the pair of them until tears ran down their faces.

'It was a long time ago,' gasped Amy, searching for her handkerchief.

'A lot of things have happened since then.' Jessie too was mopping her eyes. She became suddenly serious. 'How I went on at John because he would insist upon sending to a London workhouse for a girl. But he was right; he usually is. Otherwise, you wouldn't have come. I'm glad you did.'

This was quite an admission. Amy stretched out and grasped her sister-in-law's hand.

'And I'm glad I came,' she replied in a choked voice. 'I wouldn't be anywhere else.'

Jessie's air of contentment was contagious. Amy, too, felt that life was good as her days were filled with her child, her home and her work.

Sometimes, looking at Effie, she thought of Seth. No one had ever heard of him again after he had run off in Bristol. Where was he? she wondered. How was he getting on? How sad that he had no knowledge of his lovely daughter. But perhaps it was all for the best.

A major change came to Amy's routine; Effie started school, with such enthusiasm that she was invariably up betimes, and berating her mother for fear she might be late.

'Don't be in such a hurry. We've plenty of time,' protested Amy as Effie towed her up the steep hill.

'But, Ma, we've got singing today,' insisted the child. 'I must be in time for singing. It's my favourite.'

The trouble was that sums were her favourite, too, and reading and scripture and writing. In fact, every day had some incentive for her to be there in good time. Amy smiled fondly, and hoped her daughter's eagerness would survive the chilly mornings of winter. The prompt starts suited her very well. They meant that she could get to work early.

Prout's Yard had just laid down a new boat. Amy always found this intensely interesting, and kept interrupting her own work to peep through the door to keep abreast of what was going on. The heavy keel had already been laid and she watched as the stout stern-post was being raised, under John's critical eye.

What happened next she could not tell. There was a shout of 'Look out, Maister!' and the stern-post began to topple. To Amy's horrified eyes it seemed to fall in slow motion, but in reality it fell quickly. Too quickly for John to get out of its way. As he tried to escape, his feet slithering among the pebbles, he tripped. When the stern-post hit him he was sprawled across one of the timbers set aside to support the boat during its construction.

Already Amy was running towards the scene. By the time she reached John some of the men were lifting the post off him. She gasped in horror at the injury it had caused. The piece of timber was heavy enough to inflict severe damage on its own, but it had also struck John at an awkward angle, trapping his leg against the rough timber. His thigh was shattered and blood was gushing from a deep gash.

Instinctively she pressed her thumbs above the open wound, trying to stop the flow of blood. If only she knew what to do next… Anger at her own ignorance gripped her. To her relief Charlie Bowden came hurrying up.

'Oh, my lor'!' he exclaimed in horror, dropping to his knees beside John.

A lifetime as a shipwright among the dangers and sharp tools of a boatyard had taught Charlie a lot about coping with injury.

'Quick, girl, your petticoat. Idn't no time for modesty,' he said, his work-worn fingers taking over the task of stemming the blood.

Amy did not need to be told. She had wriggled out of her underskirt and ripped part of the white cambric into strips. The rest she folded into a firm pad which she handed to Charlie.

'Thank heaven he'm fainted, poor devil, else he'd be in agony,' said Charlie.

With infinite care he managed to staunch the flow and bandage the wound, then he improvised a splint. Amy did what she could to help him, but she felt it was little enough. John lay so white and still when they had finished that her heart missed a beat.

'He's not… ?'

'No.' Charlie shook his head at her unfinished question. 'And he'm not bleeding so desperate, thanks be. 'Tis as bad a break as I've seen, though. The sooner us gets him to hospital the better.'

One of the apprentices approached, out of breath. He looked shaken and grey, but triumphant.

'I— I've been up to the road,' he puffed. 'Just caught the station carrier passing – he'm backing his cart as close as he can – the lady across the road – her'm sending some blankets and such—'

'Good lad! Oh, you good lad!' Amy wished she could say something more to praise such quick thinking, but her mind was concentrated on John.

The men fashioned a stretcher from poles and canvas and, under Charlie's guidance, carefully lifted John on to it. As they took him to the carrier's cart, Amy followed behind feeling helpless.

'I'll go to the hospital with him,' she said, hoping to have found a way of being useful.

Charlie was not so sure. 'I think me and a couple of the lads should go,' he said. 'We'm going to have to hold tight to him going up they hills. Us don't want the poor soul sliding down to the bottom of the cart and making things worse.'

He was right, of course. Amy stood aside, feeling more useless than ever.

Then Charlie said the words she had been dreading. 'Someone'll have to tell his missus,' he said, looking straight at her.

He was right. Who else could go? Amy grabbed her coat and set off at a run. Before she reached Furzeham she was gasping for breath and a stitch stabbed at her side. She barely noticed the discomfort. She had other, far more serious worries. How could she break the news? How was she to tell Jessie that her days of perfect happiness had come to an end?

Chapter Fourteen

The new cottage hospital, Brixham's pride and joy, stood on a hillside overlooking the centre of the town. Neither Amy nor Jessie had breath to spare as they sped in that direction. Hurriedly they climbed the final precipitous flight of steps leading from Fore Street to the road above. The idea of calling a cab never occurred to either of them; the slopes were too steep and the ways too narrow. It was quicker to go on foot, ignoring bursting lungs and agonized muscles.

Charlie was waiting for them in the entrance hall. In his working clothes he looked out of place amidst the white tiles and pristine paintwork.

'The doctor's just come,' he said. 'He'm in there with the maister now.'

At that moment a nurse approached, rustling with starch.

'Mrs Prout?' she asked, looking from Amy to Jessie.

Jessie stepped forward.

'Where is he? Can I see him?' she begged.

'Not for a while.' The snowy wings of her cap shook regretfully. 'If you would care to sit down, the doctor will have a word with you as soon as he can.'

The nurse rustled away again, leaving them in the eerie silence of the corridor. Amy slid her arm comfortingly about Jessie as they sank on to the hard wooden chairs. She could feel her sister-in-law trembling through her thick coat. Amy had never been in a hospital before. Nor, she suspected, had Jessie, and the unfamiliar atmosphere, redolent of carbolic and ether, seemed to add to the nightmarish quality of the day.

'Grand place this,' remarked Charlie, looking round.

'Yes, isn't it?' agreed Amy. 'Thank goodness we've got a hospital at long last.'

'That's true. Got the latest of everything up yer, they say. Maister's being looked after in the proper place, instead of just up the doctor's.'

'That he is. The best treatment and the best equipment.'

'It took long enough getting the money together, but 'tis worth every penny, I reckon. Every penny...'

The conversation between Amy and Charlie faded and died. It had been aimed solely at heartening Jessie, who showed no sign of having heard a word. She sat hunched up, her hands clasped tightly on her lap. The look of bleak despair on her face reminded Amy painfully of John's expression on the night that young Todd had been born. Here she was again, trying to give comfort when she was not certain there was much comfort to give.

Charlie was beginning to fidget. Amy looked at him over Jessie's bowed head.

'If 'ee don't need me no more, Mizz Prout, I'll be getting back,' he said. 'Don't 'ee worry none about the yard. I'll see to everything.'

'Very well, you go,' Amy said. 'We'll let you know how Mr Prout gets on.'

Charlie rose and turned to Jessie, clearly wanting to say something encouraging, yet not knowing how. He briefly put a hand on her shoulder before leaving. As he was going through the door, Amy suddenly hurried after him, conscious of how much had been left unsaid.

'Charlie,' she said quietly. 'We haven't begun to thank you for what you did today. However severe Mr Prout's injury turns out to be... whatever the outcome... it would all have been much worse if you hadn't been there.'

'There idn't no call for thanks.' Charlie looked uncomfortable at the idea. ''Tis only what anyone'd have done.'

'Not everyone would have known what to do. Me, for instance. I've never felt so useless in my life. Mrs Prout isn't taking much in at the moment, but when she can I'll be sure and tell her what you did.'

'There idn't no need,' Charlie repeated. 'I justs wants Mr Prout back safe and sound. He'm a good maister, and there idn't so many of they about as us can afford to spare them.'

After Charlie had gone the silence seemed more intense than ever, adding to their growing tension. Every door that opened, every voice that rang along the empty corridor made them jump. After what seemed an interminable wait Dr Searle approached, looking unfamiliar and informal in his shirt-sleeves. There was nothing informal about his expression. That was grim. Jessie leapt to her feet at the sight of him.

'John?' she said. 'My John?'

Dr Searle guided her back into her seat and took the chair recently vacated by Charlie.

'Mrs Prout,' he said gently. 'Your husband is suffering from a serious compound fracture of his thigh-bone. The only way I can even try to put it together again is by operating. He is being prepared now.'

'An operation? Oh no!' Jessie's already pinched features grew more haggard, and she raised her clenched fists to her mouth as if to hold back the horror.

The doctor took her hands in his.

'I know how much that word must alarm you,' he said. 'Doubtless your fears stem from the bad old days, when such things were little short of butchery. I promise you it won't be like that. Medical knowledge has advanced tremendously in these last few years. I will be treating your husband in a fully-equipped modern operating theatre, with properly trained and efficient staff to help me. Everything that can be done will be done, I assure you.'

'I know,' whispered Jessie through white lips. 'And thank you, doctor.'

'However, it will be some hours before you can see your husband. Apart from the operation he will need time to recover from the anaesthetic. Perhaps it would be better for you to go home and come back…' He stopped, brought to a halt by the outraged look in Jessie's eyes.

'I'm staying,' she said.

'Very well.' The doctor stood up. 'They will be ready for me now. I promise you will have news of your husband as soon as possible.'

The long wait continued. The only interlude was when a fresh-faced young nurse brought them some tea. Amy had lost track of time when the doctor returned. He was wearing his overcoat and in his hand he carried his hat and his bag.

'Your husband is sleeping, Mrs Prout,' he said, 'It will be some while before he regains consciousness, but you may go and see him if you wish.'

Jessie was on her feet and following the nurse almost before the words were out of his mouth.

'How is he, doctor?' asked Amy.

'As well as can be expected,' was the non-committal reply. He gave a tired smile, tinged with compassion. 'Your sister-in-law is fortunate to have your support, Mrs Prout. She's going to need it for a long while yet, I'm afraid.'

'You don't mean——? John's life isn't in danger, is it?' Amy asked in alarm.

'Not his life,' replied Dr Searle, and with a brief, 'Goodbye', he departed, leaving her wondering what he meant.

Amy waited, breaking her vigil only once to fetch Effie from school and take her up to the house at Furzeham.

'Don't 'ee worry, I'll stay until 'ee gets back,' said Aggie. 'I won't leave they babes to Millie, never fear.'

'Thank you,' said Amy gratefully. 'And perhaps you'd make up a bed for us. I think we'd better spend the night here.'

It was dark before Jessie could be persuaded to leave the hospital.

'He looks so ill, and he's in such pain,' she kept saying on the way home.

'He's in good hands,' was the only comfort Amy could give.

The next few days fell into a set pattern, with Amy and Effie continuing to stay at Furzeham, and Jessie spending as much time as she was permitted at the hospital. At first Amy accompanied her sister-in-law, but as she was never allowed to see John she found herself spending her time uselessly sitting in the corridor.

'If you've no objection, I think I'll go in to the boatyard this morning and see how things are going on there,' she said.

'Would you?' Jessie was grateful. 'Poor John's very concerned about the business, for all his mind's foggy with the stuff they give him to ease the pain. If you're there it might make him more settled.'

'Right, I'll bring back a report that you can pass on to him, if you're sure he's up to being bothered with such things.'

'He's not really, poor lad, but you try and stop him. Tossing and turning with fretting, he was, and it causes him agony to move.'

'I'll bring you the news to tell him – and I'll make sure it's good.'

When Amy returned to the boatyard she soon saw that she would not need to falsify any of her reports to John. Under Charlie's supervision, the boat on the stocks was progressing well. Nevertheless, her appearance was greeted with frank relief by the foreman shipwright.

'I be glad to see 'ee and no mistake, Mizz Prout,' Charlie said, after he had asked about John. 'Us've managed fair enough so far, but there's been letters and bills and such coming in, and us didn't know what to do about they. They'm stacked on your desk, and you'm welcome to 'em.'

'It sounds as though I've got some work to catch up on,' smiled Amy. 'Apart from that everything's going all right?'

'Us've managed, I suppose.'

'We have to go on managing,' replied Amy. 'The alternative is for us to be looking for other jobs.'

'That's true enough.'

He looked as if there was something else he wanted to say, but when Amy asked, 'Is there anything bothering you?' he shook his head and went back to work.

Amy made for the office. There was certainly a fair amount of letters and messages waiting for her attention, and she settled down to tackle them. It soon became apparent that while there were some matters she could deal with on her own initiative there were many more that were in John's province. They could manage for a while without him, maybe for as long as three or four weeks, but any longer and she wondered how they would cope.

Charlie came into the office half-way through the morning. He looked decidedly uncomfortable.

'Can I have a word, Mizz Prout?' he asked.

Amy laid down her pen.

'I knew there was something troubling you,' she said. 'Come on, tell me what it is.'

'I don't hardly like to ask, not with the maister so poorly, but some of the lads are a bit bothered... They wants to know when they'm getting paid.'

'My stars!' Amy clasped her head in dismay. 'Friday's come and gone... No, it must be two Fridays, and we didn't even notice.'

'Not surprising, really. And if one or two of the lads wadn't a bit pushed – they with young childer – I wouldn't have mentioned un.'

'No, you were right to tell me. Now, let me think... I will have to ask Mrs John for authority to draw money. Tell the men not to worry, they'll be paid tomorrow if possible, the day after at the latest.'

'Good, they'm going to be pleased about that. I'll go and tell un.' Charlie was going out of the door when Amy called him back. 'Two days can be a long time if you've no money,' she said. 'Especially if you've children to feed. Are any of the men really hard pressed? They're to come to me if they are. There's a bit of petty cash to hand, I could manage something immediate.'

Charlie smiled. 'Bless 'ee, my dear, there idn't no call for that, much as the lads'll appreciate it. No, us've made sure among ourselves that everyone's managing. Us knowd it was only temporary.'

'That'll be one good message I can pass on to Mr Prout, the fact that his men are going to be paid. I wouldn't be surprised if that wasn't one of the things that's been worrying him.'

'Restless, be he?'

'Yes, Mrs John says he has the boatyard on his mind constantly, no matter what they give him to dim the pain.'

'Idn't that typical? Didn't I say he were a good maister? Us'll make danged sure the yard carries on proper, then he won't have no reason to worrit hisself.'

'Good, I'll tell him that.'

'Do that, maid! Anything as'll help.'

It seemed strange working at the yard without John being there. He was such an easy-going, unassuming man that Amy had never realized what a tight control he kept on his business. A skilled craftsman himself, he oversaw everything. Nothing slipped past his keen gaze. Amy gave a sigh. She wondered how they were going to keep up the same standard of work in his absence. One thing was clear: while John was still incapacitated she would have to come into the yard every day instead of just three mornings a week.

Jessie looked drawn and exhausted when she returned from the hospital.

'I wish he was making better progress,' she declared. 'He doesn't seem one jot better. I keep asking the nurses how he's getting on and all they'll say is, "It's early days!"'

'They're right. It was a very bad break that John suffered, we both know that. It's bound to take longer than a simple fracture. But he's strong and healthy and he's always led an active life. That'll stand him in good stead.'

'I wish I could think that. I'd be much happier if someone would tell me something. It's being kept in the dark that's so hard to take.'

'Why don't you make a point of seeing the doctor? He goes up every day, doesn't he?'

'Yes, he'll be there tomorrow afternoon. That's a good idea; I'll see him and demand some answers.' Jessie's brief moment of assertiveness died. 'Will you come with me?'

'Of course I will. Now there's something I need to ask you. The men haven't been paid for two weeks and there are other bills. If I could have some sort of authority, with you countersigning...' Amy explained what was needed with great care. She could have saved herself the bother.

Jessie said, 'Do whatever you think best,' without having seemed to have heard a word.

'We could call in at the bank on the way to the hospital?'

The word 'hospital' penetrated Jessie's consciousness.

'If it doesn't make us late for seeing the doctor and visiting John,' she said.

At the bank it was Amy who made the arrangements; Jessie was too distracted to take any interest.

'I wish I could get her to understand more,' Amy said to the bank manager. 'At the moment she would put her name to anything I set in front of her. It is a very delicate situation for me. I've never had control of such large sums of money before, and I'd be happier if someone else shared the responsibility with me.'

'From what I have seen of your accounting, Mrs Prout, I am sure you have nothing to worry about,' said the bank manager. 'However, I understand your predicament, and if you have any difficulties please come to me. Also, if it would make it easier for you I will give Mr Prout's account my personal attention until he is fit again.'

'Thank you.' Amy was much relieved.

'And how is Mr Prout getting on? Is his leg mending well?'

'That's what we're going to find out now,' said Amy, and for some reason she felt a cold spasm of dread.

The sense of foreboding stayed with her on the way to the hospital, and was not lessened by the solemn face of the doctor when they were ushered in to him.

Once in the doctor's consulting room, Jessie's tense lethargy left her and she became quite belligerent.

'I want to know how my husband is progressing, Dr Searle,' she stated. 'I want to know the truth instead of always being fobbed off with "As well as can be expected" and pointless statements like that. Tell me frankly, is his leg mending properly?'

The doctor considered his words carefully before he spoke.

'The honest answer to your question, Mrs Prout, is that we do not know,' he said. 'We can only wait and pray. A compound fracture as serious as the one your husband suffered does not knit together easily.'

'But his leg will mend?'

'We hope it will.'

'You say that as though you have doubts. You mean my John might have a crippled leg for life?'

'If the bone does not knit that is one possibility.'

'And what is the other possibility?' asked Jessie, anxiety driving away the last vestige of her aggression. Then, when the doctor did not reply she whispered, 'Oh no! Not that! Never that!'

'I'm afraid so,' said the doctor quietly. 'I regret to say that amputation is something we might have to consider.'

Jessie buried her face in her hands. Amy put her arms about her and held her tightly, rocking her gently as the sobs shook her sister-in-law. The thought that John might lose his leg made her feel physically sick. A sudden picture came back to her of the night she first arrived in Brixham, of John striding out, her box carried effortlessly on his shoulder. The prospect of that same man trying to hobble about on one leg filled her with horror.

'It's not certain he'll lose his leg, is it?' she demanded, determined to find cause for hope. 'The bone might still mend?'

'It might.' The doctor was not optimistic.

'What are his chances?'

'About fifty-fifty.'

It did not sound good, and the sick dread inside Amy grew. Aloud she said confidently, 'Then he has an equal chance. That can't be bad. We mustn't lose hope.' To her ears her voice sounded false and over-bright, but perhaps she could manage to encourage Jessie.

'How soon will we…?' Jessie's words faded away.

'That I cannot say,' replied the doctor. 'Another fortnight, a month… If only we had some means of seeing how the fragments of bone are knitting then I could be more definite. Since we have not then we can only wait and pray.'

'Does John know?' asked Jessie.

'No, we thought it best not to worry him unnecessarily.'

'Good.' Unexpectedly Jessie sat upright in her chair, and scrubbed away her tears, an expression of intense determination on her face. 'And he need never know because it idn't going to happen. The poor lad's got enough to pull him down, what with the pain and me drooping over him weeping and wailing. Well, not any more! My John's only going to hear good news and see people with cheerful faces. He'm going to get better because I idn't going to let un do nothing else.' Her brief lapse into broad Devon dialect was ample proof of the strain she was under.

She stood up and caught sight of herself in the mirror.

'Good gracious! The way I look isn't going to do anything to brighten John's day, that's for certain. First thing tomorrow I'm going down Decent's to buy myself a new hat. Until then the poor soul's going to have to put up with me as I am.' As she made for the door she paused, glancing back at the doctor. 'I know what'd cheer him up. Ten minutes of my sister-in-law's company. It's time he was seeing faces other than mine and the nurses', and besides, he's getting desperate for proper news of his yard.'

She swept out, leaving Amy and the doctor staring after her in amazement.

'Can I go and see him?' asked Amy.

'I don't seem to have any say in the matter,' smiled Dr Searle. 'Perhaps Mrs Prout is right. Cheerful patients always mend quicker than miserable ones. But no more than ten minutes, please.'

Amy was shocked when she saw John. Not only did he look pale and ill, his face furrowed with pain, he appeared to have aged.

'Well, have I a boatyard left?' he asked weakly, making a manful attempt to smile.

'Just about. There was a plank or two still lying about when I came away,' Amy grinned back.

'Jessie says you're going in every day. That's good of you.'

'Someone's got to go down there and crack the whip. No, I have to be honest. Charlie's got everything under control and the men are working well.'

'And what about the boat?'

'That's going on splendidly. The owner was in yesterday, all the way from Hull, and he was very pleased…'

The ten minutes sped by. The way John drank in every detail betrayed how anxious he was about his business. The snippets of news she had sent via Jessie had evidently not been enough.

'Chatting to you did John the world of good,' said Jessie later that evening, after she had returned from her second visit of the day to the hospital. 'The nurse said he had a lovely restful sleep after we'd gone.'

'In that case, I'll drop in every day for a few minutes, if it will help, just to give him news of the yard.'

'Would you?' Jessie looked grateful. 'There's no doubt it eases his mind, and that's bound to help him. Between us we'll have him walking about again as good as new.'

For the rest of the evening Jessie was optimistic and lull of plans to help John. Amy admired this new spirit in her sister-in-law. She might have believed in it completely if, during the night, she had not been woken by muffled sobs coming through the wall that divided her bedroom from Jessie's.

Amy kept her word and visited John every day, telling him of the things going on in the yard. She was always selective in what she told him, relaying only the positive news. He was not strong enough to tolerate problems or anything controversial. In the meantime she and Jessie kept an eagle eye on him, eager for the least sign of progress, dreading the grim look on the doctor's face. One week passed, then two... The waiting seemed interminable.

In the days and weeks which followed, Jessie and Amy began to snatch at anything hopeful. Any suggestion of a lessening of inflammation or an easing of swelling was enough to send their hopes soaring, to have them plummet again at some other setback. Every day they dreaded the ominous summons into the doctor's presence, every night they heaved a sigh of relief that it had not come.

Conditions at the boatyard were becoming more complicated. For a while everything went along relatively smoothly, but as John continued to be incapacitated the number of matters requiring his attention grew.

One day Charlie clumped across the pebbles towards Amy, a glum expression on his face.

Concerned, Amy asked him what the matter was.

'If 'ee wants to know I'll be glad when Maister's back, and that's the truth of it.'

'Is something wrong? It can't be the boat, surely? I thought this morning how splendidly the planking's going.'

'The boat's going well enough, there's no denying. What frazzles me is having to decide things.'

'What sort of things?'

'When to order this and that, and whether us should buy or not. You see, over to Churston Quay they'm breaking up the *Mary Jane* Good li'l craft her were until her broke her back being put up on the blocks – danged fools made a hash of it. Any road, there's some fine timber coming out of her, decent seasoned stuff. Normally the maister'd be after it like a shot, but I don't know what to do.'

'You've seen it and it's good?'

'Yes. I don't suppose you could mention it to the maister, to see what he wants doing?'

Amy considered carefully. 'No, I don't think we should bother him about such things yet,' she said. 'He takes a great interest in the yard and asks questions, but I honestly don't think he's up to making decisions at the moment.'

'I didn't think he would be. Trouble is, if us leaves un much longer then someone else'll have un.'

'Could we ask to have it held for us until Mr Prout's a bit better?'

'That's going to be a long time, bain't it, Mizz Prout? And they wouldn't hold un for long, there's too many folks eager to find well-seasoned timber.'

'Then what are we to do? Do you think we should have it?'

Charlie shuffled uncomfortably.

'That idn't for me to say. I can do aught you ask concerning building a boat, and I can choose the right timber for the right job, but buying…! I want naught to do with un. Buying timber, that's always been the maister's job. If he idn't yer, then I suppose 'tis youm.'

Amy took a deep breath.

'I'm not in charge of the yard,' she protested.

'Then if you idn't, who is? Us've muddled through so far, but with Maister likely to be abed for a long time, us've got to have someone to say what's what.'

'But not me. I don't know enough, for one thing, and the men would resent it for another.'

'Maybe they would, but they could take their choice. A maister in petticoats who pays regular, or no maister and no pay. You'm the one as deals with the bank and handles the money, so you'm in charge.'

Amy was rather alarmed by the responsibility being thrust upon her. There was a lot of sense in what Charlie said; someone had to be in control until John was strong enough to take over again. The fact that he might never return to the yard was something she refused to consider.

'You've looked at this timber, you say?' she said. 'Have you made a list of what we could use?'

'Yes, yer 'tis, along with the rough prices.' He tore a page from his notebook and handed it to her.

'Right, then I'll have a look at it.' Amy went back to the office.

The matter of the timbers from the *Mary Jane* occupied her for some time. Carefully she balanced the costs scribbled down by Charlie against the current prices of new wood and what they had paid for reclaimed stuff on other occasions. Timber was John's major financial outlay, and he had a lot of capital tied up in the piles of planks and logs which littered the beach. But these were assets which were quickly used up. They needed constant replenishing. Should they buy the timber? Could they afford not to? She had to come to a decision one way or another. After much consideration Amy went out to find Charlie.

'I don't think we should miss these timbers from the *Mary Jane*,' she said. 'Would you mind going over this afternoon and seeing about it? Everything you've got on your list, if we can get it.'

'Right you are, Mizz Prout,' beamed Charlie, happy that the responsibility had been lifted from him. 'I'll go straight after my dinner.'

He looked pleased. Amy felt less sure. This was her first big decision. Instead of feeling elated at this major step, she was consumed with doubts. It was a fair bit of John's money she was spending without his authority. What if she were making a grave mistake? Then she shook herself, as if to dispel her uncertainties. She had not made any mistake.

In Charlie's expert opinion the timber was of good quality and what they wanted. From her own calculations it was a bargain. John might not approve of what she had done, but he would not lose financially by it, that was the important thing. However, although Amy knew she would have to tell Jessie of her purchase, she decided it might be better to wait before passing the news on to John.

The fortnight the doctor had given as a possible deadline for a decision on John's leg passed, then the month. January came, bringing with it not only a new year but a new century. 1900! Still the dread word 'amputation' was never mentioned. The doctor began to use phrases such as, 'Not deteriorating' and, 'Progress seems to be being maintained'.

John continued to suffer a great deal of pain which, combined with his unaccustomed weakness and inactivity, made him irritable.

'My poor lad, is it any wonder?' said Jessie, excusing an uncharacteristic outburst of temper from her husband. 'Lying there day after day with hardly anything to take his mind off his suffering. He's missing the babe too. He feels the boy's growing away without him there to see it.'

'Maybe the sister will let you bring Todd up one afternoon, even just to peep round the door,' suggested Amy.

'That's a thought; I could ask.' Jessie considered the idea. 'The only blessing is that John doesn't know this awful worry that's hanging over him. He'd never be able to bear it, never!'

'He'll never need to find out,' said Amy with confidence.

Jessie smiled at her, a hint of tears in her eyes. 'Oh, Amy,' she said, 'what would I do without you?'

Amy was only too glad to be on hand and to give Jessie her support, but she missed her own home. She went back regularly to the cottage in Paradise Place, to air the rooms and to pick out some of Todd's books to take up to John. Every time she entered through the front door her heart yearned to be there permanently. The furnishings were modest, some of them were downright shabby, yet they were hers, and she longed to be back amongst them with Effie. She began to wonder if she would ever live there again.

One afternoon Jessie came back from the hospital with her face aglow.

'I saw the doctor today,' she exclaimed. 'And I asked him bluntly, "Is my John's leg to come off or not?" And do you know what he said? He said, "Barring unforeseen circumstances I do not think such severe measures will be necessary." What do you think of that?'

'Not necessary?' Amy stared at her in delight. 'That's marvellous! Absolutely marvellous!'

'It is, isn't it? My John's leg's safe! He's getting better!' In her excitement Jessie caught hold of Amy and together they danced a jig, then they collapsed into each other's arms, weeping with relief.

'Aren't we a pair of fools?' gasped Amy between sobs. 'The best news we've heard in months and here we are in tears.'

'I know. I'm happy, truly I am, but somehow I can't stop crying.' Jessie mopped ineffectually at her eyes with a handkerchief which was already soggy.

'Don't even try to stop. A nice cry's what we both need, it'll do us more good than anything else.'

Amy was right. They wept away the anxiety and tension which had been gathering during the recent weeks. When at last they ceased they were tired and limp, yet they both felt more cheerful and relaxed than they had done since before John's accident.

'You will come up with me to see him tonight, won't you?' begged Jessie. 'It'll be a sort of celebration, though he'll have no idea what a dreadful thing was threatening him. He'll see us looking happy and that's bound to make him more cheerful.'

'My, both of you tonight,' said John when they appeared at his bedside. 'Folk'll think I'm one of they pashas with a harem.'

For some reason Jessie and Amy found the remark funny and started to laugh. Ever since the afternoon they had been chuckling and giggling, light-headed with relief.

'It weren't that funny,' John pointed out.

'It was! I was picturing you with a turban round your head, blowing smoke through one of those things that looks like a pickle jar. What's it called?' demanded Jessie breathlessly.

'A hubble-bubble pipe,' supplied Amy, and that set them off again.

'You two had best quieten down afore Sister slings the pair of you out for being rowdy,' John cautioned. 'I can't think what's the matter with you. Been at the scrumpy or summat?'

'No, we haven't,' Jessie assured him between chuckles. 'We're just happy because...' Lost for a plausible explanation she looked at Amy.

'We're happy because – we're happy,' she said, straggling to control her mirth.

'You're sure you bain't tiddly, the pair of you?' insisted John.

'John Prout, what a thing to suggest. When did you ever see me inebriated?' Jessie tried to sound indignant, only to finish up helpless with laughter again.

'Then if it idn't the booze, and it idn't nothing you wants to tell me about, then it must be summat pretty special that's happened. Summat like me not having my leg cut off, for instance,' said John calmly.

The laughter died instantly.

'You knew!' gasped Jessie and Amy together.

''Course I did. There idn't many secrets in a place like this.'

'But how long have you known?' Jessie demanded.

'I knowd it was serious from the beginning, and then when Dr Searle always went away with a grim face after looking at me I soon put two and two together.'

'All this time, keeping it to yourself, and you never told me. Why?' Jessie clutched at his hand.

'I wanted to save you worry. I didn't think you knowd, you see. Not until you two came in acting proper mazed.'

'Oh, John! Oh, John!' cried Jessie, as she clutched her husband's hand against her heart. 'Oh, John!'

Very quietly, Amy crept away.

'Would you please tell Mrs Prout I've gone on home?' she asked the nurse on duty, then hurried out into the night.

As she walked through the darkened streets she thought the lump in her throat would choke her. John's bravery occupied her thoughts to the exclusion of everything else. It was some time before the footsteps behind her registered. She was not normally nervous on her own at night, but the streets were narrow and ill-lit, and there was no one else about. Prudence rather than fear made her lengthen her stride and hasten her pace.

'If you go on hurrying like that I'll never be able to catch you,' said an all too familiar voice.

'Jed Greenway! You frightened the life out of me,' she said, turning to face him.

'No I didn't. You're only saying that to make me feel uncomfortable.' He was grinning at her; in die gloom she could see the gleam of his white teeth. 'What are you doing out at this time of night?'

'I might ask the same of you. If you must know, I've been to see John.'

'How is he?'

'Improving at long last.' Then because she had to confide in someone she said with a rush, 'There was a chance that he would lose his leg. We've been desperate with worry.'

'That would have been grim. There's no risk of it now?'

'No, thank goodness, not unless there is a serious setback. We never told John what might happen. We didn't want him to fret. Then tonight we discovered he'd known all along. The poor man had kept it to himself to save us. I can't get over that, I really can't. He must have been suffering in his mind as well as with his leg, yet he never let slip once.'

'That's typical of John Prout. There aren't many men like him.'

'How true.' She felt better for having unburdened herself.

Although the streets held no terrors for her she found Jed's presence reassuring. Then she realized that he was heading in the wrong direction, away from the Prestons' house.

'You don't have to walk me back to Furzeham, you know,' she said.

'I know, but I will, anyway. You're quite a stranger, I haven't seen much of you lately. When are you going back to your own home?'

'I don't know. Not until Jessie no longer needs me, I suppose.'

'Pity. I miss dropping in at Paradise Place. I haven't had a decent bit of saffron cake in weeks; don't tell Sally I said so.'

'You could come up to Jessie's house. She wouldn't mind.'

'Maybe, but it wouldn't be the same.'

'You seem to have been calling on someone. It's unusual to see you out on a weeknight,' she remarked.

'How do you know? You don't go out much yourself.'

'I'm going by what Sally says.'

'Sally doesn't know everything I do.'

'Did you have a pleasant time?'

'Where?'

'Wherever it is you've been.'

'Very enjoyable.'

There was a pause while Amy fought to quell her growing inquisitiveness. She lost.

'Aren't you going to tell me where you've been?' she asked.

'No,' he replied. 'Let's just say I've been out for the evening, having some time off. That's what you're always telling me to do, isn't it?' She was taken aback by his response. When he spoke in that calm, offhand voice it always confused her. She never knew whether he was serious or not.

'And you enjoyed yourself, you say?'

'Yes, thank you.'

Again he did not elaborate and she wondered why he was being so reticent. Was it perhaps that where he had been was not fit for her ears? In that case, where had he spent the evening? It was obvious he had not been drinking; and she knew him too well to suspect him of gambling. That left women – or a woman. He was not walking out with anyone, or she would have known. There was another sort of female, of course. Brixham had its share of such creatures, and she knew two or three of them by sight. The thought of Jed going with any of them was repugnant.

'Had you been following me long?' she asked in a tight voice, determined not to probe further into his activities. Too late she had remembered that what Jed did was no concern of hers.

'From the end of Brewery Lane.'

Brewery Lane! There was a house in one of the courts down there which had a lurid reputation. Was that where he had been?

They walked on in silence for a way, then he said, 'Are you feeling all right?'

'Yes, why?'

'Because you usually go on at me until you've found out what you want.'

'How can you say such a thing?' she retorted indignantly. 'I don't pry. Well, not often. And how you spend your evening is none of my business.'

She waited, certain that now he would tell her.

Instead he replied, 'It wouldn't have interested you, anyway.' Then promptly changed the subject.

By the time they reached the house at Furzeham, Jed had still not given a single clue as to his activities that evening. He would not come in, but as they said goodnight he thrust a piece of paper into her hand, saying, 'This is for you.'

Frustrated, tired, and filled with painful emotions she could not recognize, Amy stuffed it into her coat pocket unread. Later, when she was getting ready for bed, she retrieved it. The paper proved to be a handbill. It was advertising a lecture with lantern slides on Africa, to be held at the Assembly Rooms that evening. That was where he had been! The wretch had been teasing her all the time, and she had not realized it. There had been no loose women, no lustful assignations. He had been no closer to the house of ill-repute than walking past the end of the lane.

Usually the knowledge that she had jumped to the wrong conclusions so dramatically would have made her laugh and swear a terrible vengeance on Jed. This time was different. Her own reaction disturbed her. She had spent a miserable evening, really distressed at the thought of Jed with some over-painted hussy. Finding out that he had spent that time at an innocent travel lecture made no difference. The feeling of dejection had remained with her, incomprehensible and bewildering, far into the night.

—

With John improving at long last there was no longer any reason for Amy to stay on at Furzeham. She had always looked forward to moving back into her cottage, but when she and Effie finally returned she was surprised by the surge of emotion she felt at being back in the tiny rooms, surrounded by her own things.

Jed was one of her first callers. She had not seen him since their encounter that evening, and when he walked in, for some reason she felt a twinge of awkwardness, sure that he had guessed what stupid ideas she had harboured about him.

'Aren't you going to ask me about the lecture on Africa?' he demanded mischievously.

'No, though I dare say you'll tell me anyway.'

'My, you do sound vinegary. Where did you think I'd been? In some den of vice?'

'Certainly not!' she retorted, rather too quickly. 'If you must know, I thought you'd been courting Lucy Burton again.'

'I never courted her a first time, so I couldn't do it again,' he declared. 'You didn't really think that, did you?'

'No,' she said suddenly. 'I thought you'd spent the time with that Lizzie creature. The one with the hair that's dyed ginger.'

No sooner were the words out of her mouth than she regretted them. What had possessed her to blurt out the truth in such a way? Yet she had to know his reaction. She waited, tense and horror-stricken. The result was not what she expected.

'What? Me spend an evening with Sixpenny Liz?' He stared at her in disbelief, then burst out laughing. He did not often laugh aloud, but now mirth had him helpless.

'A respectable widow woman like you shouldn't know about such females,' he gasped, when he had control of himself. 'Certainly you shouldn't suggest that a decent fisher-lad like me might visit one.' He wiped his eyes with the back of his hand.

Amy suddenly felt extraordinarily relieved. Jed considered a visit to Sixpenny Liz to be a cause for hilarity, nothing more. She began to laugh too.

–

Every day Amy continued to call on John to give him news of the yard and of the boatbuilding business in general. As he gained strength his interest grew stronger and sharper. On one occasion, after they had been discussing the progress of the boat currently under construction, John looked rather pensive.

'Her'll soon be ready for launching at this rate. We'd best start thinking of the next one. Us've got a decent order-book ahead of us thank goodness!'

'That we have. There's the smack for the fellow over at Teignmouth, and Ned Turner's spoken up for us to build a mumble bee for him.'

John nodded with satisfaction. 'That should keep us going for a while, if we'm able to manage.'

'Of course we'll manage,' said Amy confidently. 'You're getting steadily better, aren't you? By the time we're ready to get the next boat on the stocks you'll be out of here. I don't suppose you'll be quite running round like a two-year-old at first, but you'll be able to keep an eye on us.'

'I hope you'm right, maid,' said John earnestly. 'But I'm a bit bothered about the stocks of timber. I never likes to let them get low – you always has to think well ahead with timber.'

'Shall I bring you a list of what's in hand? I'm sure Charlie would help me; then if there's anything you think we should get we'll see about it.'

'That's a grand idea.' For a moment John was enthusiastic, then he looked doubtful. 'It idn't that I don't trust you and Charlie to do your best, but buying in timber – that's something I've always liked to do for myself. And now's the time to choose un, afore the spring growth starts.' He gave a regretful sigh. 'There was some seasoned timber I had my eye on out of a ketch that broke her back. The *Mary Jane*. There should've been some grand stuff out of her. It's too late now. We'm missed un.' He gave another deeper sigh. 'I wonder who got un.'

Amy hesitated for an instant, then said, 'We did.'

'What?'

'We bought *Mary Jane's* timbers. Well, a good number of them.'

'You didn't tell me!'

'We didn't like to, you weren't fit enough. Charlie said it was decent quality, and the price seemed reasonable, so I paid up.'

329

'With my money?'

'With your money.'

Amy waited for his outburst of anger. Instead John demanded, 'Did you get any curved stuff among it? Any crooks?'

'Yes. I can't recall offhand how many. I'll bring you a list next time I come.' She paused, regarding him cautiously. 'Did I do the right thing?'

'You did the right thing, girl.' John lay back against his pillows. 'Provided you bain't paid a fortune for un.'

'No, I compared it with new timber, and with the beams you got from the old barge at Galmpton. It was a fair price.'

'You know, I'm going to have to watch it, or I'm going to be put out to pasture and you'm going to be running the show,' he observed.

'Give me fair warning, then,' she smiled back. 'I'll need to buy myself an adze and a bradawl before I can start serving my time as a shipwright.'

'I wouldn't put it past you,' said John, and he chuckled.

Charlie shared Amy's relief next morning when she told him of John's reaction.

'If that idn't a weight off my mind!' he said. 'It's been bothering me since us bought the danged stuff. Mind, it would've bothered me just as much if us hadn't!'

'Everything's all right now. We can breathe again,' smiled Amy. 'Neither of us will get our marching orders the minute Mr Prout's on his feet again.'

Her optimistic mood lasted until she opened the morning post 'Oh no!' she exclaimed in dismay.

'What's the matter, Mizz Prout. I heard 'ee call!' Charlie put his head back in the office.

'Oh, Charlie, this is bad news! Mr Pritchard has cancelled his order for the smack.'

'What, the fellow from Teignmouth? He can't do that, surely?'

'I'm afraid he can. Nothing's been signed.'

'No, but 'twere a gentleman's agreement atween him and the maister.'

'That seems to be the snag. He says that his agreement was with John Prout, and seeing as Mr Prout is no longer supervising the yard, nor is likely to in the foreseeable future, he considers himself to be released from all promises.'

'That idn't right. A good twelvemonth ago he spoke for that smack, and now he'm backing down. How'd he hear about Maister's accident right over to Teignmouth, that's what I'd like to know?'

'There's plenty of boats go between here and there. I suppose it wasn't surprising.'

'What's us to do now?'

'I'll write to him and try to persuade him to change his mind. I'm not too hopeful, though. At the bottom of the letter he's written, "I've already made arrangements for my boat to be constructed elsewhere."'

'He were quick off the mark! As you says, Mizz Prout, it don't sound too hopeful.'

Amy's pessimism was justified. Although she wrote several times, assuring Mr. Pritchard that the high quality of workmanship would be maintained, the letters in return were adamant. Prout's Boatyard would be building no craft for Mr Pritchard.

'Us best tell Ned Turner he'm moved up the list, then,' said Charlie. 'He weren't expecting to get un this soon, I hopes he'm got the money together.'

The response from Ned Turner was more friendly but just as disappointing. The message was clear. He had no wish to have any boat built unless John Prout supervised.

'It sounds as though he'd be willing to wait until Maister's better,' said Charlie. 'How long do 'ee reckon that'll be?'

'Months at the very least,' said Amy. 'Mr Prout's been on crutches a bit, and we had hoped he'd be home soon, but the doctor won't even suggest any sort of a date. And he tires quickly. He's a long way off supervising anything.'

'Months! Us can't wait too long. This boat's due for launching soon, then all us've got is a refit. That idn't going to keep us going long.'

'I know. I dread the thought of having to lay off any of the men.'

'Maybe us could find some other order, build a boat for someone else until Maister's back.'

331

'That's easier said than done. Already the news is out that we've lost one certain order. When it gets abroad that we've as good as lost a second then folks will be even more reluctant to come to us. It's because I'm here,' Amy said despondently. 'Men don't like the idea of a woman having anything to do with building their precious boats. I've heard them. "Females and boats don't mix. Never have!" Anyone would think I was trying to build the wretched things with my own hands! No, the yard should have had a man in charge.'

'It's a bit late for that now. I reckon you'm doing a good job. The lads've got used to things as they are, and the maister habn't got no complaints seemingly. You've no call to give up.'

'I won't give up. I'll write to Ned Turner instead. And, Charlie, Mr Prout's not to hear of this yet. He's better, but he's not that much better!'

The reply from Ned Turner brought no joy. He still wanted John to be in charge.

'We've got to think of something,' said Amy. 'You know what it's like once a yard starts losing business. It takes years to build it back up. If it ever does!'

'And Maister's built this yard back up once already,' said Charlie glumly.

'There's nothing for it, we've got to get a contract for another boat from somewhere, to show people we're still building decent craft. We've got to restore confidence in Prout's. We can't have Mr Prout getting better again and coming back to nothing. I think I'll call on Ned Turner and see if I can persuade him to change his mind.'

Ned Turner lived in a trim terraced house overlooking the harbour. 'I think I can guess why you'm here, Mizz Prout,' he said as soon as he saw Amy. ''Tis about the boat, bain't it?'

'It is, Mr Turner. Can we talk about it?'

'Us can talk, my dear, but I don't think it'll change nothing.' He led the way into the parlour and gestured for her to take a seat by the roaring fire. 'If you must know, I'm glad to have a word with you, for to tell the truth I feels bad about withdrawing my boat. I'm real sorry about it. I knows it must seem like kicking a man – and a good man

332

at that – when he'm down, but I idn't a rich man. I know 'tis only a small boat, a mumble bee, but it'll cost me everything I've got and a bit more besides. I've thought it over again and again, and I can't take no chances.'

'We realize that there might be difficulties for you, beginning your vessel earlier than expected. If any of those problems are financial I'm sure we can come to some arrangement. Deferred payment, for example.'

'It idn't the money. Leastways, not entirely. I must speak out straight, 'tis only fair. I've got to say it. John Prout's yard without John Prout bain' what I was hoping for.'

'We've got the same workers, fine craftsmen all of them.'

'That may be so, but you bain' got John Prout. There's some as can do, and there's some as can tell others what to do. Old John, he can do both – when he'm got two legs to stand on. Nothing gets past he.'

'We guarantee the workmanship will be of top quality.'

'I knows you'll try your best, but with John I'd know it'd be the best. That's the difference. I'm willing to wait for John to come back, even if it takes a year, but I must have him in charge of my boat. I'm sorry, Mizz Prout. My mind's made up.'

He spoke with real regret, and although she was disappointed, Amy understood his plight. No doubt other people were involved. It was quite usual to have mortgagors to help finance a fishing boat. Ned Turner was too dependable a character to risk money that belonged to someone else.

He had said he would wait a year, which was very fair of him. Unfortunately she knew the business could not last a year without new orders. She felt very depressed as she made her way home.

When she and Effie had had their evening meal and she had put the child to bed, Amy sat alone by her fireside consumed with gloom. She pictured John recovering from one blow only to be struck by another. Ruin! The few inquiries that had arrived in the post had come to nothing. The discreet adverts in the local papers and fishing periodicals had brought no joy. Ned Turner had been their last hope. She knew that what they needed was one boat, built entirely without

John's influence, to prove that Prout's Yard was still turning out fine craft.

After a while she came to the conclusion that black thoughts and misery were getting her nowhere. She needed to think of some plan of action. That was easier said than done. She considered half a dozen schemes – building a smack on spec, going for some other form of craft, concentrating on repairs and refits – only to discard them as too risky or impractical. She kept coming back to Ned Turner. What would it take to make him change his mind? His reasons for withdrawing or at least delaying his boat seemed twofold. He was concerned about the quality of workmanship and also its financial implications. Workmanship and finance! There had to be a solution somewhere.

It was dawn before she managed to resolve the problem. She could hardly wait to put her idea to Charlie later that morning. When she did he listened open-mouthed.

'That's danged clever, Mizz Prout,' he said in admiration. 'If that don't change Ned Turner's mind us might as well give up.'

'You think it's worth a try? Good, I'll go to Mr Turner's right away.'

'What, you again, Mizz Prout?' Ned said when he saw her.

'Yes, Mr Turner, it's me again. I've a proposition to put to you.'

'You don't give up, I'll say that for you. Come along in and tell me about it.'

'Right, now last time we talked you were very honest and told me why you had withdrawn your order from Prout's. As I see it you had two main reasons: you were doubtful about the workmanship and, although you didn't quite put it into words, you implied that you might have problems financing the boat because John was not in charge. Is that right?'

'It is, although by the sound of it I wadn't so much honest as downright blunt,' replied Ned, looking rather shamefaced.

'No, it was good that you were outspoken. It means we know exactly where we stand. I'll be equally frank with you. You aren't the only one who has backed off. We need another order to prove to everyone that we're still in business. That's why I've come up with this

334

idea: we put a special clause in your contract which will state that if you are dissatisfied with the boat in any way we will rectify the causes for complaint and refund ten per cent of the cost of completion. What do you say?'

'Say? I don't say nothing. I be struck dumb. Let's see if I've got the hang of this. If I idn't satisfied with the boat you'll give me back ten per cent of my money?'

'Plus putting right any causes of complaint. It shows how confident I am that we can do a decent job.'

'It sounds too good to be true. There'm bound to be snags somewhere. I could find all sorts of things to complain about, just to get my money back.'

'You'll be insuring the boat, won't you? And Mr Jenkins, of the Fishing Smack Insurance Society, will be surveying her? Then we'll be happy to accept his surveyor's report. We'll even pay half his fee as a gesture of confidence and goodwill. What do you think of that?'

'I think I haven't never heard the like!' Ned regarded her with a mixture of bemusement and respect. 'If this be a taste of what'll happen when you wenches take over then heaven help us, that be what I says.'

'Will you consider it?'

'I'll consider un, right enough. Don't see as how I can afford not to. I needs a bit of time, though.'

'Of course.'

Amy knew it was not his decision alone. Being Ned he would consult his financial backers. She hoped it would not take him long. Not even her most optimistic hopes anticipated seeing him next day, but there he was, at the yard.

'Morning, Mizz Prout,' he greeted her. 'I be yer with my decision. Before I says anything there be a couple of points. First, can I have a look over the smack you'm working on?'

'Certainly you can.'

'Thanks.'

Before Amy could say another word he was off, leaving her on tenterhooks. He was thorough, she had to give him that. There did not seem to be a square inch of the craft that he missed.

'Did you like what you saw?' she asked when he returned.

'A decent bit of shipwrighting, I'll say that,' he admitted. 'Mind, her were started when John Prout was here.'

'Only just. The stem-post was being set up when the accident happened,' she reminded him. 'I think you mentioned some other point?'

'Yes. What does old John think of this yer scheme of youm?'

For the first time Amy's enthusiasm was deflated.

'I haven't told him yet,' she admitted.

To her relief Ned Turner roared with laughter.

'I likes the way you say "told" and not "asked",' he chuckled. 'Poor boy, he didn't know what he were letting hisself in for when he took you on, I'll wager. Never mind. If John be agreeable to the special clause then 'tis all right by me.'

'You mean it? You really mean it? Oh Mr Turner I could hug you!'

'Go right ahead, my lover. I idn't never been hugged by a yard manager afore!'

It was an apprehensive Amy who hurried along to the hospital that afternoon. She was worried not only about John's reaction to her idea, but what effect it might have on him. There was no help for it. This was too important a decision for her to make on her own.

John listened carefully to everything she had to say.

'You'm putting me in something of a cleft stick,' he said when she had finished. 'On one hand I don't want my yard going downhill, and on the other I idn't keen to find you'm managing too well without me. Either way I can't win.'

'Oh, John, I'm sorry. I didn't mean to worry you in any way but—' She stopped, for he was grinning all over his face.

'Don't take on. I was only pulling your leg, girl,' he said. ''Pon consideration I'd sooner have a business that's making money. That way if my pride be sore at least I can nurse un in comfort.'

'Then you approve?'

'Of course I approve. You'd best go down the solicitor's to make sure there idn't no problems, but I reckon 'tis a splendid notion. There be only one snag as far as I can see.'

'What's that?' asked Amy, her face falling.

''Tis a pity 'tis only a tiddy li'l mumble bee. Next time make sure you signs up a danged big smack.'

'A smack could cost you more in repayments,' she teased.

'Never! You can tell they lads down the yard if I has to repay one penny piece I'll be down there and thrash the lot of them with my crutch, do you understand?'

Smiling, Amy left the ward. As she did so she could still hear John chuckling. She reflected it was a long time since she had heard him laugh so heartily. It had to be a very good sign indeed.

Chapter Fifteen

'We'm getting low, there idn't no two ways about it!' Propped up in his hospital bed, John waved the paper he held in his hand. It was the list of timber stocks that Amy had brought him.

'There's enough there for Ned Turner's mumble bee, surely,' she said.

'Yes, and no doubt us could manage longer, but I likes to have stuff by, seasoning proper. Us'd better buy some in.'

'Right, I'll see what's at the timber yard.'

'The timber yard'd do at a pinch, but I always likes to see my timber growing, leastways, fresh-felled.'

'You aren't suggesting I go into the woods and pick out which trees we want?' she asked in alarm.

'Why not?' John's eyes twinkled. 'You'm running the yard, by all accounts, and no boatbuilder worth his — or her — salt'd stick to the bits and pieces the timber yard's got on offer.'

'I don't know anything about trees,' protested Amy. 'I can just about tell one sort from another.'

'Then you'm going to have to learn, maid!' John grinned. 'Don't look like that. I wadn't suggesting you goes alone. Take Charlie. To be honest, he could do it hisself, he'm a fair judge of a bit of timber, but you knows what he'm like about deciding things. Aught to do with business and he don't want to know. You'll have to go along with him and look as if you'm responsible.'

'You'd like us to go soon?' asked Amy, somewhat relieved.

'Yes, please. While they'm still doing the winter cut. See what you can get. Some folks like the spring growth. 'Tis easier to get the bark off for one thing, and bark fetches a fair price. But I prefers winter wood, especially oak, if I can get it. They'm probably felling up to Southdown about now. Charlie'll know.'

Charlie did know! 'Yes, they'm cutting. But 'ee idn't saying the maister wants me to go up there and choose some stuff?'

'I am.'

'What if I chooses wrong and wastes Maister's money?'

'You won't,' said Amy assuredly. 'Supposing you did make a bad choice, the yard would still have some timber to work with. That would be better than no timber at all.'

'I don't know… The old shipwright was still doubtful.'

'You'll do splendidly, and I'll be there too. I'll be the one responsible for everything.'

'You'll be there, Mizz Prout?' The worried expression went from Charlie's wrinkled face. 'Why didn't 'ee say so in the first place?'

On a bright, bitterly cold day, Amy, clad in stout boots and her thickest clothes, accompanied Charlie to the stretch of woodland. It was not far from town but, as ever in Brixham, their way led up a steep hill. She had never been to these woods before, but she could have found her way even without Charlie; the rhythmical sound of saws and the dull thud as axes bit into trunks would have led her to the spot.

As they approached the clearing work stopped. Most of the men knew Charlie and greeted him by name, but the presence of a woman in their midst was a cause for curiosity. One burly fellow leaned on his axe and gave an appreciative whistle as Amy passed by. Straight away Charlie rounded on him.

''Ee can stop that, Ernie Street,' he snapped. 'Be a bit more respectful. Mizz Prout's yer on business.'

He sought out a tall man clad in corduroys.

'This be Percy Williams, Mizz Prout,' he declared. 'He'm the foreman round yer. Perce, Mizz Prout and me, us be yer to look at this timber of youm.'

The woodsman was evidently nonplussed at having to deal with a woman. He half put out his huge fist to shake hands, then changed his mind and tipped his bowler hat instead.

'Mr Prout have broke his leg real bad,' said Charlie. 'Mizz Prout'm running things till he'm better.' He spoke as if it were the most natural thing in the world.

Percy Williams did not accept the situation so readily. Disapproval glared from his eyes as he said, 'Sorry to hear about your husband, Mizz Prout.'

'Thank you, but Mr Prout is my brother-in-law,' Amy explained.

The disapproval intensified. Amy recognized the look immediately. A wife could be justified in controlling a business while her husband was incapacitated, but some other female…

'Perhaps we could see what you've got cut, Mr Williams?' she suggested in a brisk, no-nonsense voice. 'Then we'll look at your standing timber.' She moved towards the pile of logs at the side of the track, leaving the men no option but to follow in her wake.

'That be a fine piece of elm. Look at the girth.' Percy Williams slapped his hand on the topmost log. The look he gave Amy was challenging.

She was equal to him. 'What, with a twist to the growth like that, Mr Williams?' she said, smiling sweetly. 'It's boats we're building you know, not corkscrews.'

'Should've warned 'ee, Perce, boy,' chuckled Charlie, giving the woodsman a friendly jab in the ribs with his elbow. 'Don't 'ee try no tricks on Mizz Prout. 'Tidn't worth the bother. Now let's be seeing some real timber.'

As she had expected, once he got started Charlie forgot his misgivings. He went systematically through the stand of trees, rejecting some, chalking his mark on others. But when Perce Williams tried to discuss the tally with him he said, ''Ee must deal with Mizz Prout there, Perce. Her handles the business end.'

It took some haggling to get Percy Williams down to a price she was prepared to pay. As they left after having made the arrangements, including transport, she suspected she was still being charged over the odds.

John, however, was delighted. 'Winter-cut oak's always hard to get, and well worth paying a bit extra for. You did well to get some.'

'I suppose I did,' Amy said with a wry smile. 'If it had been left to the foreman I'd have been sent away with a flea in my ear. He didn't think much of having to deal with a woman.'

'Oh!' John looked apologetic. 'Made things difficult for you, did he? I'm sorry. Jessie's already said what she thinks of me, sending you off into the woods with a load of men. I should've thought before I asked you to go.'

'I didn't mind,' said Amy. 'My back's broad.'

'I don't know about that,' John said. 'But you'm only got yourself to blame if I forgets and sends you to places as idn't right for a woman. If you wadn't doing such a good job down the yard I wouldn't suggest such danged stupid things.'

Amy could almost feel herself swelling with pride. In her heart she feared that she was doing no more than muddling through at the boatyard; perhaps she was managing better than she realized: if John approved of her efforts she must be doing a good job. It was very gratifying.

Her sense of self-satisfaction lasted until that evening when Jed called. His face was grim, and his dark brows were drawn together in an expression of extreme anger.

'My, you're looking like a thunder cloud,' she remarked. 'What's upset you?'

'You have!'

'Me? What have I done?'

'I couldn't believe my ears! I never thought you'd do anything so stupid.'

'What are you on about?' she demanded, taken aback. She could not recollect Jed ever being annoyed with her, and she did not like it.

'You going up to the woods at Southdown with Charlie Bowden,' he retorted.

Amy stared in disbelief, then gave a chuckle.

'Are you suggesting we went up there for a bit of courting?' she asked. 'Honestly, Jed, what are you thinking of? Charlie's all of seventy, and happily married into the bargain.'

'Of course I'm not suggesting there's anything between you and Charlie,' snapped Jed. 'I know you went to buy timber. But you should have had more sense. You were the only woman up there. Didn't you know you'd get yourself talked about?'

'Is that all? I thought it was something serious.' Amy dismissed his comments with a shrug. 'To be honest, no, I didn't think about such things. Does it matter?'

'How can you say that? Of course your good name matters.'

'I don't see how I've done anything to affect it.'

'Don't you? Doesn't being alone with a lot of men affect your reputation?'

'I work among a lot of men every day. I'm the only woman at the yard.'

'That's different. You're working for your brother-in-law, and under normal circumstances he'd be there with you.'

'I was working for John then. He was the one who suggested I should go.'

'Then I'm surprised at him. He should have a greater regard for you.'

'He has a regard for me,' answered Amy with increasing irritability. 'He thinks I am doing a good job looking after the boatyard. That was why he asked me to go up to Southdown. As he couldn't go himself he sent someone responsible instead. I don't see what you're objecting to.'

'I'm objecting to hearing your name bandied about the harbour and elsewhere. You went where you had no business to be. Can you imagine what those men must have thought when you turned up? They didn't like it, I can tell you!'

'Ah, we're getting to the truth of it now, are we?' exclaimed Amy. 'It's nothing to do with my reputation, is it? All this fuss is because a woman has dared to poach on a man's preserve.'

'I might have known you'd take that attitude. Just because you go down to the yard to write a few letters and pay a few bills—'

'Write a few letters and pay a few bills!' repeated Amy furiously. 'I do a deal more than that. I keep the business side of that yard running. It's because I'm female that you refuse to acknowledge it. You men think that there are too many things that only you can do. As for me having no business up at Southdown, that's nonsense and you know it. I'd a perfect right to be in those woods. I was there on legitimate business, and anyone who can put any other interpretation on it has got a nasty, petty mind.'

'Thank you for thinking me nasty and petty,' answered Jed, his voice low with suppressed anger. 'I thought I was pointing out something obvious: that to go about the countryside flaunting yourself the way you've just done makes a woman the subject of gossip. And to be the subject of gossip is degrading.'

'The subject of gossip, am I?' cried Amy. 'Degrading? What you mean is that I should know my womanly place and take a job fitting for a silly, witless female. If I was bruising my knees scrubbing other folks' floors all day you wouldn't have said a word. If I was breaking my back washing their foul linen, that would be all right, because that's a job fit for a woman in your eyes. You're narrow-minded, Jed Greenway, and I've never realized it before.'

'Thank you!' he retorted sarcastically. 'I appreciate your opinion of me. That's all the gratitude I get for trying to protect your reputation.'

'My reputation can take care of itself. It's none of your concern.'

'You are quite right. In future I'll keep my nose out of your affairs.' With that he strode out of the house.

Amy stared after him, unable to believe what had happened. It was unthinkable. She had quarrelled with Jed. Her oldest, dearest friend. She had never thought to hear him say such harsh, hurtful things to her. And she had said harsh, hurtful things back to him. How could she have called him narrow-minded and nasty and petty? Worse still, she had accused him of interfering in her affairs. How dared she, when she was the one who interfered shamelessly in his?

She rushed to the door and wrenched it open.

'Jed!' she called, then stopped abruptly as she came face to face with Jed himself.

He was standing on the doorstep. The anger had gone from his expression. He looked white and shaken.

'Amy,' he said. 'Amy, we quarrelled.' He sounded shocked at the enormity of what had happened.

'We've never done that before, have we?' she replied, equally perturbed. 'Not in all the years we've known each other.'

'I–I don't know what got into me, rushing here and going on at you like that. I'm sorry.'

'You've nothing to be sorry for. It was me, taking everything the wrong way. Goodness knows, I've no cause to accuse you of meddling in my business. Look how often I do the same to you, and you never lose your temper over it.'

'That's different. You do it for my own good, because you're bothered about me.'

'And aren't you bothered about me?' she asked.

There was a silence between them, filled with a sudden tense anticipation.

'Of course,' he said, almost roughly. 'You've got to have someone to look out for you now that Todd's gone and John's laid up. Who else is there but me… ?'

'Who else indeed!'

The silence returned, and with it the same odd sense of expectancy.

'…Until you find yourself another husband,' Jed went on, almost hurriedly.

'That's not likely.'

'Oh, I don't know. Until the right fellow comes along, you can rely on me.'

'I know, and thank you… Look, we don't have to continue this conversation on the doorstep. You can come in again, you know.'

'Perhaps another time. I–I'll call again tomorrow, if that suits you?'

'Of course it does.'

'And, Amy – everything is all right again, isn't it?'

'Yes,' she said forcefully. 'We just had a barmy ten minutes, that's all. It's over and done with now.'

He smiled, as he always did, at her use of the old London expression. Smiling cost him quite an effort.

'I'll see you tomorrow, then.'

As he stood there preparing to leave, there was something almost forlorn about him. Forlorn? Jed had never been that, even as a little boy. Solitary, taciturn, resolute, but never forlorn. Their disagreement had disturbed him badly, as it had Amy. She longed to give him comfort, to show how sorry she was, to drive away the hurt bewilderment which lurked in his eyes. For one lunatic instant she felt like flinging her arms about him and holding him close, giving him solace as she would Effie. She did not, of course. Poor Jed, he'd think the end of the world had come, she observed to herself with a wry smile.

'See you tomorrow,' she replied.

Their disagreement was never mentioned again. Yet somehow its influence continued to touch their relationship, certainly as far as Amy was concerned. Until then she had taken the bond between them for granted. The quarrel, brief though it had been, had proved that their friendship was vulnerable. She tried to picture life without Jed. She could not. It was like trying to imagine a world without the sky. It made her determined never to quarrel with him again.

–

The great event of the spring was that John came home. He looked thin and wasted from his long weeks of inactivity, but his spirit was undimmed.

'Young Todd there's twice the man I am at the moment,' he said, cheerfully watching his son hurling wooden bricks against the furniture. 'What I needs is a few of Jessie's meat puddings inside me. Then you'm going to see a difference!'

'I'm sure we will,' smiled Amy. 'You'll be over at the yard in no time, telling us where we've been going wrong.'

'Ah, it'll take Jessie's meat puddings *and* a few of her pasties afore I'm quite up to that, I reckon,' John replied. 'Ned Turner's boat is going to be up to you and Charlie. I'm aiming to having a say in the one after that.'

'If there is one,' muttered Amy to herself.

She did not mutter quietly enough, for John retorted with mock severity, 'There'd better be, maid! I'll know who to come for if there bain't; I be getting danged nippy with this old prop.' And he swished the crutch experimentally in her direction.

'In that case there's certain to be a next boat,' Amy grinned, nimbly dodging out of the way.

Although she might joke with John, the prospect of starting a new boat completely from scratch made her anxious. It would have been a different matter if there had been some sort of standard design. There was not, of course. That would have been too much to hope for. She knew from experience that each craft was individual, its design the result of much discussion between the owner and the shipwright. This was very much John's province, and she wondered how Charlie would react to being solely in charge.

'You'm going to be there when Ned Turner comes, bain't you?' Charlie asked.

'Yes, I'll be there,' Amy replied, knowing full well her contribution would be nothing more than moral support.

It was unfortunate she was delayed at the bank on the morning that Ned arrived. She need not have worried. By the time she reached the yard there was much evidence of scribbled pages from notebooks and chalked sketches on odd pieces of wood. Ned and Charlie were too deep in argument to notice her arrival.

'I tell 'ee, that's too sharp in the bow,' Ned was protesting. 'A danged wet boat's what that'll give us. If I wants to pitch up and down I'll go up the fair come regatta and spend my money on they swing-boats.'

'Sharp? That idn't sharp,' protested Charlie. 'As for the bow you'm wanting, I've seen bulldogs with more snout than that!'

Amy could not help chuckling. At the sound both men looked up. 'Why, hullo, Mizz Prout. Didn't see 'ee there.' Ned greeted her.

'Good morning to the pair of you. I hope you're making good progress, Mr Turner.'

'That we are. We'm getting on fine, idn't we, boy?'

'Doing fine, Mizz Prout,' Charlie agreed.

Both men's eyes were sparkling, and Amy realized they were thoroughly enjoying their argument.

'Us've got file basics down.' Charlie indicated his precious notebook. 'Now we'm discussing the important bits.'

'Yes, I heard the discussion!' smiled Amy. 'I was wondering – what do you think of making a half model for Mr Turner, Charlie? That way he can see everything's exactly as he wants it before we begin building.'

'They's my thoughts exactly, Mizz Prout.' Charlie nodded in agreement.

'I can see you'm determined not to give me no refund,' chortled Ned.

'Us idn't giving no refund,' declared Charlie. 'There won't be no cause. No, this half model will make sure there won't be no argument about what you want. You'll be able to see how that snub bow of youm idn't no good. It'd do fine for shovelling up mud, mind. 'Ee could always use un for dredging out the harbour.'

'Joke away, boy! Just give me a nice easy bow, and us'll soon see who has the last laugh,' declared Ned.

Amy crept away unseen, leaving them to enjoy their amicable arguing. Their long and sometimes heated discussions must have had some purpose because before long the final list of specifications was set before her for costing. Charlie himself made a model of half of the hull, from bow to stem, exactly to scale. It was a superb piece of craftsmanship. Amy noticed that compromise had been reached over the question of the bow, which was neither as sharp as Charlie had insisted nor as blunt as Ned had demanded. The finished model met with John's unstinting approval.

'That's grand,' he said when Amy showed it to him. 'Ned Turner's going to have a fine craft there.'

'Can I tell him you said so?' asked Amy, pleased.

'No you can't! This be your boat, youm and Charlie's. You'm proving a point, that Prout's Yard turns out first-rate smacks even when John Prout idn't there. That's it, idn't it, maid?'

'Something like that,' she admitted.

'Right then, I say that's a top-class design, but that's for your ears and for Charlie's only. As far as anyone else's concerned I idn't involved. I be still recuperating.'

'You're doing that right enough. I can practically see you getting fatter as I sit here,' teased Amy.

'Beef stew and dumplings, that's what I had for my dinner.' John pretended to ease his belt. 'If a man can't get better on that he may as well give up.'

Although he might pretend not to have any part in the early planning, nevertheless, Amy found it very reassuring to have John's approval. The grunt of relief that Charlie gave when she passed on John's message told her that she had not been alone in her anxieties.

'That's the maister satisfied and Ned satisfied,' he said. 'I'll take this yer model up to the lads in the mould loft. They can draw up the lines full size for us.'

For Amy the next few weeks were the most nerve-racking and the most exciting she had ever endured. Time and again she neglected her own duties to see some new stage in the development of Ned Turner's boat. They cut their own timber from logs stacked at the yard. Not the ones she and Charlie had ordered from Southdown, they were too fresh, but well seasoned ones bought by John a long time ago. With her heart in her mouth she would stand beside the sawpit across which the log was laid, and watch as Jack, the top sawyer, guided the long saw the length of the timber, following a mere chalk line. His skill, and that of his sawdust-covered mate who stood down in the pit, never failed to amaze her.

'There us be, Mizz Prout,' Jack would exclaim triumphantly. 'Us've managed to cut port and starboard sides from one timber again. Tell Maister his ten per cent be safe.'

'Keeping Maister's ten per cent safe' had touched the pride and the imagination of the men, and it became almost a motto during the building of the boat. Nor was it just John's workmen who showed an interest. Although their place of work was termed a yard, this was simply convention. There was no boundary round them, they build their boats on the beach, and people were free to wander about at will. It was quite usual to have a few curious souls coming round to watch progress, but the interest taken in Ned's boat exceeded anything Amy had ever experienced.

'I think I should go round with a hat and take up a collection,' she remarked to Jed one day. 'You'd think no one had ever built a boat before.'

'Ah, that's because everyone's keeping a weather eye on you,' said Jed.

'They are? Why?'

'They're watching to see if Ned Turner collects his ten per cent or not.'

'You mean the story's got round town already?'

'Certainly it has. What did you expect? Every prospective boat owner in Brixham is watching events very closely. They want to see if Ned gets a decent boat or his ten per cent.'

'He'll get a decent boat, no doubt about it.'

'But just supposing he doesn't! Everyone's waiting to see if this ten per cent thing'll work.'

'Of course it'll work. It's legally binding and everything.'

'Yes, but you know Brixham fishermen. They're a cautious lot where money's concerned. They want to see if everything goes smoothly. Even legally binding clauses have been known to cause trouble.'

'Everything will go smoothly, you'll see.'

'Good, because it will make quite a lot of difference to your order book.'

'You really think so?'

'I do.'

Amy gave a satisfied sigh. 'I hope you're right,' she said. 'That is what I've been working towards.'

'Well, your extra clause has certainly made you the talk of the place.'

'I thought you disapproved of me being talked about?' she said, then immediately regretted her words. They reminded her uncomfortably of their quarrel.

Jed gave a grin. 'That was different,' he said. 'This time, if anyone has made any critical remarks about you then I haven't heard them. Everyone seems to think that clause is a grand idea.'

'Good.' Amy sighed again. 'John's hoping to be back at work part-time after we finish Ned's boat. Wouldn't it be wonderful if we had a full order book for him to come back to?'

'If the present amount of interest is anything to go by, then I can see him having to expand,' said Jed. 'Two boats on the stocks at once. How about that?'

'It sounds wonderful. He can look to one boat, and I can look to the other.'

'You enjoy working here don't you?' Jed was suddenly serious. 'Yes, you know I do.' She was puzzled by his question. 'Why do you ask?'

'I was wondering if you'd got tired of earning your own living. It's a lot to do when you've got Effie to look after, and the house.'

'No, I'm not tired of it. Nor do I think I ever will be, which is just as well because I've no alternative.'

'What if you marry again?'

'You seem determined to marry me off. If it's all the same to you I'd sooner not take on a husband just to pay my rent.'

'Isn't there anyone you'd like to marry?'

'There might have been once,' said Amy suddenly quiet, remembering Daniel, 'but not any longer. I much prefer working.' She smiled cheerfully again. 'Anyway, John will soon be fit for work, and I'll go back to my three mornings a week, which suits me fine. Don't you go setting up as a matchmaker on my behalf, please. It's very kind of you, but I'm happy as I am.'

'That's all that matters, then.' He said it in such an odd way that she looked at him sharply.

'Is something wrong?' she asked.

'No. You're happy, nothing else matters.'

'And what about you? Are you happy?'

'Of course. The fishing's been good and my debts are getting less.'

It did not seem to Amy much to want out of life, and she said so.

'It'll do for me,' answered Jed, with such an air of finality that she changed the subject.

Gradually Ned's boat took shape on the stocks, progressing from a gaunt skeleton of wood to a recognizable hull. The interest in her grew, not to mention the amount of advice offered by 'informed' bystanders. Charlie took these helpful comments in his stride.

'I'd suggest 'ee has a go with this yer adze and show me how 'tis done,' he would say, waving the tool in the direction of the 'expert'. 'But I knows the first thing 'ee'd do is slice off they toes of youm, so I won't.' At which the 'expert' would disappear, knowing that his prediction was probably right.

As the boat neared completion, tension in the yard mounted and speculation in the town grew. Then the day was fixed for Mr Jenkins from the Fishing Smack Insurance Company to come and survey the craft. To Amy's disappointment they had not one fresh order on the books.

'I was sure that this boat would make a difference,' she complained, 'and it hasn't.'

'Don't be impatient,' John replied. 'Let's see what happens after Mr Jenkins has had his say.'

Quite a crowd had gathered for the arrival of Mr Jenkins. Amy felt her stomach churning with nervous anticipation as she watched him go aboard, a business-like notebook sticking out of his pocket and a large ball of chalk in his hand.

'He'm intending to do the job proper, at any road,' commented Ned, much impressed. 'Just like one of they fancy surveyors down to Lloyds.'

'Let's hope that chalk of his doesn't grow any smaller,' said Amy earnestly. 'We don't want him marking too many faults.'

'He won't find much,' said Charlie stoutly. For once it was he who was confident and Amy who needed reassurance.

The crowd waited expectantly for the reappearance of Mr Jenkins. If they hoped for some dramatic announcement delivered from the deck of the mumble bee they were doomed to disappointment. He was determined to carry things out correctly, down to the last letter.

'I shall send both of you a written report,' he informed Amy and Ned.

'Can't you give us a hint of your findings?' Amy pleaded.

'I regret I must decline, Mrs Prout.' He looked quite shocked at the idea. 'It would not be proper. I prefer to give a carefiil evaluation of my survey and commit my findings to paper.'

'What's he on about?' asked Charlie, none too quietly. 'Can't understand a danged word he says. Never could.'

'He says we must wait,' whispered Amy in his ear.

'You will receive the result of my survey by second post tomorrow,' said Mr Jenkins, glaring coldly in Charlie's direction.

'Second post tomorrow,' said Amy in dismay after he had gone. 'That's ages away!'

The wait for the postman next day was agonizing. When he finally came striding along the beach, Amy rushed to meet him.

'That's the one you'm waiting for, Mizz Prout,' he said cheerfully. 'On the top of the pile.' And whistling blithely he went away.

Amy's hands shook as she held the envelope.

'This should be John's job. He should open it,' she said.

'Well, he bain't yer, and us habn't got time to traipse up to Furzeham,' retorted Charlie. 'You'm in charge, maid. You open that letter, afore the strain gives us all apoplexy.'

Glancing up Amy was surprised to see that the men had abandoned work altogether and were clustered round outside the door, eagerly awaiting the result.

'Very well.' She took a deep breath before slitting open the envelope. Swiftly her eyes went down the detailed comments on the sheet of paper until she came to the vital conclusion at the bottom. 'We've done it,' she said very quietly. 'In Mr Jenkins' own words, "To conclude, I find this craft sound, seaworthy and of excellent workmanship." Do you hear that? Excellent workmanship! Not just good! Excellent! We don't pay the ten per cent!'

Her final words went unheard, drowned in the burst of cheering from the men.

'Now 'ee can go up and tell the maister,' said Charlie, who was beaming all over his face. 'Bad news could've waited, but good news, that's different.'

'You're right,' she said, already reaching for her hat. At the doorway she paused and looked at the men who were still shaking hands and slapping each other on the back. 'You were the ones who did this,' she said. 'And simply to say thank you falls far short of what I want to say.

As for Charlie, he's the one who made everything possible. Without his skill and experience the lot of us would have been out of a job long since. As a token of appreciation there will be something extra in everyone's pay this week.' This was greeted with more cheering, but Amy had not finished. 'And for an immediate celebration there's a barrel of cider in the corner here if I can have two volunteers to roll it out.'

Amidst renewed cheering, Amy would have set off to Furzeham if Jack, the top-sawyer, hadn't called out, 'Not so fast, Mizz Prout. You'm idn't going until us've drank your health.'

'Indeed you idn't,' agreed Charlie. 'Maybe I does know what I be doing when it comes to boatbuilding. Considering how many years I've been working in boatyards it'd be a poor look-out if I didn't. But, my word, us'd have been in a sorry state if the rest had been left to me.' This was greeted with laughter. 'No, 'tis true,' he insisted. 'Us've needed Mizz Prout to keep us on the straight and narrow, and I says, Yer's to Mizz Prout, God bless her, and having petticoat rule idn't half bad!'

The cry went up 'To Mizz Prout!' as a variety of tin mugs and chipped cups were raised in her direction. Amy was so overcome her throat went tight.

She was saved from having to respond by Ned Turner's voice demanding, 'Be this a private celebration or can anyone join in?'

'Join in! Join in!' cried Charlie. 'Hand Ned a mug of cider, someone.'

'We'm celebrating the fact that you'm going to be sailing in a first-class mumble bee.'

'So Mr Jenkins says in his report.' Ned waved his copy of the letter, then held out his hand to accept the cider. 'I'll drink to his findings,' he said happily. 'I suppose I couldn't lose either way, but of the two give me a really good boat every time. Ten per cent of the cost idn't much good to you if you'm out sailing in an unseaworthy craft in a force nine. Let's drink to Prout's Yard and the fine boats you build, mine in particular.'

'You'll be sailing in her afore 'ee knows it,' said Charlie, after this latest toast had been drunk.

'You'm right there. I can send off to Dartmouth to register her now. Once her'm finally signed over to me us'll be off across the bay. Then you'll see naught but our stern, and that's a promise.'

'There's some talk of getting the port registration moved to Brixham,' said Charlie.

'There's always been talk of that,' replied Ned disparagingly. 'I'll believe it when it comes. Still, I don't mind drinking to that day.'

And the mugs were raised one more time...

'It was quite a party,' Amy informed John, after she had managed to creep away.

'They deserve it.'

'And it was all right to say they'd get something extra at the end of the week?'

'Certainly it was.' John looked at her keenly. 'There's a good few folks I'm in debt to for what they've done these last few months. I knows what I owe them. I won't forget.'

'Good, because I wanted to talk to you about Charlie. He's been magnificent, he really should be rewarded in some way.'

'I haven't forgotten Charlie, but he idn't the only one. What about you?'

'You don't owe me anything other than my regular wages. No, you see to Charlie, and a bonus for the men. That will do. That will have to do.'

'Why do you say that?'

'Because we've no work in hand. A few repairs to a barge, nothing more.'

John did not share her despondency.

'Don't be so gloomy,' he said. 'Let today's news get round town a couple of times. We'll get work, never fear.'

He was right. The inquiries, written and verbal, came flooding in, to be followed by film orders. The yard was secure for the foreseeable future.

John got his wish and returned to work for the beginning of their next craft. He arrived in a hired cab, and the men cheered until the horse bucked and shied. At first he came for only one morning a week. That was sufficient. By the time the cab came back for him he was white and drawn.

'Hasten slowly,' Amy advised when he spoke of trying to come for an extra day. 'You're back at work, that's the main thing. Once a week is enough for the owners to feel their boat's under the expert eye of John Prout. Unless you're hinting you don't think the place is being properly run when you aren't here?'

'That's the nail hit right on the head,' John said gravely. 'Enough orders for a year or more, the men working well with no serious complaints, the timber stock high. Yes, I be mortal worried about my business. Worried that it don't need me.'

'Now I have to say that of course we need you, John. We want you back full time, you know that. But it would be foolish to undo months of patient effort by coming back for too long too soon. Do it gradually. We can manage on our own for a bit longer.'

'I know you can, maid, and I'm grateful. You'm right, of course. One day a week's enough for the moment.'

'Good. It'll give me time to get accustomed to taking orders again, too.'

'You? Taking orders?' scoffed John. 'That'll be the day.'

–

The months ahead were busy and prosperous. John followed Amy's advice and took his time returning to work. By the following winter he was back at the yard every day, though he was never as mobile as he had been. And there were times when the pain and weakness in his leg forced him to stay in the office. Somehow Amy never did go back to her simple clerking job.

One day he remarked, 'I don't know whether you'm my right arm or my right leg, girl, but I'm real glad to have you. I owes you a deal and I think 'tis time to pay my debts. How about being a full partner in the business?'

Amy was thunderstruck. 'A partner? I couldn't,' she gasped.

'Why not? You've earned it.'

'I haven't. I've just muddled through.'

'Then your muddling be better than some folk's best efforts. It'd be proper and legal.'

'I'm sure it would be, but… Oh, I don't know. What about Charlie? Has he been taken care of?'

'That he has. We've talked it over, and what he'd like most is a regular pension, and that's what he'll get. Stop worritting about him and consider yourself! The partnership's there if you want it.'

'It's very tempting, but there are things to consider. It would mean extra work, and there's Effie. Can I think about it?'

'Certainly you can. There idn't no rush.'

This new and unexpected offer buzzed in Amy's brain like a nest of wasps all morning, until she was forced to take a walk along the beach to clear her head. She came across Charlie contentedly whistling to himself as he measured up some timber.

'You sound happy,' she remarked.

'I got plenty to sing about,' he said with a grin.

'Your pension?'

'Maister's told 'ee about that, has he? Yes, I be like a dog with two tails about un. 'Tis time I give up work. I were eleven when I started. Come Lady Day I'll have put in sixty years building boats. That's enough for anyone. I wants to enjoy myself tending my garden and maybe go fishing on the breakwater when I feels like it. Maister offered me a lump sum, but that would mean banks and things and I can't be doing with they. Us've a bit in the post office for emergencies, and enough in the burial club to see us both off decent. That's all us wants to bother with. Maister's been proper generous. He'm giving me a danged good pension regular every week, and it'll be for my missus as well, if I goes first.'

'You aren't retiring straight away, are you?' Amy asked in alarm. 'We'd miss you terribly.'

'That be nice of 'ee to say so, Mizz Prout. No, I be going on until Lady Day. I'd like to do the full sixty years.'

'Good, because the place wouldn't be the same without you.' She paused. 'Mr Prout's offered me a partnership,' she said. 'I don't know whether to accept or not.'

Charlie did not look particularly surprised.

''Ee can do the job,' he said. 'And if 'ee was a man 'ee'd be mazed not to jump at it. But being a woman be different, I can understand that. There's that li'l maid of youm to think of. Maybe 'ee'll be looking about for another pa for her one day. You'm too young and pretty to stay a widow for long, I reckon, and there's some men as wouldn't take kindly to a wife working at a boatyard. Still, 'ee knows what the job's about, and you'm the only one as can decide. Sleep on it. That's the best thing.'

'You're right, I'll sleep on it,' said Amy.

Later she found Charlie gazing up at the boatyard sign, a perplexed expression on his face.

'What's the matter?' she asked.

'I be trying to work out how much wood us'll need for the new sign,' he said. 'It'll be a rare bit bigger than this one.'

'Why is that?'

'Well, us can find room for "Prout and Son" easy enough, but I be danged if I can work out how to get "Prout, and Son, *and* Sister-in-law" on into the bargain.'

'I haven't accepted yet,' she laughed.

'Maybe not, but I likes to be prepared,' said Charlie. 'I think I'll have the timber measured up ready for when 'ee says yes.'

His confidence was justified. After much deliberation Amy gave John her answer.

'I accept your offer, with many thanks,' she said.

'That's grand.' John's face lit up. 'Jessie'll be as pleased as Punch, for one. And as for me, I'd dance a jig if this leg would let me. You won't regret it. It'll mean more money for you and Effie, money you'll have to take as your due now. There won't be none of this "No, my wages are good enough" nonsense.'

'Am I as bad as that?' grinned Amy.

'Worse, maid! Worse!' John shook Ms head in mock despair. Then he grinned. 'To be honest, girl, I needs you. This leg of mine idn't what it was, nor ever will be, I reckon. Oh, I idn't complaining. I be too thankful it's still there. But I idn't the lad I was, and no mistake.

I needs help running this yard, and with Charlie going soon I be real grateful you accepted, I can tell you.'

John's words came as a relief to Amy. She had feared his offer of a partnership had come from an exaggerated sense of gratitude. If that had been the reason she could have foreseen all sorts of complications ahead. But John needed her, and that put a different complexion on things. She felt justified in accepting now.

'You'll have to move,' was Jessie's immediate reaction.

'Why? We're cosy as we are,' protested Amy.

'Cosy? Is that your name for it? I call it being damp and cramped and grubby. Somewhere more open and airy, with a bit of garden, that's what you need. I'll keep my eyes and ears open for you.'

Amy's protests died on her lips as she remembered: a better house, with a garden for Effie to play in – that had been Todd's ambition. She had almost forgotten.

'Thank you,' she said. 'There's no rush, please don't go to any trouble.'

'It won't be any trouble.' House-hunting was just the sort of project that suited Jessie.

In the new year the unthinkable happened. Queen Victoria died. Ordinary plans such as moving house were forgotten as a stunned nation hung up black crape and tried to cope with the news.

'I can just remember her coronation,' said Charlie. 'Leastways, I recall seeing the streets decorated and hearing bands playing, and being told it was because us had a new queen. My word, that were a good few year ago! About sixty-four, I reckon. I knows I wadn't long out of petticoats.'

'She certainly ruled for a long time,' agreed Amy. 'It's going to seem odd having a king.'

'I wonder if old Edward'll still come into the bay on his yacht now he'm king.'

'Well, let us know if he invites you on board for a drink,' said Amy.

'I will,' grinned Charlie. 'Who knows, he just might, and come Lady Day I'll be free for socializing.'

Charlie's retirement was the second momentous happening of 1901. To Amy the yard did not seem the same without him, and she knew

John felt the same. One of the other shipwrights, Matt Lupton, was appointed foreman in his place. He was an excellent craftsman and a pleasant fellow, but he was not Charlie.

'Perhaps we'm expecting too much too soon,' commented John. 'Matt's only got twenty years' experience behind him. Once he's put in another forty years he'll be every bit as good as Charlie.'

There was another upheaval that summer.

'I've found just the house for you,' Jessie informed Amy. 'It's at North View, on the other side of the harbour, which will be handy for work. Good sized rooms, a fine outlook, and it's nice and airy, not like that place you're in. The garden's not too big, and the rent's reasonable. Come and look at it.'

Amy had looked at countless of her sister-in-law's 'finds' only to declare them unsuitable. On this occasion, however, she liked what she saw, and decided to take the terraced house.

'It will do until you are ready to buy something of your own,' said Jessie with satisfaction.

'Buy?' exclaimed Amy. 'I'll never be able to afford to buy a house.'

'Yes, you will.' Jessie had no doubts. 'You're a partner in the business now, don't forget. You'll be buying before long, you wait and see.'

Amy did not believe her. To be in a position to buy even the humblest of houses seemed way beyond her reach, partner or no partner.

It was a wrench leaving Paradise Place, for all its inconveniences. It had been her home at a time when she had thought she would never have a real home of her own again. For that reason alone it would have a permanent niche in her heart. But there were other things: her life with Todd, Effie growing up, the friendship of Lizzie and Mrs Cobb. When Amy left Paradise Place she felt as if part of herself had been torn away.

Nevertheless, when moving home this time she found her new affluence made quite a difference. There was no whitewashing for economy's sake as there had been when she and Todd had moved into the other house, nor plain muslin curtains because they were the best she could afford. In the new house she had wallpaper on the walls, and pretty cretonne to hang at the windows. For the first time she had the luxury of a front parlour, separate from the kitchen, and in a great fit of extravagance she bought a carpet. Jed helped her with the decorating and the moving in.

'I'd better make the most of this, I don't suppose I'll be allowed in here again,' he remarked as he deposited a 'new' second-hand armchair on the carpet.

'Not with your boots on, you won't,' said Amy.

'I will be allowed in then? That's a relief. Pity it's more out of the way than Paradise Place. That was nice and handy.'

'It was nice and handy for the rats and mice too. You will come and see me just as often, won't you?' she asked, suddenly serious. 'I mean, it's only a bit further out of your way.'

'Of course I will. Mind, if I'm going to have to slog up Sheepy Lane regularly I shall expect it to be worth my while. Gingerbread at the very least, if not saffron cake.'

'Honestly, here I am, a woman of business with a responsible job, and you still expect me to make you gingerbread.'

'You expect me to come up that hill to visit you,' pointed out Jed reasonably.

'In that case, I suppose I've no alternative.' She paused, diverted by the scene from the window. 'Do you know, I hadn't realized how much I'd missed looking out over the harbour and the bay. I'm seeing it from a different direction now from when I was at Furzeham, but it's wonderful to have a view again.'

'You'll be able to keep an eye on me sailing in and out of the harbour, like you used to.'

'So I will. I hadn't thought of that. Oh, but I won't be at home quite so much as I was then. I know! Every night I'll have a light shining in the window here, then you can see it from the *Swan*.' She spoke jokingly.

'Make sure you do. I'll always look out for it,' he replied. He was serious.

Although her promise had been made in jest, Amy kept her word. Each night she lit a brass-bowled oil-lamp and stood it in the parlour window. Whether Jed ever looked up and saw it she was not sure. She rather suspected that he did.

Settling in to her new home was surprisingly easy. Effie loved having a garden to play in, and they both appreciated the extra space and open aspect. However, the open aspect was at times a mixed blessing.

'There I was, thinking how much cleaner our clothes stayed up here compared to down in Paradise Place, and this has to happen,' complained Amy when a stiff gale blew her washing off the line.

'I'll catch it! I'll catch it, Ma!' cried Effie excitedly, dashing after a runaway chemise.

The wind filled it, sending it whirling upwards into the terraced garden which rose behind the house. Amy was suddenly reminded of Daisy's drawers hanging from the railway carriage window and being carried away by the breeze. What a long time ago that had been, and how far she and Jed had come since then. They were the lucky ones. Of Seth there had been no news, not since he had run away all those years since, and as for Daisy... Poor Daisy, her life had been bitter and wasted and short... Yes, she and Jed had been lucky. They were both prospering and were respected in the town. They had found their place among the people of Brixham. At least, she had; she was not so sure about Jed. She hoped he had, but there was no telling with him. He never seemed to belong anywhere.

'I've got my chimmy, Ma,' called Effie, coming back down the steps, the errant garment held up like a flag. 'It fell in among the gooseberry bushes! It's all muddy.'

'There's no need to tell everyone,' laughed Amy. 'Come on, we'll have to wash it again, and those pillowcases that came off too. I'll be glad when the September storms are finished.'

Amy was not alone in her sentiments. Everyone heaved a sigh of relief when the autumn equinox was over, for once leaving behind remarkably little damage. Then, just as the fishing fleet returned to sea, the belated storm struck.

'We're in for a bit of a blow,' remarked John above the rattles and bangs as every loose piece of timber, canvas or rope flapped violently in the wind. 'The black ball's been hoisted up to Berry Head.'

'But the boats have already gone!' exclaimed Amy.

'They'll be all right,' said John. 'A stiff breeze won't worry them.'

Brixham men always referred to any wind as a breeze, but Amy knew that if the storm warning had been hoisted they were threatened with something a great deal stronger. Throughout the day the winds freshened, soon reaching gale force. A few boats came back into port. Faces round the harbour began to take on an anxious look. The crew of each smack that made it back into harbour was questioned as to the whereabouts of other boats.

''Tis to be hoped they've sense enough to run for shelter,' was the most frequently expressed comment.

What everyone knew was that sense did not enter into it. In the conditions that were building up every skipper would be trying to make for a haven somewhere. The entire town prayed silently that they would all make it.

Setting the lamp on the windowsill that evening Amy turned the flame up brighter than usual. The *Swan* was not back yet. The beating rain obscured the view from the windows, so she had gone down to the harbour to check. No one had seen Jed, no one had any news. Soaking wet she had climbed back up the hill to the house, where the windows rattled in the force of the gale, and where the wind now shrieked about the chimney-pots.

Long after Effie had gone to bed, Amy sat by the fire, ignoring the puffs of smoke sent downwards by the storm. Frequently she would get up and peer out of the window. It was no use. All she could ever see was blackness, and water streaming endlessly down the pane. Finally she went to bed. She did not sleep, thinking of Jed out there in the tumult. Then the gale must have lessened, for she dozed off.

The storm returned with a suddenness and a violence which had her awake in an instant. She had never experienced anything like it. In the years that she had lived in Brixham she had grown accustomed to gales and thought she had long since stopped being afraid; but this was different. The whole house shook, sturdily built though it was, and the windows seemed about to be blown in. Hastily Amy rose and went into every room, drawing the curtains as a precaution. All except the parlour. That window she left alone. A feeling of terrible helplessness swept over her. If Jed were out there, battling against this fury, there was nothing she could do to aid him. She could only wait.

It was still dark, not much past midnight at a guess. Incredibly Effie, whose room was at the back, remained sound asleep. Amy had just finished retucking her blankets when there was a hammering at the door. It took her a moment to recognize the drenched creature on her doorstep; then by the light of her upraised lamp she saw that it was Sally Preston. She dragged her inside and closed the door.

'Wood,' gasped Sally. 'I'm getting wood – anything that'll burn… Have you got some?'

'Yes, I've some kindling in the shippen,' said Amy bemused. 'You're welcome to it, but why?'

'The light on the breakwater's out – and the guiding light on the pier's been blown away – *Vigilant* got in a while back… The boats couldn't get to shelter – most of them – they hoped to ride out the storm then the wind shifted… Now they'm trying to get back and there's no light… *Devon Maid's* just smashed against the pier wall – in the dark they couldn't get the men… My sister's boy, he were on the *Devon Maid*…' For a moment Sally seemed on the point of collapse, then with an effort she rallied. 'Us can't do naught about the breakwater – too dangerous – but we'm trying to keep a fire going on the pier to guide the boats home… Us've done it before in my grandma's time, in the Great Gale – That's why I want wood… 'Tis burning away like paper in this wind.'

Amy had heard the old story before, how in 1866, during the worst storm for a hundred years, the wives of Brixham stayed out all night burning everything they could lay their hands on, even their furniture, to keep a guiding light ablaze for their men. Now it seemed history was repeating itself. Her feeling of uselessness faded. 'You'll need more than my bit of firewood,' she said. 'We'll go to the boatyard. There's plenty there.'

'The boatyard?' Sally's face brightened. 'Us needs more help then. I'll knock a few folks up while you'm getting some clothes on.'

Amy was already part way up the stairs. 'As you go, ask my neighbor if she'll sit with Effie, will you please?' she called over her shoulder.

Sally did not need to do much knocking up. Few people in Brixham were asleep that night. By the time Amy left the house there was a gang of women waiting in the street, well muffled against the storm and most carrying hurricane-lamps.

'Right, to Prout's Yard,' cried Sally.

'Why Prout's?' demanded someone. 'There's boatyards nearer than that.'

'True, but tramping round a yard on a night like this could be tricky, not to say dangerous,' shouted Amy as well as she could above the storm. 'Does anyone know their way about any of the other yards? No? Then we'd best stick to Prout's. I know which timber stacks to go to there, for all it's dark.'

The women made their way to the yard, clinging to one another to prevent being blown over as they struggled towards Breakwater Beach. They dodged tree branches and roof tiles that came hurtling at them out of the darkness. Simply going along the road was difficult enough; Amy wondered if she had been over-confident in claiming to know her way about the yard. Eventually, soaked to the skin by the sea-spray as well as the rain, they reached the point where the breakwater joined the road.

'Danged useless object!' cried one woman, shaking an impotent fist towards where the crumbling stone jetty thrust into the sea. 'Suppose to prevent all this it were, but it be too danged short! Not enough money, that was it! They wouldn't spend the money!'

'Save your breath, Kitty, my lover,' her friends advised her, drawing her back into the group that was now following Amy.

It was hard going. The glow of the hurricane lamps seemed too feeble to penetrate far into the pitch darkness, and pieces of wood had been strewn across the beach by the wind.

'Go slowly and carefully,' advised Amy. 'We don't want accidents.'

Much of the timber in the yard would be useless to them she knew. The logs were too large for them to haul and would be difficult to burn. She made for the part of the beach where the smaller timbers and off-cuts were stored. The women fell on the pieces of wood, gathering them in their arms, filling their skirts with them.

'Us needs a barrow,' cried Sally.

There was no barrow, but Amy found some good alternatives. Large pieces of stout canvas.

'We'll use them to drag the wood along,' she shouted. 'Start filling them up while I find some rope.'

It was not the easiest way of transporting timber, but somehow they made their way back into town, four women pulling on the ropes of each improvised sled, other women retrieving pieces of precious wood that kept falling off. Amy and Sally followed behind pulling their own canvas sled. The boatyard had plenty of other combustible materials as well as timber, and the pair of them had plundered the store sheds as well of things like oakum and hemp and pitch.

Amy's arms were one massive ache as she pulled, her hands red-raw from the coarse rope, but she never slackened her pace. She kept thinking of Jed heading towards land only to be greeted by inky blackness. If the fire went out he would never find his way back. She would never see him again.

Soon they could see across the harbour to where a glimmer of flame marked the end of the pier. There was no question of taking a short cut across the inner harbour by boat in those conditions: they had to drag their burdens all the way round. No one spoke now. They were too exhausted.

Waves were breaking over the pier wall when they got there, impeding their progress and making the task of those tending the fire infinitely more difficult. Amy's sodden skirt wrapped itself about her legs. Water welled and sucked round her feet as she shuffled along with Sally. They both tried to ignore the flotsam they could see bobbing violently about in the harbour. Those spars and timbers were the remains of what had once been a fishing boat.

A metal basket held the fire at the end of the pier. The flames were spluttering as they approached. She and Sally thrust their offering forward.

'There's oakum and pitch there,' Amy screamed against the wind.

One of the women tending the fire turned. It was Lizzie Drew. An almost unrecognizable Lizzie who had aged ten years with worry and fatigue.

'Oakum and pitch,' repeated Amy, as loudly as she could. 'Put some on before the fire burns out.'

Lizzie glared at her, eyes red-rimmed in the lamplight, and something seemed to snap.

'What be 'ee doing yer, high and mighty Amy Prout?' she screamed. 'What right have 'ee to come yer giving orders? Us've got men out there. 'Ee haven't. There idn't no one of youm out at sea.' Then she burst into tears.

Amy watched her being led away, while another woman silently took her place at the fire.

She thinks I haven't got a man out there like everyone else, thought Amy. But I have. I have! I've always had, only I was too stupid to realize it before. Now it might be too late!

Chapter Sixteen

The cold light of morning brought an eerie silence to the harbour, where normally there was cheerful noise and bustle. There were plenty of people about. Men were already aboard the boats, trying to make sense of the jumble of shattered masts and tangled rigging, or on the water attempting to clear away the pathetic debris of splintered timbers. Women stood in groups on the quays, their clothes still sodden, their eyes bleak. No one sang or whistled, voices were subdued, even the cobbles seemed to echo more quietly to the clatter of nailed boots and iron-shod wheels.

The storm had died dramatically with the turning of the tide, and for Amy the present calm added to her sense of unreality. Jed had not come back. It was growing less likely that he ever would. The *Our Violet* had struggled in just before dawn, an exhausted Harry on board. That had been some hours ago, and since then no other smack had been sighted. There was little hope now for anyone else.

Part of her refused to accept that she would never see Jed again. In her head her image of him was vivid, his strong face with those heavy dark brows, so often serious, yet which could light with sudden laughter. Jed could not be gone. He could not have departed from her life so completely. But in her heart she knew she might have to accept his loss. She had lived in Brixham too long and comforted too many sorrowing widows to believe otherwise.

How bitter! She had not realized how much she loved him until it was too late. She thought back to Todd. Why was she destined only to know how much she cared for a man after she had lost him? Was it because she still measured her feelings by the deep passion she had felt for Daniel? That had been the hot, heady emotion of youth, tinged with being in love with love itself. A very different sensation from what she felt now.

When had her feeling for Jed changed, deepening into this awful ache? It had been such a gradual process she could not tell. Perhaps it had been going on for years, a gentle maturing of the senses in the same way that timber became seasoned. And just as well-seasoned timber became strong and long-lasting, so did time-ripened love. She knew now, with absolute certainty, that whether Jed came back or not, he would be her last and only love.

'I'd better be getting home, I suppose. I'll be more use there than here.' One of the other women spoke with hopelessness.

Amy was stirred into action by her words. She looked at the sodden ashes of last night's fire. There was nothing for her to do here. She, too, would be better employed going back home. Effie would be waiting.

'Is Uncle Jed home yet?'

The hurried words, and the look of anxiety in the light-blue eyes, stung Amy. She had been so bound up in her own grief she had not considered Effie. The child was old enough to understand the implications of a storm at sea, and she loved Jed too.

'Not yet, sweetheart,' Amy said, taking the little girl in her arms. 'We've just got to be patient and wait.' She dared not offer false hope.

Effie clung to her for a while before releasing her, saying, 'You're all wet, Ma. Go and get some dry clothes on before you catch your death of cold.'

This unexpected reversal of roles brought an involuntary smile to Amy's face. It felt ages since she had last smiled. She feared it would be a long time before she did so again.

'I'll go straight away,' she said. 'Then I'd better make us both some breakfast or you'll be late for school.'

The kindly neighbour who had sat with Effie all night had also built up the fire in the kitchen range and set the kettle to boil. Amy blessed her thoughtfulness as she poured herself a jug of hot water to take up to her room. Disasters such as the storm drew everyone much closer. In a community like Brixham it was not only those who had lost men at sea who were affected, it was everyone.

She did not feel like eating, but she forced herself to swallow a few mouthfuls to encourage Effie.

'You will come and tell me when Uncle Jed gets home, won't you?' said the child as Amy left her at the school gate.

'I can't promise, because I might not know,' she said.

'You'll know,' replied the child with complete conviction, 'Say you'll come and tell me. Please! Please!'

'Very well, if I hear anything I'll come up to school,' Amy promised.

The rest of the day stretched before her, empty and meaningless. Along with the fear came the added agony of waiting. She was not alone. Several boats were still unaccounted for, a score of families grieving and waiting. Amy knew she was one of the lucky ones; she had a job to occupy her, she did not have the increased anxiety of having lost a breadwinner. She had just lost her man. Just? The word struck in a shaft of pain. Just! What an inadequate, useless word. As if the loss of Jed could be just anything.

She had reached the Quay and was making her way to the boatyard when a commotion disrupted the unnatural quiet of the harbour.

'There's men coming in! Another crew!' Word spread like a grass fire.

Amy turned her gaze toward the harbour entrance, expecting to see a boat arriving, then she realized that the excitement was focused away from the harbour. These men were coming in on foot.

Down the Shade, the road which ran between Overgang and the sea, trudged seven men. Their faces were grey, their clothes were soaked. Several had makeshift bandages. They moved mechanically, looking straight ahead, not noticing the growing number of people who were beginning to join them, attaching themselves to the caval-cade as if it were a procession.

Running hopefully towards the group the first person Amy made out was Matthew Burton's son, Isaac, his arm in a rough sling. This was the crew of the *Jupiter*. She tried hard to be pleased. It was wonderful that the men from one of the missing boats were back safely, and she was truly glad. Or she would be when she recovered from the sick disappointment that they were not from the *Swan*.

Then she saw him; Jed, plodding along in the middle of the group, his face more ashen, his expression more taut than any of the others.

'Jed! Jed!' Eagerly she ran towards him, pushing her way through the crowd.

One by one the men were being claimed by their loved ones, encircled by arms, supported and led away. All except Jed.

When Amy reached him he was still trudging on, his pace not slackening.

'Jed! You're safe! Thank God!'

She flung her arms about him, and pressed her face against his sleeve, not caring that it was soaking wet and smelled of the sea. As she embraced him she had to trot to keep up. His arm went about her, his sole response to her presence, although Iris fingers gripped her shoulder.

'You're safe! You're safe!' she kept repeating.

She knew better than to ask what had happened. How she wished he would lean on her. She wanted to give him her support, her comfort, something of herself to ease the inner pain he was suffering. But this was Jed, who had never leaned on anyone – only his fingers flexed ceaselessly round the curved of her shoulder as if continuing to confirm that she was there. When he eventually spoke his voice was dull with exhaustion and distress.

'Frank's gone,' he said.

'Oh no! His poor wife!'

Frank Bartlett had been one of the hands on the *Swan*. His wife, Harry Preston's sister, was expecting her fourth child any day.

'I've lost a man. A good man. It should never have happened.'

'You can't blame yourself, not in those conditions.'

'I could have got the *Swan* through the storm. She would have taken it, but for the sails. The cross-threads! Everyone said I shouldn't have them – but I knew best. I knew what I was doing. I could keep out of trouble. That's what I thought. Now, because of my pride, Frank is dead.' His voice had been getting lower and increasingly bitter.

Amy said nothing. This was not the time to interrupt. She tightened her hold about his waist, pressed her face against him once more, waiting for him to continue.

'The storm took everyone by surprise. It blew up out of nowhere. One minute we were managing fine, the next there were huge gusts. I didn't have time to reduce canvas. A great sea came aboard, the mainsail held it, and we went over. The *Jupiter* picked us up. All except Frank. We never saw any sign of him.' His voice was devoid of emotion, as if the tragic events had not touched him. Amy knew better.

'Where's the *Jupiter* now?' she asked quietly.

'At Broadsands. Isaac Burton managed to beach her. We've made her secure. She'll sail again.'

Amy wondered at the stamina of these men. After the terrors of the storm, and the perils of being shipwrecked, they had found the energy to save the smack. Then they had walked more than two miles along the cliffs back to Brixham. Such bitter irony! Jed had helped to save the *Jupiter* but he had lost his own boat. For the moment, however, the loss of Frank occupied his mind to the exclusion of everything else.

'I'd better go and tell his wife.' The words were full of anguish.

'Let me go. You go home, you look about to collapse. Harry's back safely. He and Sally will be relieved to see you.'

'No.' He released his grip on her shoulder, and gently but firmly disengaged her arm from about his waist. 'His death was my fault. I must be the one to face her.'

'You can't blame yourself,' she protested. 'In a storm like that...' But she could see she was wasting her breath. 'Then let me come with you?'

He shook his head. 'I'll go alone. I won't have you sharing the blame.' He swayed, as if to step away. Suddenly he swung round and flung his arms about her, clinging to her so tightly she could scarcely breathe. Then abruptly, as if he regarded his momentary urge for contact with another human being as a weakness, he released her and walked away.

She watched him go, his gait unsteady with weariness, and inside she ached with love for him.

'Oh, Jed,' she whispered. 'Don't always be so alone. I'm here. You need me. Please admit it.' She knew it was a vain plea, even if he could have heard her.

Jed was no longer in view, and Amy stood for a moment, limp with emotion. Mingled with her overwhelming relief that he was safe was her feeling of love for him, and also an odd sense of despair, he needed support and solace, that was obvious, yet he would not let her help – the brief embrace she discounted as a momentary aberration. It was the inner independence that had dogged him since childhood that would not break and let her come close. She feared she was destined always to be held on the fringes of his life.

Amy stirred herself, remembering she had a promise to keep. Retracing her steps back up to the school she gave her whispered message to the teacher at the classroom door.

'Thank goodness for some happy news.' The teacher glanced back into the room, at the scattering of empty places among her pupils. 'Poor little souls,' she said softly. 'This is a sorrowful time for quite a few, I'm afraid.'

Amy nodded in agreement, thinking of Nellie Bartlett waiting in vain for Frank to come home. Then she crept quietly away to her own work.

There was plenty to do at the yard. The gale had caused terrible damage, with debris everywhere. Worst of all the half-finished boat in the stocks was leaning drunkenly. When she arrived the men were already trying to right it. It was a tricky job, and she waited until matters were past the critical stage before she approached John. She had an admission to make to him.

'I reckon we can spare a few off-cuts and log ends,' he said, when she told him how she had plundered the yard for firewood.

'It was more than that,' she admitted. 'We were dragging stuff along wholesale, using canvases as sleds. Our canvases,' she added. 'I'm afraid they're ruined. And we helped ourselves to pitch and oakum and stuff from the store.'

'That was you, was it? I thought the storm had blown the door in or something.'

'I'll tally up what we took, and pay for it.'

'No you won't!' For once John's voice was sharp. 'It wadn't that much, not when you hear what other folks lost last night. I'm glad

Prout's Yard did something to help. I did precious little. Jessie fair near had hysterics when I suggested coming down.' He sounded almost bitter.

'She was right,' said Amy firmly. 'One slip in the dark and wet... Be content, the yard made a sizeable contribution. We didn't need you damaging your leg again into the bargain.'

'I hear Jed got back safe.'

'Yes. He lost one man. Frank Bartlett went down with *Swan*.'

'That's ten men gone at the last count,' he said. 'Two boats sunk with all hands, and the skipper of the *Serenity* had the mast fall on him. Ten men, and ten families in trouble. 'Tis terrible.'

'It is,' agreed Amy. 'And when you include the other boats that were wrecked or badly damaged. I'm afraid there'll be a lot of people who'll have a hard time this winter.'

She was thinking of Jed. How would he fare now that the *Swan* had sunk? At the moment the blow had not struck him, but it would, and soon. Her every instinct was to be with him. If only she had the right; but she had not. She was an old friend, nothing more.

Throughout the next day, Jed was never out of her mind. Uncertainty beset her. Should she call on him at the Prestons' house, or wait until he came to her? She feared to intrude. Sally Preston would have more than enough to occupy her. Then she met Sally herself.

'He'm taken it terrible hard, what with losing Frank and his boat,' Harry's wife informed her. ''Tis going to take a time for him to get over it. He thinks he'm to blame, and he idn't going to forgive hisself easy. It'd do him good to talk to someone.'

'I'll come, if you think it would help.'

'I do,' said Sally emphatically. She considered for a moment. 'It might be best if you called tomorrow. Today he'm still wore out, and when he idn't brooding he'm sleeping. Come tomorrow, when he'm rested.'

'I will,' Amy assured her.

When she went to the Prestons' house next afternoon after work, however, she was met by an apologetic Sally.

'He idn't in,' she said. 'Went out straight after his breakfast, what he ate of un, and us habn't seed him since.'

373

'But where can he have gone?'

'Goodness knows. Harry's been down on the *Our Violet* all morning, and he habn't seed hide nor hair of him.'

'Never mind, I'll call again some other time if I may.'

'You do that, maid. You'm always welcome.'

But although Amy called again and again, Jed was never home. ''Tidn't no wonder you keeps missing him. He idn't never yer!' declared Sally. 'Out first thing he goes, and that's the last us sees of un till supper.'

'Where does he go? What does he do?' asked Amy with growing concern.

'Us knows that. He goes all over the place! He'm taken to walking, that's what he'm doing. The carrier's lad seed him right over to Totnes the other day.'

'Totnes? That's miles away! What on earth was he doing there?'

'Walking along like one of they clockwork toys, according to the lad. Didn't seem to see nothing nor recognize no one. Other folks have seed him too, in the most unlikely places, and they says the same thing.'

'That's not like Jed.'

'No, it idn't. Us've told him every time you've called, and he just says, "Oh." We'm beginning to get worried about that boy, I don't mind admitting.'

Amy shared her anxiety, and with it she felt hurt. It was as if Jed were avoiding her. Every part of her wanted to help and comfort him, yet he was evading her. It proved to be not just her he was shunning. He was never seen round the harbour or at the Seamen's Rooms or any of his usual haunts. Sightings of him were by chance and usually miles away from Brixham. Amy grew increasingly perturbed. Jed was suffering and she could do nothing to help. How could she, when she was never with him? She calculated how long ago it was since last she had seen him. It had been the morning after the storm, almost a month ago. Since then he had not been near her, and she did not know what to do.

Her trepidation was not eased by a worried-looking Sally knocking on her door one day.

'I be sorry to trouble you,' Sally said. 'But us don't know who else to mm to and that be the truth. There just idn't no getting through to Jed, and it can't go on. He'm tramping the countryside come rain, come shine, till supper, then he sits staring at the fire till bed. There idn't no talking to him, nor arguing. He just don't hear. I don't know what's to become of him, I really don't.'

'I'll do anything I can, of course – but what?'

'If you could come and talk, you might get through to him. It'd have to be late, I'm afraid. He don't get back until near dark. He still blames hisself for Frank's death, that's the root of the matter. And there's no denying the loss of the *Swan* have hit him a sorry blow too. Now he habn't a boat, no job and no prospects. That's enough to hit any man. But he thinks 'tis all his fault, that's what makes un worse. I've told un till I be blue in the face, "There's plenty of folk who sail with crossthreads and never had a hint of trouble. You was just unlucky. That storm was something out of the ordinary." It don't make no difference, though. Goes in one ear and out t'other.'

'Will tonight do? I can get someone to stay with Effie for an hour or two.'

'If you would.' Sally looked relieved. 'If you could get un to eat, that'd be something. There's never been so many dinners wasted in our house. The dog thinks he'm died and gone to heaven he'm getting that well fed.'

'I'll come!' stated Amy. 'And I'll get through to him, even if I have to— to hit him over the head.'

It was dark when she reached the Prestons' house that evening.

'Well, look who's yer!' declared Harry with well-simulated surprise. 'Jed boy, you'm got a visitor.' He gave Amy a huge wink, while at the same time gesturing to his family to go, leaving Jed and Amy alone.

She entered the small room with an assurance she was far from feeling. All day she had been considering what she would say to Jed, how she could penetrate the depths of his misery and make him take notice. He did not seem aware of her presence. He was sitting on a chair, staring into the fire, his hands clasped in front of him. She was shocked by the change in him. He had lost weight; his woollen guernsey hung on him, and even in the ruddy glow of the fire his face looked haggard and gaunt. It was going to take something startling to reach him.

She swallowed hard. 'Hullo, Jed,' she said in a brisk, business-like tone. 'I've come to ask when do you want us to start on your new boat?'

It took a moment for her words to sink in, almost as if he needed time for his brain to function.

'Boat?' he said at last. 'What boat?'

'The replacement for the *Swan*, of course.'

He gave a harsh laugh. 'A replacement for the *Swan*? Talk sense, woman! How am I going to get a new boat? I had one smack and I sank her. I don't deserve another.'

'Is that so? In that case how are you going to support Nellie Bartlett and her children? Her man went down with your boat. Surely you owe her something?'

He drew in his breath sharply. For the first time, he turned to look at her. It wrenched at her to see the anguish in his face, but having got his attention she dared not relent.

'Traipsing through the countryside might be doing something for you but it isn't helping those poor little ones,' she went on inexorably. 'You're going to need money for that. How do you propose to earn it without a boat?'

'The insurance money!' he said harshly. 'I'm going to give Nellie that.'

'A nice gesture!' Amy winced at the sarcasm in her voice, yet she continued without pity. 'And how much will that be? Not much shared among the boats which were lost or damaged beyond repair. It will do for a start, I suppose. It won't support four children for long, though. Not when one of them's barely a month old. After that Nellie can always go on the parish or scrub floors to feed them.'

'No!' Jed gave a shout of protest. 'I'll see they're all right.'

'And I repeat, how do you propose to do it without a boat? There aren't many share fishermen who can support other men's families.'

'I can earn enough. I've no family of my own. I don't need money.'

'No, but Sally does. Or is she expected to feed you out of thin air? You certainly haven't given her any rent recently.'

He had got to his feet, facing her, ready to give a brusque reply. But at her words the retort died on his lips.

'I–I'll pay her when I've got a job. She knows that.'

'Certainly. What she doesn't know is how long she'll have to wait. As far as I can see you've made no effort to find work.'

'Amy, I thought you were my friend.'

It was a cry of pain. She needed every bit of her self-control not to enfold him in her arms and tell him it was just a charade. A ploy to jolt him out of his depression.

'I can't see that anything has changed. I haven't spoken one word that isn't the truth. I agree you've had a hard time. You've every right to feel sorry for yourself, but I don't see why Nellie Bartlett and her children should have to go into the workhouse while you indulge in self-pity.'

Mention of the workhouse was a cruel blow. For a moment she thought she had gone too far. His face, already pale, lost its last vestige of colour, causing his lips to turn white. His eyes burned dark with distress against his pallor.

'I'm giving her the insurance money, I tell you!' he cried in anguish.

'And I say you can do better than that!' she shouted back. 'Invest that money in a new boat. That way you'll be able to give Nellie an allowance for years to come.'

'You say yourself the insurance won't amount to much, not with so many claims. Where's the rest of the money to come from?'

'From mortgagors. That's how other men finance their boats.'

'And you expect people in this town to risk their money with a man who's sunk his own smack?'

'No, but they might risk it on a man who's had bad luck. Provided, of course, he shows some backbone and doesn't skulk around like a whipped dog.'

'Is that what you think of me?' he demanded.

She saw the sudden fury flood into his face as he reached out and grasped her arms. He shook her, his fingers biting into her flesh.

'A whipped dog? Is that your opinion of me? I never thought to hear you say such things. I thought I knew you, Amy Prout, and I don't! I never realized you had such a hard, cruel streak in you. Just as I never realized you would kick a man when he's down. You shouldn't be here, breathing the same air as a man with no backbone. You'd better leave, and quickly, before it chokes you. Go on! Get out! Get out, I say!' And he hustled her through the door, slamming it behind her with a violence which shook the small house.

Once out in the darkened street, Amy leaned against the cob wall and began to sob. She was vaguely conscious of the door opening again and someone approaching. Arms went about her comfortingly, but they were not Jed's arms.

'There, my lover, don't take on so,' said Sally's voice consolingly.

'Oh, Sally, I haven't helped him… I've only made things worse,' wept Amy. 'I should have been kind and gentle to him but I wasn't… I don't know what got into me… I said such awful cruel things to him you wouldn't believe… Beastly hurtful words seemed to come into my mouth and I couldn't stop them… And when he's already suffering so much too… How could I have done it, Sally? How could I? I've done him terrible harm.'

'Now as to that, let's not be too sure,' replied Sally. 'There's some ailments respond to honey and some to vinegar. Us've tried being kind and understanding and it didn't get us nowhere. Maybe this touch of vinegar of youm might do the trick. Leastways, you'm got him proper riled up, which is more'n anyone else has managed.'

'That's because he thought I was his friend,' cried Amy even more bitterly. 'And he thinks I've betrayed him. Is it any wonder he's angry?'

'Let's just wait and see,' was Sally's gentle advice.

Amy's weeping racked her until her ribs ached, only then did her sobs begin to abate.

'Shall my Harry walk you home?' Sally asked solicitously.

'No, thank you. It's not far.' Amy scrubbed at her eyes with the heel of her hand. 'But can I ask a favour of you? Take care of Jed, please. He won't want to see me again; and he does need friends. He'll deny it with his last breath, but he's not nearly as hard and independent as he thinks he is. He needs someone very much.'

'I know he does, maid, and never fear. Harry and me, us'll care for un as if he were one of our own. Whether he wants un or no.'

There was no sleep for Amy that night. Hour after hour in the darkness she went over the things she should have said to Jed. The gentle, reasonable approach she should have taken, the kind words she should have spoken. Then she went over what she had actually said. Those words tore at her like steel claws. To have been so cruel. If she could she would have taken back every word, no matter what it might cost. But that was impossible. The words had been said.

Although it was not yet dawn, Amy felt too restless and miserable to lie any longer. She was about to get up when a hammering on the door sent her leaping from the bed. Such urgency at this hour could only be one of her neighbours in trouble. Pausing to fling a shawl about her shoulders, she hurried downstairs.

It was not one of her neighbours. It was Jed. He, too, looked as if he had not slept, but in the lamplight she saw that his eyes had lost their awful defeated look. 'I know you're disgusted with me, but please don't turn me away,' he urged. 'I must talk to you.'

She hesitated for the briefest of moments, for she was clad only in her nightgown and shawl, her thick honey-coloured hair tumbling loose down her back. Then she stood aside to let him in. He marched ahead into the parlour. It was cold in there but he did not seem to notice. When she went towards the grate to build a fire he stepped forward to prevent her.

'Don't bother with that,' he said, taking hold of her arms, gently this time. His fingers caressed the soft cotton of her nightgown as if he could sense the bruises beneath the fabric. 'I was rough with you last night,' he said apologetically. 'What a fool I was. I'm ashamed of myself for treating you in such a way. Accusing you of not being my friend. You, of all people! Will you forgive me?'

'I'm the one who should ask forgiveness. The things I said—'

'Exactly!' he interrupted. 'Who else but you would have known how to help me? Everyone else was sympathizing with me, and saying what bad luck I'd had. That was the last thing I needed! Goodness knows, I was more than sorry enough for myself! Then along you came and told me exactly what I needed to hear. That sitting in a corner brooding isn't going to help anyone. Not me, and certainly not Frank Bartlett's family.'

'Oh,' said Amy weakly.

'You're right, I've got to get another boat somehow. Not a large smack, that would cost too much for now, but what about a mumble bee? Do you think that's a good idea?'

'I think that's an excellent idea,' Amy agreed. 'Being smaller it would be quicker to build. You'd be back fishing sooner, and you'd have fewer overheads. I'm sure you'd have an easier time getting the money together.'

'Yes, the money.' Jed pulled a wry face. 'Do you really think there are people in Brixham who'd back me? I've already lost one boat.'

'Yes, I think you'll find folk who'd be willing to invest in a man who's already proved himself to be a good seaman and a reliable skipper. The record of catches you got with the *Swan* speak for themselves. And you've already proved your determination in the way you restored the *Swan*.'

'Only to lose her.' A trace of the old bitterness crept back into his voice.

'No one can hold you to blame in those conditions,' she retorted firmly, 'so don't start all that again.'

He gave a sudden laugh, as welcome to Amy's ears as it was unexpected.

'You certainly mean to keep me up to the mark, don't you?' he said. 'Yes!' said Amy decisively. 'And don't you forget it.'

'I can't see you letting me. It's decided then. I go for a mumble bee. To be built at Prout's Yard?'

'Of course. That is if you want unfair preferential treatment and have your boat put at the head of the list.'

'It sounds very tempting, though I'm not sure I'll have got the money together by then.'

'You'll have the money.' She spoke with absolute conviction. 'We've a deal of repair work in after the storm. You'll have time. Let's see — the insurance share-out will be paid soon, won't it? That means you've got some capital. What you need is one good backer to start with. Someone well-known and respected. Once the news gets round that they're supporting you then others will follow. Now, who can you approach? I know! George Beale!'

'The very man I was considering. How's that for two minds thinking as one? Now what's the matter? You're looking serious.'

'It's nothing,' said Amy. She was so delighted to see him full of enthusiasm again that she was unwilling to introduce a gloomy note into the conversation.

'Come on, tell me! I've got my backbone almost back in place now, I won't collapse under the weight of what you've got to say.'

She winced at this reminder of her previous day's sharp words, more determined than ever not to say what was on her mind.

'Come on,' Jed urged gently. 'I want to know.'

'Very well,' she said reluctantly. 'I was just wondering what you're going to do until your boat is built.'

'Anything legal that will earn money,' was the prompt reply. 'Potman at the George, sweeping the streets, anything.' He grew serious. 'There won't be many places going in the fishing for a while, not with so many smacks out of the water after the storm. That was one more thing that made me see the sense of going for my own boat again. I thought that for a spell I'd try and get on one of the coasters – Falmouth, Weymouth, Southampton, maybe round to Bristol. The conditions aren't great, I hear, and the money's not wonderful, but they always need men. I should earn enough to give something to Nellie and have some left over for Sally.' He gave another laugh. 'I sound as though I've got a woman in every port, don't I?'

Amy did not answer. She did not want to break the spell, for as he talked Jed had loosed his grip on her and unconsciously slid his arms about her. Resting against his chest, encircled in his embrace, she scarcely dared to breathe. His lips were close to her, she could feel the warmth of his breath stirring her hair. Another inch and his mouth would be caressing her. She waited, tense and expectant.

Absorbed in his topic he tightened his hold on her, not noticing that he drew her even closer.

'Thank goodness you came when you did,' he said. 'Mind you, I lay awake for the first part of the night wanting to strangle you. You didn't pull any punches, did you? But then, sometime after midnight, it began to come to me that what you said made sense. A lot more sense than the addled rubbish that's been going on in my brain these last few weeks.' His voice went suddenly quiet. 'All I could think about was that Frank was dead. Because of my stupidity a decent woman was widowed and four children fatherless. I began to think that the loss of the *Swan* was some sort of just punishment. Then you gave me a talking to. It hasn't changed how I think about Frank's death, or its consequences. I'll always blame myself. But I see now that feeling responsible doesn't stop me doing something useful at the same time, does it... ? Does it?' he repeated when he got no reply. Then he realized the intimate closeness between them. He gave an embarrassed gasp and let her go.

'Oh,' he said awkwardly, taking a step back from her. 'Oh, Amy, I'm sorry.'

'I'm not,' she replied promptly. 'It's freezing in here. No wonder we huddled together for warmth.'

Her brisk tone did not match her true mood. She was sadly disappointed by their abrupt parting. For her every instant she had been close to him was a precious moment to be treasured. For him it had been no more than an absent-minded gesture, something for which he should apologize.

'I–I'd better be going.' He continued to look awkward. 'It's getting light. You've things to do, I dare say.'

'You're welcome to stay to breakfast.'

'No, thanks. I think I'll be getting back. Sally and Harry'll have a fit if they see my bed hasn't been slept in.'

'Very well, if you must go. But please be extra quiet on your way out. If the neighbours see you leaving at this hour they'll think the worst.'

'Will they?' He looked both stricken and surprised. 'I suppose they will. I didn't think. I'm sorry, I shouldn't have come.'

'Yes, you should,' she said emphatically. 'You've no idea how glad I am to see you looking something like your old self again. I was sure the Jed I knew would never give way under any circumstances, no matter how hard they were. And I was right.'

'Only just,' he admitted. 'I did need a sharp slap to get going again. And talking of going…' He paused at the door, and looked at her. He moved towards her as if he might kiss her. Then he thought better of it, cleared his throat and said, 'Goodbye for now – and thanks.'

He forgot about closing the door quietly, and the clatter of his boots on the stony road echoed in the frosty air. Amy allowed herself a sad smile. She was truly delighted he was managing to put his troubles behind him, and just as pleased he was thinking positively of the future. Without doubt he was grateful to her, and had expressed his gratitude for her advice and her friendship. But how she wished he had thought of her as a woman for once.

Amy went to work that morning with more than usual resolution. When discussing the financing of the new boat with Jed she had suggested he should approach George Beale. She continued to consider him a hopeful prospect, but she knew very well that money was going to be a scarce commodity in Brixham that winter. She had an idea for another mortgagor.

'Hullo,' John greeted her. 'I recognize that expression on your face. You'm wanting something.'

'Yes,' admitted Amy. 'Though it's more in the nature of a trade. I want you to help finance Jed Greenway's new mumble bee in return for my share of the business.'

'That's plain enough, any road. Why don't you advance him the money yourself? You'm a partner, when all's said and done.'

'Two reasons. One, I haven't got those sort of savings together yet, and two, Jed wouldn't accept money from me even if I had.'

She was not being quite truthful. She knew she could probably have raised a loan from the bank, but the one thing she did not want was for Jed ever to be beholden to her, especially where matters of finance were concerned.

John regarded her keenly. 'He'm going for a mumble bee this time, eh?'

'He has to have something. He's got it into his head he's responsible for Nellie Bartlett and her children, and he'll never support them as a share fisherman.'

'He'm a sound enough fellow, I'll give him that. And did well at the fishing so I've heard. I'll tell you what, ask him to come up Furzeham one evening soon, and us'll have a chat. If he'm got any account books and whatnot he can bring them, too.'

'Thank you, you're a lovely man. Do you know that?'

'I've had my suspicions about that for some time. As regards Jed, don't go getting excited, mind. I habn't said yes to nothing. Us'm just going to have a talk.'

'That's fine. Oh, there's one thing... Please don't let on about me giving up the partnership.'

'No, I won't let on because it idn't going to happen. The partnership idn't nothing to do with it.'

'What? Oh no... !'

'I idn't arguing. If I agrees to back Jed it'll be because I thinks 'tis a good investment, and that'll be the only consideration.'

She knew there was no point in discussing the matter further, when John made up his mind to something he would not move.

'Thank you,' she said, 'if you're sure... ?'

'Now what be you up to?' John cried, for Amy had lifted down the leather-spined order book.

'I'm pencilling in Jed's boat, there, after the repairs to the *Southern Cross* and before the ketch for the man in Ramsgate.'

'You'll get us hung,' protested John, half laughing.

'You didn't promise any date for the Ramsgate boat, did you? There certainly isn't anything written down here. We'll say Jed's was an emergency job. Besides, it's only a little mumble bee. That won't take long.'

John shook his head in amused disbelief.

'If the man from Ramsgate complains I'll tell him us have problems beyond our control – us have a female working yer. That'll be reason enough,' he chuckled.

When next Amy met Jed he was looking serious.

'Don't frown like that,' she scolded. 'It makes you look bad-tempered.'

'I'm not angry, I've got a problem,' he said. 'George Beale is going to back me.'

'That's wonderful. What's the problem?'

'It's his reason for agreeing. He says it's because he feels guilty for having sold me the cross-threads in the first place. That's why I don't think I can accept his money. I was the one who wanted them, he warned me about them. He has no reason to feel guilty—'

'If ever a man worked at complicating his life it's you, Jed Greenway!' declared Amy. 'George Beale has agreed to be a mortgagor for your boat, right? Is he going to lose his money?'

'Of course not. With the interest he'll gain.'

'Then that's the end of the problem. Say "Thank you very much, Mr Beale" and accept. When you've done that you can get yourself up to Furzeham and have a talk with John. He isn't promising anything, but he might be your second mortgagor.'

'John Prout? With George Beale and John Prout behind me I'll have people queuing up to finance my boat. What did you do to the poor fellow?'

'Nothing much. Kicked his bad leg, threatened to burn down the boatyard, a few minor things like that. You will go, won't you?'

'I'll go, and if he says yes I'll know it's all due to you, no matter what methods of persuasion you used.'

'When he says yes, not if,' Amy contradicted.

She was right. Before the week was out both John and George Beale had signed the mortgages. In less than two months Jed had full financing. The work in hand at the boatyard was completed, then they were ready to lay the keel for the new mumble bee. Jed was not there to see it. He was sailing on a coaster bound for Poole.

'If we'm sharpish like, Jed's going to find himself with a Brixham port mark,' observed John.

'Has it been decided at long last?'

'Yes, due to start in May, I've been told. Brixham's to have its own registration after all these years. 'Tis going to seem strange having it on the boats after seeing DH for Dartmouth. You'm going to have to leam a couple of new letters, idn't you, Dick?' He addressed the yard's painter, who was passing by.

'I'll manage if I practise long enough,' Dick assured them cheerfully.

'It will seem strange,' agreed Amy. 'But very nice. Much more fitting, somehow, since far more fishing boats sail from Brixham than from Dartmouth. I wonder it wasn't done years ago.'

'You'm idn't the only one, maid,' said John. He continued to regard the embryo vessel, half formed, its ribs showing. 'There's some decent work going into that boat of Jed's, although I says it as shouldn't.'

'It would be a bad job if there wasn't,' retorted Amy. 'Seeing as you've got money tied up in her.' And they both chuckled.

'He were wise to have a mumble bee. A smaller boat'll give him a chance to get established again. Did you nag him into it?'

'No, I didn't,' said Amy. 'It was his own idea.'

'Any road, I expect he thinks it was,' John said with a grin. 'I don't suppose he'll keep her long, though. He'm a man with a way to go, be Jed Greenway. Give him a couple of years and he'll be selling her to buy a bigger boat.'

'That's how George Beale started, and look at him now.'

'Exactly!' said John.

The building of the mumble bee continued steadily, and Amy watched her progress with particular interest. So much rested on the success of the craft: Jed's future, and that of Nellie Bartlett and her children.

'What are you going to call her?' she asked, when Jed was home for a spell. 'How about *Swan II*?'

'No, I don't think so. The *Swan* wasn't a very lucky craft, was she?'

'You've got to choose something, and soon,' persisted Amy.

'I will,' he assured her. 'I've been giving the matter a lot of thought. I have had one idea.'

'Yes, what is it?'

'I wondered about calling her the *Lucy Burton*.'

She looked up at him sharply and caught the glint of laughter in his.

'You do and you've as good as announced your engagement to her,' she said.

'What, has the fellow from the chemist's escaped from her clutches?'

'He has. Lucy's on the marriage market again.'

'In that case I'll think again, and quickly. How about Towser? Towser was the Prestons' dog.

'It's a possibility,' replied Amy. 'No one would think you were planning to marry him.'

It delighted her to hear him joking again. Some people who did not know him well might say that he was restored to being the old Jed again, but she knew otherwise. The scars of the storm remained and, being Jed, they had bitten deep. But he was learning to live with them, and that gave her cause for much happiness.

Amy was quietly reading the *Chronicle* later that week when the past suddenly reached out and assailed her. It was a small notice: 'Sir John and Lady Robertson, of Redcombe Grange, Torquay, are happy to announce the engagement of their eldest daughter, Mary, to Captain Daniel Newton, only son of Captain and Mrs William Newton of Capstan House, Brixham.'

She read and re-read the announcement several times, not certain of her reaction. She felt an immediate pang of regret certainly. Daniel had been an important part of her girlhood. Then she realized her regret was as much concerned with nostalgia for the past as for a lost love. Even the nostalgia was selective. Her love affair with Daniel and their stolen meetings had been causes of joy, but there were large parts of her youth she would not want to relive. She was far happier now.

She could not help trying to compare the feelings she had had for Daniel with the love she felt for Jed. It was an impossible comparison. It was like trying to equate the transitory brilliance of a firework with a long-lasting, slow-burning fire. There had never been any real hope of a future for Daniel and her, that was obvious now, and she wished him well with his Mary.

–

Although Amy plagued Jed, he refused to tell her what name he had chosen for his boat.

'You'll have to make your mind up soon,' she urged as they crossed the beach together to see how the mumble bee was progressing. 'The men have done painting her. You can't have Dick standing about with his brushes waiting while you decide.'

'*Towser* is as good a name as any,' Jed persisted. He had said it so frequently she was beginning to fear he might be serious.

'You can't call a boat after a dog,' she protested, then stopped.

Dick was busily at work on the vessel's side. A skilful sign-writer, he had painstakingly completed the letters BM and was just beginning on the number 1.

'BM 1!' exclaimed Amy in astonishment. 'She's registered in Brixham! You've got the first Brixham port mark! Why on earth didn't you tell me?'

'I didn't think you'd be interested.' He said it in an offhand way, as if it were something of no importance.

'You always say that!' she declared. 'You don't mean it, though. I can tell. You knew jolly well I'd be interested, and pleased and excited. Oh, aren't you thrilled that your boat is the first?'

Jed shrugged, determined not to show emotion. 'It's as good a number as any other,' he said.

'Oh you… !' Amy began, then for a second time words failed her. They had strolled further round the vessel and were now regarding her from the rear. Dick had certainly been busy. In neat letters on the stern was written the port of registration. 'Brixham'. Above it, in gleaming white for everyone to see was one word: *Amy*.

'*Amy!* You've called her Amy! After me?' she asked in disbelief.

'I don't know any other Amy,' was the gruff reply. 'And you objected to Towser.'

'You've called her *Amy*!' She was totally stunned. His most prized possession, the most valuable thing in his life, and he had called it after her. She was at a loss for words.

'You don't mind?' There was uncertainty in his voice.

'Mind? It's the nicest thing that's ever happened to me. It's a compliment. It's—' She stopped, aware that the workmen were watching them, grinning all over their faces.

They had evidently been in on the secret. The colour rose in her face as she considered what they must be thinking. Boats were named after someone close to the new owner's heart. Even the *Our Violet* had been named in honour of Matthew Burton's sinewy wife. What sort of a relationship would the men think existed between her and Jed when they saw *Amy* written up?

In the midst of her embarrassment she felt a stirring of hope. Could this mean that Jed thought her more than a friend? When he had suggested calling his boat the *Lucy Burton* she had joked that it was tantamount to announcing his engagement. The joke was not far short of the truth. Was calling his boat *Amy* his way of declaring he loved her? She glanced furtively at him but he was as inscrutable as ever. Frustration made her want to shake him hard. If only he would give, just once…

'Mizz Prout, carrier's come with a parcel to be signed for!' The call of duty sent Amy hurrying back to the office, not certain whether she was loved or not.

The launch of the *Amy* was a crowded affair. By comparison the celebration for the refitted *Swan* seemed quiet indeed. The beach swarmed with people, causing Amy some misgivings when she looked at the refreshments set on trestle-tables above the water-line. They had seemed more than ample when she, Sally and Jessie had laid them out. Now she wondered if there would be enough to go round. She held out little hope that the sandwiches, cakes, buns and biscuits would be consumed only by those actually invited.

'That's some nice hat,' remarked John, looking at her head. 'I've seen fewer flowers at the annual show than you'm got there.'

'I thought I'd splash out.' Amy raised a self-conscious hand to the confection she was wearing. 'I couldn't afford a new hat for the *Swan*. I thought the *Amy* deserved a better send-off.'

She could have added that Jed, for whose benefit she had bought the hat, had not noticed it. The boat *Amy* had his complete attention, her flesh-and-blood namesake would have to wait.

Not until the boat was safely in the water and the cheering done did he remark, 'I haven't seen that hat before, have I?'

'I've been wearing it all day, but apart from that, no,' she replied.

He gave a sigh of contentment that had nothing to do with millinery. His eyes were once more fixed on the new hull.

'She's there because of you,' he said. 'Without you pushing me I don't know where I'd be today.'

'Probably here, doing exactly what you are doing.'

'No, I refuse to accept that. Perhaps I would have had another boat but a long, long time in the future. The way I felt I didn't even want to go to sea again, never mind have a boat. Then you came along and bullied me into action.'

'Oh dear, was I so terrible?' asked Amy in dismay.

'Terrible? No.' He seemed puzzled by the idea. 'You were exactly what I needed.' He looked about him. 'Where's Effie?' he asked.

'Gone with Jessie to spend the night at Furzeham as a special treat.'

'You're on your own?'

'Yes, I suppose so.'

'Then come for a walk. There's nothing more I can do here, and I'm restless.'

The beach had cleared rapidly. Amy and Jed were almost the only people left. There was nothing more for her to do either.

'All right,' she said.

They strolled out along the coast towards Berry Head. Before they reached the great limestone headland, by mutual consent, they turned back towards the town, taking a higher route that ran across the crest of the hill. On their way they talked of the launch, of the people who were there, and of the boat's future; but Amy did not pay full attention to the conversation. Her mind was occupied with other things.

Jed did love her, she was becoming more and more convinced of it. Not that he showed it. It was as if he were making a conscious effort to smother his emotions and avoid contact with her. They were walking through fields now, secluded and private, but he did not so much as attempt to take her hand. If they touched by accident he moved away.

Yet he could not find her repugnant. Not if he sought her company and named his boat after her. It was a ludicrous situation.

We could go on like this for another thirty or forty years, thought Amy. Loving each other and doing absolutely nothing about it.

Some women might be able to adore from afar. She was not one of them. In her years of widowhood she had realized how much she missed the physical side of love. To Amy love was an act of giving – her caring, her presence, herself. She knew no other way of expressing her deepest feelings. Words were not enough. At that moment she wanted to give her love to Jed very much indeed. He needed loving, there was no doubt about it: a lifetime of standing alone had starved him of affection, an affection she longed to give him. There was only one way out of the dilemma: he would never ask for love, so she must offer it.

They paused at a field gate to look down on the scene below them, the crowded harbour and the rows of cottages climbing the slopes that surrounded it. Amy gripped the top rail tightly to give her support.

'When are you going to ask me?' she demanded.

'Ask you what?'

'To marry you!'

Jed did not reply immediately, and his lack of surprise gave her hope. Had he been thinking about it?

'Effie does need a father, I suppose…' he said.

'I wasn't thinking of a father for my child,' Amy protested.

'…I'm not the right man,' Jed went on, as if she had not spoken. 'I've got too many responsibilities already. I'm up to my ears in debt again.'

'I don't want someone to support us. I can do that!'

'You can find a far better husband than me. There are some fine men who'd be only too glad to wed you, and who'd make you happy. Choose one of them. I've nothing to give.'

'I don't want anything from you.'

He was deliberately staring out across the fields, his chin determined, his mouth grim. Shutting her out in a way she recognized only too well. 'It wouldn't be a good idea for us to marry.' He spoke emphatically.

'I brought the subject up for one reason,' she said, trying hard to be equally dispassionate. 'I didn't suggest marriage because I need someone to help me raise Effie, nor to keep us fed. I suggested it because I love you.'

There, the words were said and the die cast.

He made no response, and she felt her self-control crumbling as she went on, 'I-I thought you loved me too. I seem to have been mistaken. Just forget I ever said anything. I wish I'd never spoken...'

Tears were coursing down her cheeks and she bent her head so that he could not see them. She was not quick enough.

'I've made you cry!' He turned towards her, horror-stricken. 'How could I have done such a thing? I'm sorry, truly I am.'

He reached out his arms to her, but she resisted him.

'Don't,' she pleaded. 'Don't do anything you don't mean, just because you can't bear the sight of tears. I'm the one to be sorry. I've made a fool of myself and misjudged your feelings, and now everything's spoiled. It's all gone wrong.'

It took great determination for her not to put her head against his chest and howl out her misery. Instead, she bit her lips tightly together and averted her head in an attempt to control herself. When he took hold of her she tried to keep her grip on the gate so that she would not have to face him. With unexpected persistence he prised her fingers off the bar and pulled her gently towards him.

'You didn't misjudge anything,' he said. 'I do love you.'

'You do?' She looked up at him through her tears.

'Of course.' He spoke as if it were the most obvious thing in the world.

'Then why did you never say anything?'

'I didn't think—'

'And don't say you didn't think I'd be interested,' she retorted.

'Very well, I won't.' He said it with a hint of a smile.

'Why didn't you tell me before?' she asked, more gently.

'Because I can give you nothing.'

'But I love you. I want nothing from you, only yourself.' As she spoke she knew that would be the hardest thing for him to give.

'I'd be no good at sharing my life; I've been on my own too long.'

She could feel his fingers tensing against her shoulders, and she sensed he was fighting an inner battle with himself.

'Yet you say you love me,' she urged gently.

'I do.' The pressure of his fingers grew greater as he pulled her closer. When he spoke again it was hurriedly, as if he could not restrain the words. 'Even when you were a girl, with cropped hair and workhouse hand–me–downs, you were the most beautiful thing in my life.'

'Oh… !' The exclamation was no more than a sigh. For Jed to have admitted so much was a revelation, a great crack in the protective shell he had built about himself.

'You've felt like that all those years?' she whispered. 'Then won't you let me love you now? Can't we be together?'

'It wouldn't work,' he protested, almost angrily, making her fear he was already regretting his one sign of softening.

'Why not? We love each other, don't we?'

He did not reply and she could feel him distancing himself from her once more.

'For pity's sake! Do you always want to be on your own?' When he still did not reply she twisted out of his grasp and stepped away, unable to stand being torn apart inside any more. 'Then be alone, Jed Greenway!' she cried, her voice shaken by sobs. 'Be alone and don't blame anyone else when you're lonely. I've tried to get close to you, and all you've done is push me away.'

She stumbled from him blindly, not caring which way she went.

'No!' From behind her came a great bellow of pain, and the sound of running feet. In an instant Jed had her in his arms. 'Don't go, Amy,' he begged. 'Don't leave me—'

He could say no more, he could only grasp her tightly, his face pressed against her hair. She felt him shaking with emotion he was unable to express. But he had admitted his love for her, and his need. That was more than sufficient for the moment. Gently she drew his face down to hers and kissed him on the lips, a kiss that grew in warmth and passion as Jed's inner reserve slowly melted. He would have to learn to give of himself, she knew. It would not be an easy task, nor a swift one, but she would be happy to teach him.

The air was heavy with scents of a May evening, and early bats flittered on silent leather wings. Below them a pale mist in the dimpsey light had turned the sea to pearl and cast a soft veil over the town. It looked beautiful, and familiar, and very welcoming.

'We'd best be getting home,' said Jed eventually.

'Is that how you think of it now?' she asked. 'As home? There was a time when you felt you belonged nowhere. Has that changed?'

As ever he considered his words before he spoke. 'I've changed,' he corrected. 'And yes, this feels like home to me. I never thought it would, I was not even sure of the meaning of the word. I am now, though. Everything I need and cherish is here: good friends, a good harbour... and you. What more could I want?'

Such an admission from Jed. Where was his old reserve now? Amy looked up into his eyes and saw only love reflected there – love for her. With a single finger she traced the lines of his mouth, no longer tightly pressed and dour, but tender and vulnerable. She could hardly believe her own happiness.

'Let's go home,' she said softly.

There was no walking apart this time. They were in love and they admitted it. Their aims were intertwined about each other as they headed downhill together. Back to the place that had become a safe haven for them both.